WHAT MARKS YOUR PATH?

WHAT MARKS YOUR PATH?

CAROLYN P. SCHRIBER

Two roads diverged in a wood, and I—
I took the one less traveled by,
And that has made all the difference.

—Robert Frost

CONTENTS

Chapter One

SAWDUST AND COTTON FLUFF

Friday, August 7, 2009

"What the . . .! What chicken truck drove through here?"

Sarah stepped off the elevator on the third floor of Bailey Hall and froze in place. Something white and fuzzy coated the familiar history department hallway, reminding Sarah of a highway through midwestern farmland right after a truckload of live chickens had passed on its way to a processing plant. Except these weren't feathers. They were soft fibers, so light they stirred in the slightest breeze and floated in the air before settling into white drifts on every horizontal surface.

Gwen Le Pham, the department secretary, looked up, her almond eyes twinkling in amusement above the surgical mask that covered the lower part of her face. "Welcome to Cotton Central, home of the Tennessee Cotton Growers Alliance and location of this year's three-week seminar in Grading Cotton Fibers. You're just in time to fill your lungs with fuzz."

"They're meeting in our hallway?"

"Well, in our classrooms, to be exact, but this stuff is so tiny that it sifts through the cracks and follows in the wake of everyone who goes in or out of those rooms. The attendees have been here for a week, so we have another two weeks to enjoy living in the clouds." She waved an impatient hand in front of her face. "Oh, be careful where you walk. The fibers make the floor slippery. Dr. Chalmers keeps telling me I'll get used to it, but I don't believe him for a minute."

"It's awful—reminds me of those stories we read of young girls dying from lung disease in the cotton mills of the Industrial Revolution. I always though they must be exaggerated, but . . . a-choo! Sorry."

"Here, have a mask. I bought a box of them for the department. They help you breathe."

"Thanks, but I'll . . . a-choo! . . . try to hold my breath till I get to my office."

"You can't escape. The fibers follow you everywhere!"

Shaking her head in disbelief, Sarah fumbled for her keys and noted with dismay a small white drift that had formed on the threshold of her office. As she pushed the door open, the fibers swirled in response and danced into the room ahead of her. She turned back to the secretary's desk. "Changed my . . . a-choo! . . . mind. I'll take a mask, thank you."

Before Gwen could answer, the silence shattered as a jackhammer ground its way into some flooring tiles and an electric saw buzzed through a softer piece of wood. Their concert finished with a crash. Sarah covered her ears. Gwen shook her head and reached for another box hidden in her desk drawer. "How about some ear-plugs?"

"What was that?"

"Dr. Chalmers' latest remodeling project down at the

other end of the hall. He has a crew creating new faculty offices for the people we haven't even hired yet."

"I'm guessing no one else is here, right? There's no way to work in this chaos."

"Tell me about it! We haven't seen Dr. Monroe all summer. Dr. Winthrop and her summer assistant are over in the computer center working on the latest job applications. But before you just duck and run, Dr. Chalmers asked me to let him know if you came in. He wants to talk to you."

～

Sarah was plowing through a stack of unopened and unwanted mail when the knock came at her office door.

"Come in. It's open."

Kevin Chalmers, the new department chair, slipped in, shutting the door behind him. "Welcome back, Dr. Chomsky. Sorry the place is in such a mess, but this is work that we must complete before the beginning of the semester."

"What? Oh! I forgot I was still wearing the earplugs. How do you get anything done in this racket?"

"Well, it makes a difference if you're the one making the noise. When the workmen get too loud, I just go down and join them. It's fun to run one of those jackhammers, although I suppose you might not enjoy it."

"I suppose not! Gwen said they're building new offices?"

"Yes, that's part of what I wanted to talk to you about. I was concerned about how the department was running last year, so I'm taking advantage of my new position to make some changes around here. But first, let's talk about you. I understand you've been off on a research trip. How did that go?"

"Well, I've spent most of the last six weeks in Charleston and Columbia, South Carolina, gathering evidence for my thesis that unhappy slaves used water symbolism in their spirituals and sermons to pass along guidance for those trying to escape their bonds."

"An interesting concept. Sounds like a good conference proposal, or even a journal article."

"Both, I hope. But it's hard to know when to stop researching and start writing."

"If I may nag you just a little, it's vital that you get some original research added to your *curriculum vitae* before the end of this year."

"I do have an invited lecture on my schedule from the local Daughters of the Confederacy. I'm to be the speaker at their November luncheon."

"That's fine. But you need to understand that an invited talk to a bunch of people who know little but have their minds already made up is not the same as producing a paper for your learned colleagues."

"Yes, sir." Sarah had a vague feeling that she had just been sent to the principal's office.

Kevin changed the subject. "How's David doing? Recuperation from his shattered shoulder coming along as expected?"

"He's doing well, or so he tells me. I just got home last night, so I haven't seen him, but we talked for a while on the phone. You may have heard that he just spent six weeks at Johns Hopkins getting an artificial shoulder blade."

"Amazing what they can do these days."

"He now claims to be an official member of the Bionic Men's Club. I'm encouraged to hear his reports, but I'll know better after tomorrow night. We're going out for a welcome home dinner. I'm looking forward to watching him cut his steak!"

"Please give him my best wishes. Now come. Let me show you what all we've been doing."

~

K evin led the way down the sawdust-filled hallway, stopping at the door to his old office. "You may remember what my office looked like—the same size as the chair's chamber and much more space than I needed. When I realized that we were going to be short one office in 2010, it was ones of the first spaces I wanted to remodel."

He pushed the door open and nodded at the west wall. "You'll see that the demolition guys have chopped off a good third of it. This reduced area will now house one of our new hires—either Colonial or Modern World."

He continued down the hall to where the workmen were framing a new doorway and a fellow on tall metal stilts was busy hanging drywall. "And this will be the other new person's office, using the rest of my old digs and about half of what used to be the graduate student lounge."

Sarah caught her breath. "But . . . that doesn't leave the students much room. Won't they object?"

Kevin gave her a side-eye glance and then shrugged. "Yes, I suppose they will complain that they have no space left at all. At the end of the corridor, a third room will serve as History Reading Room. It will have bookshelves on all the walls, and in the center, four connected and partitioned reading desks—the kind you see in old libraries, complete with clamshell design to discourage chatting with one's neighbor."

Sarah was pressing her lips together to keep from blurting out any more critical comments, but she couldn't help but glance across the hall to the open kitchenette used by both faculty and graduate students. There, too, a worker was building the framework for a wall and doorway.

"And what you're looking at now will become the Faculty Room, complete with a new round conference table and chairs. The kitchen will remain intact, still brewing our coffee and chilling our brown bag lunches, but no longer overrun with students. This will give the faculty our own space, where we can relax, share a snack, or hold a private meeting. As for the graduate students, they will still be able to get together in the Grub Hub for a gossip session, and the library is always available for the boring stuff like studying."

"I'm sure you have your . . ."

". . . my reasons? I do, indeed. From its very inception, I thought it was a mistake to share such a large part of our floor with our graduate students. And I found it even more worrisome when they kicked out all the underclassmen and expanded their own territorial rights into the faculty corner. You need look no further than the excesses of last year to understand why it is important to maintain certain academic boundaries between faculty and those we teach."

"But why so quickly? I mean, our new faculty won't be arriving for a year or more. Why this rush to get everything done before the students come back?"

"Maybe because I'm the new broom?"

Sarah gave him a skeptical look.

"No, you're right. It's more than that. The opportunity is now. We're down to five continuing graduate students, one of whom will finish in December. And they are pleasant people who are as upset by the events of last spring as we are. I'm betting they will accept the changes without a protest. They'll also get some benefit from the new facilities. As you pointed out, the new faculty members won't arrive until next year. In the meantime, I intend to have the two new offices furnished with work tables and chairs, computers and telephones. Mike McGarrity will have the use of one of them as our temporary adjunct instructor, and he will share the space with Jeff, who will be working on our job search files on weekends. The other empty office will go to the two teaching assistants, Jean and Matt, where they can do their grading and whatever else they need. That will leave only Ellie, and she'll be busy in the Reading Room, enjoying the quiet while she works on her master's thesis."

"What about new grad students? Didn't we have several applications?"

"Yes, indeed. And we've accepted six of them so far. They are another reason to act now. They will come into the completed changes and accept them as *status quo*. By the time our new faculty arrive and move into their new offices, our graduate contingent will already be used to getting together in other locations."

K evin steered Sarah back toward her office. "We've just one more matter to discuss, and then I'll let you get back to work. In the turmoil of those last days of spring semester, neither Robert nor I remembered to provide you with an appropriate end-of-year review. Let's correct that now. How would you describe your first year of teaching?"

Sarah took a deep breath to give herself a few moments before answering. "It was exciting. Exhilarating. Fun. Instructive. Surprising. Challenging. And . . . terrifying."

"I'm sure it was all of those things. But what stands out in your memory—besides the obvious last act?"

"Well, when I had lunch with my dissertation director over the holidays, all I could talk about was how different our students were from the people with whom I went through school. I wanted him to understand how excited I was to have such a diverse group of graduate students—people with all kinds of backgrounds and opposing ideas. They made every discussion lively, and we all ended up learning from one another."

"And what did you tell him about our undergraduates?"

She frowned. "Not much that I can remember. Oh, I think the classes went well. They were lectures, and the students were clear in understanding the major concepts. There weren't many problems . . ."

"No. And few high points, either, I'm guessing."

Sarah looked away, embarrassed to have him point out her failures.

"No, but . . ."

"You need not cringe. I don't intend to scold you. In fact, I recognize that your classes were no better or worse than those of your most experienced colleagues. You reflected the prevailing attitude of the department, and that's a matter I hope to correct across the board. I want us to reach out to our youngest students in the coming year. And you can help."

"I'll try harder, I promise."

"That's not what I meant. Think back. Were you a member of Phi Alpha Theta as an undergraduate at Boston College?"

"Of course. Phi Alpha Theta was a big part of our lives. There was something validating about being elected to a national honorary fraternity of historians. It put us on a scholarly footing with our instructors and . . ." She hesitated and cocked her head. "And we don't have a chapter here, do we?"

"No, we don't, but you are about to change that. I'm asking you to take that on as your project for the next year. Let's create a PAT chapter here, involve our young majors and minors, and give them a reason to take pride in that historian label."

"I'm not sure I know where to start."

"Research it, my dear. You are a historian, are you not?"

Chapter Two

WHEN ALL ELSE FAILS, GET PIZZA

Friday, August 7, 2009

Alone at last, Sarah faced the pile of unopened mail on her desk with distaste—grocery ads, a pitch for the local street fair, several book release notices, a new dentistry office opening, a sale catalog from the local office supply store, the opening of a new Japanese crêperie, the schedule of cheerleader demonstrations, and several departmental flyers touting the best new courses on offer this fall. She shuffled the pile, looking for any sign of real correspondence. Seeing none, she swept the entire collection into the wastebasket, gathered her tote bag, and turned out the lights. At Gwen's desk, she dropped off the mask and ear plugs. "I give up. The next person who comes looking for me can find me at home. I'm out of here until things settle down."

Feeling like a tourist in an unfamiliar city, she hesitated at the outer doors to check for fast-moving cheerleader squads. Then she headed for the faculty parking lot and the relative safety and silence of her car.

"Sarah! Wait up!" The familiar shout came just as she dropped her tote bag onto the front seat, and she turned to spot Julia Winthrop jogging toward her. "Not that I blame you for wanting to clear out of here as fast as possible, but I was hoping to catch you in time for lunch. Welcome home!"

Sarah hugged her colleague and mentor. "Julia! How good to see you. I've been floundering amid all this campus upheaval. Thank goodness something is still the same. You look great—rested and happy, unlike my other encounter this morning."

"You must have come from Third Floor Bailey. Sawdust and cotton fluff are not your favorite decor accessories, I take it."

"No, and neither are cheerleaders, cotton farmers, or a freshly minted department chair with a penchant for lecturing anyone who comes his way."

"Kevin on a high horse this morning, is he?"

"Well, toward me he is, at any rate. In the first few minutes of our impromptu meeting, I learned that I am stuck in my ways and unwilling to entertain new ideas. I have also been a total failure at reaching out to our undergraduate population, a disappointment to those who expected me to have published something by now, and a slacker at carrying my share of the load within the department."

"Wow! And were you ashamed of yourself?"

"No, although I apologized for my flaws. I also promised not to mention the invited lecture I'm giving to the local Daughters of the Confederacy because they are hopelessly biased and won't hear a thing I have to say. And I've agreed to create a new Phi Alpha Theta chapter for our campus."

"That should keep you busy for a while. Sounds like you need sustenance. How about a pizza?"

"For lunch?"

"Why not?"

"Why not, indeed? Your car or mine?"

"I'll drive, and you can fill me in on where you've been and what you've been doing."

Sarah drew a deep breath as they drove deep into the mountains surrounding their little college town. "I'd almost forgotten how much I love the Smokies. Just smell that fresh air and the tang of pine needles warmed by the sun. Even if you can't see them, you know the leafy trees are full of birds and wildlife. And look—there next to the road— a family of raccoons, showing the little ones how to check for traffic."

Julia slowed to be sure the tiny creatures would not venture beyond the verge. "They are cute, aren't they? Even though I don't think so when they knock my garbage can over in the middle of the night. And speaking of furry things, how's my favorite cat? Did Elijah enjoy his trip to South Carolina?"

"Oh, he did! We stayed with my old college roommate, who has two little cat-crazy girls. They spoiled him outrageously. He's developed quite a taste for shrimp, although I've warned him that they are too expensive for cat food when I have to buy them rather than just scooping them out of the bay with a net."

"How did he feel about oysters? That's what I remember about South Carolina."

"Wrong season for oysters, although I'm sure he'll love them if we go back in the fall."

"So, you hit the South Carolina Historical Society's archives, and Elijah stayed home to eat and sleep."

"Oh, he had long sessions of entertainment, I promise you. There were dozens of little green lizards in the yard, and they spent their days sunning themselves on the walls. Elijah went crazy every time he spotted them, although to my knowledge he never caught one. Their tails break off if a predator tries to sink a claw into them.

"Oh, and you should have seen him at the beach! We took him to explore the Atlantic one day. The waves scared him at first, but I had him leashed and harnessed to keep him from getting swept out to sea. And then he looked around and realized that he was standing on sand—the world's biggest kitty litter box. He scratched, squatted, and covered. I think he planned to mark every inch of that sand—but only until he uncovered a crab who snapped back at him."

"I love that cat!"

"Me, too. I'm never lonely if he's with me."

"You didn't even miss David?"

"Well, I did, but I get more accomplished when he isn't around to distract me."

"I hear he's doing well with his recovery."

"I'll know more after we have dinner tomorrow night."

A few minutes later, Julia turned into a dirt parking area in front of an anonymous-looking diner.

Sarah frowned. "There aren't any other cars here. Are you sure they're open for lunch?"

"Most of their regular customers are working folks, not the lucky few like us who have the summer months free. But Momma will be in the kitchen, stirring the sauces and chopping the vegetables. She'll be happy to see us."

The familiar bell rang as they pushed the door open and caught their first whiff of garlic-infused tomato essence. A red-faced little woman bustled her way through the kitchen's swinging door and wiped her face with a corner of her apron.

Then a smile lit up her face as she recognized two of her favorite customers. "Bambinos! You back in town so early? Come. Come in and let me look at you."

She hugged Julia and then grasped Sarah by the shoulders to stare at her face. "You, Sarah. You look much better than the last time I saw you. Life is treating you better, eh?"

"Yes, Momma. Everything is fine. And how are you?"

"Eh. So-so. I don't like this summer weather and the biting bugs it brings."

The response was so unusual for the cheerful little woman that Sarah and Julia exchanged a worried look. "Where's Papa?" Julia asked, looking around the empty dining area.

"Is long story. I tell you all about it once I get your pizzas in the oven. Sit down and be comfortable. I bring you some cold *limonata* when I come back."

Julia was still frowning. "Her English only deteriorates when she's upset. Something's not right. I had expected Papa to be trotting out of the back by now."

"Maybe it's just an early fight."

"Could be, but I intend to find out."

She didn't have to wait long. Momma brought a tray with three glasses of lemon soda garnished with mint leaves and plopped down on the end chair. "Papa in hospital. He fall down in street, but doctor say nothing wrong with his legs. He think maybe it's his heart. So they do tests, and we wait to hear results. He not happy, and me, neither."

"Oh, Momma, I'm so sorry. Which hospital?"

"He's in Cookeville . . ." She hesitated as she struggled to recall the formal name. "Cookeville Regional Medical Center. It was the closest when the ambulance came to get him after the fall."

"How long will he be there? Have they told you?"

"No. Depends on what his tests show, maybe."

"What can we do to help?"

"Nothing. I work because he can't stand to have me hanging around the hospital bed, and he worries about the business running without his help. I visit him early in mornings before restaurant opens. But there's nothing else to be done for now. It seems strange that he's not under foot. No one to fight with. I get your pizzas." She gave them a brave smile as she headed for the kitchen.

Julia grimaced with frustration. "Poor dear soul. This might be the first time they have slept apart."

"I'm sure you're right. And I know from my own reactions that when I miss David, no one else can make me feel better. We must keep checking on her, though, just in case . . ."

For a few minutes, both young women appeared lost in thought. "Maybe we could take her to visit him, or . . ."

"I wonder if she needs help here, not that I'm equipped to be a waitress, but . . ."

"I heard that! Just stop it. Both of you. Don't sit there feeling sorry for me. Yes, I miss Papa, and I worry about him. But you can't fix things for me." Momma slid the pizzas across the table and rejoined them.

"Uh oh, time for one of your lectures?"

"Maybe so. Let me tell you about how people act when they have troubles. Small children don't have any sense of time. They only know what they are feeling. So a child with a boo-boo only knows it hurts, and it doesn't help when her mother tells her it will only hurt for a few days. All she knows is that it hurts now. And teenagers are just as bad. Tell a fourteen-year-old she can't attend an unchaperoned drinking party, and she'll throw a tantrum about how you have just ruined her social standing—maybe even her entire life."

"You're right. My little sister has her entire life ruined every couple of weeks!"

"Most people outgrow that stage when they fall in love

and marry. For the first time, they are putting someone else's needs ahead of their own. The two of you are splendid examples—you've reached that age of awareness when you experience your first meaningful love affair. That is why you are sitting here worrying about what I need and wanting to fix things for me. You're happy and you want everyone else to be happy, too. It's sweet of you, but you don't yet understand the nature of sadness. The older you get, the further you'll try to stretch. You'll work within your community, reach out to people through charitable organizations, try to make the world a better place. But in the long run, you can't ever protect people from injury or grief or fear."

"We have to try."

"And you're bound to fail, because all those bad things—pain, sorrow, despair—they are all necessary parts of life. You can't take them away. Without pain, a person wouldn't appreciate good health. Without fear there would be no relief. Without grief, no joy."

"So, what should we do? Ignore the pain of others? That seems hard-hearted."

"Not ignore, but share, hug, smile, understand. You can't fix the problem, but you can help carry the load. When your friend cries, you must not tell her to smile. Instead, you tell her it's all right to cry. And in old age, most people will discover how to accept—a realization that all experiences serve a purpose if we can be still and try to discover what lesson life is trying to teach us.

"I'm learning that now, and I find the process comforting. I learn that I can cope with this series of setbacks, and that reassures me that I'll be able to cope with the next one, whatever it turns out to be. So you must not try to solve my problems. Just tell me I still make a good pizza, and we'll all move on."

Sarah and Julia stood and moved toward the tiny Italian

lady, each one planting a kiss on one of her withered cheeks. "Momma, you still make the best pizza in Tennessee!"

Sarah had a far-away expression on her face as they left the restaurant. Julia let her explore her feelings for a while before putting forth a gentle prod. "Mama's lecture must have touched a memory for you."

"It did. If her theory is correct, all that drama—and trauma—surrounding Cassie last year must have taught me a lesson. I was wondering what that lesson might be. So far, all I remember is my fear of her stalking behavior and the pain she caused everyone who knew her. David's wounds were so severe that they remain in a class of their own. But when I close my eyes, I also see the terrible hurt that shattered Dr. Brokowski and drove him into retirement.

"I think there are lessons for all of us in those events. But perhaps we're still too young to appreciate them. Remember, Mama was talking about the understanding that comes with age and experience. Perhaps this school year will suggest some comparisons."

Chapter Three

REUNION

Saturday, August 8, 2009

The next afternoon, Sarah dithered over what to wear for her reunion dinner with David Cohen, her on-again-off-again boyfriend. She had not seen him since graduation day back in May, and both of them had experienced major changes since then. A long, celebratory brunch that day had repaired some issues that had driven them apart, and they had renewed a commitment to their friendship. But time and circumstances had not allowed them enough time to put their mutual attraction to a test. They had parted on good terms, both determined to make their relationship work even as their individual lives pulled them in opposite directions.

Sarah had left town almost immediately to immerse herself in research for a book that would satisfy the college's 'publish-or-perish' policy toward new faculty members. Dragging her cat Elijah with her as a traveling companion, she had headed first to the University of North Carolina and its library holdings in Southern history. Then she had spent a week in the old-fashioned Carolingiana Library in Columbia, South Carolina, before heading to the delights of Charleston and its rich cultural attractions.

Her Boston College roommate, Bettina Malmesbury, had proved to be an excellent hostess and guide, escorting Sarah deep into the Low Country that still harbored the descendants of cotton-growing slaves. The history faculty at Charleston College had also made her feel welcome and had worked eagerly to include her in their plans for a Jubilee Year celebration in 2012.

In stark contrast to Sarah's combination of research and touristy activities, David had spent his summer in the hospital at Johns Hopkins, where he had undergone an experimental reconstruction of his entire right shoulder—the result of the shooting incident that had nearly taken his life and had put an end to his police career. And no matter how much he—and Sarah, too—tried to put that recent trauma behind them, neither of them could forget the horrors of that night.

A mentally ill young woman, one of Sarah's students, had set out to pull a prank on the history department's faculty. But the incident escalated and spiraled out of control. Wild flowers the woman had thought would cause an irritating rash turned out to be deadly poisonous. The college summoned hazmat teams and police. The student broke into Sarah's apartment looking for a place to hide, and David found himself in the line of fire when the young woman panicked. While Sarah was rushing David to the hospital, the student fled from police in her husband's truck. At the first turn, she hit a bridge abutment. The truck flipped over a viaduct into a fiery crash that claimed her life and changed the futures of many who had known her.

This dinner, Sarah realized, represented much more than a simple welcome home. Questions lingered after the crash.

Would Sarah be able to forget the disastrous conclusion to her first year of teaching and make a fresh start with a new class of students? Would David find that his newly created job was as satisfying in reality as it had sounded when the police chief had proposed it? And had their relationship survived the past weeks of separation?

Sarah stared at her closet, mired in doubt. She rejected anything that might seem too sexy and a number of little black dresses that were too somber. She fingered an embroidered denim that seemed too casual, and a block print that was too controlling and formal. A paisley print? No. At last she settled on a neutral linen sheath enlivened only by a long chain necklace of golden flowers, colored glass beads, and wooden shell carvings. Low-heeled sandals completed a picture of simplicity and comfort. This evening was a final exam—a test that might determine the shape of the rest of their lives. The coolness of her outfit belied the inner turmoil she felt.

Sarah froze when the doorbell rang. Then, taking a deep breath, she opened the door, and her fears disappeared. At that moment, the world might have stopped spinning without her noticing.

"Hi, beautiful!"

"David. Oh, David!" With an enormous smile, she threw herself into his arms and curled herself into the safety of his embrace.

"Wow! It's a good thing I'm not the mailman."

Sarah giggled. "You're not the mailman? Darn it! I had such high hopes."

Refusing to rise to the bait, David pushed his face into the tangle of her curls and pulled her closer. The two stood wrapped in a single contented package. At last Sarah realized both his arms were around her, and she pulled away far enough to stare into his eyes. "David. Your arm. It's holding me in a tight embrace, just as it always did. How wonderful that feels."

"I told you the surgery was a success."

"I didn't dare hope . . ."

"The arm gets stronger every day. I still have a hard time reaching over my head, and I try not to lift too many heavy objects, but for embracing the people I love, it works just fine."

"You've been experimenting, have you? With whom?" Sarah was laughing as she teased him. All her fears had evaporated, leaving behind nothing but a familiar cloud of belonging.

David grinned back at her. "My sister? My grandmother? My old first-grade teacher? Who did you think I meant?"

"I don't know—an attractive physical therapist or your new secretary?"

"Not a chance. The therapist was a crusty old Marine, and my new secretary is sixty if she's a day."

"Good!"

The banter had put any lingering doubts to rest for both of them. They forgot they had ever been apart. Hand in hand, they moved into the living room, and David looked around. "Where's your furry roommate?"

"Elijah? He was here just a minute ago. Maybe you scared him."

"Do cats forget so quickly?"

"Well, he hasn't seen you since the night you . . ." She stopped, not wanting to stir up painful memories.

"He needn't worry. I may not have been around for a while, but I haven't forgotten him." He reached into his pocket and pulled out a catnip mouse. "Elijah? Come on out, little buddy. I have something for you."

"The bedroom door," Sarah whispered and nodded toward the hall.

Slowly, stomach close to the floor and tail tucked in, the little black cat crept down the hall toward the living room.

David crouched and dangled the mouse by its tail—a move no self-respecting cat could resist. As the cat reached for the toy, David pulled it away. "Not so fast, there, fellow. You could at least say hello before you grab your treat and run off to have a nip party."

Obligingly, Elijah wrapped himself around David's ankles, purring loudly.

"That's better. Still up for a game of fetch?" David tossed the mouse down the hall and watched as the cat flew after it. "Now bring it back."

Elijah carried the mouse gently in his teeth, dropped it at David's feet, and then watched eagerly for the next toss. But the second time he retrieved the mouse, he carried it off into the kitchen.

Sarah shook her head in mock embarrassment. "Once a catnip addict, always an addict."

"That was my plan. Now he won't miss us while we go off for a celebratory dinner. Ready?"

I solde's was their favorite restaurant. It reminded them of their first proper date—a college cocktail reception after which the younger faculty fled to Isolde's back room for dessert crêpes amid the warmth of a piano bar. Sarah and David had felt at home that night and returned for a Valentine's Day dinner. And that had been the night they had fallen in love, sharing their hopes and dreams until the wait staff had politely but firmly pushed them out the door long after closing hours.

"I love this place," Sarah admitted as the *maitre d'* settled her chair at just the right moment. "It has such great ambiance that I almost forget we're here to eat. I'd be happy just absorbing the old mahogany furnishings, damask table-cloths, the chandeliers, piano music coming from the back room, candles on the table, rosebuds in crystal vases, sparkling silver . . ."

"*Pardon*," a voice at her elbow interrupted. "The chef sends his greetings and offers this evening's am*use-bouche* to tempt your palates." He placed a tiny silver plate in front of each of them. The plates held what appeared to be an Asian soup spoon bearing a perfectly grilled stuffed mushroom topped with a sliver of shimmering glacé. With a tentative finger, Sarah touched the spoon handle and then drew back in surprise.

The waiter nodded, never cracking a smile. "We make the spoon of bread—perfectly edible. *Bon appétit.*"

"How brilliant! But it's almost too perfect to eat."

"Not for me," David mumbled through his first bite. "Just wait till you taste it."

Sarah stared at hers a moment longer, wanting to remember every image. Then she, too, succumbed and ate every crumb. When the waiter had removed their service plates, they sat back and stole glances at each other.

"This is the awkward time, isn't it—when you flounder around trying to think of a conversation starter?" David's smile was warm and adoring.

"It is. I'd usually fill the silence by picking up the menu and pretending to study it, but . . ." She looked around the table, aware for the first time that no such time filler was available.

"Sorry, but there will be no menu tonight. The chef has

been planning your welcome home meal all week. You have no decisions to make, except for what to enjoy next."

"You've had a hand in this, I suspect."

"Only now and then." The sommelier had arrived bearing a silver ice bucket wrapped in a damask napkin. With a flourish he extracted his trusty waiter's tool, twisted off the wire guard, and popped the champagne cork. He poured a small amount into David's glass and waited for his nod of approval before filing the two champagne flutes he had supplied. "*Salut*," he nodded before disappearing as quietly as he had come.

"Here's to a wonderful year to come." David clicked the rim of his glass to hers and threw her a silent kiss.

The champagne loosened their tongues, and they chattered comfortably about their plans for the weeks ahead. David was excited about his new office, which the mayor's staff had furnished and decorated while he was recuperating in Baltimore. Sarah countered with her description of the sawdust and cotton fibers that had greeted her upon her return.

At some point, a platter of tomato bruschetta and hot spiced olives had arrived, and they plunged into it as if starved. "These are wonderful! I've never had an olive that wasn't cold from the fridge, but heating them gives them another whole layer of flavor. Your buddy the chef is a genius. I wonder if he teaches classes."

"Oh, no, you don't. He'd steal your heart in an instant. You must settle for an occasional sampling of his wares."

The bustling arrival of more waiters interrupted their conversation. The youngest removed the empty appetizer platter and their service plates, brushing the crumbs away with his handy brass butler's helper. A second young man supplied fresh plates and different silverware. The sommelier returned to refill their champagne flutes.

Then, with a flourish, the head waiter appeared, pushing a cart upon which rested a domed silver platter. He placed the cart next to David's right elbow and lifted the lid to reveal the feast within—a perfectly cooked filet of beef surrounded by tiny frill-topped carrots, slender spears of spring asparagus, and tempura-fried baby squashes still with their blossoms attached, the whole swimming in a sea of glistening red wine reduction. "Your chateaubriand, sir. Would you like me to carve for you?"

"Yes, please. While I trust my new skills with my bionic arm, I try not to over-extend them. If someone is going to send that beautiful piece of meat flying off the platter, I'd rather it be you than me."

The waiter deftly sliced the filet and filled each of their plates before replacing the silver lid. "Your second servings will be warm and waiting when you are ready. Or we can pack them up for your midnight snacking, whichever you prefer." With a barely suppressed smile, he withdrew quietly. David chuckled and Sarah blushed.

S arah took a few moments to absorb the perfection of the plate in front of her before taking a tentative first taste. "Oh, that sauce is amazing! The filet itself would win me over, but the added flavor—what is it?"

"I believe I detect a black truffle or two," David suggested. "And do you approve of finding edible flowers on the menu?"

"They're squash blossoms, aren't they? I've only read about them, but I like their crunchiness as a counter note to the creaminess of the carrots and asparagus. It's all delicious."

Their conversation died away as they gave themselves over to enjoying the meal. After several minutes, however, David looked up and found Sarah staring at him.

"You're not eating. Is something wrong?"

"No. It's just . . . I can't help noticing that you eat like a Frenchman. Why have I never noticed that before?"

"Ah, the left-handed fork! It's a newly acquired skill."

"To accommodate your injury?"

"Not exactly, although it was a physical therapist who insisted I make the change. He ridiculed the way Americans wield their silverware. Watch. We eat with a fork on our right hand, tines pointed up. But to cut a bite of meat, we switch the fork to the left, pick up the knife in our right, impale the piece of meat on the fork with tines down, cut a chewable piece from the whole, lay the knife down, switch the fork back to the right with tines up, and then chase the bite around the plate trying to catch it." He demonstrated the American style while making a parody of it.

"A proper European holds his fork in the left hand with tines pointed down, his knife in the right, and never puts either of them down. The fork holds the bite while the knife cuts it, and then it goes straight to the mouth. Much more efficient! And it's so much easier. My injured arm had to re-learn only one motion, not a whole series of changes. Beyond that, it allows for much quicker eating, which conceals how much you have consumed. At least that's my excuse for gaining several pounds while in Baltimore."

"In that case, you'll not sell many women on your new method."

"Perhaps not, but it makes me ready for seconds. Can I serve you?"

"Heavens, no! I'll be lucky to finish this plate. But you go right ahead. It would be a shame to turn this fantastic meal into leftovers."

As David turned his attention to the covered platter on their table-side cart, Sarah experimented with a left-handed fork. But when David noticed, she shook her head in dismay. "It feels awkward and clumsy."

"That's because you're clutching the fork in your fist like a child." He smiled indulgently. "Here, let me show you. Put the fork down and imagine that you have no silverware at all. See that piece of meat on your plate? Pick it up with your left hand and eat it from your fingers."

Sarah looked around to be sure no one was watching. Then she did as he asked. As her index finger and thumb reached her lips, David put out his hand and stopped her.

"Look at the position of your hand. See how your index finger points toward the bite of food? Now, put it down and try it with the fork. Hold your hand in that same position and slide the fork between your thumb and index finger. Tines down. Put your finger on the slender neck of the fork, so that the tines become an extension of your index finger. Feel that position." His hand rested on hers and then began a slow caress. "Now eat your bite of steak and see how good it feels."

As she took that bite of food, his hand moved slightly to trace the line of her jaw. The air around them felt charged with electricity, and every word they spoke whispered an innuendo. With a visible effort, David pulled his hand away, although his eyes never left her face. "Don't let your dinner get cold."

Slightly puzzled by his on-again, off-again advances, Sarah once again turned her own attention to the food in front of her. When they had finished their meal, she leaned back in repletion. "I may never need to eat again."

"You'll change your mind soon enough," he warned as the waiters once again descended on the table and whisked away all traces of dinner. On cue, the *maitre d'* arrived with another of his silver trays. "The chef suggests an appropriate *entremets* —a palate cleanser. We have for you a *trou Normand*—an apple sorbet drizzled with Calvados, an apple brandy. It creates a 'Norman hole' to make room for what is yet to come."

Sarah used her spoon to sample the puddle of Calvados on the bottom of the dessert glass. Both David and the waiter watched in trepidation as she sputtered and choked on the straight liqueur. When her eyes stopped running and she could breathe again, she grinned. "That's wonderful stuff!"

"Indeed, it is, but best taken with some cooling sorbet to ease its passage."

They had almost finished the *entremets* before Sarah noticed that the waiter's silver tray had delivered not just the two dessert glasses but also a third crystal container—a tiny lidded box.

"After-dinner mints?" she asked, nodding at the little box.

"No, we're not nearly finished yet. This was just a break between events."

David reached for the box and held it out to her.

"Sarah Rebecca Chomsky, I have adored you since the first day I met you. I have waited patiently through our history of ups and downs. I have accepted your career goals and your five-year plans for your life. I have loved your cat and not asked that you love my interfering Jewish mother. I have shown my devotion by putting my life on the line for yours. But now I have a favor to ask of you.

"In this tiny box is a pledge of my fidelity and a circle of my hopes and dreams. It is not an engagement ring. It goes on your right hand, not your left, at least for now. It asks no promises and makes none. It is not a diamond. I will not offer you a diamond in anything other than an engagement ring. I offer you my heart and hope that you are ready to admit that a bond of love ties us together—that we are a couple, and that we intend to go on moving through life as a team. I want the world to know that I love you and that you love me in return."

Sarah's heart was beating wildly as she took the box from

his hand. She lifted the hinged lid and gasped at a brilliant blue star sapphire surrounded by a circle of tiny seed pearls. Her hands were shaking so badly that she was afraid to touch it. She handed the box back to David and extended her hand.

"Will you put it on?"

As he lifted the ring and slipped it onto her finger, they might have been alone on a mountaintop. But they were in a crowded restaurant, and there was no way to hide what had just happened. The pianist burst into a medley of love songs, the other diners applauded, and the chef himself approached their table bearing a chocolate tart adorned with raspberries and a tiny sparkler.

Chapter Four

REVELATIONS

Sunday, August 9, 2009

Sarah struggled with her awakening. Several layers of cloth bound her arms, and she couldn't find her pillow. Her head ached, her lips felt cracked, and her eyes were gummy. A beam of sunlight made her wince with pain, but she recognized her own bedroom, the bedspread she lay upon, and the throw that had wrapped itself around her. Only her feet felt free—and cold. As she peered beneath the throw, she also recognized the simple linen sheath she had worn to dinner, although now it was a mass of wrinkles.

Trying to decide if she was alive or dead, she pushed herself to her feet and made her way to the bathroom. The cold tiles reminded her she had not found her slippers. One glance into the mirror was enough to make her question the wisdom of getting out of bed. She closed her eyes and splashed water on her makeup-smeared face, wiped the streaks off with a washcloth, and pushed her fingers through her tangled curls. The improvement was marginal. She stripped off the wrinkled dress, dropped it into the hamper, and cuddled into the plush robe she had left hanging behind the door. Two headache capsules and several deep breaths somewhat relieved the pain at the base of her skull, and she felt almost ready to face the morning.

"Coffee," she muttered to herself as she found her slippers and shuffled across the hall to the kitchen. A plaintive meow answered her. "Look out, cat. This is not the time to practice your ankle-weaving. Why can't you learn something useful, like how to plug in the coffee pot?"

"Sounds like a dangerous idea to me. Knowing Elijah, he'd brew you a cup of catnip tea instead of coffee."

At the sound of an unexpected voice, Sarah had clutched her throat, her heart racing and fear blurring her ability to think. She groped for a butcher knife and turned to face the intruder.

"David! What are you doing here? How did you . . .?" Then she noticed his tousled hair and his wrinkled clothes.

"Did you stay here all night?"

"Didn't intend to, but I guess I did."

"Oh no, don't tell me. We didn't . . . uh, we didn't, did we?"

"No. That I would have remembered. Your virtue is safe for another day, my lady."

"But what happened? I'm fuzzy on the details of coming home."

"Well, you kept falling asleep on the drive from the restaurant. I suspect that last shot of Calvados did you in. When we got here, I thought you were awake, but once inside the apartment you just wandered away from me and fell across the bed, out like the proverbial light. I pulled your shoes off and covered you with the throw from the rocking chair, but then I was afraid to leave you. I stretched out on your couch to wait for you to wake up again. And here we are, halfway through the morning."

"I'm embarrassed!"

"Don't be. You were a charming drunk, gentle and peaceful in your sleep. And I drank as much as you did. If I had been a cop, I'd have pulled me over for DWI."

Sarah giggled at the image and then winced as another pain stabbed through her forehead. "We both need coffee!"

~

Sarah poured fresh coffee into two large mugs. "Cream and sugar?"

"Ugh! No. Black, please."

"I agree." She moved their mugs to the kitchen island, and they settled themselves side by side on the stools that turned the island into a countertop table. They remained quiet for several minutes while the coffee cooled enough to drink. Sarah's hand rested on the counter, displaying her new ring.

"It's beautiful, and I love it, but . . ."

"But? Please don't tell me you're having second thoughts. We're way beyond that point." David was frowning at her.

"They're not second thoughts, exactly, but . . ."

"Well, come on. Spit it out." His night on the couch left him too frazzled to display his usual patience.

"There's something you don't know, and I don't think I can wear this ring while keeping a major secret from you." She slid the ring from her finger and placed it on the counter between them. "And I can't control your reaction. It's for you to decide."

"I'm waiting. Get to the point."

She took a deep breath. "I'm not the innocent single woman you think I am. My first marriage ended in divorce while I was still a teenager."

Despite his resolve to remain non-judgmental, David's face changed. His eyes widened, his nostrils flared as if he couldn't get enough air, and his lips compressed into a tight line. She was right about the effect her pronouncement had upon him. He had no words.

"It was a high school romance. I was seventeen and convinced that Aaron Lehman was the love of my life. In our senior year, I realized my parents expected me to go off to university. They pushed me to apply to Boston College, and when I did, I received an early acceptance and a sizable scholarship. Everyone congratulated me, except Aaron. He came from a working-class family; his father ran a small kosher[1] butcher shop. Aaron had neither the money, nor the grades, nor the desire for further education. He wanted me to stay home with him. Naturally, my parents would not hear of such a thing. One weekend, I let Aaron talk me into eloping. We ran off to New Jersey, lied about our ages, and persuaded a small-town judge to marry us in the courthouse. We kept the marriage a secret just long enough to graduate from high school.

"The morning after graduation we told our parents, and they were furious. My father quit speaking to me for several days, but the Lehmans tried to help us find a solution. Aaron's father gave him a job at the butcher shop. Aaron hated the shop. His mother took me in hand and tried to teach me the fine points of keeping a kosher kitchen. I hated the kitchen. They gave us a place to live, and we both hated the damp basement apartment in their house. Everyone was miserable, and it didn't take long for us to realize the marriage was a mistake. My parents wanted to declare the wedding invalid because we had lied about our ages on the license, but we had waited too long to do anything but go through a regular divorce procedure.

"The details were unpleasant, and I've tried my best to forget it ever happened. I delayed my matriculation at Boston College until the second semester, and once there, I took extra classes to make sure I graduated on time with the rest of my class. And if I'm honest, I'll admit that I went to graduate school because I felt safer when I was in school. I've been hiding out from marriage ever since."

David studied her face while she finished the story. "Where is he now—this Aaron?"

"I don't know. We haven't spoken since the day we signed the divorce papers."

"Your parents? The neighbors? No gossip?"

"My folks moved out of the Bronx and into a new neighborhood in Brooklyn shortly after I went to Boston. I've never gone back, nor do I want to. That period of my life is long buried, David. I never think about it—or didn't until your family started talking about our marriage, and I realized that I would have to answer questions about it from the rabbi.[2] I didn't want the news to blindside you."

David picked up the ring and twisted it in his fingers. "I told you last night that this ring represents my heart, which I have already given you. Nothing you have told me has changed how I feel about you. If anything, I trust you more because you felt compelled to tell me the truth. Let's put it back on that finger where it belongs. And then I'm going to declare a general policy. We will spend our lives looking toward the future, not glancing back at our regrets.

"Easy enough for you to say. You don't have any regrets or early indiscretions."

"You think not? That's where you would be wrong. I guess it's my turn to play 'True Confessions.'"

"What did you do that now embarrasses you?"

"Well, I have a criminal record."

David stretched and fidgeted for a minute. "This may not sound as serious as an elopement, but it's something I never talk about. I was fourteen, maybe fifteen, a bored teenager not interested in much besides our local minor league baseball team. A bunch of us guys were walking home one Saturday afternoon after another losing game. The big debate was about our incompetent pitching staff. One fellow suggested that they must have trained by throwing rocks because none of them knew how to handle a baseball. Somebody else thought real rock-throwing could have taught them all a thing or two. And from there the discussion went to our own rock-throwing talents.

"It so happened that there was an empty office building at the end of our block, and I bragged that I could throw a rock clear over the top of that building. The guys jeered at me and suggested I was only willing to try that because iron grillwork protected all the windows from breaking. One thing led to another, and we soon had a regular contest going. It wasn't as hard as it looked, and we soon had a real barrage of missiles sailing over the roof.

"The fun ended when alarms went off, and a police car swooped down upon us. We thought of running away, but the sight of real police guns changed our minds. We tried to explain that we were just having fun, but they accused us of breaking and entering. After all, something had set off the burglar alarms. One of the investigating officers returned to report that the door locks were still intact, but broken glass littered the floor. Our rocks had shattered the skylights on the roof of the building. So much for window protection! The police needed to locate the building owner so that he could get some tarps placed over the broken windows before the next big rain arrived. What happened to us—the perpetrators—didn't seem to matter much.

"The cops crammed us all into the back seat of the patrol car and took us to the police station. They interviewed each of us, wrote down our parents' contact information, took our pictures and fingerprints, and then pushed us into their holding tank. It wasn't long before our parents started showing up. My father—lawyer that he was—glowered when he found his son sitting on a bench in a bare jail cell.

"As I look back on it now, I can see that the cops went easy on us, but at the time I was too scared to appreciate it. They asked for ten dollars as a security pledge, signed us out into our parents' custody, and sent us home with instructions to report to the courthouse on Monday for our arraignments. After listening to our parents tell us how stupid we had been, we were all prepared to do jail time. Instead, the arresting officer argued for our oblivious ignorance of the damage we were causing, the judge gave us a lecture on civic responsibility, the warden of the juvenile detention center argued that he didn't have room for us, and the building owner agreed not to press further charges if our families paid to have his skylights repaired.

"Thus ended my crime spree. After my first promotion as a cop, I checked the files for my name. And there it was. According to the police record, I was still little pimply-faced Davey Cohen—mug shot and fingerprints still on file and a notation on the police report that I was guilty as charged according to my confession but not convicted because the victim refused to prosecute."

"And that's why you wanted to become a cop?"

"I don't know. Maybe so. I suspect we both have taken our early life lessons and translated them into behaviors we continue to act upon today. I want to understand what makes our suspects act as they do, and you want to rescue those who make poor decisions from ruining their own lives."

"It's the same thing, isn't it? Some folks would call it 'paying it forward.'"

"Just two do-gooders—that's us."

David stood up again and stretched. "I need to go home and take a shower to loosen up my back muscles. That sofa of yours is lovely, but it's not designed for healthful sleep. Believe me or not, I really didn't intend to spend the night and monopolize your morning."

"I didn't mind. It was kind of fun to wake up and find you here. And we've learned a lot about each other, I think."

"All to the good. Oh, before I leave, I need to warn you that you will find a kitty bag inside your fridge with the remains of our chateaubriand."

"Chateaubriand for the cat? I think not! Sounds like supper to me."

"But I promised him . . ."

"Maybe a bite or two, but I'm only willing to share, not sacrifice the whole thing."

"Fair enough. We didn't talk about your plans for the week, either."

"It's a busy week, I'm afraid. I have only ten days before I go back to work full time, and I need to spend them writing. Dr. Chalmers has made his publish-or-perish expectations clear—with his emphasis on the threat of perishing. Fortunately, I have most of the research completed. Now it's just a matter of pulling it all together."

"You're still talking about slaves and conch shells?"

"Yes, and they will appear in three different publications."

"Isn't that confusing?"

"No. It's a natural progression. I'll start this afternoon. If you were a fly on the wall (and I'm not recommending that!)

you'd find me puttering and talking to myself as I hash out my arguments. By Monday I should be ready to sit down and outline a twenty-minute lecture, like the stories I tell in the classroom. I'll talk about finding the slave cemetery and the questions raised by the conch shells. That's designed as an entertaining conference presentation. I never write out a lecture and read it aloud. It's much more believable and interesting if I tell it off the cuff. As soon as I'm satisfied with it, I'll condense it to a one-page proposal and send it off to the next available conference organizer.

"Then I'll write the same thing out in formal language, adding scholarly references and footnotes. In this longer version, I'll explain the meaning behind the conch shells. That's the format of an article aimed at a scholarly reading audience. It will get a day or so of editing, and off it goes to one or more academic journals.

"And then comes the third iteration, this time as the introductory chapter of a much broader topic. The third version puts its emphasis not just on the conch shells themselves, but on their symbolism in the minds of the slaves. That gives me at least a start at formulating a book proposal. And putting the three steps together satisfies all the demands my department chair has in mind.

"It's a simple approach, but it works best if I can concentrate on producing one format right after another. Ten days should be more than enough time. And then maybe—just maybe—I'll be free by next weekend." She grinned up at him.

"That sounds like a bribe: leave me alone for this week and I'll repay you by Saturday."

"You're an absolute mind reader. Now, go home and let me get started."

∽

To mark the start of the new school year, Sarah invited David; Julia Winthrop; Julia's usual escort, Bert Wheeler, the basketball coach; along with two other good friends, Beth Wilkerson from the English department and Lyle Agaretti from Biology, to join her for wine and heavy snacks in her apartment on Saturday evening. It was a casual and relaxed affair, the friends happy to be back together after being scattered across the country all summer. There was enough chill in the mountain air to suggest a fire, and the group sprawled around the fireplace, munching on snacks as they exchanged funny stories about their summer adventures.

Everyone wanted to hear about David's surgery, and he regaled them with tales of passing through airport security checks now that he was a bionic mixture of bones, porcelain plates, and stainless-steel pins and braces. Bert had spent his summer working hand in hand with the construction crew building his new gymnasium and civic center. When he challenged David to test his recovery with an arm-wrestling match, David declined, bowing to the muscles bulging Bert's forearm. Lyle had spent his summer in the woods of Maine, fighting nothing meaner than some blood-sucking mosquitoes. He had, however, discovered what appeared to be a heretofore unrecognized species of mushroom—a find that might provide the stuff of several academic papers.

Beth described her adventures in the Bodleian Library in Oxford, where she had traveled in search of early editions of Chaucer's *Canterbury Tales*. Several of the handwritten editions contained pornographic sketches made by the pious monks who copied the manuscript. Despite the rules against photography, she had captured some delightful images on her phone. She passed the phone around for all to see, although she admitted she wouldn't have the courage to describe them in an academic publication.

"Oh, but you have to write about them. That legitimizes them. Otherwise they just become your private porn stash." Lyle was laughing at her blushing cheeks. To draw attention away from Beth's embarrassment, Sarah described her own adventures in bathroom humor, using the story of Elijah trying to use the entire South Carolina beach as his personal toilet.

At last, they turned to Julia. "How were things in Birch Falls, Julia? You weren't traveling, were you?" She glared at them and grumbled at having had to stay home all summer to read job applications and deal with sawdust and cotton fluff.

"I've heard your time wasn't all spent that way," David jibed. "To hear Bert tell it, you had some exciting moments at one point."

Now it was Julia's turn to blush. She caught her lower lip between her teeth as she glanced at her left hand and moved it out of sight.

Sarah stared at her, took the hidden hand in her own, and turned it over. "That's much too beautiful a diamond to keep hidden under your sleeve." The room filled with shouts of congratulation as the friends realized what had happened.

"When's the wedding?" Beth demanded. "Tell us every detail."

"We don't have any details yet. It's all new to us, too. But I'm guessing . . ." She looked at Bert, whose face had gone soft with adoration.

"Go ahead, hon. I'm as curious as anyone. What are you thinking?"

"Well, I have a year's sabbatical starting next September, and it might be good for us to have that year to adjust to married life. So, maybe . . . a late summer wedding? What do you think, Sarah? Should we make it a double?"

And now it was Sarah's turn to blush as she realized she was making the same gesture of concealment. Taking a deep breath, she held out her right hand. "It's not an engagement ring—wrong hand. But, yes, it is a symbol of a 'committed relationship.'"

"How could you not tell us?" Beth demanded.

"It's only been a week," Sarah pleaded. "This is the first time we've all been together."

"Well, I think it's wonderful. And say what you will about which finger it's on, it's beautiful enough to serve as an engagement ring, too."

"Is that a hidden message for me?" Lyle was giving Beth a look of mock horror. "Hey, I bought you some mushrooms."

"It's true. He did. He brought me a pair of mushroom earrings, and they are adorable."

"I've at least branded you."

"Maybe so, but you're still on probation. And you don't get to follow along on your friends' coattails. You must concoct your own romantic gestures."

It was a lovely conclusion to the evening, and the three couples parted in a haze of happiness. But now it was time to start the new semester.

Chapter Five

RETURNING STUDENTS

Monday, August 17, 2009

Sarah sat in her car for several minutes. She looked out across the campus with mixed feelings. One part of her was eager to begin the new school year, while in the corners of her mind, niggling little fears reminded her of the disastrous climax to her first year of teaching. She gave herself a mental shaking and a stern lecture. "The past is over. You're an experienced teacher, and your colleagues are your friends. Just look around. The cheerleaders and cotton farmers have departed. Maintenance men have mowed the lawns and swept the sidewalks; construction crews have finished their tasks; and the first students are showing up, eager for new discoveries. This is a new year, and you are lucky to be a part of it. Get on with the program."

The path to her office led her past the amphitheater, the old orchard, and the paddock where the veterinary school kept its animals. Each vista made her smile, none more so than the paddock with its small group of bouncing goats who tracked her movements and ran to the fence to see if she had brought a treat. The imposing façade of Bailey Hall welcomed her, and she noted that her steps were quicker and more determined as she entered the building.

Her friend and mentor, Julia Winthrop, held the elevator door for her, and they rode to the third floor together. "Here we go, ready or not! Gwen told me you've been working from home so you could concentrate on your research project. How's it coming?"

"Good, I think. I have submitted two paper proposals, but I will not talk about them until I see if they draw a response. I've at least had the time to synthesize all the information I picked up over the summer, and I can now concentrate on what's going to be happening in my classroom." She wrinkled her forehead. "I know the university expects us to accomplish great things in teaching and research, but for the life of me, I can't figure out how to do both at the same time. Is there a secret method I'm missing?"

"No, I don't think so. Everyone I know struggles with the conflicting demands on our time. You're handling it well, although I was just thinking about how complicated your calendar must be, what with your Jewish High Holy Days[1] happening so early this year. Are you going to need some help again?

"To be honest, I haven't thought about it yet. And that's because I don't want to think about it." She gave a rueful laugh.

"Is there a particular reason?"

"Since I didn't spend any time in New York this summer, my devoted parents are going to visit me here over part of the High Holy Days. They plan to fly down Thursday, September 17th, rather than travel on the sabbath, and they'll return on the Monday morning flight out of Nashville. Rosh Hashana[2] falls on that Saturday, thank goodness, which makes it more convenient for everyone. I don't have to hostess the dinner, either. My parents also wanted to visit with Rabbi Leibowicz, and he has invited us to celebrate the holiday dinner with him and his family. That's all to the good, except that Mrs. Leibowicz in her usual generosity has also invited the Cohens to dinner. That will also be the first time my folks have met David, and I can't imagine how stressful that will be."

"You can always hope that the religious setting for that meeting will keep everyone on their best behavior."

"From your lips to HaShem's[3] ears!" She rolled her eyes. "As for the rest of the High Holy Days, I suspect I will have many evil thoughts to atone for, but Yom Kippur[4] shouldn't be a problem this year. The fast occurs on Monday, September 28th, and I only have one morning class on that day. I won't need anyone to fill in for me. But thanks for reminding me to write this schedule on the calendar."

"Well, hold that thought for a while. It looks like you already have a small line of eager students waiting to see you."

~

"Good morning, Doc! Are you open for business?" The speaker was a slender young man who looked familiar, but Sarah couldn't place him at first. Then she scrutinized his face, and a memory clicked in.

"Chad? Chad Overstreet? Famous unpacker of my office library?"

"You got it. I'm surprised, though. Lots of people don't recognize me this year."

It seemed a curious comment, but she let it pass. "I assume you're not here looking for more hard labor, so what can I do for you?"

"I need some guidance, but I'm not in a hurry. I believe this young woman was here before me."

Embarrassed that she had spoken first to the male student while ignoring the young woman, Sarah turned to the perky girl who had been leaning on the door frame to watch their conversation. "And what can I do for you, Olivia?"

"You remember me, too? You must have a fantastic memory. I might rather have expected you to remember my father."

"The formidable Mr. Cartwright? That was a parent confrontation I'd rather not recall. How's that family discussion going?"

"That's why I'm here, but it's complicated." She turned to Chad with a dazzling smile. "Are you sure you don't mind waiting? I could come back later in the day if . . ."

"No, no. Go ahead. I'll read the department bulletin board or something."

Sarah busied herself with unlocking the door, turning on the lights, and moving the latest stack of mail to the far side of her desk. Then she settled back into her chair and swiveled to face the young woman waiting just inside the door. "Come, come. As one of my advisees, you're always a priority for me. Sit. How can I help you?"

"Well, I gather that you remember my father ordering you to make me sign up as a business major?"

"Yes, and I told him that should be your decision. Are you still set on pursuing a history degree?"

"We're still both standing behind the lines we've drawn in the sand. Neither of us has been willing to give an inch."

"That must make life at your house rather difficult."

"Which is why I'm living in the dorms, and he's willing to pay the extra room and board money to escape the daily arguments. But I may have come up with an idea, and I need to run it past you."

"Shoot."

"I'm willing to do a double major—business and history

—if that's possible. I know you've never had me in a class, but I promise you I'm an excellent student. The business courses still sound boring, but most seem to be about math, and I'm a numbers whiz. And history is what I do for fun. It's not the course content that worries me; it's the number of required hours. Is there any way to pull this off without taking an extra year to graduate?"

"It won't be easy, but yes, it's possible to double-major and still graduate on schedule."

"When I add up all the required hours, I don't see how, at least not without adding one extra semester, and I know Dad wouldn't like that. He's already scheduled my May 2012 graduation party at the country club." She made a face. "Gah! That sounds so pretentious, but it's exactly the way he thinks." She shuffled through several loose notes and handed one to Sarah. "Here's what I'm seeing."

Sarah glanced at the list of degree requirements and then smiled. "And here's what's confusing you. The university requires every graduate to have a broad general education besides the in-depth studies in your major field. You've listed those required hours as 'Core Courses.' But re-read those requirements, and you'll see they include six hours of the same foreign language. If I recall your record, you had four years of French in high school, right? And you took and passed the qualifying exam during your first week last year. I remember because you were the only one of my advisees who passed. You can scratch those six hours of requirements.

"Next comes the real core, which requires nine hours of social studies, six of which can be history courses. You can double up because you will already have those as a history major. They require you to have six hours of economics, doubling up again as a business major. So your count is eighteen hours off, right from the start. In terms of numbers, you can do this double major and still have room for two electives in the mix."

"Oh, Dr. Chomsky, you're wonderful! And you could remain as my advisor, right?"

"Ah, yes and no on that one. You'll have both a history advisor and a business advisor. But one of those will have to take the lead and make any major decisions on your behalf. The college rule is that when there are two advisors, the senior one prevails. Your business advisor will outrank me, because I'm still the new kid on the block."

"That'll do. You will at least have a hand in my affairs."

"One other problem could arise during your senior year. Both majors require an intensive senior project, and you don't want to be doing them both in the same semester. But we can make sure that doesn't happen. Now the only question is whether you can convince your father to buy the arrangement."

"That I can handle. I've lived with him all my life. I know his soft spots and his tantrum triggers. Trust me. And thank you. You've lifted an enormous weight off my shoulders."

~

"Next!" Chad was smiling, his eyes still following the departure of the young woman who had made his breath come a little quicker than usual. "Do you need some time, or are you ready to take on the next kid with a problem?"

"I'm ready, Chad. Come on in and try out the interview chair you guys found for me. What kind of guidance do you need that your advisor can't handle?"

"That's just it. I don't have an advisor, and I need one."

"Why not? Were you such a problem child that your last

advisor fired you? By my calculation, this is your junior year. You should have made that decision last year."

"It should be my junior year, but it's not. It's the start of my sophomore year again, and I don't have a declared major."

"You've lost me!"

"Wait. You don't know what happened to me, do you? I thought everyone had heard." He gave a rueful chuckle. "Maybe I'm not as important as I assumed."

"Maybe I'm just out of the loop. But you'd better start from scratch and tell me what happened."

"I got hurt—bad—in the second football game last year. Two brutish-looking tackles hit me behind the lines with two head butts, one on either side of my helmet. Have you ever wondered what it would be like to be a fly caught between two cymbals as they crashed together? I found out. There was this huge clanging noise, and then the lights went out. When I woke up, I was lying on the football turf, with the entire team taking a knee in a circle around me and the coaching staff all prodding me to see if I could move. They carted me off the field, but about halfway to the exit ramp I sat up and declared myself to be just fine, thank you. The team doctor looked me over, studied my eyeballs, and told me I was to warm the bench for the whole first half. What a bummer! But when we headed for the locker room at the half, I only made it a few steps before I keeled over again, and that time I didn't wake up.

"At the hospital, the doctor diagnosed a severe concussion and told the nurses to try to wake me every hour. I didn't respond. After several more hours, they diagnosed a traumatic brain injury and admitted that I was in a coma. I didn't wake up for nineteen days, and when I did, I . . ." His voice broke, and he looked away to keep Sarah from seeing the tears in his eyes. "I was a baby again—couldn't talk, couldn't walk, couldn't control . . ."

"Oy veh![5] How frightened you must have been."

"One of the hardest parts was seeing the reactions of my family. My father yelled and threw things in sheer frustration. My mother sat in a chair and sobbed. And my little sisters, when they were finally allowed to visit reverted to childish habits—thumb-sucking, hair-twirling, and such. I knew how scared everyone was, and I was sure it was all my fault—not the best attitude for getting over a TBI."

"But you did get over it. You're here."

"Yes, I did, mostly, but it took months of physical therapy and lots of psychiatric help, too. For the longest time, a wall blocked my path. Words made sense in my head, but all that came out were some sounds like 'an-oh, an-oh.' Movement was like that, too. I could picture myself running down a football grid, zigging and zagging to outrun the tacklers, but when I tried to walk, my legs just flopped around.

"And then one day, it all came back. The concrete wall dissolved, and I could walk and talk again. I can't explain how it happened. My mom says I didn't learn to talk until I was three, but my first words came out in a complete sentence. And that's how it happened again. After five months, I got out of the hospital. I was hungry again—ate everything in sight— and couldn't get enough exercise. The PT folks had to run me out of their gym when their day was over.

"I had missed the whole football season of my sophomore year—not to mention the classes—but I vowed to get back to playing strength. And then came the most crushing blow of all. The doctors called me in for a conference and declared that my football-playing days were over forever. Another hard bump to the head would kill me. I almost said, 'Good!'"

"Eh! It's just a game for little boys, Chad."

"No, you can't understand, I know, but football was my life. That's what I believed from the time I was big enough to hold a ball. I was already a football hero in junior high school, and when I went on to high school, I was the sopho-more starting quarterback, the first the school had ever had. I wasn't big enough to be of interest to one of the big name universities, but a triple-A school fit into my scheme of things because I knew I'd be the star of the show. From the begin-ning, my major was Kinesiology, so I'd understand how the human body worked and moved.

"I planned to play college ball and then take a shot at the NFL draft, showing up as a walk-on if I had to. I thought I'd spend several years playing pro ball, save my huge salaries, and then go into coaching, moving up through the ranks of college coaches. And if the coaching jobs ran out, I'd become a sportscaster, still talking about the game when I could no longer play it.

"But one shot, one good block to the head, and my careful plans burst like a soap bubble, leaving me with nothing. Which is why I'm here. Kinesiology is no longer of any use to me. I missed my entire sophomore year of college, along with a chance to be one of the few underclassmen to win a Heisman trophy. The team went on without me, and they had an excellent record at it, too, I have to admit. Their new quar-terback is the star now in his senior year, and nobody much even remembers me."

"I'm sure that's not true."

"It is. Let me tell you what happened to me just the other day. A scrawny young kid, maybe thirteen or fourteen, all feet and hands, was following me around the grocery store. When he got up enough nerve to approach, he said, 'Hey, didn't you used to be Chad Overstreet, the star quarterback?'"

"Used to be?" Sarah smiled despite his seriousness.

"Yeah. Used to be. As if, without a football, I quit being Chad. And then I realized I believe that, too. My life is over."

"You don't really believe that. You're here, back in school, moving on."

"Into a giant void! I came back to good old Smoky Mountain because the college was generous and refunded all my scholarship money for the year I missed. My folks insisted that I use the money to come back and re-do my sophomore year. It's pretty much a waste of time, because there won't be any money for two more years. My dad's a line foreman at the local toy factory, but he just earns enough to keep us all fed and clothed. Still, I have to have a new major, and I figured history was as good a topic as anything. I know a lot of small schools hire guys to be football coaches in the fall and history teachers the rest of the year."

"Well, if you're asking me to take you on as an advisee, I'd be happy to, but I'll warn you that I won't allow a defeatist attitude within the ranks of my advisee group."

"So long as that little blonde just in here is part of your group, I promise to be sincerely optimistic." He wagged his eyebrows and grinned.

"Her name's Olivia Cartwright, in case you were wondering."

"Cartwright?" Oh, crap! Pardon my French, but she must be my dad's boss's daughter. A fat lot of a chance I'll have there."

Chapter Six

FALL IS A BEGINNING, NOT AN END

August 17–23, 2009

S arah noticed how different she felt this year. Last year she had spent this opening week terrified that she might not make the right moves. She had nightmares about showing up late for a faculty meeting and discovering she was naked. She panicked at every knock at her office door and kept piles of scribbled notes to herself about what she still had to do. She revised her class syllabi several times. She practiced opening lectures in the shower and revisited every waiting classroom to make sure she knew how everything worked.

This year she felt at home. From her office window, she watched the incoming freshmen with gentle amusement, seeing them as untapped potential scholars rather than threatening challengers. She enjoyed talking with returning colleagues and welcomed chat sessions with mid-course graduate students.

Chad and Olivia were only the first of many undergraduate students to visit Sarah's office. She found it rewarding that many of those she had taught last year stopped by to ask what she was teaching in the current semester. Their eagerness spurred her own, and she realized she was impatient to get started with this year's classes.

But first, there were rituals. The faculty came together for the first time on Wednesday morning. They conducted the traditional Pledge of Allegiance, a prayer for a successful year, and the singing of the Alma Mater. Then came the committee reports that contained nothing at this early date except for their list of good intentions, most of which would end up being postponed to some later year. The same disgruntled professors pointed out that Monday-Wednesday-Friday classes had more student contact hours than did the Tuesday-Thursday classes, a factor of mathematics that the dean once again noted and ignored. The president announced the schedule of kick-off events, and the dean gave his usual lecture on infractions of college policies.

Wednesday afternoon should have provided a restful break from faculty responsibilities, but—just as had happened the previous year—a knock on her door interrupted Sarah's peace. The visitor was Jamison Chandler Cartwright, factory owner and egotistical blowhard.

"I assume you remember me," he announced as he bustled his way into the office and plopped down in one of the visitor chairs.

"I do, Mr. Cartwright. You left an unforgettable impression last year. Won't you have a seat and tell me how I can be of help?"

"I'm already sitting down, in case you've not been paying attention."

"Oh, I noticed. I was just trying to excuse your rude behavior. This is my office, in case you haven't noticed." Sarah's wide-eyed stare conveyed an open challenge.

'Humph! Let's get right to it, shall we? My daughter Olivia

still refers to you as her advisor, even though I have made it clear to her that I expect her to enroll as a business major. What do you intend to do about that?"

"What do I intend to do? Nothing. Students at Smoky Mountain have until the end of their sophomore year to declare a major, and they do so without needing permission from any but their own interests and desires. It's not my decision—nor yours."

"What has she told you?"

"I am not at liberty to discuss my private conversations with a student. In fact, there are laws against my doing so. I refer you to the Family Educational Rights and Privacy Act (FERPA) and Health Insurance Portability and Accountability Act (HIPAA) privacy rules. Since most college students are eighteen or older, their educational records are private, and we may not discuss them with their parents without the student's consent."

"But you know what she's thinking."

"Mr. Cartwright, you are wasting your time—and mine." Sarah moved to the door and held it open, inviting his departure.

Cartwright stomped out, yanking the door from her grip and slamming it behind him. Within a few seconds, both Gwen Pham and Kevin Chalmers appeared in the hall to check on the cause of the commotion.

"Is everything all right, Sarah?"

"Yes, sorry for the disturbance."

"What was that all about?" Kevin was not about to leave without an explanation.

"The father of one of my advisees wants access to his adult daughter's academic records. I explained the FERPA policies to him, and he went storming off to take the matter up with the federal government."

"I seem to remember you having the same altercation

with a parent last year. This will not become a pattern, I hope."

Sarah shook her head in frustration. "Same topic . . . and same parent. I promise you, I was as polite as I could be under the circumstances."

~

Thursday was move-in day, with anxious parents hovering over their offspring's last moments of being a kid. The new students, picking up on the tension all around them, wondered if they had made the right choice. That day ended, just as it had the year before, with parents being lured to buffet tables overflowing with finger sandwiches and lemon bars. Meanwhile, the students gathered in the auditorium to hear a series of lectures from the upperclassmen on the Smoky Mountain traditions that they pledged to support and carry forward. The students' day ended with the solemn signing of the honor code, while the faculty hustled their parents off to their cars without further agonizing over their goodbyes.

On Friday morning, the campus awoke to a raging all-day rain that forced the administration to move the lovely ceremonies of Convocation from the amphitheater to the shelter of the auditorium. That limited space, not designed to hold the entire faculty and the incoming freshman class, let alone the orchestra, choir, and student government leaders, squashed everyone together in packed rows. The rain conspired to turn the air into something of a sauna, replete with the odor of mothballs from the professorial gowns worn only twice a year. Even Sarah, who loved ceremonies like this, squirmed and wished this last ritual a speedy end.

~

T he rain was giving way to muggy nightfall by the time David and Sarah returned to her apartment after Friday night prayers at their synagogue.[1] Sarah excused herself to change out of her wet clothes into some cozy sweats. They were debating the possibilities of ordering a pizza delivery when the phone rang. Sarah grimaced as she reached for her cell, knowing that a call on Friday night did not bode well for the prospect of a peaceful evening.

The caller was Matt Garrison, graduate student and teaching assistant by day, and at night, the owner of a some-times-gay bar called The Conference Room.

"This better be important, Matt. It's been a long week!"

"I'm sorry to bother you, but I have an ongoing crisis here in the bar, and I thought you'd better know about it before it blows itself up into a major news story."

"What have you done now?"

"It's not me, ma'am. It's that little blond advisee of yours —name's Olivia something?"

"Olivia Cartwright? What would she be doing in your bar —what's it called? The Conference Room?"

"Yeah, and that's what I wondered, too. We don't encourage the college crowd. But it's her, all right. The wait-ress carded her at the door and flagged her as a minor. She's with an older guy, though, and that's where the problem starts. The waitress won't serve her anything but a coke, but the guy is ordering shots of bourbon with a beer chaser. He makes a show of downing the shot, but the waitress says he pours most of the bourbon into Olivia's coke. She's seen him do it twice now, and he just ordered a third."

"And what is it you want from me?" Sarah took a deep breath to control her growing irritation. She noted that David was watching her, his brow wrinkled with concern.

"Well, as the bar owner, I have to stop what's going on. If I let her consume alcohol on my premises, I could lose my liquor license and The Conference Room would be out of business. But if I call the cops, she's going to get arrested, with her name in the paper and all. I thought maybe you could ride to the rescue, so to speak, and get her out of here before anyone realizes what's going on."

"I don't think that regulating a student's alcohol consumption is part of my job description."

"Maybe not, but I know you care about her, and . . ."

"Can't the waitress just pick up her glass—or spill it—or something?"

"I thought of that, but it would just destroy the evidence, not do anything to put a stop to this guy's evil intentions."

"I can't control him, either."

"No, but you can step between them and protect her as one of your responsibilities. I suspect he'll give way to your air of authority."

"All right. I'll come, but I'm bringing my friend, the former policeman, with me. You must keep them there until we arrive, though. Offer them a free appetizer or something. I'll pay for it."

She disconnected the call and shrugged her shoulders in guilt when David frowned at her. "What else can I do? The girl is one of my responsibilities. I need to change clothes again."

"Wait. I'm familiar with The Conference Room. Trust me. You'll fit in better wearing those sweats than you would in your professorial garb. Let's just go. You can fill me in on the way. Just remember, I'm no longer a policeman. I can throw a scare into somebody, but I can't arrest him."

Matt was waiting for them near the door. He nodded toward a booth near the back of the room and then left them to position himself near the phone behind the bar. Sarah led the way, catching Olivia's attention and smiling to reassure her.

"Hi, Olivia. Does everyone have the same plans for starting a busy semester? Would you mind if my friend and I shared your booth for a few minutes? It's getting crowded in here."

The girl's face flushed, and she stammered a bit as she tried to make the introductions. "This is Jack Dunlap, a . . . a family friend. I'm just showing him around town. And Jack, Dr. Chomsky is my academic advisor at the college."

When Dunlap glanced up in obvious disinterest, David took over. "And I'm Lieutenant David Cohen, Birch Falls Police Department." His smile did not reach his eyes as he extended his hand. Dunlap's jaw tightened, and he gave a brief nod in acknowledgement. He did not move to shake hands. The four of them settled into an uneasy silence.

"Can I get you anything else?" The waitress asked as her eyes darted back and forth across the table.

"Yes," David answered. "You can remove this young woman's drink and bring her a fresh, unadulterated coke. And for my friend here," he went on, nodding across the table, "a cup of hot, black coffee would help—along with his check, please."

"I don't want coffee," Dunlap protested.

"Yes, you do. I count three shot glasses and three empty beer bottles, and since this young lady is only nineteen, I have to assume she did not help to consume any of the alcoholic beverages. That amount places you well over the limit for DWI, and I doubt you are in any shape to walk across a room in a straight line."

"I'm fine, thank you. I am not inebriated."

"Then I will have to make a further assumption that you shared these beverages with the young lady. And that being the case, the law requires me to tell you that contributing to the delinquency of a minor by providing alcohol is a felony punishable by a hefty fine and several years' imprisonment. Do you understand me?"

"I . . . I . . ."

"So let me explain what's going to happen next." He smiled at the waitress as she delivered the coke and coffee. "You are going to drink that coffee while our waitress here runs your credit card through to settle your tab. I'm going to be on my phone arranging for a patrol car to stop by, pick you up, and take you home, wherever that might be. Dr. Chomsky will take care of helping Olivia to get some fresh air before we drive her back to campus and get her settled in her dorm. The police will tow your car to our impound lot, where you may pick it up on Monday by paying the towing and storing costs."

"Am I under arrest?"

"No, sir, you are not. We record this incident as a 'customer service call,' and file it away, where it will not see the light of day again . . . unless you repeat the behavior with Olivia or any other woman . . . in which case we will throw the book at you for both incidents. Is that clear?"

On the sidewalk outside, Olivia turned to Sarah in embarrassment. "Just so you know, I didn't ask Jack to spike my coke, and I only drank one sip of it. It tasted horrible! He surprised me because he has never done something like that before. Jack works for my dad and spends a lot of time at the house. I regard him as a family friend, along with the fact that he's available if I need a date for some occasion. Tonight, he called and offered to take me out to celebrate the start of the school year, and I thought we were going to get dinner. Instead, he took me to that bar, and it scared me to realize the guy behind the counter was your teaching assistant. I hoped he wouldn't recognize me, but I guess he did."

"Yes, he did, and I'm happy he called me instead of the

cops. But Olivia, Mr. Dunlap is much too old for you, and when a guy like that goes after a much younger girl, his intentions are seldom honorable. Promise me you'll stay away from him."

"Are you going to tell my dad?"

"No. There are laws about what an educator can and cannot tell a parent about a child's behaviors. Here, the law considers you an adult, and I cannot tell your parents anything about what you do. I had a similar discussion with your father earlier in the week. And I'm tired of finding myself in the middle of the Cartwright family's affairs. I am only your academic advisor, not your family therapist. However, I recommend that you wake up tomorrow morning determined to start this new semester as an adult."

"Yes, ma'am. But . . ."

"But what?"

"I appreciate your help tonight, and I don't want to impose further, but . . . I'm hungry. Could we maybe stop for a hamburger on the way back to the dorm?"

Determined to take her own advice about starting the semester afresh, Sarah arrived on campus early Monday morning, but not soon enough to escape the traffic jams as returning students lined up to move back into the dorms. Her fixed smile was looking strained as she headed to her office. She knew that students who needed to make last-minutes changes to their schedules would commandeer the next two days. Several familiar faces already surrounded Gwen's desk, some looking for lists of classes that still had openings, others with questions about prerequisites.

"Dr. Chomsky! Wait a minute, please." Gwen made a shooing motion with both hands to chase the students away from her desk as she swiveled her chair and caught Sarah's free arm. "Wait. You need to know there's a man in your office."

"What? Who is he, and what's he doing there?"

"I don't know. Dr. Chalmers let him in earlier. I just didn't want you to walk in and have him scare you to death."

"Oh, please. It's not Mr. Cartwright again, is it? If so, I swear I'll..."

"No, not him. This guy's young—maybe a new grad student."

Shaking her head, Sarah marched toward her office, ready to do battle. She pushed the door opened and stopped short as she recognized her visitor.

"Mr. Dunlap, isn't it? What on earth are you doing in my office? Didn't we have enough of a confrontation the other night, or were you too drunk to remember it?"

"Please, Dr. Chomsky. I'm here to apologize. That incident on Friday was a terrible mistake on my part, and I remain grateful that you folks stepped in and kept the situation from getting out of hand."

"I wasn't trying to help you. My only concern was Olivia."

"And that should have been mine, too. Look, I'll feel better if you know the entire story. I work for Mr. Cartwright. I first met him while doing an internship in his factory for my marketing degree from Vanderbilt. He liked some of my ideas and hired me, and I took the job without finding out what he wanted from me.

"He was looking for someone who could not only help sell his products but who would also court his daughter and convince her to come to work for the company."

"What? That sounds nasty."

"I know. In effect, he was pimping for his daughter. At first, I thought I could handle it for a few months and then leave, but it didn't prove to be that simple—maybe because I like Olivia—almost as much as I hate her father. He's obsessed with the idea that she must take over the company from him. He's willing to do anything to get his way. And now I'm afraid to leave because of what he may do to her to break her will."

"Do you realize how bizarre this sounds?"

"I do, and it won't surprise me if you don't believe me. But I wanted you to know that I'm on your side—and on Olivia's, too. I'll do whatever I can to protect her from that man. If you ever see that she needs help, you can call on me. Here's my card and my private cell number. And now I need to go bail my car out of the impound lot." He grinned. "That's why I was here so early. You were on the way. Once again, I'm sorry for what happened Friday night, and it won't happen again."

Sarah watched him leave with mixed feelings. On one hand, she wanted to believe him; on the other, she had no reason to trust him.

Chapter Seven

TRICKS OF THE TRADE

August 26, 2009

S arah's first class of the week met on Wednesday morning. The announced title of the course was "Cotton as Catalyst," and Sarah was sure that few of her students understood what that meant. She entered the lecture hall with a bundle of cotton stems and distributed them among the members of the class.

"Pretty, aren't they? For those of you who aren't cotton farmers, take a little time to examine these fuzz balls. Note the symmetry of their four lobes, and the contrast with the shells from which they have sprung. Pass them around. Make sure everyone gets a close look because you're going to be spending a lot of time this semester discussing cotton. Why? Those fuzzy little puffs contained the power to make or break a great nation."

"I've never seen one," she overheard a young woman whisper. "I had no idea."

"Can we keep them?" another voice asked.

"I don't have enough to go around, I'm afraid, but if you

want one, see me after class and I can tell you where to go to get your own stem. There's a florist in town who specializes in cotton-themed bouquets."

Now that she had their attention, she walked the students through the syllabus to describe what lay ahead. Classes would start with the earliest planters and their experiments with crops such as tea, rice, and indigo before they turned their efforts to cotton. How the planters developed South Carolina's long staple cotton would get a class all to itself. And then they would turn to the huge issue of needing slave labor to produce the world's finest fibers. That would lead them to discuss how the state built an entire economy based on producing cotton—and why its citizens voted to legalize slavery.

Next would come the overseas expansion of the cotton trade, spurred by steam-powered shipping, and then to cotton's role in the Civil War. The era of blockade-running would provide some excitement for the war-lovers as it challenged the entire fabric of international relations. At the end of the semester, they would debate the role of cotton as a major cause of the Civil War.

Sarah had noted Olivia Cartwright's presence in the class but had tried not to single her out. However, at the end of the session, Olivia waited to have a private word.

"You didn't tell me that you are knowledgeable in economics, too. From the syllabus, I think I could make a case for counting this course as both history and business."

Sarah smiled but shook her head. "Don't push your luck. But am I to take it that your esteemed father bought our plan for your education?"

"He did. Took the bait and swallowed the whole deal. Now all I have to do is pull it off."

"I'm sure it will work out. And you are right in assuming that this course will help you see the connections between your two fields. There is such a thing as an economic historian. Keep that in mind."

"I will. What did you make of that odd-looking black creature in the front row—the one with the dreadlocks, the hoodie, and the Converse high-top sneakers?"

"You mean Maria Hernandez?" Her emphasis on the name was a gentle reprimand against de-humanizing those who didn't fit some preconceived standard. Sarah cringed when she remembered her own initial reaction to the same student. As she called the names on the class roster, she had been trying to decide whether the person in question was male or female.

"Yeah, that was her name. She looked out of place."

"I assume she is here because of her intellectual ability, not because of her fashion sense. But whatever the case, I don't discuss one student with another."

It was a clear dismissal.

Sarah had objected when she learned that one of her assigned courses was the in-depth class on the American Revolution. Oh, she understood why. The topic had been Dr. Brokowski's specialty, but he was off somewhere enjoying his new retirement. And the graduate student hired as an adjunct to replace him for a year could not handle anything beyond the introductory surveys.

Still, Sarah struggled to find a fresh approach to the subject. What was a revolution, anyhow? Where did rebellion arise? And why? For the new colonies, the suggestion that they break away from the mother was both startling and frightening. Were there precedents? Were there rules? Patterns? Those were questions for historians to answer.

At the first meeting on Thursday morning, Sarah

proposed an avenue of exploration that seemed almost revolutionary. Each week they would consider one aspect of British rule over the American colonies. On Tuesdays, the students were to think like colonists, outlining their specific grievances and presenting their demands for changes in the British policies. On Thursdays, they were to be Englishmen, loyal supporters of king and crown, trying to govern a colony of unruly ruffians and finding them impossible to please. Their final exam would ask them to choose one side or the other and to defend their willingness to go to war over the areas of disagreement.

As she described the plan, she could see the students exchanging puzzled glances. This was not the usual lecture course, they realized—not one to sleep through and rely on someone else's notes to fill in the blanks or pick the correct answers out of a multiple-choice exam. This one was going to force them to think. At the end of the first class, Chad approached her desk.

"You didn't warn me that you were a different kettle of fish from our usual stew of lecturers."

Sarah laughed. "I'm not sure I like that metaphor, but I don't mind being different. Never have. And if this course keeps you awake during this nap-inducing hour, I will have achieved my goal."

"I think it sounds like great fun, but I talked my friend Buster into taking the course with me, and he thinks I lied to him about how nice you are."

"Buster? Who . . ."

"Oh, you called him Benjamin when you were taking attendance, but I thought you might remember him from the day we unpacked your books."

"Yes, now I remember. I thought one of those fellows looked familiar."

"Yeah, Buster was my 'go-to' receiver on the football team,

and he's one of the few guys who stuck by me through that year of recovery."

"Well, if he was that loyal, he'll survive this course, too. Who knows? He might even enjoy it."

S arah's third class was the graduate-level course in historical research, which meant it would include all six of their new enrollees and none of the people she considered as friends from the previous year. She was disappointed to be starting out with a whole new group, but at least it meant she could replay an old scheme for getting to know the new people. On the first Tuesday evening, the six of them wandered into the small classroom, not sure what to expect, and their uneasiness somehow gave Sarah more confidence in her own ability, even though several of these students were older than she was.

"This semester you'll be getting a brief introduction to the various approaches to historical study," she told them. "We'll talk about methods, schools of thought, resources, and the logistics of probing into the hidden facts of history. You'll also be getting to know each other and sharing your experiences. Our introductions come first, and I'll start with my own.

"I'm Sarah Chomsky, and this is my second year of tenure-track college teaching. I attended Boston College as an undergraduate and then completed my masters and doctoral degrees at Columbia University in New York City. My field of specialization is the American Civil War, although my interests extend on either end of that period—from England's Civil War in the seventeenth century to current clashes in the modern world.

"On a personal level, I grew up in a Conservative Jewish family[1]—the only child of a rabbi who spurred my love of languages and intellectual challenges. I am unmarried, although I am seeing someone in law enforcement regularly, and I live alone except for a black cat named Elijah. In my intellectual life, I am investigating the coded language used by black slaves in the American South to discuss their hopes for freedom and equality. I'll be talking about my research now and then, and I hope to bring in the other members of the department to discuss their scholarly efforts.

"For now, I want you to get to know one another, and my favorite way of accomplishing that is to let you practice interviewing each other. I will give you your pairings and we'll take a break to allow private conversations. Then we will reassemble and have each of you introduce one of your new colleagues. Your goal should be to discover some interesting facts about those you interview—their life experiences, their goals, their reasons for being here.

"Here are your pairings. Reginald Dunkeld will interview Erica Scott. Thomas Watkins will interview Michelle Brownlee, and Rick McBride will interview Abigail Martin in the first session. Then we switch. Erica Scott will talk to Thomas Watkins, Michelle Brownlee will take on Rick McBride, and Abigail Martin will interview Reginald Dunkeld. Please locate your partner, go off to a quiet corner, and start prying.

Sarah busied herself at the desk for a few minutes so that the students would not feel they were being watched. Then she leaned back and enjoyed the scenes unfolding in front of her. Soon the discussions became more animated. Laughter increased. Shoulders dropped as tensions gave way to relaxation. Friendships blossomed.

When the groups reassembled, Reginald Dunkeld was the first up. He was much older than the rest of the class, so

Erica Scott had been shy at first. "She kept calling me Mr. Dunkeld until I insisted that she call me Reggie. Her politeness was a good sign that she had had a proper upbringing, but I wanted her to feel comfortable with me. Once she used my first name, she relaxed a little and was soon chattering on about her new job as a community activist. I didn't want to make an issue of her race, but when I asked her about role models, she launched into a lengthy explanation of what the Obamas were doing to make black people like her feel that they had a role to play in the world. She insisted that Michelle Obama had convinced her to stand up for herself.

"By then, I was probing further back in her life. She told me she had graduated from Spelman, a black college for women, and I asked how she had felt about having no men on campus. She said at first it was exhilarating to speak in class, but by the time she graduated, she was ready to challenge the typical male dominance of the classroom. And she was comfortable lecturing me at that point. I also asked why she came to Smoky Mountain to do graduate work. Well, she had grown up around here, but what convinced her was finding out that our history department had hired a Spelman graduate in a tenure-track position. She said she hasn't yet met Professor Winthrop because she doesn't want to push their alumna connection, but she's looking forward to taking classes from her.

"My last question was about what she planned to do with a history degree, and her answer, I thought, was telling. She said she would wait and see what the college had to teach her. She said something like, 'I know my family sheltered me for too much of my life. Now I'm ready to open up to all possibilities.' I suspect she's going to find her choices to be wide open. The world needs more young people like her."

Next up was Thomas Watkins, a fellow in his mid-thirties who looked like what he was—a farmer. He wore jeans and a plaid shirt, with boots that suggested he could do a better job of cleaning the mud from his feet. His assigned partner was Margaret Brownlee, a middle-aged woman who had a soft, motherly look to her. Watkins, however, directed his first comments at Sarah. "I hear you're offering a course on the history of cotton this semester. I'd be happy to help you with that—anything you need."

Sarah opened her mouth as if to answer him and then closed it. As if she hadn't even heard the inappropriate remark, she gestured toward Margaret as if to say, "Get on with it."

To everyone's relief, Thomas got the message. "OK, then. Margaret and I got on together right away because we're both feeling sort of old on this campus full of young folks. She's been a wife and a mother for going on twenty years, and she's ready for a change. Oh, I don't mean that to sound like she's ready to walk out on her family, but she's not feeling as needed as she used to. Her kids are adults—or almost ready to leave the nest—and she says she's through trying to change her husband. So she's thinking about going back to teaching.

"Oh, yeah, I meant to mention that she graduated from here twenty-some years ago with a teaching degree, and she spent a few years in the junior high school. I got the impression that she did not enjoy that age group and was glad to quit when she got married. Now she's ready to go back, either with grade-schoolers or high school classes. She was less than happy to learn that those courses she took back in the eighties don't count for much these days. She applied to renew her license to teach and learned she needed to do at least fifteen hours of graduate work to qualify. So here she is."

Sarah stepped in to show the kinds of things Thomas had missed. "How old are your children, Margaret?"

"Johnny's nineteen and headed off to the army like his dad did. Betty Jane's sixteen, a junior in high school, and her brother Charlie is just emerging from that awkward fourteen-year-old clumsiness."

"And your husband? You mentioned the army ..."

"Yeah. He missed Vietnam, thank goodness, and then was a drill sergeant most of his career—training the younger recruits to go off and 'play in the sand' as he called Iraq and Afghanistan. He's retired now with full benefits, which gives us a nice cushion, and he works for a wood-carving shop in town. They turn out those crafty touristy things you see on the sidewalks downtown every summer. He enjoys what he's doing now, and I figured it was time I did the same."

"Take note, Thomas. You missed some interesting topics."

Rick McBride was up next. He had noted Thomas's failures, but he had little to say about Abigail Martin as a historian. "Abbie's the proud holder of a B.A. from our mother campus in Knoxville. She graduated in May but was too late for the teacher-hiring season, and she couldn't find any other job that paid well enough to allow her to support herself. Her adviser recommended that she take the GRE, which she did. She must have scored some impressive marks there, because Smoky Mountain offered her a hefty fellowship to go on and get her master's degree.

"So here she is. The decision to go the graduate student route just happened, and she hasn't had time to think much about what era of history she wants to specialize in, or what she'll do with an advanced degree once she gets it. I think she's putting those decisions off for as long as possible.

"We finished by talking about her hobbies, which are interesting. She's been an ice skater since she was four years old and has competed up to the national levels. She says that's all behind her now. You age out of skating as a career in your early twenties and then have nothing else to do. Turin in 2006 should have been her Olympics year, but she had a terrible fall at the Nationals and broke an ankle. By the time it healed, younger skaters were lining up to compete at Vancouver in 2010, and she had lost the competitive edge.

"So now, in her spare time, she has taken up dog training. Her family raises Golden Retrievers, and she's learning how to show them in the ring as they work toward championship levels. She has her eye on the Westminster Kennel Club Show in 2010 for her debut. I think she'll bring some interesting variety to our group."

E rica Scott was next, and her interviewing subject was Thomas. She reminded everyone that he had mentioned he was a cotton producer, so that's where she started her questioning. "He tells me the cotton farm has been in his family's possession since the Civil War." For a moment she turned to make sure Sarah had caught that point. Then she continued. "But the land's pretty well depleted, and the crops are becoming less and less profitable. So he's looking for an alternative career path. I don't think he knows what he wants to do yet. He mentioned teaching, law enforcement, corrections, politics. Like so many of us at this stage, he's hoping that his studies will point him in a new direction.

"On a personal level, Thomas has a wife named Daisy— no kids—and they share the farmhouse with his brother Henry and his family. Henry wants out of the farming business, too, so they'll be looking to sell off the land, maybe to a housing development, or something like that to bring in the big bucks. The conversation got vague at that point, because he didn't want to talk to me about how you raise cotton without slave labor. So that's about all I know."

Margaret Brownlee had better luck with Rick McBride's interview. "Rick's a great conversationalist," she reported, and we had some interesting discussions about the current school situation. As you've heard, I'm trying to get back into teaching, and he's trying his best to get out. Maybe that's just a case of greener grass on both sides.

"Anyhow, he's an assistant football coach at the local high school, and he has some frightening stories to tell about the dangers those school kids face with every football game. I got the impression that he's bothered by the responsibility he bears for sending them out to play with inadequate equipment and preparation. And the stories he can tell about difficult parents who insist that junior must play in every game will make your hair stand on end.

"He wasn't trying to discourage me from becoming a teacher again. I think he loves the profession, but he'd be better off teaching a subject he enjoys and not being a coach at all. From what he tells me, his wife Rebecca feels the same way. They have two little boys—Billy and Mike—and she is determined to keep them off the playing field, which she won't be able to do if Rick remains a coach. So that's why he's here. Like all the rest of us, he's hoping this next couple of years will put his life on a better trajectory."

"**W**hat a pairing this was," exclaimed Abigail Martin as she took over to do the last report. "The youngest member of the group interviewing the oldest one. But I enjoyed it. It was like talking to my grandfather—and I mean that with the greatest respect, Reggie, because I love my grandfather. But he's losing his memory, so I can't ask him about his past life. Reggie is sharp as ever, and he has one tale after another.

"I wanted to know why he waited so long to go back to school, and he corrected me. He's not going 'back to school' because he never went, at least not beyond high school. His father died when he was a teenager—fell off a combine and got pulled into the blades. Reggie had to step up and take care of the farm because there was no one else to support his mother and sisters. He didn't marry because he had more than enough women in his life telling him what to do. So he took care of three old ladies until they all passed away, and by then he was already in his seventies.

"He says he doesn't regret all those lost years. He had a responsibility, and he accepted it. He used to read at night—anything he could get his hands on—as a replacement for his education. He learned an amazing amount. He has a prodigious memory—I tried to stump him with questions and failed. But he says what he learned the most was how much he still has to learn. And that's why he's here. No career goals —just pure hunger for knowledge. I stand in awe of him."

Chapter Eight

A FLURRY OF SOCIAL OBLIGATIONS

September 4, 2009

S arah had spent all Friday afternoon holding office hours. One after another, the students had wandered in to ask questions about textbooks or syllabus issues, to introduce themselves, or to ask for leniency because of their special needs. She could tell how tired she was by the sound of her feet shuffling through the door. She dropped her tote bag on the table and sank into the welcome comfort of her couch. Her eyes drooped shut of their own volition, and she sat unmoving for several minutes. When the phone rang, she mumbled at it.

"Go away, whoever you are. I don't want to hear it."

The ringing persisted until she reached for the receiver, growling, "Yeah?"

"Wow! That was not the reception I was expecting!"

"Oh, David. Sorry. I'm just wiped out. No one reminded me how difficult the first full week of teaching can be. I feel like I've delivered several one-person filibusters to a room full of stuffed rag dolls. They sat there staring at me as if I crawled out of the woodwork somewhere. And I kept tap dancing faster and faster, hoping that one of them would show a spark of understanding. Does that make sense, or am I mixing metaphors beyond comprehension?"

"You sound tired. I called to find out if I would see you at the synagogue tonight, but I think I got my answer."

"You're right. I don't want to move out of this room unless it's to change into sweats and tuck my bare feet under a blanket. I'll do sabbath prayers[1] in the morning."

"How about eating something? You sound as if you need nourishment."

"Not if I have to cook it first. I'd rather starve."

"OK. So you're not up to going out, either, I guess. How about takeout?"

"Do I have to chew?"

"How about something chopped into tiny pieces?"

"You're getting closer. Soup?"

"Can do. Do you like Thai food?"

"In Birch Falls?"

"Yep. A new place just opened, and they do a respectable job with Tom Yum soup. You go find your sweats and blanket, and I'll come bearing food fit for the gods. See you around six?"

"Wonderful. I'll try to stay awake."

~

David arrived on cue, bearing an assortment of white bags and folded buckets with flimsy wire handles. From a pocket he pulled chopsticks, packets of hot mustard, soy sauce, and the mandatory fortune cookies. "I thought you advertised Thai, not Chinese," she teased.

"Hey, this is Appalachia. You have to take what you can get. If we were eating at the restaurant, we'd be having mango ice cream for dessert. For takeout, you'll have to settle for fortune cookies."

The spread he laid out on the coffee table began with the advertised Tom Yum soup, hot and mellowed by coconut, with sliced mushrooms and tiny twisted fried noodles. Then came fresh vegetable spring rolls, missing their traditional shrimp filling in deference to Jewish dietary restrictions against eating shellfish but overflowing with cucumber spears, fresh mint, Thai basil, cilantro, and cold rice noodles, with a dip of spicy peanut sauce. To accompany the spring rolls, David opened another sack to reveal several bottles of Singha beer. And then came the centerpiece—a shared bucket of chicken Pad Thai, containing noodles flavored with the traditional tamarind, palm sugar, and fish sauce, and topped with lime wedges, chopped peanuts, and crisp bean sprouts.

At last, Sarah leaned back on the couch pillows, wiggling a bare foot at him. "You were right, as usual. That was what I needed. Now I'm stuffed, warm, relaxed by the beer, and reeking of onion and garlic."

"Must not forget your fortune cookie." He grinned and handed her one last bag. "Choose your own fate. I refuse to take responsibility."

"She picked one at random, cracked it open, and then hesitated to pull the little strip of paper. "What if I don't like it? Can I get a do-over?"

"That depends on what this one says."

"It says '7-90-43-8-26.'"

"Silly. That's your safe lottery combination. Turn it over."

As she read it, a slight smile spread across her face. "Confucius say: 'Always follow your heart. It knows the way home.' Now you."

David read his fortune aloud. "'Great treasure requires great patience.' That's not as good as I hoped. What does it mean? Must I wait patiently while you go off to follow your heart? Doesn't seem fair."

"No, but it suggests you'll win the treasure at the end, and if I'm the treasure, I'll find my path home."

"Maybe so, but next time, we're going for the mango ice cream. Here. Let me help you clean up our mess, and then I'm sending you off to an early bedtime. I want to hear about your new classes, but not until you're rested. Do you have plans for the weekend?"

"Nothing exciting. Lecture writing and class roster memorizing. But it's a three-day weekend, so . . ."

"Maybe you can find time for the Labor Day parade and community picnic on Monday? You might have missed it last year because you were so new, but it's quite the tradition around here. Besides, my dad's the honorary parade marshal this year, so I have to be there."

"I'd love to. And can we join your folks for the picnic? I haven't seen them since the accident, and I feel like I should. It's bound to be a little uncomfortable, but the public setting will help, I suspect."

"You, my dear, are a born diplomat. I'll pick you up around 9:30 on Monday morning."

"You're on."

That was the trouble with parents, Sarah told herself. Not only did they try to manage and direct their children's love lives as soon as a boy turned thirteen or a girl turned twelve; they devoted the rest of their lives to it. Dating was both feared and encouraged. In orthodox communities, families encouraged boys to marry before they turned eighteen, and girls could marry at much younger ages. Even in conservative and reform circles, marriages traditionally took place before the early twenties. And for single adults, as she and David were, entire families felt it their responsibility to help locate a "nice Jewish boy or girl." Those pressures meant that modern young people who wanted to establish them-selves in careers had to maintain a complicated balancing act between independence and adherence to family tradition.

From her bat mitzvah[2] forward, Sarah had rebelled against the encouragement to find a "nice Jewish boy." Such a fellow sounded, boring, stupid, and under his mother's thumb. Sarah had hoped to find a strong, independent Jewish man, not a boy. But until David had entered her life, no one had met her mother's expectations or her own. The saving grace in her family had come from her rabbi father, who supported her academic efforts, despite her mother's disap-proval. David had suffered even more parental criticism. While his mother bewailed the image of a thirty-five-year-old son who had never married, his father had threatened to disown him for turning down the solid income of a law firm partnership to pursue a poorly-paid career in police work.

Now that their friendship had become a committed rela-tionship, David and Sarah still faced the daunting need to gain parental approval of their chosen partners. No Jewish mother was likely to rejoice in a decision over which she had had no part. And ready or not, Sarah and David could no longer avoid the issue.

Sarah's relationship with the Cohens was already on shaky ground. The last time Sarah and Mrs. Cohen met had been in a hospital corridor outside the room where David lay with a shattered arm and shoulder, the result of a shootout at Sarah's apartment. Mrs. Cohen had lunged at Sarah, blaming her for causing David's injury. "He shouldn't have ever met you! This is all your fault," she had shouted until a nurse intervened to put an end to the commotion. David assured Sarah that his mother had gotten over her rage and now understood that Sarah had saved his life by getting him to immediate medical treatment. Still, Sarah quivered inside when she thought of facing the woman again. Well, better to get it over with before the next crisis.

And the next crisis was already on her schedule. Her parents had invited themselves to Birch Falls for their first visit to Sarah's new home. She agreed before she realized the visit would take place over Rosh Hashana. When Sarah informed her local rabbi that she could not attend their scheduled dinner, Rabbi Leibowicz reacted as she should have known he would. She had almost forgotten that the rabbi and her father were boyhood friends. Now the rabbi rejoiced that they could renew their friendship. A Rosh Hashana dinner table could always expand to include old friends like Solomon and Ruth Chomsky, he claimed. His wife joined in with an even more elaborate plan. Leonard and Miriam Cohen also attended the Leibowicz synagogue. Why not include their family, Sheila suggested, so that everyone could get to know one another? Sarah had nodded in agreement, but she was already imagining how many things could go wrong.

September 7, 2009

Labor Day turned out to be the perfect introduction to fall. Although the sun was still hot, there was a cool edge to the breeze. The poplar trees, always the first to announce a change of seasons, suddenly showed clusters of golden leaves. An occasional v-formation of geese flew overhead, and horses groomed to show off in the parade sported the first signs of their warmer winter coats.

Leonard Cohen led the parade, sitting in the back of an

antique convertible with his devoted wife at his side. As if
they had studied the moves of the English royal family, they
now lifted their hands and twisted them at those who
cheered their appearance. Sarah and David waited near the
grandstand to greet his parents when they left their vehicle to
observe and judge the parade. To Sarah's great relief, Mrs.
Cohen beamed at her, as if in denial that any hard feelings
had ever existed between them.

At the end of the parade, Mr. Cohen made his way to the
podium and tested the loudspeakers to be sure his words
would reach everyone in the crowd. After a brief welcome, he
announced the winners of each category among the parade
entrants: marching bands; floats representing various unions,
civic clubs, and businesses; equestrian units; decorated bicycles; and pompom squads. Mrs. Cohen passed out the
winners' certificates, although only a few people coveted the
awards. Most of the crowd was simply waiting for the
announcement that food was ready.

"We want to thank all the restaurants participating in
today's picnic lunch. You will find an amazing assortment of
foods on offer, each variety selling for a single dollar. We have
submarine sandwiches of all kinds, soups, salads, pizza slices,
hamburgers, sausages, and ethnic specialties. All booths
open and close at the same time, so make your choices
quickly. At the end of the hour—that is, at one o'clock—the
booths will close and the cooks will turn in their proceeds.
The entrant having sold the most will win the honor of
displaying this banner—Birch Falls' Favorite Lunch Spot—
for the next year. And in case you are wondering, all proceeds
from winners and losers will go toward the purchase of new
holiday decorations for Main Street."

He closed his speech as the crowd broke up and headed
for the food tents. David, who had pulled Sarah away early,
now pointed her toward one of several umbrella-shaded

tables for four lining Main Street. "Grab that one and make sure everyone knows you are holding it for His Highness the Parade Marshal. I'll round up the grub for everyone. What is your preference?"

"Um, the potato pirogies with the side of cucumbers in sour cream—and lavender lemonade. That sounds delightful."

"You and my mother are so much alike," he mused. "That's what she ordered. The two of you will have to forgive us if my father and I prefer burned bratwursts with onions and kraut. Back soon. Keep watching for the parents to arrive."

Sarah didn't know whether to laugh or cry at being compared to his mother, but, she decided, it was better than being told they disagreed. For the rest of the day, no harsh words spoiled the relaxed ambiance of a holiday from work, and Sarah's worst fears about the upcoming family meeting subsided, if only for a little while.

September 17-19, 2009

The Chomsky's visit two weeks later also started off well. Sarah and David had tried to choreograph every step without making the meeting seem more important than it was. Sarah had met their plane in Nashville on Thursday afternoon and delivered them to their hotel in Birch Falls. When her mother had asked where David was, Sarah explained that he was testifying in court that afternoon, serving as an expert witness in an ongoing corruption case. He had also suggested that this first day was a day for a family reunion, not one in which to introduce strangers. Sarah took her parents to dinner in the hotel dining room and then settled them in for an early night.

On Friday morning, she treated them to a tour of her college campus, allowing them to sit in on her Civil War class and then taking them to lunch at the Faculty Club. Her mother was quiet and wide-eyed during their tours, although she enjoyed the stories of the college's years as a nunnery. Rabbi Chomsky loved seeing his little girl in such a professional setting. Every time he heard a student address her as Dr. Chomsky, his smile grew broader.

In mid-afternoon, Sarah took them to her apartment, where they renewed their acquaintance with Elijah, and Ruth Chomsky relaxed. Just as they had planned it, David arrived around five, bearing a catnip mouse for Elijah and winning Ruth's heart because of his obvious affection for the cat. Sarah offered wine and bruschetta while they waited for the proper moment to light the Shabbat candles.[3] Then they made their way on foot to the synagogue for prayers, where the two rabbis fell into one another's arms, erasing decades of distance between them.

On Saturday, Sarah and her mother baked an elaborate kugel[4] to take to that evening's Rosh Hashana dinner, while Rabbi Chomsky joined Rabbi Leibowicz in his study for hours of reminiscing. David called Sarah once to find out how things were going. Tensions were running high at his parents' house, he reported, as the Cohens worried about meeting Sarah's family. She responded with an observation that her mother, too, was suffering from a case of nerves. Sarah sighed and admitted that she was nervous, too.

Jacob Leibowicz, however, had no intention of allowing this meeting of families to be anything but a joyful occasion. That afternoon he reminded Solomon of their stay at the Israeli kibbutz and their first lesson on how to blow the shofar[5] on Rosh Hashana. That led to the two of them hunting down the synagogue's ceremonial shofar and conducting a private contest to see which of them could make it sound most like the blast of a trumpet. Their efforts were feeble, but they continued the rivalry before dinner. As the families gathered at the table, Jacob gave the initial sounding, which came out as a squeak. Solomon Chomsky took his turn, laughing so hard he missed the mouthpiece. Leonard Cohen asked if he could try but produced only a puffing sound. Soon everyone was laughing, and the celebratory meal began on that raucous note.

David had once remarked to Sarah that he always hated the Rosh Hashana dinners because every food item was sugary. Sheila Leibowicz had carried out that tradition. Besides the kugel the Chomskys had brought as a gift—its noodles soaking up honey, apple slices, and raisins—the table featured both a sweet tomato barbequed brisket and a chicken roasted in a sweet apple and honey-based sauce. Surrounding the meats was an assortment of vegetables, but only those whose starches also turned to sugar under the high heat of the oven—potatoes, broccoli, asparagus, squash, and yams. And topping the meal came a honey cake, daring anyone to introduce a sour note.[6]

At last, having gorged themselves on the sweetness of dinner, exhausted their repertoire of old stories, and sipped the last of the wine, Rabbi Leibowicz cleared his official rabbi throat and commanded their attention.

"What a pleasure it has been to share this holiday table among our dearest friends. I know, however, that some of you have been expecting me to deliver a sermon on the values of marriage." He stopped and raised an eyebrow in Sarah's direction. She stared at her lap until he continued.

"There is an elephant in the room—a lovely star sapphire elephant worn with pride but upon an untraditional finger." Now he was looking straight at David, who also refused to meet his gaze.

"Three married couples sit here—my old friend Solomon

and his wife Ruth, Leonard and Miriam, faithful congregants, and my Sheila, my own life's companion. We have weathered the pains and the joys of life, and we know that our shared devotion has smoothed the paths we have walked. Should I bore you all with platitudes, knowledge you have gained in the flesh during—if my calculations are correct—some 123 years of married life? As for you, Sarah and David, I need not say more because you have grown up in the hearts of these families. I can offer you no finer examples of the rewards of married life. I have only two messages to share with you.

"The first is a corrective I would like to see written into our holy books. Jewish tradition has always favored marriage at a young age as a shield against the distractions of the world. But in our modern age, it has become more and more necessary that intelligent young people take as much time as they need to develop the talents HaShem has given them. I therefore commend you both for the career paths you have followed, even though a motherly voice followed your every footstep, asking when you intended to find a nice Jewish partner and get down to the business of actual life.

"The second message is an open secret—a secret every married couple knows. Life is harsh, and troubles come to everyone. We all face disappointments, disasters, disease, death, destruction, but most of us overcome those 'd-words.' How? Because we also know that we have our very own person, someone who will always be there to catch us when we stumble and love us without fail in our darkest moments. That's the real secret of marriage, and my greatest wish for each of you—that you will find your own person to come home to—and that when you find that person you will be sure enough to make that commitment the priority in your lives.

"Now go in peace as we enter the most solemn days of the Jewish year—the Days of Atonement. If you have made mistakes, correct them where you are able. If you have quarreled, seek agreement. If you have had doubts or suspicions, rise above them. If you have harmed another, make amends. Then may you enter the new year with a clear conscience and trust that all will be well."

As they made their way home from the synagogue, Ruth linked her arm with Sarah's and drew her to a slower pace, while David and her husband moved ahead. She patted Sarah's hand and murmured, "Nice Jewish boy!" For the first time in days, Sarah relaxed.

Chapter Nine

DAYS OF ATONEMENT AND RECONCILIATION

September 20–28, 2009

I n the days that followed their Rosh Hashana dinner, Sarah found a sense of peace she had not expected. She attended sunrise prayers every morning before classes started, and she ended each day's work back at the synagogue for evening prayers. It was the ritual her rabbi father had taught her to follow during the High Holy Days, but this year she listened to the Hebrew words as if she were hearing them for the first time. They spoke to her deepest thoughts and soothed doubts she hadn't realized were bothering her.

The good feelings followed her throughout her days. This year she hadn't felt the need to explain the religious significance of the High Holy Days, and her colleagues respected her privacy. Her classes went well, her lectures sparkled with tidbits of human interest that kept her students engaged, and individual conferences resulted in more than a few solved crises.

Even a phone call from Miriam Cohen did nothing to shake Sarah's sense of equilibrium, although she was surprised that the older woman had overcome her distrust of the telephone. David's mother explained that both David and his father would spend the Sunday before Yom Kippur[1] at the synagogue, while she stayed home to prepare the nourishing casseroles and sweet cake with which the family would break their fast on Monday evening. Would Sarah be willing to drop by and help with some preparations, she wondered? Sarah did not hesitate to accept, and she looked forward to picking up some new recipes to add to her collection.

Sarah arrived at the Cohen's house early on Sunday morning and found Miriam Cohen already hard at work in the kitchen. She moved from stove to cutting board and back, brushing pita rounds with seasoned olive oil, grilling them in a cast-iron skillet, flipping them to mark the reverse side, and then dropping them onto the cutting board to be sliced into wedges.

"These will be done in a jiffy, and then I can take a break before we launch into the supper preparations," she explained. "The wedges accompany the salad course, but they stay crisp for days, so I try to get them finished early. There. That's the last one. Now we can chat about what comes next. Coffee? It's not wise to consume too much caffeine in the days leading up to a fast, but a single cup this early won't be a problem."

Over steaming coffee and almond biscotti, Mrs. Cohen probed into Sarah's family traditions. "I'm sure you must have fond memories of Yom Kippur suppers with your family. Is there any dish you associate with ending the fast?"

"No." Sarah confessed. "When father assumed his duties at the Brooklyn synagogue, the women of the congregation already had a long tradition of creating a cold buffet spread in the hall for the entire congregation after Yom Kippur prayers. Each one of them had her own specialty, and father was wise enough not to interfere with the tradition. Mother and I offered our services in the kitchen, snatching a few bites wherever we could."

"What about last year? You were already in town here, weren't you?"

"It was strange not to have anywhere to go. I headed home, poured a glass of wine, and discovered that I didn't have an appetite to eat alone. So I just went to bed." She laughed at the memory. "By midnight I was starving and raiding the refrigerator."

"Well, we will expect you here with us this year. Hannah and her family will be here, too, and it would upset the family to see any changes to the menu we resort to every year. We'll start with a crisp and colorful Mediterranean salad served with those pita wedges. That's what we'll organize first. I'll stir up a batch of the dressing, and you can work at chopping the lettuce, cucumbers, tomatoes, and kalamata olives. We'll refrigerate all the ingredients. Then all we have to do Monday evening is toss them together with a can of cannellini beans, sprinkle some feta cheese on top, and dinner is off to a splendid start.

"Sounds wonderful."

"The centerpiece of the dinner, however, is a creamy tuna noodle casserole,[2] the children's perennial favorite. We can complete the casserole except for the breadcrumb topping this morning and refrigerate it until we return from the synagogue tomorrow evening. It will go into the oven and will be hot and bubbly by the time we are finished with the salad.

"We top off the evening with a lemon-glazed poppy seed cake.[3] It's usually served during Purim, but since we spend that holiday helping with a dinner for the poor, we've moved our poppy seed cake to our breaking of the Yom Kippur fast."

Sarah noted how the mere mention of her family traditions turned the quiet Miriam Cohen into an animated whirlwind of activity. "This is part and parcel of what Rabbi

Leibowicz was referring to when he talked about the privileges of growing up in the heart of a family, isn't it? We are so lucky to have traditions like these." On an impulse, Sarah reached over and hugged Mrs. Cohen, which left them both flustered.

They worked without speaking for a while, Sarah concentrating on chopping the salad vegetables while Miriam drizzled the olive oil into her salad dressing to keep the emulsion from breaking. Their silence, however, was not uncomfortable. It left them both with the feeling that they had become a team working toward a common good.

Once they began the cake recipe, Miriam grinned and turned to Sarah. "I'm going to let you settle a long-standing argument in this family. There are two ways to handle the poppy seeds. One demands that the seeds be ground into a smooth paste, which will give the cake a darker color and a somewhat more intense poppy flavor, while the other recommends adding the seeds whole, which keeps the batter lighter and gives the cake a certain crunchiness. I've done it both ways. One of my children likes the dark cake; the other wants distinct crunches. This year, you get to choose."

"And you will not tell me which one is David's choice, will you? Is this a compatibility quiz?"

"No. I'm just avoiding making the choice."

"All right, then. I've never understood the need to grind up something so small as a poppy seed. I choose crunchy. But then, I enjoy popping the cells of bubble wrap, too."

"And David will be proud of you!"

Around eleven, with everything prepared except for the tuna casserole, Miriam called for a lunch break. "As a family, we treat these hours before the fast with care. The men setting up the synagogue will have one of Sheila's meat-filled meals about now. I thought you and I might break for a cold chicken sandwich on seeded rye bread, along with pure water and some fruit salad, all of which are waiting in the refrigerator. Sound good?"

"High fiber, high protein, no added sugar, no more caffeine—sounds perfect."

"And then in the dinner hour before sunset, after the men come home, we'll have a chicken soup filled with noodles and vegetables, along with challah.[4] You will stay for dinner, I hope."

"No, no, I can't. I must go home for a while—take care of the cat, change clothes—."

"Then I will send you home with a container of soup to reheat. The soup is ready. That's what's been simmering on the back of the stove. It's important to eat well before a fast," she reminded Sarah.

"You're too kind. But how do you find time to do all this?"

"Today I cook for tomorrow. Yesterday, I cooked for today. We always know where our next meal is coming from."

"You amaze me."

"Well, there's one more thing I have neglected to do, and I must take care of it before sundown. I . . . I owe you an apology."

"Why?"

"For all those terrible things I said to you on the day of David's accident."

"That's long behind us."

"Not for me. And not in HaShem's book of transgressions. It terrified me to imagine losing my son. I was angry that such a fate had befallen him and frustrated that I could not take my anger out on the foolish young girl who had caused it."

"We were all afraid and angry. No one is responsible for what gets said in the heat of a moment."

"Not so. We are always responsible. What's worse, I was jealous of you because when I walked into David's hospital room, the first thing he asked me was where you were. I saw you as a thief, stealing my son from me, not as the woman who had saved his life. I'm so sorry. Sorry for everything I said and did. I can't ask for your forgiveness because I don't deserve it. But I can ask you to believe that I have learned to love and respect you and to be grateful to you for making my son happy. I thought you were taking him away from me. Instead, you have given him a new life. He has come back into the heart of our family because of you and your love. I shall always be grateful for that."

Sarah had no words to offer—only another hug and a silent prayer of gratitude that this struggle was behind them.

Tuesday, September 29, 2009

Strengthened by the period of intense self-reflection and prayerfulness, warmed by how the Cohens had accepted her as one of their family, and reassured by how well her classes were running, Sarah did not notice that the semester was half over. Thus she was caught unawares as her life took a more complicated turn.

The first warning sign was one she almost missed. When she returned to her office on the day after Yom Kippur, she found a three-day-old telephone notice waiting for her. Gwen had noted "URGENT" at the top of the message. "Please contact Professor Robert Yearwood at the College of Charleston" followed by a 843 exchange and a semi-familiar number. A moment's thought reminded her that the number belonged to the history department at the college.

"Something to do with the Jubilee Project," she told

herself as she laid the memo aside while she checked the rest of her mail for pressing issues. Then, finding none, she tapped in the number and waited as the automated system spelled out her options. "For Professor Yearwood, press nine" was the last choice.

The voice that answered was brusque and impatient. "Yes, yes, what is it?"

When Sarah identified herself, he interrupted her. "Well, at last!"

"I'm sorry, but I just received your message. It's only a few minutes after eight here, you know."

"Oh, I forgot you're in a different time zone. Well, no matter. We have a crisis here, and I'm told you can solve it. Are you planning to go to Louisville for the Southern Historical Society meeting in November?"

"Yes, I'll be there."

"Good. I'm chairing a session on slave rebellions, and one of our speakers has just cancelled. I'm told you were here this past summer doing some interesting work on the symbolism found in Gullah cemeteries. If you can whip your notes into a presentation, we need you to fill that empty slot. Can you do that?"

Sarah's eyes had widened as she listened, and she gulped before answering. "I . . . I can. I assume it's the usual twenty-minute time limit?"

"Yes, yes, plus time for questions at the end. What's the title?"

"I don't have a title yet. Give me some time to . . ."

"No time to think about it. The program goes to print tonight. Your title? Make one up."

"Uh . . . Listening for Water."

"Listening to Water?"

"No, Listening FOR Water."

"And your full name, academic position, and affiliation?"

"Dr. Sarah R. Chomsky, Assistant Professor, Department of History, Smoky Mountain University at Birch Falls."

"Thank you. See you in Louisville. The session is Friday morning."

Sarah was still staring wide-eyed after he had hung up. "Now what have I done?"

She was still asking herself that question when she found a notice of a departmental meeting the next afternoon. The topic under discussion was "Louisville."

Kevin Chalmers wasted no time in making his wishes known. "As you all know, we are seeking applicants for three teaching positions in our department. We've received over two hundred inquiries, and we need to winnow them down to a manageable few. The Southern meeting gives us the perfect opportunity to get a preview of the candidates before the AHA interviews begin. It's safe to assume that serious applicants will attend, many of them with their advisors. I want all our faculty members to be there, checking them out, talking to people who know them, and listening to their presentations. As for the T.A.s and adjuncts, we'll need you to hold the fort here on Friday—November 6th—by covering our classes. This is an 'all-hands-on-deck' occasion."

Julia frowned. "Isn't that a little unethical, Kevin? I mean, sneaking into their talks without them knowing they are being judged?"

"Not at all. If you volunteer to give a talk, you expect people to come and judge you. That's what these meetings are all about."

"I'm not sure I can afford to go," Trevor Monroe interrupted. "Since my wife has decamped for the lure of Wall Street, I'm left paying all the house expenses here instead of just my half." He looked embarrassed by having to drag his personal troubles into the open.

"Ah, no problem. The department will cover our

expenses, provided we do it on the cheap. I thought we could all drive up together in one car and double up in twin rooms at the hotel. We can leave here Thursday afternoon. It's a straight three-hour drive on I-65, and we can grab a burger on the way. Receptions on Friday and Saturday nights are free, and we can eat from the free buffet instead of going out for dinner. We'll leave right after the last presentations on Sunday morning and be home by mid-afternoon."

"How many sessions will we have to attend?" Sarah frowned as she thought about the weekend. "I mean, I planned to attend the Phi Alpha Theta Luncheon on Friday, although I don't think that conflicts with any paper presentations. However, there are some late afternoon Phi Alpha Theta sessions on Friday that may overlap. That's what you wanted me to work on this year, isn't it?"

"Yes, but the recruitment issues may be more important. As for how many talks we need to cover, that's for Julia to figure out."

"Well, I can't answer that question until I see the program. Then it will just be a matter of asking Jeff to run a sort on our data base and pull up all the names that appear in the program. I've already asked the organizers for a computer listing of all speakers, but I've been told they didn't close entries until last night, so . . ."

"I can confirm that, Julia, because they added my name yesterday at the last minute."

Kevin looked shocked. "Sarah? You're on the program? You won't have time to do that."

"I beg your pardon? Aren't you the chair who lectured me recently about doing conference presentations and then following up with publication?"

"Well, yes, but I didn't expect you to run right out and . . . How come I hadn't heard you were submitting a proposal?"

"That's because I didn't submit one. A session ended up

with an empty slot, and someone from the College of Charleston remembered my work from this summer. The chair of the session called me yesterday and issued an invitation. I accepted. I didn't know you had already planned my weekend." She glared at him.

"Well, OK. We can do without you for that one session. When is it?"

"Friday morning."

"That takes you out of service for both Friday morning and Friday lunchtime. Not helpful!"

"I'll be happy to help Friday afternoon, but on Saturday there may also be some meetings about the Jubilee Project. I'll do what I can, but I can't be two places at once."

"The Jubilee Project? Isn't that a College of Charleston program?"

"Yes, it is, but it includes committee members like me from all over the South."

"Maybe you need to remember which institution you work for." Kevin glared at her before closing the meeting.

As they walked back to their offices, Sarah linked arms with Julia. "So we're to be roomies in Louisville. What fun! I'll bring a batch of cheddar cheese straws if you'll smuggle in a bottle of wine."

In response, Julia pushed Sarah into her office and closed the door behind them. "What game are you playing, Sarah? Is this your version of Russian roulette?"

Shocked, Sarah stared at her friend. "What do you mean? What did I do?"

"You just defied your department chair in front of his entire staff. Were you trying to get yourself fired?"

"No, and I wasn't defying him. I was just reminding him that he has already loaded me with other responsibilities."

"Didn't anyone warn you that at this stage of your career, you must pull rabbits out of hats, turn straw into gold, and perform miracles of time management? Look, sweetheart, Kevin may sometimes seem to be an overbearing bully, but he's the bully who holds the key to your academic future. During your third-year review—that's next year, I may remind you—during that review, the dean is going to ask Kevin if he wants to give you a one-year terminal extension of your contract or if he wishes to offer you another three-year contract with the assumption that you will petition for tenure and promotion during year five. If you have made him look foolish at every turn, what do you think he's going to recommend?"

"I . . . I hadn't even considered that. It just feels like he's been picking at me ever since the Cassie debacle, and I get frustrated when he criticizes me at every turn."

"There are no excuses, Sarah. Nobody cares how you feel. You have just one job, and that is to keep your department chair happy at all costs. That's the dirty little secret of academic life. No department chair can afford to have a strong-minded underling threatening his position. If you fight against him, you'll lose, and I don't want to see that happen."

"You challenged him, asking if his plan wasn't a little unethical."

"But I asked. I didn't tell him. And besides, I now have tenure. I can afford to raise issues. You can't."

"So, how can I fix it?"

"You might start by adjusting your plans. You should attend the Phi Alpha Theta luncheon. You can pick up a lot of pointers from table talk. The afternoon Phi Alpha Theta sessions will be student talks, however, and you're better off skipping those. Everyone does. As for the Jubilee Project, that's not even on the program, and if they have some impromptu meetings, you can plead that you have no open spots on your dance card. Reconcile yourself to skipping those personal choices and then go in and apologize to Kevin for complicating his plans. You will help Friday afternoon, all day Saturday, and Sunday morning. Period."

"Will that satisfy him?"

"It's a start. And from now on, don't make any academic plans without clearing them with Kevin. If you're going to submit a conference proposal, ask him for permission first, and make sure he knows when you have submitted and when you get a response. You could have avoided some of today's issues if you had told him when you got the call to fill in that last minute session. Beyond that, attempt to show him some respect. Ask for his advice, even when you don't intend to follow it. Volunteer. Be nice. Think before you give him a sharp response. Can you do that? It's only for three more years."

"I'll try. I suppose you still want those cheese straws."

"No cheese straws, no wine. And remember, if something happens to Kevin, I'm next in line for the chair. You need to keep me happy, too."

Chapter Ten

FALLING BY THE WAYSIDE

October 14–16, 2009

Kevin Chalmers accepted Sarah's apology without gloating, which allowed her to swallow her bites of humble pie without choking.

"I've been making some Phi Alpha Theta contacts online, and they all tell me the same thing—to attend the Friday luncheon but skip the individual sessions. So, I'll be available to listen to our candidates on Friday afternoon, all day on Saturday, and Sunday morning before we leave."

"Thank you, Sarah. I appreciate your attempting to clear your schedule. But while we're on the subject, have you made any other conference plans for this year?"

"Well, I know we'll all need to work at the AHA meeting when we're interviewing our candidates, so I'm not making any other plans there. And to be honest, I've seen enough AHA meetings to know they favor sessions that come to them already mapped out with a moderator, three presenters, and a well-defined narrow topic. Single paper proposals don't have a chance.

"I have, however, submitted a proposal to the Nineteenth-Century Studies Conference, which takes place during our spring break. It's a small enough group—and with a narrow enough focus—to at least consider a newcomer's work."

"So, even if you get accepted, it won't interfere with our campus visits. That's nice timing, but let me know when you hear from them."

"Yes, sir."

"How's your semester going so far?"

"Good. You know I'm doing the intro research course for our new graduate students, and they seem to be adjusting well. As for the undergraduate courses, I'm finding them exciting. In both the Revolutionary War course and the one on cotton as a political issue, I want the students to understand both sides of controversial questions, and most of them are eager participants."

"No witches or stalkers this time around, eh?"

"Not that I've discovered!" Sarah laughed as she relaxed. "No trouble-makers—just a few interesting characters, including a young man with traumatic brain damage and a girl who dresses like a street hoodlum but has a perfect SAT score. Things are running smoothly, although like everyone else, I'm looking forward to the upcoming fall break. I'll use it to put in some intense writing days, I suspect. Do you have any interesting plans?"

"No, although I suspect my wife has a surprise list of chores, including lots of leaf-raking. A break in the routine is healthy, though. I like to encourage the faculty not to spend all our off time indoors. If all else fails, I can furnish an extra rake."

"Thanks for the offer. I might even take you up on it."

~

arah's good mood carried her through the rest of the day and then burst like a bubble on the following day when she entered the women's lavatory and heard sobbing coming from the stalls. At the sound of her heels on the tile floor, the mysterious weeper stifled her tears, but ragged breathing and sniffles suggested that the storm of tears was not over. Sarah glanced at the only closed stall and recognized a familiar pair of Converse high-top sneakers.

"Maria? It's Professor Chomsky. Are you all right?"

"Yes, ma'am. I'm . . . fine."

"You don't sound fine. You sound like you need a shoulder to cry on. There's no one else here. Would you like to come out and talk to me about what has so upset you?"

After a long pause, during which Sarah hoped the younger woman was not rejecting her overtures, she tried a different tack. "Better yet, I'll go on down to my office. If you feel ready to talk, you can come down there, where no one else will walk in."

"I . . . I don't want to impose . . ."

"You're not imposing. I have nothing but free time before class this evening, and I'm a good listener. I'll leave now, and you can take time to pull yourself together."

Sarah stopped by the faculty lounge to retrieve two small bottles of water from the refrigerator. Back in her office, she moved a box of facial tissues closer to the guest chair next to her desk. Then she waited. She gave a sigh of relief when, after just a few minutes, Maria tapped at the door.

"Come in, Maria, and close the door. I'm glad you decided to share whatever is bothering you. We haven't had time to get to know one another so far this semester, but I've enjoyed having you in class. Teachers always appreciate seeing their students respond to new ideas."

"I love your class. I did not realize that a simple plant like cotton could change the course of history. It's fascinating. I just wish..."

"What?"

"I wish I could have felt that way about my other classes." She gave a deep sigh and straightened her back before continuing. "I just failed my mid-term calculus exam, which means my college career is over before it has begun."

"Whoa! You're making some big assumptions there. First, how do you know you failed the test? Mid-term grades don't appear until after break. You can't have seen the grade already. Second, no matter how low this grade may be, early exams are just a sign of progress, not an eventual outcome. And third, a college career does not hinge on a single course. If it did, half our student body would have disappeared."

"A zero is easy to figure out. I turned in a blank paper. I . . . I couldn't even understand the questions, let alone attempt to answer them." Tears glistened again as she cringed at her own words.

Sarah frowned in sympathy. "Introduction to Calculus is notorious for the number of students who fall victim to its mysteries, so I hear. I never got that far. I floundered at the level of solid geometry in high school. My teacher bargained with me. She agreed to pass me if I promised never to take another math class as long as I lived. I was happy to oblige."

Maria smiled at the story but kept shaking her head. "I have to live up to my reputation. I'm known as the girl with the perfect SAT scores, and that test included problems in calculus. So, people are going to ask: did I cheat on the SATs or am I just a quitter, somebody who can't take the pressure of real academia?"

"I will not ask either of those questions. I'm going to help you look for solutions. Here, would you like some water? Tears leave you dehydrated." She handed the girl a bottle of water and smiled as she drank.

"Now, let's start with this. How did you do in your calculus class in high school?"

"What class? I went to a small-town high school—Muddy Bottom High—where most girls took home economics classes and the boys went in for welding or woodworking. A few of us petitioned to get a second year of algebra, but that's as far as we went."

"So how did you . . .?"

"A college recruiter came through town, and he singled me out because I had scored high on my PSAT. He said I would have to have trigonometry and calculus to get a high score on the tests that mattered. He offered to enroll me in a preparatory class that would train me to take the SAT and ACT, but I couldn't afford it. So I went to a used book sale at the public library, where everything cost just fifty cents. I plundered the math table and found an old textbook on calculus. I taught myself late at night and on weekends, and I got some help from a neighbor, an old gentleman who was a retired engineer. I thought I understood the basic operations, and I did—at least enough to satisfy the demands of the SAT board.

"But here? Our class is full of math majors, and they might as well be talking in Swahili. I don't recognize the terms they use, and the sample problems we work with are far above anything I found in that old textbook. They lost me from the very first day."

"Then why struggle with it?"

"Because I'm competing for the Pre-Med Track. That's my goal—to become a doctor so I can help families like my own without access to good medical care. There was a meeting for everyone considering health-related careers that first week of school, and they gave us a list of the courses we needed to take. Top of the list—prerequisites for everything to follow— are three courses at the 100-level. They include trigonometry-based calculus, molecular biology, and inorganic chemistry. They're all introductory freshman-level courses. If I fail even one of those, I'll not get into the Pre-Med Track."

"But you haven't had trigonometry, let alone calculus."

"No."

"So you may have to adjust your goals, but that still does not mean the end of your college career."

"Yes, it does. I received the Presidential Scholarship as the top-entering student in the freshman class. If I don't maintain a 3.5 average, I lose the scholarship, and I have no other source of funds."

"Can't your family . . .? Or are there loans?"

"You want the whole sordid story, do you? OK. Here goes. I'm a first-generation American. I was born in New York City, so I'm a U.S. citizen. My father was Puerto Rican, but my mother's family fled Haiti and sought refugee status in Puerto Rico after the fall of Jean-Claude Duvalier. When my father claimed his right to come to the United States, my mother and my grandmother used forged papers to accompany him to New York. They are still illegal immigrants, subject to deportation if they are caught. When street robbers shot and killed my father in Harlem, my mother moved our family into the Appalachians to escape the big city violence. We drove until we ran out of gas and then put down roots where we stopped, which was the tiny mountain town of Muddy Bottom.

"Now my grandmother is too sick to work, and my mother cleans houses for people who don't ask to see her green card. I've worked at one job or another ever since I turned fourteen because we needed the money to eat. When the possibility of my getting a college scholarship arose, mother moved us to Birch Falls to be close to the campus. But I still have to work. I'm a presser in a Chinese laundry and dry cleaner, where I work from four o'clock to midnight. We live in a fourth-floor walkup in an old bank building downtown. We have two rooms—a living area with a sink, a gas stove, and an old refrigerator, and a smaller room with twin beds. Mama and my grandmother sleep in one bed; my two younger sisters split the other. I work nights, so when I come home, I sleep on the old sofa in the living area. We share a bathroom—a shower and toilet—with two other families.

"We struggle to survive. The family depends on my salary as the largest portion of their income and on my strength to help take care of grandmother and the little girls. I study whenever I can snatch some free time from classes and work. Eating and sleeping come second in my life, and I often miss doing one or the other. College is my great luxury, the privilege I earned by my grade-point average. But I have only this one chance. If—when—I fail, my college career screeches to a halt. I can't even think about a loan because it would open my family to scrutiny and the probable deportation of my mother and grandmother.

"That's my story, Dr. Chomsky, and I appreciate your listening and caring. But there is no happy ending."

Sarah sat stunned as the girl left her office. Like many of her privileged college friends, she had not understood the depths of poverty from which others struggled to survive. After chasing her thoughts around in hopeless circles for a while, she walked down to Julia's office.

"Do you have a few minutes to listen to a terrible story?"

"Did something happen in your last class?"

"No. I found a student crying in the restroom. She's in my Civil War class, but I didn't know much about her—only that she dressed like a street thug and had made a perfect score on her SAT."

"Oh, dear. You're describing the Hernandez girl, aren't you?"

"You know her?"

"I know of her. Several people have called her to my attention, hoping their only black faculty member could deal with a brilliant black student. I'm hoping that's not why you are here."

"I'm here because you've always given me friendly advice."

"Advice about what?"

"What can I do about the fact that she just failed a calculus exam and is going to lose her scholarship, which will force her out of college altogether because she is the main support of a family of illegal immigrants."

"A calculus exam? Then you have only one course of action—to butt out. You cannot interfere in the affairs of another department, Sarah. That's a sure way to get yourself expelled from the college right along with the student."

"But there must be something we can do to help. I mean, she holds our Presidential Scholarship. We can't just boot her out the first time she stumbles."

"That's your first problem. You're assuming responsibility for her fate, when you have no say in what happens to her."

"But she confided in me to . . ."

"What she thought you might do doesn't matter. You can tell her to consult her assigned academic advisor. You can recommend that she talk to her calculus prof, explaining that she lacks the background and prerequisites to finish the course. He may have solutions we know nothing about—like departmental tutors or the ability to switch her to a more basic level. But that's your limit. You can't go to bat for her."

Sarah sighed. "You're right about the rules, I know, but it just feels wrong."

"There's one other resource that might help her. I'm the

appointed faculty sponsor of a small group of African-American women who want to establish a chapter of Alpha Kappa Alpha on our campus."

"I don't even know what that is."

"I didn't expect you to. AKA is a sorority for college-educated black women. The first chapter had its beginnings at Howard University over one hundred years ago, and it's now the largest Hellenic group of its kind. At the moment, we don't have enough black students on campus to receive our charter, but there's a fledgling group of black women who are working to improve the educational experiences of their sisters. They offer every sort of help—from scholarly tutoring to fashion advice. From the sounds of what you have told me, I suspect your Miss Hernandez could use a little of both."

"Yes, but how do we . . .?"

"Turn the problem over to me. I'll send word to their leadership and leave the specific details to them. Trust me on this one, Sarah, because the racial divide is firm in matters like this. We'd all agree that her dreadlocks and high-top sneakers need to go, but you couldn't tell her that without sounding racist. That has to come from her peers, as does any suggestion on how to survive the rigors of the college's red tape.

"The next time you talk to this young woman, you can offer her the two permitted bits of advice: talk to your professor and ask your advisor for help. That's it. No motherly advice, no sympathetic shoulder to cry on, no offers to intercede in her life. She needs to learn how to handle her own problems."

∾

C hastened once again as the neophyte professor who had failed to follow the rules, Sarah looked forward to fall break with as much enthusiasm as her students. The strains of her busy schedule weighed upon her. She had decided not to give midterm exams, but she still had papers to grade and mid-term warnings to issue. Her newly appointed position on the faculty admissions committee was taking up more of her free time than she had planned. And there was the paper presentation for the Southern. While she had a basic outline of what she wanted to say, the details needed much polishing.

The promise of four days without a single meeting or class had dangled before her all week. She looked forward to sleeping in, wearing her most comfortable sweats, and eating junk food that required little preparation. Most of all, she visualized some much-needed solitude—no e-mails, no distressed students, no demanding supervisors—just a small black cat to comfort her when she needed a hug.

By Friday, that anticipation was enough to keep a smile on her face. It was an ordinary Friday, no stranger than any other, except for the promise of pleasant days to come. No momentous changes occurred, but just beyond the reach of her senses, a series of small decisions were taking place—decisions that would affect the lives of several of her favorite students and all those who knew them.

Chapter Eleven

MARIA: TRANSFORMATIONS

Friday, October 16, 2009

In the math and science building, Maria Hernandez waited for her calculus class to be over so she could approach Professor Higgins. As usual, students swarmed around his desk at the end of class, and Maria hovered on the edge of their group, waiting to be the last one in line.

"Excuse me, Dr. Higgins, but I was wondering if you have a few minutes to talk to me concerning my progress in this course. I'm having a problem..."

"Not now, Miss... uh, Maria, is it? I have a plane to catch, and I'm running late. Students are not the only ones leaving for a vacation, you know."

"I just..."

"I said, not now. Ask the department secretary to schedule an appointment for after break." He swept a pile of papers into his briefcase and hustled out of the room without another glance in Maria's direction. Her mouth puckered, tears formed, and she sank into a nearby desk before her knees buckled.

"Hey, girlfriend, never let them see you cry. Tears have the wrong effect on old white guys—making a black girl cry gives them a sense of false power."

Startled, Maria looked up to find a dark-skinned young woman leaning over her. "I ... I don't ... do I know you?"

"No, but you should. I'm Brandy Johnson, a junior here at Smoky Mountain and a Kappa. Our advisor asked me to check on you and see if you're settling into college life. Looks as if I've located you not a moment too soon."

"I'm sorry. I don't understand. What's a 'kappa?' And who ...?"

"I'm a member of Alpha Kappa Alpha, or at least I hope to be once we get our official charter. It's a national sorority for college-educated black women. While we wait to get enough members to qualify, we're just a group of friends who try to make life easier for our black sisters here on this lily-white campus."

"I'm sorry, but I don't have the time—or the money—to discuss sororities."

"That's not why I'm here. Our faculty advisor, Dr. Winthrop, suggested that you might need a little friendly support, so she asked me to get in touch with you to see if we can help."

"I don't even know a Dr. Winthrop." Maria knew she sound petulant and uncooperative, but she floundered in unfamiliar territory.

"Maybe you don't, but Dr. Winthrop is a friend of your history professor, Dr. Chomsky, which may explain the chain by which your name reached us. I traced you here and overheard Higgins ignore your request. Are you having a problem with his class?"

"That's obvious, isn't it? And it's more than a problem. I'm failing the class and in imminent danger of losing my scholarship, which will mean the end of my college career. I was hoping to get help from him, but you saw. . . . As for his suggestion, I won't schedule an appointment because I don't even know where to find the math secretary. Offers of friendship from successful upperclassmen are nice, but much too late."

"No, that's not so. My word, are you always this hardnosed when someone offers a helping hand?" Brandy pulled a chair over and settled into it. "If the problem is this class, I'll introduce you to our president, Christina Babcock. She's a math whiz and has helped several of us muddle through calculus. Look, what are you doing over break?"

"Just what I do every day. I live at home to help take care of my grandmother and younger sisters in the mornings and after school. I attend my own classes in the middle of the day and study in whatever few minutes I can find. And I work nights—forty hours a week as a presser in a Chinese laundry. That fills my days, vacation or no vacation. With what free time I have, I'll be studying in the library." Maria stood up to put an end to the conversation.

"Wait, please. You're not alone, and your problems are common. Kappas are not rich prima donnas. We've struggled through poverty-ridden childhoods, living in slums, battling gang pressures and drug pushers, and facing discrimination, both intentional and the kinds that result from ignorance. Some give up and sink deeper into the same abyss they've always known, and others rise above it, hoping to pull others up with them."

"Sounds hopeless from where I stand—or sink."

"We're reaching out to you. Give us a chance. Meet us for lunch on Monday. If you're going to be in the library, we'll plan to gather in the Grub Hub. It will be just a few black girls who have had the same experiences. We'll buy you a sandwich and talk while we eat. Maybe you'll reject what we offer, but you owe it to yourself to listen before you shake your head again. We'll look for you around noon on Monday."

≈

On Monday morning, as promised, Maria Hernandez headed to the library and its section on mathematics. She chose a small introductory calculus text and read from page one. She wanted to gain enough understanding to talk to Dr. Higgins. Her concentration crumbled as the morning passed. She had agreed to meet Brandy and her friends for lunch, but she hesitated to follow through on that promise. The young woman's offer of friendship was tempting, but Maria had little time for friends. She had no time for sororities. And since she knew her test sealed her college fate, it was pointless to accept offers of help. It was too late.

As the hands on the library clock moved closer to to twelve o'clock, she walked toward the Grub Hub. She paused in the doorway and spotted the girls clustered around a table in the corner. Their dark faces stood out in contrast to the white customers now lining up at the counter. Maria turned to leave, but curiosity tempted her. She approached the table, feeling conscious of her ragged clothes and messy hair.

Five friendly faces turned to greet her, and she read no criticism in their expressions. She sat at the table as they passed a platter of submarine sandwiches around and distributed large glasses of iced tea. One by one, the girls introduced themselves to her and told her their stories.

"I'm Louisa Brewster and I grew up near you in Harlem. I don't know what school you attended in New York, but I know what it was like. The black schools were disasters. I was lucky that my father got a job here in Birch Falls and moved us before I finished junior high. Still, I had a lot of catching up to do."

"So did I. I'm Dolores Middleton, and my family lives in the black section of Nashville. We're descendants of the slaves who worked for Nashville's founding families. Even with all the schools available in the city, I'm the first to attend college, just as you are."

"I'm Natasha Abbott, and I'm sure you realize that I'm older than most of these girls. I went to cosmetology school after high school because I needed a quick way to make money. I'm an orphan, raised in foster families and on my own as soon as I turned eighteen. My last foster family paid for me to go to hair-cutting classes. Then I had to work for several years and save enough money to go to a real college. My progress is slow because I still work part time in a salon, but I'm getting there."

"And I'm Christina Babcock. I'm the math major Brandy mentioned—one of the lucky ones who received a good education in the public schools. A teacher realized that I had a knack for figures and encouraged me to take the tough math courses. Now that I've figured out what language these mathematicians speak, I try to help others when I can.

Maria smiled at her. "So, it's not my imagination that the other students in my calculus class do not speak English?"

"Math is a unique language, but not one that's hard to master, once you find the key. I know I can help you with that."

"I'm sure you could, but . . . it's too late, I'm afraid. I turned in a blank test, so I know my grade is a zero. And I know enough basic arithmetic to understand that with only four more tests to go, I have no hope of getting any grade higher than a D, even if I do well on the other tests. And that is doubtful, given my lack of understanding. There goes my scholarship, along with my college career."

"Well, there's one dirty little secret you don't know. We math majors keep this discovery private among ourselves, but I'll share it with you. Dr. Higgins always—always—drops your lowest test grade before he averages your higher marks. Your zero is a horror, I admit, but it won't ever count against you."

For a moment, Maria felt the room spin around her. Her breath caught in her throat, and she had to grasp the edge of the table to keep herself upright. "If you're kidding, that isn't funny."

"It's not a joke. It's a hard and fast rule among math professors. You are going to survive. We're going to help you succeed. You are the first black woman to win the prestigious Presidential Scholarship, so you can't drop out now. Our reputation is on the line along with yours, so we're your defense team."

"No, thanks. You may try to help, but I can't believe that you have no ulterior motives. Whatever you want from me, I don't have time for it. I have responsibilities up to my ears and social weaknesses you can't imagine. I haven't asked for your help, and I wish you'd quit trying to interfere in my life. It's complicated enough." Maria stood up, pushed her plate away, and headed for the door.

~

Christina had been on the alert for just such a move. She stepped between Maria and the door. "Please don't turn your back on this opportunity. We are trying to help. It's what we do. If we are rushing you into a scary decision, it's because we're late in getting started. You can trust us. And someday, you can pay it forward by helping another young woman transform her life."

"But I have so much working against me—just look at me!

How do you plan to rescue a piece of grubby street trash and turn her into the school's top scholar?"

"We start with the calculus problem. You're going to spend at least an hour a day with me until you've mastered every one of these foreign sounding principles and surpassed the star students in your regular class. We'll find the time that works for both of us," Christina promised.

Brandy was eager to move on to other problems. "Next, we're going to solve your work schedule. What does your Chinese laundry pay?"

"Five dollars an hour, but he doesn't take out any deductions, so I get a little over $800 a month, which is enough to feed my family and pay our utility bills. The family needs every cent."

"Your laundryman is cheating you. It's illegal to pay you less than the minimum wage that just went up to $7.25 an hour."

"He knows I can't complain, or he'll report my family to Immigration. They will send my mother and grandmother back to Haiti, and my little sisters will end up in horrid foster homes."

"No, he won't report you, because he's cheating the government, too," Brandy explained. "But you're going to quit that job. You're eligible for a work-study position on campus, where they pay $10.50 an hour and you work in a safe and pleasant office. You'll work twenty hours a week, but you'll earn more than you get now for a forty-hour week. I've found an outstanding job for you, working for the kindest woman on campus."

"I can't work in an office. Look at me!"

"By the time I take you to meet Mrs. Wright, you'll look the part. Tell her, Natasha."

"I'm a hairdresser, remember? I'm hoping you wear your hair in those dreadlocks because it's convenient. If you insist on keeping them, I'll show you a way to style them with a wide headband that keeps them from flopping over your eyes. But I'll be happier if you'll let me take my scissors to them and give you a simple and fashionable cut to emphasize your elegant bone structure. My salon is closed on Mondays, so I can take you into the empty shop this afternoon and give you a makeover."

"I . . . I don't know what to say."

"Don't say anything," Louisa said, patting her hand. "Dolores and I will take over after your hair styling. We run a clothing exchange in my family's garage. We encourage our college friends to turn in their good used outfits instead of sending them to a place that chops them into rags. Everything we have is free for the taking. I know we can find several outfits to suit you."

"One last step," Brandy said. "As a full scholarship holder, you get your room and board included. I know you've chosen to live at home, but there's a dorm room assigned to you, and a full meal ticket. I'll take you by housing in the morning. We'll pick up your room key and find your new living quarters."

"But I can't . . ."

"Yes, you can. You'll have more money coming in, more free time to study, and still be close enough to see your family every day. Plus, you'll have a private room, your own bath, shared with just one other girl, a good bed, a closet for your new clothes, a desk to work at, and three healthy meals a day. Why didn't you move into the dorm when school started?"

"I didn't know how."

"See? That's why you need our help. We'll stick close and show you around until you make your own friends and understand the routines."

"But my family needs . . ."

"No, they just think they do. They know you will move

out, eventually. You might as well do it now, while you have this great opportunity to get your room and board."

"But my mother . . ."

"Your mother knows she can't keep you a child forever. You'll see. They'll adjust, and so will you. They'll have one less mouth to feed, one less body to clothe, and more room to spread out. Besides, you will have more time for them than you did when you were working every day from four to midnight."

"This is a good move, Maria. Enjoy it."

Chapter Twelve

CHAD: NO GOOD DEED GOES UNPUNISHED

Friday, October 16, 2009

C had whistled a nameless tune as he drove down the country road to his grandmother's farm. It was a glorious day, the kind that often followed a violent storm like the one that hit the region the previous night. Grandma Overstreet had called early in the morning to report that the winds had felled one of her old white pine trees. It now lay across her driveway, blocking her ability to back her car out of the garage. Could Chad find time before supper to come by and take a chain saw to it—the tree, not the car, that is? He could. Chad loved the old lady and knew that she'd be baking his favorite snickerdoodle cookies when he got there.

He had always enjoyed bright October afternoons, the sun's warmth with an edge of coolness, the trees mellowing into riotous shades of red and gold, the tang of smoke suggesting that a nearby farmer was clearing land or burning leaves. But the changing season also reminded him that this was football weather and elicited a brief wave of regret for his lost career hopes. The college team would play on Saturday without their former quarterback. He would be in the stands, watching, cheering, second-guessing the calls, and resenting the traumatic brain injury that had sidelined him last year. Try as he might, he could not get past those memories.

He felt his jaw tighten and his right foot tromped down on the gas pedal as he crested the top of a hill. In a flashback, he was dashing for the goal line, the football tucked into the crook of his elbow. Fans cheered. The band hit the first notes of the school's pep song. Cheerleaders waved their shakers and flipped a series of somersaults. Then, just in time, he saw the two little girls walking in the middle of the road ahead. He shouted an expletive as he stood on the brake pedal and swerved the car onto the gravel verge. Small rocks peppered the undercarriage of the car, and dust rose in a cloud as he came to a stop.

Still shaking, he pushed the door open and jumped out to confront the careless children who had come so close to disaster. They stood stock still, mouths hanging open and hands clutching each other. "Get out of the road," he shouted at them. "Don't you have any better sense than to walk in the middle of the road with your backs to traffic? I could have killed you."

The smaller child, who appeared to be about five, broke into tears. The older girl—maybe eight or nine—put her arm around the little one. "Don't yell at her. You were going too fast." Defiant but trembling, she glared back at Chad.

"What are you doing out here, anyway? There's not even a sidewalk. Where do you live?"

"Up there." The girl pointed to the top of the hill where a white board fence surrounded an enclave of one-story condominium residences. "We were pushing our animals in the doll's baby buggy at the top of the driveway. But my shoe came untied, and I stopped to fix it. The buggy rolled down the drive, and I couldn't catch it. It crashed into the ditch over there, and Tabitha jumped out."

"Tabitha? Who is . . .?"

"Tabitha's our kitten. She was being so good. We dressed her in a little pink dress, and she just cuddled right down with our teddy bears. But I guess she got scared when the buggy fell over."

"And where is Tabitha now?"

"I don't know. She ran into the bushes, but the dress tangled her paws and she was moving funny." The little girl's bravado was dissolving, and her bottom lip trembled.

Chad's fright and anger had also faded, and he looked at the two tear-stained faces with sympathy. "Hey! Don't cry. I'll bet we can find her. Come on. Let's walk along the edge of the road here. You will be safest if you walk facing the approaching traffic. Now, about this kitten—what color is she?"

"Orange, with stripes."

"Ah. A tabby cat. I get the name now. I'm Chad. Do you girls have names, too?

"I'm Lilibet, and this is my little sister, Abbie."

"Well, how do you do, Abbie?" Chad reached out to take her hand, but Lilibet flared at him again. "Don't you touch her. Mommy says we should never let a stranger touch us."

"She's right. I apologize."

They meandered, scanning the underbrush, but there was no sign of a kitten.

"Look," Chad said, "I have to get to my grandmother's farm, and I can't leave you two down here on this road by yourselves. Maybe Tabitha ran back up the hill and went home. Cats find their way by smell. Why don't you let me drive you back to your house, so you can wait for her to find her own way home? My car's right here. Hop in."

"No! Go away! Leave us alone! Mommy says we must never get into a stranger's car."

"I'm not a stranger. I'm Chad, and my grandma lives right around the corner here."

"No. You're a bad man. Run, Abbie!"

Chad watched as the two little girls fled for their lives, back up the sloping driveway, Lilibet dragging the doll buggy behind her. With a sigh of frustration, Chad drove on to his appointment with the chain saw.

Two hours later, the old pine tree chopped into manageable logs, Chad swallowed a last snickerdoodle and headed home. He slowed as he approached the condominium complex, scanning the road on either side for a glimpse of orange fur. This time he was lucky. He spotted a bedraggled and mud-spattered little cat crouched at the edge of the road. Stopping his car again, he got out and approached the animal. He had trouble seeing any orange fur because she was covered in mud, but around the cat's stomach some pink fabric proved that this little kitten had once worn a pink dress to go for a buggy ride.

With as much care as possible, he picked her up and carried her to his car. She was wet and shivering from cold and fright. In the trunk, he unearthed a cardboard box to contain her while he drove. He was just about to start the car when a police vehicle approached with lights and siren going full blast.

Chad's first reaction was fear. Had he done something wrong? It couldn't be a moving violation because the engine wasn't even running. A parking ticket, maybe? He tried to control his shaking as he clutched the steering wheel and waited for the officer to approach. He watched in the rearview mirror, trying to figure out what was taking so long.

At last, two patrolmen emerged from the police cruiser and approached, one on either side of Chad's car. The older officer tapped on the glass, and Chad rolled down the window. "Is there a problem, sir?"

"I'm Sergeant Murphey. That's my partner, Officer Duncan. License and registration, please."

"I have to wiggle around. I'm sitting on my wallet, and the registration is in the glove box."

"Got a gun in the car, son?"

"No, sir!" Chad's voice shook.

"OK, let's get the paperwork, but move slow and try to keep your hands where I can see them."

With fumbling fingers, Chad located his license and handed it over. Then he reached for the glove box.

"Hold it. Is it OK if my partner opens the glove compartment first?"

"Yes, sure."

"You're Chad Overstreet? Where have I heard that name?"

"You a football fan? I was the quarterback for the college last year—at least until an illegal hit rattled my brains."

"I remember now. Badly hurt, weren't you?"

"Yeah, you might say that."

"Brains still rattled?"

"No, I'm lots better, but the doctors won't let me play anymore."

"Hmmm. Would you step outside, please? And place both hands on the roof of your car."

"What's the problem, officer?" Chad complied with the request but wrinkled his brow. "Is this a no-parking zone or something?"

Instead of answering, the officer peered into the car again. "What's in that box on the front seat?"

"Nothing but a cat."

"A . . . cat? What . . .?"

"Well, it's a mud-covered kitten wearing a pink dress, but I didn't think you'd believe that."

"I've heard sillier excuses. Officer Duncan, look in that box while I get our young friend settled. Hands down, Mr. Overstreet. You just have a seat here in the patrol car while we check some details."

"What's going on?"

The cop did not bother to answer as he pulled out a cell phone and punched a quick-dial button. Then he turned his back to conceal his conversation.

"It's a dirty cat, all right," Duncan confirmed as he leaned into the patrol car. "Where did you get it?"

"I found her alongside of the road. I was going to take her back to the little girls looking for her earlier."

"Sergeant Murphey. Did he Mirandize you just now?"

"What? I don't know . . ."

"Did he read you your rights?"

"Why? I have done nothing wrong."

"That's for us to decide. Hang on. Let's take care of the formalities before you say anything else." The young cop pulled a ragged card from his breast pocket and read:

You have the right to remain silent. Anything you say can and will be used against you in a court of law. You have the right to an attorney. If you cannot afford an attorney, one will be—

"What are you doing, Duncan? This young man is not under arrest." The older officer glared at his partner.

"He will be. He's ready to talk." He turned back to Chad and finished reading from the card. Then he asked again, "Tell us where you got that cat."

"I found her alongside of the road just now. I was going to take her back to the little girls who were looking for her."

"And what little girls were those?"

"They were walking in the middle of the road two hours ago. I thought maybe they had gotten lost, and I stopped to see if they needed help." Chad looked puzzled. "What would you have me do—leave them out there in traffic?"

"No. It's just that we got a report of a lost cat a while ago—might be the same one."

"I don't imagine there are many cats wandering around in a pink dress." Chad grinned and shook his head as he reached in to pet the kitten.

"But about these little girls . . . do you know them? How did you know where they live?"

"I didn't, exactly, but they said they lived up there in the condos. I was going to go around there and see if I could spot them, or maybe ask someone if they knew whose cat it is."

"Hmmm." Officer Murphey frowned as if puzzled." Well, you sit back and keep that cat from tracking mud all over our back seat. We'll take you up there and see who we can find." Sergeant Murphey slammed the door and nodded at Duncan to get in the front seat.

"It's OK, sir. My car's right here. I can take care of this myself. You don't need to . . ."

The roar of the car engine was his only answer.

The condo houses were all the same color and style, differing only in the minor details of windows, door placements, and landscaping. A few had cars parked in the driveways, while others featured yards filled with bicycles. Chad stared out the back window looking for familiar faces, but there was no one around. The emptiness did not seem to bother Officer Murphey, however, as he drove down the main street and pulled into a driveway as if he knew where he was.

"This must be it," Chad said. "That's the little girls' doll buggy—the one the cat was riding in."

"Yes. Thought it might be. You can get out of the car, Mr. Overstreet, but stay right here unless I call you over. I'll take the cat." He hoisted the box, which was now rocking a little as the cat sought a way out.

Taking a firmer grip on the box, he approached the front door and rang the bell. A frazzled woman opened the door. "Yes? Oh, Sergeant Murphey! I wasn't expecting you to be back so soon."

"I think we've found your cat, Mrs. Grimsby. Does this look like her—under all the mud, that is?" He opened the box and tipped it to show her the contents.

"Oh, Tabitha! What have you gotten yourself into?" The woman pulled the bedraggled kitten from the box and held her at arm's length. "Girls! Come quick! Tabitha's home, and she needs a bath!"

Lilibet and Abby came running from somewhere inside the house. "She got her dress all dirty," Abby scolded.

But Lilibet was staring at the police car in the driveway. She tugged at her mother's arm. "Mommy! That's him. That's the bad man who tried to nap us." She pointed at Chad and then ducked behind her mother.

"You mean 'kidnap,' dear."

Sergeant Murphey waited no longer. He nodded at his partner and shouted, "Cuff him, Duncan."

Chad stared at the house in disbelief as Officer Duncan twisted his arms behind his back and clamped the cuffs around his wrists.

Chapter Thirteen

OLIVIA: WHAT HAPPENS ON BREAK

October 16–18, 2009

O livia Cartwright was in her dorm room Friday afternoon, carelessly packing a few things to take home for the duration of fall break. Her roommate watched her and shook her head. "You couldn't be gloomier if you were Anne Boleyn headed for the chopping block. Won't you enjoy having a few days away from this pressure cooker?"

"Well, if you want to play with metaphors, I'm not escaping the pressure cooker; I'm just jumping from that cooker into a frying pan."

"Bad time at home?"

"Always, but weekends are particularly grim. Oh, tonight will go all right. But there's a family ritual starting on Saturday morning. Daddy will be up early, headed for a round of golf followed by a visit to his office. He'll do a walk-through of the manufacturing facility, noting every tiny flaw, and then he'll call up the week's sales figures and rage at any perceived failure. There will be a direct correlation between his golf score and his anger, and I assure you, he's a terrible golfer. He will end his day at his favorite gentlemen's club, where he can get a steak cooked just the way he likes it and then nurse a cigar and snifter of brandy while exchanging lies with his cronies.

"Back at the house, my mother will be primping and getting ready for her weekly outing with her 'girlfriends.' They head to the country club before noon and celebrate their friendship with several rounds of mimosas, followed by a fancy luncheon. After they've sampled all the desserts, they'll turn to casual bridge games. Their understanding of bridge is no better than my father's skill at golf, but the cozy foursomes are ideal for exchanging gossip and watching who's playing tennis with whom. They'll also be checking the time to see how soon the sun will be over the yardarm so they can start on rounds of manhattans or martinis. The staff will run them out around six to make room for the dinner crowd, but by then most of them will need to be driven home. We never see my mother on Saturday nights. She comes home and goes straight to bed to indulge the start of her hangover.

"The next morning, we'll all be on time for the traditional Sunday brunch with my father's brother and his family—because no one wants to miss the latest chapter in their ongoing fraternal feud. The food's usually good, but the arguments are really stale. After that, we go our separate ways again, just trying to avoid one another."

Olivia's cell phone played a tune, interrupting her diatribe. Her roommate gave a wave and headed for the door. "See you Wednesday!"

The caller was Jack Dunlap. Olivia had been avoiding him since that awful night in Matt Garrison's bar, but almost anything would be better than what she faced at home.

"Hi, Jack."

"Hi, yourself, Princess. Got big plans for fall break?"

"None at all. I was just describing a typical Cartwright weekend to my roomie. Now that I've reminded myself, I may just unpack my suitcase and hide under the bed."

"Well, may I offer one chance for a little fun? Saturday afternoon and evening, the Rotary Club is throwing its annual Oktoberfest to raise funds for the homeless shelter. They take over City Park with games, arts and crafts, food booths, a biergarten, polka lessons, and even dachshund races. How about we pretend to be Germans for the day and share in the celebration?"

"Sounds better than what I face at home, provided you promise we won't spend all our time in the biergarten."

"I pinky-swear."

Saturday started off well for Olivia. She had slept long past her usual hour, making up for lost sleep during the week. By the time she stumbled out of bed, her parents were both gone for the day, a condition that pleased her. She headed for the kitchen, scrounged through the refrigerator for breakfast possibilities, and settled for coffee, orange juice, toast, a banana, and several slices of bacon. Then she took her time getting ready for a casual day at the park. She smiled at her image in the make-up mirror, realizing that she was primping just as her mother did on Saturdays.

She had to admit that she was looking forward to seeing Jack. She had no illusions about falling in love with him. They didn't have that kind of chemistry. But she liked him a lot and enjoyed his company. He was handsome in a rough sort of way, self-assured, and rich enough to indulge her whims when they were together. He was a significant improvement over the boys her own age, most of whom were still pimple-faced and strapped for cash.

It was another glorious October day, suited for a festival. Olivia and Jack arrived at the park in mid-afternoon and started their day by wandering through some arts and crafts displays. Fall decorations dominated the homemade items for sale, challenged only by tables full of pickles, jams and jellies, pie fillings, and chow-chows. Olivia dawdled at one table displaying jewelry made from small pebbles and colored bits of glass.

"See anything you like?" Jack asked, already reaching for his wallet.

"No. I was just curious about where people find all these interesting stones. They're not really my style. Let's move along."

At one point, they stopped at a booth to purchase flavored ices and sipped them until both of them had tongues tinted with shades of blue and purple. In another area, they found the games, which looked like the Rotarians had borrowed them from a traveling carnival. Jack proclaimed himself an expert at ball tossing and ringing coke bottles. Olivia laughed at him for sounding like a little kid. She challenged him to prove himself by winning her a stuffed animal.

"Now who's the little kid?" Jack mocked, but he could not resist a dare. After a few warm-up tosses, he lassoed five bottles in a row, and the booth owner created a show of presenting Olivia with the prize—a stuffed dachshund.

"It's an omen," Jack said, as the public address system squealed and announced that all entrants in the "Race for the Weenies" should assemble at the makeshift racetrack.

"Come on. This should be fun to watch." From all over the park, dog owners appeared, leading their long little dogs toward the starting line. Olivia clutched her stuffed dachshund and declared his name to be Dieterich. She grinned as she noticed how many of the dogs resembled their owners, but one caught her attention. The owner had dressed the poor animal in lederhosen and a leather vest. He was an older dog and so overweight that he waddled as he walked. His owner, at the other end of the leash, was a middle-aged woman wearing a dirndl skirt. She, too, waddled.

Jack noticed what Olivia was watching. "They're well suited to each other," he remarked. They turned out to be much more than that. The woman found a place at the starting line and ordered the dog to "Stay." Then she headed off to the finish line, where she squatted and dug around in the contents of her purse. The emcee read through the rules and called out the ritual, "Ready! Set! Go!"

The woman reacted by pulling a large bratwurst out of her purse and waving it at her dog. "Come to Mama," she called, and the chubby dog never took his eyes off that sausage as he speed-waddled his way down the course to win the race. After a small flurry of protests, the emcee declared that the rules did not prohibit the displaying of a sausage. The dog and his owner accepted a small trophy and waddled off. Jack was grumbling, but Olivia laughed. "I love people," she declared.

After the racetrack closed, Jack and Olivia agreed it was time to eat. The park pavilion offered an authentic German dinner next to the biergarten, which advertised mustard pretzels and pickled eggs. Olivia raised an eyebrow as she waited to see which setting was Jack's choice. He surprised her by leading the way straight to the pavilion. "Crisp, sweet cider is the beverage of the day," he announced. The menu offered only two choices: bratwurst and sauerkraut or jagerschnitzel with spaetzle and red cabbage. After the experience at the dog races, they both chose the jagerschnitzel and settled in to enjoy an unfamiliar meal.

The food was delicious, and all went well until Jack pushed his empty plate aside and leaned toward Olivia. "I have something of a confession to make," he said. "After that affair at the bar, I went to see your Dr. Chomsky and apologized for appearing to put you in danger. She didn't seem to believe my remorse and embarrassment, but I tried to assure her of my good intentions. She was shocked to hear that your father was the one who asked me to date you, but I promised her that that I am dedicated to protecting you from him. I declared that I detest your father for his bullying ways and that I care for you. I hope she believed me."

Olivia was staring at him in horror. "Wait! What are you saying? My father asked you to date me? He set us up? Did he hire you? Pay you? And you let him pimp for me?" With each question, her voice grew shriller. "That's it! I'm through! Thanks for the farewell dinner."

"Wait, Olivia! I thought you knew!"

She stood up, gathered her things, and turned away from the table. Then she hesitated and went back. "You can keep your stuffed dog. I hope you'll be happy together." Tears flowed as she threw the toy into his face and ran off.

At the edge of the park, Olivia hailed a taxi to take her home. "At last, a use for that twenty-dollar bill mother always insists I carry," she thought. The house was quiet, as she had expected, and she made it to her room without interruption.

But now the tears flowed, and her stomach heaved. The emotional jolt, on top of the unfamiliar and heavy meal she had eaten, sent her running for the bathroom. She fell to her knees in front of the toilet as the spasms took control. At last, emptied and drained, she washed her face and fell across her bed, trying to decide whether she was ill, hurt, or just angry. Without resolving that issue, she fell asleep. One last thought echoed through the corners of her mind: "And I didn't even have a beer!"

On Sunday morning, still groggy from sleep, Olivia wandered downstairs to make her command appearance at the family brunch. She kept her eyes averted from her father as she greeted her aunt and uncle and their twins—a boy and a girl. To her own surprise, she felt a pang of extreme jealousy at the sibling bond between them. "At least they have each other when the family gets too crazy."

She looked around the table for her mother, only to see her swigging a Bloody Mary as if it contained life's blood rather than tomato juice. Only Bertha, the maid, gave her a friendly greeting as she handed her a full plate. Olivia realized she was starving after last night's escapade, and she gave her full attention to her Eggs Benedict. She enjoyed them until her father's voice boomed through the room.

"Well, Olivia, how was your evening romping around the park with the German peasants? Did you and that handsome fellow of yours have a good time, or did . . ."

She didn't let him finish. Without even considering what she was doing, she hurled the biscuit she was buttering into her father's face. It hit him on the chin, causing his head to jerk back, and his arm, flailing to intercept the biscuit, caught the celery tops sticking out of his breakfast cocktail. As tomato juice spread across the starched white tablecloth and dripped into his lap, she stood, leaning her hands on the table to spew her words into his face. "Ask him yourself, you bastard. He's your paid gigolo—the guy you hired to date me so you'd always know where I was."

The dining room was silent as she pushed her way to the door. The twins were rolling their eyes at one another and giggling behind their hands. Again, she envied them. Back in her room, she moved from closet to bureau, trying to decide if she should to pack and leave.

But where was she to go? The college was closed; the dorms locked up tight. Her sorority sisters were off on their annual theater excursion to New York. She thought of trying to catch up with them, but she knew their tickets were all reserved in advance. Her father had labeled the trip frivolous and refused to fund it. There was no way to catch up now.

She couldn't call Jack. She had burned all her bridges there. Maybe Bertha would let her help wash the dishes, she thought. Instead, she locked her door, pushed a chair under the knob, and crawled back into bed, wishing there was a painless way to end her life.

Chapter Fourteen

REALITY INTRUDES

October 21–22, 2009

On Wednesday morning, Sarah hummed to herself as she made her way from the faculty parking lot to the Humanities Building. She was rested and eager to get the second half of the semester underway. There was much to do, she realized—midterm reports, the pending trip to Louisville for the Southern Conference, the final winnowing of viable job candidates, then Thanksgiving, all leading up to what would be a double whammy of Hanukkah celebrations and Finals Week. Still, her spirits soared as she realized how much she loved this job.

The icy hand of reality, however, waited for her just outside her office door. The student had her back turned to the hallway, but she was all too familiar. Olivia turned to reveal that she was wearing oversized aviator-style sunglasses.

"Wow! Hiding a massive hangover or a migraine at the thought of returning to classes?" Sarah thought she was making a joke but soon realized the situation was too serious to ignore. Olivia followed her into the office and removed her sunglasses, revealing a rainbow of bruising that extended from her right eye across the bridge of her nose, fading as it reached her eyebrow and part way down her cheek. She lifted her chin and stared back at Sarah.

"You're going to make a big thing of this, so I thought it would be better to hash it out in your office rather than in a room full of my classmates. It's not open for discussion. I just need your permission to keep the sunglasses on during class."

"Oy vey, Olivia. What happened to you? Were you in an accident?"

"So to speak. I ran into a kitchen door."

"No kitchen door inflicts that kind of damage. Did someone hit you?"

"No. I hit the door in the middle of the night. I was looking for a midnight snack and forgot about that door to the pantry."

"That's a mark left by a fist, not a door. Which of your disagreements precipitated this blow? Was it a quarrel with your father or with Jack?"

"The kitchen . . ."

"I heard you, but I can't believe you."

"That's what happened, whether or not you believe it."

"My dear, you need to realize that when a man inflicts that kind of damage on a young woman's face, it's only a short distance to more brutal treatment. The attacks will escalate. They always do."

"The door was apologetic."

"Don't be smart. You need to recognize the danger you are in."

"May I keep the sunglasses on during your class, or

should I plan to get the notes from someone until I look more presentable?"

"You may keep them on, but we're not finished with this discussion."

"Yes, we are." The young woman whirled on her heel and left the office.

Sarah sank into her desk chair and buried her face in her hands. That scene had not gone well. From force of habit, she reached for the phone to call David. An attack that left such brutal evidence required the intercession of the police. Then she drew back. It was almost time to meet her Civil War class. The news of Olivia's black eye would have to wait until later in the day.

∽

Other worries assailed Sarah as she walked to the lecture hall. Would Maria Hernandez be in class, or would she have already left school? Her discouragement had been obvious on the previous Friday, and Sarah's recommendation that she talk to her calculus professor had met with nothing but a shake of her head and a shrug of her shoulders.

Sarah's glance went straight to the far front corner of the room, only to see a stranger sitting in Maria's usual spot. Or was it a stranger? The attractive young woman smiled back at her and nodded, as if to say, "Yes, I'm still here." Maria had lost her dreadlocks, and her natural hair, now cut short in a pixie style, emphasized the girl's high cheekbones and fine chin line. A bare trace of makeup put a blush on her cheeks and softened her mouth. She wore a beige turtleneck sweater with slim-cut jeans and brown loafers. Best of all, her back was straight and her head held high.

Stunned by the transformation, Sarah gave the young

woman a concealed thumbs-up sign, and then launched into the day's lecture. There's something about standing behind a lectern and facing a room full of listeners that takes control of a professor's performance. This was one of Sarah's favorite subjects—blockade-running, as it had developed during the early years of the Civil War. As she described the ponderous movements of most naval vessels of the nineteenth century, Sarah forgot about the personal crises that beset her students. For the next forty-five minutes, all that mattered were the sneaky tricks the small blockade-runners used to slip through marshy channels as they avoided being spotted by the enemy patrols.

At the end of class, however, Maria dawdled until everyone else had left the lecture hall. Then she approached and offered Sarah a handshake. "Thank you for helping me last week. I'm not sure how you did it, but you put into motion a series of events that have changed my life."

"I don't know that I did anything, but walk down the hall with me and tell me about your eventful fall break."

"After you talked to Professor Winthrop about me, she called in a rescue crew of Kappas—black students with expert survival skills. They surrounded me after my calculus class on Friday and took over my life. It's a long story, but I now have a new job working in the dean's office instead of a Chinese laundry. And I work half the hours a week for double the pay."

"You're working with Martha Wright? That's fantastic! We all rely on her when it comes to getting things done."

"Well, so far, my only duties include answering the phone, keeping the coffee pot filled, and taking care of the dean's cat. Did you know he had a cat in his office? I've never had a pet, but I'm learning to enjoy Marmalade." Maria was bubbling with enthusiasm now.

"Next, they got me a private dorm room, sharing a bath with just one other girl instead of three entire families. And I have my very own bed. I've never slept in a real bed all by myself before. I have a meal card, too—all I can eat three times a day. It's amazing. And they took me to their clothing exchange, where I got to pick out several college-style outfits —and even a coat! Can you imagine? One of the girls is a beautician, too, so she cut my hair. Do you like it?"

"I think you look stunning, Maria, and it has changed your life, hasn't it? But—not to bring up a sore topic—what about that calculus class?"

"Oh, that's best of all. My blank test may not count, and I now have a personal math tutor. Christina Babcock is a math major, and she's working with me every day for at least an hour. Calculus is already starting to make sense."

"Wonderful. What a change-filled vacation you have had. You must feel as if you have fallen down a rabbit hole."

Maria looked at her, missing the *Alice in Wonderland* reference. Then she bit her lip and gave a rueful sigh. "That was a joke, wasn't it? And I don't have the foggiest notion of what you meant. That's an example, though, of what I've learned about myself. I thought I was doing pretty well handling the details of my life, but I didn't know how much I didn't know.

"A better example is the phrase 'room and board.' I saw that in the list of things my full-ride scholarship provided, but I didn't understand what it meant. I knew no one who went to college, and I had never heard that phrase. Oh, I knew what a room was, but I couldn't even imagine one person living in a room all by herself. And the 'board' part was even more confusing. I never connected it with food. I've been in college for weeks, sleeping on the sofa in my mother's tiny apartment, eating whatever she managed to squeeze out of her cleaning payments and the additions she gathered from the food pantry. And all this time, the college has been holding a dorm room for me and a meal ticket for three meals a day. I was—still am—overwhelmed by my own ignorance."

"Oh, Maria, we all keep learning every day. I had never heard of the Kappas until Professor Winthrop told me about them last week. And look how important they turned out to be. As for your transformation, don't beat yourself up about what you didn't know. Accept the changes and learn as they come. You're going to be fine now."

~

I t had been a stressful day, and Sarah hurried to her apartment for the peace it offered her. She couldn't help seeing the contrast, however—her lovely garden residence, which she didn't appreciate often enough, and Maria's excitement over having a proper bed for the first time in her life.

When David called to ask about her first day back, she hesitated before answering. "Some good; some bad. But let me tell you about the good side first." She bubbled with excitement as she described the changes that had turned a failing little street urchin into a confident college woman. "She looked amazing, David, and it made me ashamed to realize how much I had allowed her physical appearance to influence my assessment of her."

"From my point of view, the best thing about this entire story is that it unfolded without dragging you deep into the student's private life."

"I agree. Julia had pointed out to me that I could not make suggestions about the girl's hair or clothing without sounding arrogant and racist. That had to be done by her peers. And look at how successful they were! I just wish . . ." Her voice trailed off as her thoughts jumped back to Olivia Cartwright.

"All right. Spill it. What was the bad part of your day?"

"Olivia—again."

"Ah, no! That girl is trouble, Sarah. I warned you after the episode at the bar not to get involved with her life."

"I know you did, but she showed up this morning with a horrible black eye—a black, blue, green, and purple eye, nose, and cheek. She tried to tell me she bumped into the kitchen door in the dark, but this was a fist-sized blow. In fact, it wouldn't surprise me if she has a bit of broken cartilage in her nose, too. I tried to get her to tell me who did it—her father or Jack—but she stuck with her kitchen door story. All I could do was give her a canned speech about how physical abuse escalates unless she takes legal steps to put an end to it."

"Which she didn't believe."

"Right. I almost called you this morning to ask you for help, but I knew how you would react."

"Right again. There's nothing the police can do, Sarah, unless she files a formal complaint. We see these incidents all the time when we get a domestic disturbance call. The men beat up on their women, and the women let them get away with it out of fear."

"I understand, even if I don't agree with the rules. But I'll still worry about her."

"That won't help Olivia and will cause you unnecessary misery. Think about the purposes of a college education, Sarah. Aren't you supposed to be preparing your students to lead full adult lives? They come to you as callow eighteen-year-olds, true, but by the time they graduate, they're old enough to drink, to vote, to marry whomever they choose, to risk their lives in the military. They must also be old enough to make their own choices in life. You don't help a child become an adult by deciding for her."

"I know. You're right. And I promise to try."

～

T hat promise lasted only until ten o'clock the next day, when Sarah noticed that Chad Overstreet was not in her Revolutionary War class. At the end of her lecture, she stopped Buster Davis, Chad's best friend. "Where's Chad this morning? He's not taking a long break, is he?"

Buster cringed at the question. "I don't know, professor. Or rather, I think I know where he is, but I don't know why."

"I don't understand."

'Well, he's been missing a lot. He didn't show up for Saturday's football game, which was unusual for him. I called him to see what was up, but he didn't answer his phone. We had planned a fishing trip for Monday, and he didn't show up for that, either. I called his house and got his mother on the phone. And when I asked about him, she cried."

"Oh, dear, is he ill? Injured?"

"No, he's . . . uh, he's in jail."

"Jail! Whatever for? I can't imagine anything more unlikely."

"I know, and his mother doesn't know much, either. She said he went out to his grandmother's farm Friday afternoon to help her get rid of an old tree that blew down in last Thursday's storm. It was blocking her driveway, so he had to take his power saw out there and chop it into moveable pieces. And then, on his way home, a traffic cop pulled him over, arrested him, and took him to jail. His parents got a brief call from him, saying he had to go to traffic night court for a parking violation and might have to pay a fine before he could come home.

"They drove down to the courthouse, but when the bailiff called his case, the cops stepped in and asked the judge for a continuance. They said they were in the middle of an investigation and might want to bring more serious charges against him—charges that might land him in criminal court. The judge granted a seventy-two hour hold on him, and they returned him to his cell."

"This doesn't sound right."

"I know, but this is just what his mother told me. His case came up again in night court on Monday, and the judge allowed a second continuance. So he's been in jail ever since Friday, but his car is in the impound lot as evidence, he's not allowed visitors or phone calls, and he doesn't have a lawyer, either. He's due back in court again tonight, but who knows . . ."

"I know someone who might find out. Thanks for telling me, Buster. I'll do a little checking and see what I can discover."

Sarah sat in her office, arguing with herself. She knew David would fuss at her if she called him, but this situation seemed to demand action. Fortifying herself with a deep breath, she dialed David's cell phone.

"David? Please don't yell at me, but a student needs your help."

"Sarah! Didn't we just talk about . . ."

"Please listen. There's something very wrong about this situation. Here's what I know." As she repeated Buster's story, she could tell that David was angry although she couldn't be sure whether he was reacting to her or to the details he was hearing.

"The entire story sounds far-fetched," he protested. "Are you sure you can trust this kid who told you?"

"I have no reason to think he would lie, if that's what you mean. And I don't know the boy's mother, so I don't know how reliable she is. But, please, would you just check with your policemen buddies? See what you can find out? It sounds like a terrible miscarriage of justice to me, and that's the sort of thing you handle as Police Liaison Officer, isn't it?"

"I'll ask a few questions. That's all I can promise. And I have a busy day, so don't expect a quick answer. I have to go now. We'll talk tonight."

Chapter Fifteen

BRIDGE-BUILDING

October 22, 2009

As she often did when the pressures of academia built up, Sarah headed to Julia's office Thursday afternoon. "Do you have a few minutes to listen to me while I kvetch about my world?"

"I might, if I knew what that word meant."

"Kvetch? Sorry, it's a Yiddish expression, which will give you an idea of how irritated I am. It means to complain—or more accurately, to whine like a spoiled child."

"I must remember the word. I rather like the sound of it. Kvetch away!"

"OK. How do actual teachers keep their sanity? And note that I'm not claiming to be one of the actual teachers. I'm a total fraud, floundering away at my subject while surrounded by innocent children who need mothering rather than a faculty lecture. They are dealing with physical abuse, gut-twisting poverty, and police brutality, while I'm expecting them to get upset about someone dumping tea in Boston Harbor."

"That's a crucial issue—the waste of excellent tea, I mean."

"Don't poke fun at me. I'm serious. So far this week, I've had a lecture from Kevin on why I need to pay more attention to my undergraduates, while David is fast losing his patience with me because he thinks I spend too much time worrying about them. And while I'm trying to satisfy both the men in my life, I have these children tugging at my apron strings. One of them is trying to adapt to a complete physical and mental make-over, while another is hiding a bruised face behind a pair of oversized sunglasses. And the third is crying for help from a solitary jail cell, where he is being held without legal aid for a crime he did not commit."

"Good heavens! That sounds like a heavy load. And here I've been worrying about a guy who cracks his chewing gum. And then, there's you—the determined little problem solver and bridge builder, trying to be all things to all people. You seem to attract the problem cases. Let's see if we can winnow them out. I take it you've seen Maria Hernandez and the transformation my girls created over break?"

"Yes, and it's astounding. She looks marvelous. Her new outfit and haircut let her look the part of a scholarly college coed. Her new work-study schedule should help her keep her schoolwork under control, and she couldn't ask for a better boss and mentor than Martha Wright. I'm relieved to know she's no longer ironing some man's starched white shirt until midnight and then walking home alone through her sketchy neighborhood. But there's still what she saw as the insur-mountable obstacle—that zero grade in her calculus class. Then, too, such sudden and massive life changes can be as traumatic as any disaster. I'm not ready to put a 'case closed' sign on her just yet."

"Perhaps not, although I can put your mind at ease concerning one of those problems. This is a closely guarded secret. No math major will ever talk about it because they all know they may one day need to benefit from it. Christina revealed it to Maria only when she realized that Maria was planning to leave school. The secret was the only way to keep her here, and you must also promise never to admit you know it."

"Is this one of those typical sorority things—the pledge that binds the members together for a lifetime?"

"No. Not at all. He'll never admit it either, but Jeremy Higgins, the calculus professor, makes a firm practice of dropping a student's lowest grade, so long as the student perseveres and lasts the course. Maria's zero on her first exam will disappear. The only grades that will count are the ones she gets from here on in. And Christina assures me that Maria is determined to master the calculus, no matter what it takes. The two of them have started from page one and are making quick progress. You can quit worrying on that score. Now, what's going on with the black-eyed one?"

"She's healing, but I'm worried that she is going to continue to suffer abuse. She's dating a much older guy, and I already know, from an unfortunate situation two weeks ago, that he spiked her drinks when she was not looking. She also has a domineering father with a violent temper. Either of them might have punched her lights out without so much as an apology or an explanation."

"So which one was responsible?"

"She wouldn't tell me. She's behaving like a typical victim of gas-lighting. She's defending her abuser because he has convinced her that she is to blame—that she makes him hit her."

"I suppose about all you can do at this point is warn her. Both of the girls bear watching, although I wish you weren't the one upon whom the burden falls. What about the fellow in jail?"

"I know little—only what I get second hand from his mother by way of his best friend. He's a nice kid, still recuperating from a horrible accident that might have killed him. Two traffic cops who thought they had found a major criminal arrested him last Friday afternoon. They have held him without a lawyer or bond or contact with his family ever since. It sounds like such a miscarriage of justice that I called David and asked him to look into the case."

"And he agreed?"

"With much reluctance. I'm on my way home now to cuddle up with a cat who doesn't get into trouble, while I wait to hear from the official Police Liaison Officer."

"For what it's worth, Sarah, I think you're handling these situations well. When you see someone drowning, you can't just sit and watch it happen because you're not the lifeguard. You need to summon help."

"Thanks, Julia. You might try explaining that to David sometime."

～

Sarah was more exhausted than she realized. She dropped her tote bag on the kitchen counter, kicked off her shoes, sat down on the couch with Elijah on her lap, and drifted into a deep sleep. Several hours later, she awoke to the sound of someone banging on her front door. Still muddled, she opened the door to find a worried David staring at her straggling hair and smeared makeup.

"Are you all right? What's happened? I've been calling you, but your phone didn't answer."

"Nothing's happened. I guess I fell asleep." She ran her fingers through her unruly curls and checked to make sure she wasn't still drooling. "I must have forgotten to take the phone out of my tote. Sorry. Didn't mean to worry you."

"I thought you'd want to know the outcome of Chad's case right away." David's voice made his grievance clear.

"I do. What did you find out?"

"Your boy is fine. He's had his hearing, accepted a sentence of 'time served,' and is now free and headed home with his parents. We even got his car out of the impound lot without paying a fee. Satisfied?"

"That's wonderful news, but I want to hear the entire story."

"Not until I have time to recover from the scare you gave me. I need three things: a cuddle with my favorite feline, a beer, and a hug and kiss from you, although not quite in that order."

"The hug and kiss I can handle," she said, throwing her arms around him. "Thank you for always being around when I need you."

"We cops promise to serve and protect. Now, where is that cat?"

"Under the bed. Your banging on the door scared him, and he flew off my lap. Will he come and cuddle? I can't speak for him. He's a cat, remember. He does as he pleases. But I can handle the beer while you try to lure him out. There's a new squeaky toy on the coffee table that might help. Squeeze it once or twice, and he may come running."

She headed toward the kitchen, glanced at her watch, and turned back. "It's late. Have you eaten?"

"Nope. Been too busy putting out your little fires. You?"

"No, me neither. Maybe I should order a pizza."

"OK by me. But make it something mild and inoffensive. I'm too wound up for peppers, onions, and grease."

"How about a margarita—just tomatoes, basil, and mozzarella?"

"Perfect."

~

Later, they wiped the last of the tomato sauce from their chins, curled into a cat-topped pile on the couch, and relaxed.

"Now tell me everything. What did Chad do that landed him in jail for six days?"

"Poor kid. He was just trying to keep two small children from getting run over on a narrow road. Then he went to help his grandma get rid of a fallen tree in her driveway, and on the way back, he stopped to rescue a lost kitten. What's not to like about all of that?"

"It sounds like things Chad would do. I told you he's a good kid."

"Yeah. Well, in this case, he ran afoul of two keystone cops who were hoping they had caught a real bad guy. I got the distinct impression that they resented how nice he turned out to be.

"Chad's first mistake was offering the two little girls a ride home. He didn't want to leave them there on a country road with no sidewalks, so he meant well. But the girls' parents had told them they should never get into a stranger's car, so his offer scared them, and they went running up the hill toward the condo neighborhood where they lived. When they got home, they told their mother about 'a bad man' who offered them a ride. And the mother—panicking—called the police station and reported an attempted kidnapping.

"Chad was rescuing the kitten when the cops found him, and they jumped to the conclusion that he was going to use the kitten in his next attempt to lure the girls away. From then on, they made one procedural error after another. They didn't tell him why they stopped him, nor did they formally arrest him or Mirandize him before questioning. They put him in the back seat of the patrol car and drove off with him—in effect, kidnapping him—and then held an informal line-up of just one suspect in the driveway of the girls' house. And their only evidence of an attempted kidnapping was the statement of a small child.

"By the time they got back to the station and tried to book Chad, they realized that they only had grounds for charging him with illegal parking along a state highway. Friday night, they all ended up in Traffic Court, but the cops asked for a sidebar and told the judge that serious criminal charges were coming. So she granted a hold on Chad for seventy-two hours to give the cops time to assemble their criminal case for a higher court. From there things went downhill fast because the arresting officers had no evidence for the charges they wanted to bring—attempted kidnapping and pedophilia."

"Oy vey! What nonsense!"

"Yes, but Chad contributed to it. He told them who he was and described how he had his brains scrambled—his words —in a football game. To them, that proved their point. In their minds, he was a criminal, one who was not right in the head. And they had a good talking point there."

"Come on, David. Chad has recovered from his injury. It hasn't turned him into . . ."

"Sarah, listen to me. I spent part of this afternoon talking to some of Chad's doctors, and the picture they painted is none too promising. Based on his injuries, and those of others like him, Chad has not recovered. The degree of traumatic brain injury he suffered may have left him with impairments that will never go away. Topping the list is the tendency to make poor judgments, along with failure to consider the consequences of his actions. He may never get over that—nor other impairments such as irritability, aggression, the inability to determine right from wrong, and acting on impulse, just to name a few.

"He's still under medical treatment. He has appointments

several times a week for physical therapy, neurological programming, and psychological studies. But the doctors' prognosis is that he will never regain full cognitive health. They don't expect him to finish college or to hold down a full-time job. He's damaged, Sarah, and he may need a lifetime of supervision."

"That's such an unfair judgment! You don't know him. The doctors see him only as a medical case. To me, he seems capable of handling college. Just because he made a poor decision or two, that doesn't mean that he will . . ."

"It does. He'll be able to hold a job, so long as it doesn't require him to operate dangerous machinery or make quick decisions. He may find a place in a protected workshop, or detailing cars at a dealership, or bagging groceries, or gardening. He might even marry, so long as his wife accepts constant responsibility for him, in the same way that women take care of husbands who come home from military service with PTSD. But the adults around him should not let him function on his own.

"I'm not saying he is a bad person. He's not. He's more like one of HaShem's innocents. But he's a loose cannon. His tendency to act without thinking makes him a danger to the community. That's why he will need supervision. He shouldn't even be driving, let alone be out in public without a keeper."

"It's so sad." Her tears spilled over, and David held her as she wept.

Chapter Sixteen

THE BEST-LAID PLANS

November 5–8, 2009

As Sarah looked at her November calendar, she felt mixed emotions. On the one hand, she was looking forward to two weeks of regular classroom routines, a welcome change from the anticipation and fallout from fall break. But at the end of that period would come the Southern Historical Conference and all its accompanying obligations. She no longer worried about her paper presentation. She knew she had finished it, polished it to the nth degree, and lodged it in her automatic memory. All she had to do was find the right room, show up on time, and launch into an enthusiastic and entertaining story of a bizarre cemetery discovery. Kevin's other tasks, however, challenged her to hunt down unsuspecting job applicants and take notes on everything they did, from the subject of their talks to the appropriateness of their appearance. The very thought made her cringe.

A three-hour drive from Birch Falls to Louisville, Kentucky, did nothing to ease her reluctance. Kevin did most of the talking as he drove. He was full of gossipy tales of unsuitable candidates he had run into over the years—the awkward, the unprepared, the arrogant, the bored—all of them consigned to his dismissal as pathetic misfits. He made Sarah wonder how they would ever find three new instructors to suit his high standards. She worried, too, about Trevor Monroe, listening to this litany and testing his own chances of receiving a tenure offer in the coming months.

They took only two brief breaks—a greasy hamburger for dinner and a quick gas station stop. Still, it was almost 9:00 before they pulled into the canopied entrance to the Downtown Marriott in Louisville. The sorting out of suitcases and briefcases confused the bellhop, who did not understand why the two men were sharing one room and the two ladies another. The desk clerk, too, looked up and asked, "You're not couples?" Sarah shuddered to think of the possibility, but it made her wonder about the hotel's usual clientele. It was a four-star Marriott, however, which conveyed the promise of comfortable beds and decent food.

"Anyone up for a drink to celebrate our safe arrival?" Kevin asked. There were no takers. Sarah was the only one to offer an excuse. "They scheduled my paper for first thing tomorrow morning. I need a good night's sleep."

"I take it we're not opening the wine, either," Julia commented on the elevator.

"Not tonight. I'm too tired to enjoy it. All I want to see is a pillow." In fact, she found a whole pile of pillows, small, round, and soft as marshmallows. She curled into her bed and fell into a deep and dreamless sleep.

The good night's rest put her in a cheerful mood the next morning. When she joined her colleagues at breakfast, Julia recommended the lemon pancakes with fresh blueberries. Sarah declined.

"They sound marvelous," she said, "but I think I'll opt for

protein over carbohydrates. I'm going to need all the energy I can gather to get through this paper presentation. I'll hold off on a sugar rush until tomorrow morning."

"How you can eat a plain egg white omelette is beyond me," Julia laughed.

"It's not all that dull. See all those little green bits? Those are yummy herbs and energy drops. The hash browns help, too."

Kevin glared at both of them as he settled for a glass of tomato juice and a cup of black coffee. When he added several drops of Tabasco sauce to his tomato juice, Sarah could not resist. "How long did you spend at the bar last night, Kevin?"

"Humph," he mumbled. "I just didn't sleep well." Collegiality first thing in the morning was not his strong suit.

Sarah's paper went well. From the moment she stepped behind the podium, her classroom persona took over. Her eyes sparkled as she described her discovery of a Union Army cemetery just off the major highway on Hilton Head Island.

"I knew it was there. That wasn't a surprise. But what shocked me was finding another clearing right at the edge of the Union plot—one filled with random objects such as conch shells, lines of small stones, pieces of broken pottery, and ragged bits of cloth. Bramble bushes, small trees, and more than a few clumps of poison ivy covered the ground. But under a layer of old leaves, more man-made objects appeared. Some were chunks of dried wood with rough initials carved in them, while others appeared to be slabs of concrete bearing names written with a wet finger." She hesitated, giving herself time to make eye contact with her audience.

"Yes. This, too, was a cemetery, but a very primitive one, a slave cemetery—one whose occupants had no last names or concept of what year it was—only a familiar name, like Jake or Sue or Maddie. Under one live oak tree, a circle of stones outlined what had to be a family grouping. Nearest the trunk of the tree a concrete slab said 'Mama.' And below, small round patties bore numbers one, two, three, and four. No names." She waited again for the significance to sink in. "A mother who lost four babies before losing her own life."

She described her puzzlement that the two cemeteries lay so close to one another. Which one had come first? She had gone back the next day with a more powerful camera to take pictures of as many of the graves as she could, but nature had intervened. During the night, a powerful storm swept through the island, uprooting several of the large trees, including the one that had sheltered the mother and her babies.

When Sarah discovered the damage, she almost cried with frustration. But as she crawled through the branches and over the trunk of the tree, she spotted a more surprising find. Where the roots had pulled out of the earth, a large hole revealed a deeper layer of funeral objects and primitive grave stones. The significance did not escape her. The slaves' cemetery pre-dated that of the Union Army in 1862. But now, as often happens, the answer to one question raised several others.

Here, Sarah's attention focused upon the funeral objects in the slave cemetery. Among the stones, primitive carvings, pottery, and tattered cloth, one unusual object stood out. Almost every grave displayed one or more conch shells.

But why? Again, she paused, and she could feel the audience leaning forward, waiting for the next answer. She had reached the heart of her argument, and she led her listeners through their own childhood experiences with the large pink shells. As they remembered hearing the waves splashing within the shell, she transported them to a slave galley. In the ship's hold, captured slaves could not see the water. They could not see the direction in which they were sailing. All they could hear was the sound of the water splashing against the hull—water that was taking them away from their homes.

"The slaves longed to return home, but how? Their Christian preachers promised them that Jesus would come to carry them home, and in the literal minds of the slaves, going home meant not heaven but back to the land of their fathers. And how would they know, except by the sound of the water? Conch shells, then, became a reminder that the water that carried them away would someday carry them back. The promise was there, hidden deep within the pink folds of the echoing shell."

Applause was sincere and lasted longer than Sarah expected. At the end of the session, most of the questions concerned the conchs and their water symbolism. She found it gratifying and encouraging.

As she gathered her things to head for the Phi Alpha Theta luncheon, one member of the audience approached her. He looked familiar, but she couldn't place him until he greeted her with a question. "You went to Columbia, didn't you, and studied under Prof. Kaplan if I'm not mistaken?"

"Yes, I did, but . . ."

"Sorry. I'm Charley Prescott. I was finishing my doctorate the year you arrived. We never met, but I remember that your enthusiasm made you stand out among the new recruits. And now you're all grown up, a professor yourself, and you've mastered the Kaplan style to a T. He always had that knack of ending a lecture with a puzzle that kept the audience coming back."

"Thank you. That's quite a compliment."

"It's a sincere one. Your paper also reminded me of a research puzzle that nagged at me for a while before I let it drop. I thought it might be of help to you."

"I'm curious, but I'm on my way to the Phi Alpha Theta luncheon and don't want to be late."

"I'm headed that way myself. We can talk as we walk. What do you know about Denmark Vesey?"

"Just the basics. He was a freed black, accused of plotting a slave rebellion in Charleston in 1822. It didn't come off, but they hanged him for his efforts."

"Right. Did you know he had a wife and family?"

"No. Does it matter?"

"Well, it did to them. His first wife, Beck, was a slave. Her master allowed her to marry but refused to let Denmark buy her freedom. They had two children who were also slaves because their status followed that of their mother. The same was true of his second wife. His third wife, Susan, had also been a slave at one time, but she earned her freedom, and she took Vesey's last name. Rumor says Denmark taught Susan to read and write, and she then kept a journal of his activities until his death. The journal has never surfaced, but several historians have believed that it would reveal that Susan was the mastermind behind many of her husband's efforts to help slaves escape ."

"That would help me—how?"

"Susan Vesey may have been the originator of the water symbolism you are exploring. For example, take the song, 'Michael, Row the Boat Ashore.' It may have been a coded instruction to escaping slaves about how they were to cross the Ohio River. Or maybe Michael was just a fellow who owned a rowboat. Susan's diary might tell you the difference."

"I gather you think the diary exists."

"I do. At one point I intended to search for it, but other projects interfered. I'm just tossing the idea in your direction, in case it tempts you to pursue it."

F riday night, Sarah and Julia ate dinner in the Porch Kitchen, the hotel's casual restaurant, before attending the presidential address by Jack Kirby. "The ceremony may be dull, but it is the Southern Association's 75th anniversary, and they say the new president is an entertaining speaker," Julia said. "Besides, he's taking on Ancestry.com, and his genealogy stories should be funny." As they headed downstairs, they met Trevor Monroe, who asked to join them for dinner.

"Where is our fearless leader tonight?" Sarah asked." Is he skipping the presidential address?"

"I guess so. All he told me was that he was joining some of his old buddies from his days at UC Davis."

"Well, we'll try to get along without him." Julia giggled. "In fact, I suggest we order a bottle of wine to go with our dinner in honor of his absence."

While they waited for dinner, Sarah told her colleagues about Charley Prescott's suggestion. "What do you think? Is this something I need to look into, or should I ignore it?"

"Hmmm. It sounds to me like he was hinting that you need to prove the accuracy of your interpretations. Who was it who said, 'Sometimes a cigar is just a good smoke'?"

"Oh, I can think of so many examples. Take Faulkner's statement that every good southern novel has a dead mule in it. But maybe that mule is not a symbol of the abject poverty of the rural South. Maybe it's just a mule who died."

"Maybe Michael's boat is just a rowboat, and sometimes water is just water."

"OK, you guys, I get the point. But how do you know which is which? It's all a matter of interpretation—a discussion that perhaps should come from the English department, not History."

"But that is the point, Sarah. History bases its findings on fact, not interpretation. So maybe you do need to find Susan Vesey's diary."

"Or maybe I should just quit."

"No, you just need another glass of wine."

Saturday brought more rounds of paper presentations and other formalities. By 4:30, Sarah had reached her limit. She emerged from her last paper session to find Julia waiting for her in the hallway.

"Are you ready for the tribute buffet in honor of three dead historians?" Julia asked.

"The ones I've never heard of? No, thanks. I'm exhausted. You go ahead."

"Are you abandoning me to the dubious charms of Two Buck Chuck and tunafish finger sandwiches?"

"Whatever. I've decided that while I still love history, I hate professional historians."

"Assuming that I do not yet qualify for the latter category, I have something better on offer. After lunch I went up to the room and put a lovely bottle of Pinot Gris on ice in our bathroom sink. The room service menu suggests chicken wings with various dipping sauces accompanied by carrots and celery sticks. Bring out your tin of cheddar cheese straws, and we'll have a feast worthy of the finest dining room."

"In our pajamas?"

"Absolutely!"

"You're on."

Much later, Julia stretched, licked her fingers, and leaned back on the bed pillows. "You didn't mean what you said earlier, did you? About hating professional historians?"

"I did. I have seen all too many bad examples during this conference. One poor fellow had just finished delivering his paper when a middle-aged lady in the back of the room stood up, waved a book around and shouted, 'If you had ever bothered to read my book, you would have known the answers to the questions you raise.'"

"How rude!"

"And the older they get, the worse they get. One old guy fell asleep and snored in the middle of a presentation. Another kept snorting and mumbling, 'Young whippersnapper!' Whatever has happened to civility and good manners?"

"I hear you. Sometimes these conferences bring out the worst in older scholars who feel they are being left behind. But you know better than to condemn an entire generation for the sins of a few."

"I've seen too much rivalry, too much wrangling over meanings, too many personal attacks. It makes me wish I had followed my mother's advice and gone to secretarial school. I could have found an un-demanding job and married the boss."

"And discovered you hated the job and the boss, who was a hopeless bore. No, Sarah. I don't think that's your problem."

"OK, O Wise One. What do you think the problem is?"

"May I be honest without angering you?"

"Sure."

"I think this conference makes you uncomfortable."

"Nonsense. I've never felt stronger or more confident than I did while giving my presentation Friday morning. I had that room full of strangers eating out of my hand."

"And that feeling only lasted until your Charley Prescott made a gentle suggestion about how to improve your thesis. From then on, you have behaved like a whipped puppy. I have seen it as I watch you in a crowd. You shrink—You hunch your shoulders, fold your arms, lower your eyes, and speak in a whisper."

Sarah looked away, and Julia let the silence build. Then she continued.

"I had a similar but reversed discussion with Trevor today at lunch. He has been avoiding conferences because he felt out of place. But he is enjoying this one because he feels at home. I am seeing a world of confidence in him since we arrived in Louisville."

"Why the difference?"

"Experience, perhaps. Maturity. Or maybe it's something less tangible—the prevailing atmosphere. You are a Yankee, born and bred in New York City. Kevin grew up in Louisiana. I come from Georgia, and Trevor is a Texan—all Southerners, and this is the Southern Historical Association. We hear a chorus of southern accents just like ours. We're used to saying one thing and meaning another. That allows us to insult each other without destroying our friendship. You may teach Southern History and live in the South, but you're not a southern historian. Here, you're a cowbird in a swallow's nest. You recognize that, and you feel like a misfit."

"So what do I do? Take lessons in how to drawl?"

"No, you can't overcome Yankee-ness—nor should you want to. But you can avoid jumping to conclusions or basing life decisions on two days of uncomfortable social inter-actions."

"Yes, ma'am. But can I go home tomorrow? Please?"

Chapter Seventeen

WHICH PATH WILL YOU FOLLOW?

Sunday, November 8, 2009

On Sunday morning, the Smoky Mountain history faculty piled into the car right after the last speaker finished. "Let's drive for a bit and then stop for some lunch," Kevin suggested. "And while we drive, we can discuss the candidates whose talks we observed. Julia, do you have everyone's observation reports?"

"Yes, I think so. We started with a list of thirty-seven candidates, but we had already eliminated many of them. Some were not close enough to finishing their degrees, and others had areas of specialization that did not fit our openings. That left twenty-two potential interviewees, and I have your reports on all of them. Of that number, you recommended further consideration of only five of them. Do you want me to review them now?"

"Go ahead. It'll help pass the time."

"For the modern world tenure-track position, we liked two very different women. The first is Emily Pottersfield, an English woman whose degree comes from Lucy Cavendish

College, Cambridge. The observer said she is an expert on British Empire expansions and England's role in the European Union. I also received a second comment about her, based on a casual conversation Friday night. She confided that teaching jobs are scarce in England, and she is hoping to find a better opportunity in the States.

"The second is Louise Nakamura Breckenridge from the University of Chicago. She is an outlier in this group because she is much older than the other applicants. However, what she lacks in youthful energy, she more than makes up for with enthusiasm and experience. She's a former high school teacher, so she is comfortable speaking in public. She began her talk by revealing that her father's family lived in a Japanese internment camp during World War II, which led her to study international relations in her graduate work."

"So, she's Japanese-American. What's her marital status? Do we know?"

"Kevin, I'll recheck her application letter when we get home, but you know we're not allowed to ask questions like that unless the candidate brings it up."

"Well, it could affect her suitability."

"We'll see."

Sarah pressed her lips together to keep from laughing. Julia's tone of voice had been that of a mother speaking to an unruly child. Kevin, however, remained tone deaf. "Let's move on, shall we? For the Early American position, I liked Gabriel Ramirez."

"Any reason?"

"Well, he's a University of Florida graduate. His grandparents were Mariel Boat People in 1980, escaping from Fidel Castro's Cuba. His specialty is Latin America, but he has a good understanding of American history, much of it drummed into him by his family as they encouraged him to make a place for himself in his adopted country. And the paper he gave dealt with our indigenous people, the American Indians, so he seems well-grounded there, too."

"Sounds promising, but there was a second candidate for that position who made a good impression. You want to talk about her, Trevor?"

"You're referring to Elizabeth Bradford. She's a Harvard graduate, which is always a selling point among our Board of Trustees. There will be lots of other schools interested in her for the same reason. She is strong on American Colonial but weaker in Latin America. Her paper had much to do with genealogy, which made me hesitant after listening to Friday night's tongue-in-cheek presidential address on tracing one's ancestors. She is proud of her Daughters of the American Revolution membership and her descent from the original Plymouth Rock settlers."

"And what's wrong with that?"

"Well, nothing, except I'm not sure how her DAR credentials would resonate with the demographics of our student body. As Professor Kirby pointed out, many of our students would rather hear about Daniel Boone."

Again, Sarah had to swallow a giggle as Trevor took his shot at Kevin's absence from the Friday night lecture. And then it was her own turn.

Julia winked at her and then explained, "I'm going to let Sarah tell you about our last choice, because she would be a candidate for my one-year replacement, and I'm a little possessive about that job."

"This would be Ramona Bishop," Sarah said. "She's a University of Texas graduate and took a post-doc position there for the current academic year. Now she's willing to accept another one-year appointment to get some experience in a smaller, liberal arts school. She admits that her love of the Ren-Ref period stems from her mother's encouragement to read historical fiction. But it's obvious that she loves her field, and her paper was a wide-ranging discussion of the broad application of the term, 'Renaissance.' I admired the way she could talk about the ancient world, the fifteenth century, and today's technological transformation, all in a single paragraph. She might be someone we could use in a variety of positions. But I have a lingering doubt, too. She seems to make a habit of seeking one-year appointments, which I find puzzling."

"Lack of commitment in the long term? That points up my final warning about the search process." Kevin paused and cleared his throat, as if to emphasize what he was about to say. "Don't get too invested In any of these candidates. You've seen what they can do with a nugget of research. It's one thing to entertain a receptive audience of scholars for twenty minutes. It's quite another to interest a roomful of restless adolescents over fourteen weeks. You also have not talked to these people as candidates. They have needs and expectations you don't yet understand. How they will function as colleagues or how they will interact with the uniqueness of our eclectic bunch of students are unknown factors.

"We have a long road to travel, and I'm not just referring to the distant shores of San Diego. With only a few exceptions, you have seen no one but southerners. You have yet to encounter the Ivy League crew, the down-to-earth Midwesterners, or the West Coast crowds. Believe me. This year will be the first time the AHA has held a meeting west of the Rockies, and the University of California faculties will parade all their graduate students for our perusal.

"We'll talk to ten candidates for each of our positions. We'll be able to get a sense of who they are and what they are looking for. There will be personality clashes and obvious misfits, while others will be all-stars. But we still won't know enough to hire any of them. That's why we'll spend much of the spring semester inviting a visit from two or three of them for each position. That's when we'll watch them function in a classroom. Then, perhaps, we will have identified our best fits. But hurdles will remain. The best candidates will have multiple offers from schools that can provide more advantages than we can. There's always the chance that we'll land the perfect fit. But it's also possible that our search will fail."

"So much for a pep talk."

"Sorry, Julia. I understand how much work you're putting in on this, but you need to be ready for all eventualities. And we can't anticipate what will happen. There's one more element you all need to know. The dean has informed me of two recent additions to our search committee. Howard Kennedy from Political Science and Marilyn Fitzpatrick from Art History will join us to interview our AHA candidates. Both of them are experienced faculty members, and both of their departments rely on history courses to fill in the gaps in their own majors."

An uneasy silence settled over the car as the listeners tried to absorb this additional information. At last, Trevor broke the mood by changing the subject.

"Today's Sunday," he said. "Don't the Titans have a game today?"

"I'm sure they do, although I do not know what team they're playing. I've lost interest because their won-lost record doesn't come close to last year's division championship status. Why don't you play with the radio dial and see what you can tune in? If you find an NFL broadcast, maybe we can at least catch the score."

When the raucous cheers of a football crowd filled the car, Julia and Sarah rolled their eyes at one another and then moved closer so they could talk without disturbing the football fans in the front seat.

"Don't look so glum, Sarah. There will be a path of free time opening before you."

"Just what I need—another path." Her voice was so bitter that Julia stared at her in alarm.

"What's wrong now, girlfriend?"

"I was just remembering. About this time a year ago, I was telling David about my five-year plan for earning tenure. I told him I had one clear path, with sign post markers every few months to tell me what I needed to accomplish next. Little did I know how confusing my life was going to get."

"The plan is still there, isn't it?"

"The plan may be, but weeds have overgrown the path. No, instead of a clear path, I now have a bunch of trails—brief lines shooting off in all directions. And instead of progress markers, I have double-headed arrows pointing in opposite directions. If I come to a fork in the path, one branch goes around in a circle and comes right back to where it started, while the other heads straight for a dead-end."

"I chose the one less traveled, and it has made all the difference," Julia quoted.

"Ha! You might notice that Robert Frost never tells us what the difference was. I suspect both endings were wrong."

"So maybe it's time to start over—decide where you want to end up and work backwards."

"And if I don't know where I want to end up?"

"Then maybe you need a vacation."

Sarah would have been the first to agree that she needed some time away from everything, but her calendar offered no such hope. Thanksgiving was just two-and-a-half weeks away. While on paper, it looked like a good four-day weekend, Sarah's parents were expecting her to fly home to New York City for dinner, and David's family was hoping for a blizzard that would prevent her from going North. Both would result in a turkey dinner, but neither outcome promised relaxation as part of the bargain.

Then, after two more weeks of classes, she could look forward to eight days of conflicting obligations because the college's exam schedule corresponded to the eight days of Hanukkah.[1]

"At least you won't be teaching every day, and you can schedule your own grading times," Julia said. "I've never known much about Hanukkah, though. What's involved in each of those days?"

"Well, the religious requirements come every day at sundown, when we light one more candle on our menorah,[2] read the story of the miracle of the oil,[3] and recite the ritual prayers. That only takes about half an hour, but then everyone gathers for a festive dinner each night. The children receive small token gifts, and much visiting goes on from house to house. My days will be my own, but unless I stay home to light my solitary menorah, the evenings will be hectic."

"But that still gives you three more weeks of free time before you have to be in San Diego, doesn't it?"

"On paper, yes. But David is pressuring me to go along on his trip to Baltimore for his six-month check-up."

"What's wrong with that?"

"He's planning an elaborate road trip. We would set out by viewing some sections of the Appalachian Trail on the way to Baltimore. Then, once his medical appointments are over, we would drive from Baltimore to New York City and spend New Year's with my parents. Next, we would head to Washington, DC, as tourists, go on to Williamsburg for a day or so, and complete the circle by getting back to Birch Falls in time for me to catch my plane to San Diego."

"It sounds like a fun trip, but . . ."

"That's a big 'but,' if you'll pardon the expression. There's winter weather to worry about, not to mention my parents' disapproval when they learn I'm planning to spend several nights in motel rooms with a man to whom I am not married. Beyond that, we would have to take Elijah along because all my usual cat sitters will be out of town during that time."

"I thought Elijah was a good little traveler."

"He is, as cats go, as long as it's a short and direct trip. But dragging kitty litter and cat food in and out of motel rooms every night is not my idea of fun. Plus, after one or two days, he gets crotchety. Cats never like change."

"So, what do you want to do with those three weeks?"

"Ah. I would prefer to lock the door, close the blinds, disconnect the phone, and hibernate. In my dreams I imagine bubble baths, long winter naps, gourmet meals and second glasses of wine, mindless TV, and trashy novels. But I'd settle for time to think about my academic development and re-work my four-year plan."

"Then tell David that. It's your time off, and you need to follow whatever path is most important for you. Let me make one suggestion, however. Keep thinking in terms of five years —not just the remaining four. That fifth year will now be your sabbatical year. Think about how much research and what kind of research you could get done with a full year away from campus."

Chapter Eighteen

WELCOME TO SAN DIEGO

Wednesday, January 6, 2010

O nce again, Kevin Chalmers volunteered to drive. This time, he and his colleagues were headed to Nashville to catch their early non-stop flight to San Diego. "Assuming the flight's on time, we'll have all afternoon to get settled into the hotel, register for the conference, and locate our interview room."

"We're not doing the interviews in a hotel room, are we?" Sarah asked." I always hated those sessions."

"No, AHA has learned its lesson on that account. The hotel is providing partitioned sections in several meeting rooms, with tables and a half a dozen chairs for each college. I'm not sure what's the noise level will be, but at least you won't be sitting on somebody's unmade bed while you're talking about educational theory."

"So far, so good," Julia whispered." And since we're flying on Southwest, we can pick two seats far away from Kevin and Trevor."

After the usual entertaining talk from the flight attendant

and an uneventful takeoff, Julia and Sarah settled back to get caught up on how they had spent their time off. "You look rested and cheerful," Julia said. "I gather you convinced David to go to Baltimore on his own, while you settled into that much-deserved bubble bath."

"Yes, and even while he was at home, he gave me all the freedom I needed. We had a lovely New Year's Eve date, but most days I got up late, ate a substantial breakfast, and then curled up with a book or a stack of reading notes. After a day of research, I soaked in the long-advertised bubble bath with a glass of wine and then slept the sleep of the righteous."

"Just what you needed."

"Yes, it was."

"And have you reached any decisions about where you go from here?"

"I have, and you, my friend, helped me straighten out my thinking."

"How so?"

"Your comment about the fifth year in my new five-year plan was the key to untangling the mess I was dealing with. You—and Charley Prescott—made me realize that I don't have the time right now to explore a new research area, let alone write an authoritative book on the topic. So, the first revision was dropping my plan to investigate the codes used in slave spirituals. That idea is now a mere possibility—something to work on during a sabbatical year."

"So what are your publishing plans in the near term?"

"I've returned to the solid foundation of the original plan I developed while I was still in grad school. Dr. Kaplan insisted that I write my dissertation, not as some dense scholarly tome, but as an interesting book for a general reader."

"What was the topic?"

"Cotton as the foundation and the downfall of South Carolina's economy. It's the story of foolish and greedy men grasping their immediate profits and failing to understand the consequences of their greed. I ended up visualizing the story in terms of a fictional tale—the protagonist wanting to build the richest state in the Union and the limitations of the cotton crop as a villain waiting to destroy his shortsighted plans.

"The other distinguishing characteristic of the dissertation was its formatting. Contrary to the policy of most advisers regarding footnotes, Dr. Kaplan believed that if an idea was important enough for an expository footnote, it deserved to be in the text. If it were just an extraneous remark, he advised me to leave it out altogether."

"Wise man. Lucky you."

"He was right. The resulting dissertation received high marks for readability from everyone who vetted it. It is not ready for publication, but the bones of an interesting and informative book are there just waiting for elaboration. And that I can do in the time I have available. One or two of the chapters may serve as conference papers or journal articles. The rest will need polishing and more anecdotal material, but even that is under control. I just taught a course on this topic, and my lecture notes are full of anecdotes."

"This all sounds fascinating. You've got this, girl."

"Well, it's doable. At least it's a single path again with a clear direction. More important, it leaves me with enough free time to have a personal life." She laughed and added, "And the occasional bubble bath."

After the biting cold of Nashville in January, San Diego's heat came as a shock as they exited the plane. "I love the convenience of a direct flight, but it doesn't give us much time to adjust to the changes in climate," Sarah said. "And the time difference—how can it only be 11 o'clock in the morning and I'm starving for lunch?" She shrugged out of her coat and fished in her purse for a piece of hard candy.

"Patience, grasshopper," Kevin teased. "We take a shuttle from here to the hotel, where I'm sure we will find a lunch counter. You'll get used to the changes by the time we leave."

Sarah knew Kevin was trying to be provocative, but she ignored him. The city offered sunshine, palm trees, soft breezes. and glimpses of the Pacific Ocean. She filled her lungs with the air's salty tang and marveled at the futuristic architecture of the city center. After almost a month of isolation and introspection, she was ready for fresh adventures. Julia watched her with an indulgent expression and gave a sigh of relief that her younger colleague was back to being her usual perky self.

They were too early to check into their rooms, so they asked the desk clerk for a lunch recommendation. He pointed them toward the hotel's signature restaurant, Sally's Fish House. "Ask the *maitre d'* for a table on the patio. It offers a beautiful view of the harbor."

At the reception desk, a small sign announced, "We're dog friendly here. Sit on our patio and ask for your pet's special menu."

"How fun is that! I should have brought Elijah. Do you suppose they have a cat's menu, too?"

"Not much surprises me in California. People out here are all crazy," Kevin grumbled. "Let's eat inside. I don't want someone's pooch scratching fleas under the table while I eat."

"Spoilsport!" Sarah could not resist asking their waiter what was on the doggie menu, and he regaled them with a story of seared tuna sushi rolled in rice paper and doggy sliders featuring hamburger served on lettuce leaves.

Kevin continued to grumble as he read his own menu

featuring lobster rolls, soft-shell crab, grilled octopus, fish tacos, and raw oysters.

"It is a fish house," Trevor reminded him.

"Yes, but they don't have to be so obvious about it. And look—they build even the salads on Brussels sprouts, kale, avocado, and hearts of palm. I wonder if I can get some old-fashioned tomato and lettuce on my burger."

Sarah looked at him with mock sympathy. "Maybe not. They might save the lettuce leaves for the dogs."

Julia snorted tea through her nose.

After lunch, Kevin escorted his colleagues through the conference registration process and then led them on a search for their interview room. One entire section of ball rooms had been designated as the Job Search Center. The first door led to a waiting room where prospective candidates could perch on folding chairs until their interview time arrived.

The interview rooms proved to be functional, although not soundproof. Movable partitions divided the space into cubicles, each one furnished with a table and three chairs on each side. At the head of the table was a straight-backed chair for the interviewee. The hotel provided notepads and ball-point pens, along with a bottomless coffee pot and disposable cups at the back of the room. At the entrance to each cubicle, a fresh-faced college student waited with a list of each college and its scheduled interviewees.

The organizers had assigned Cubicle 73 for Smoky Mountain University, and Kevin gathered his colleagues around the table to explain the procedures. "Interviews start at 1:30 tomorrow and finish at 5:00. Each session will last for a half an hour, leaving a fifteen-minute break to allow candidates to move from one location to the next, while the interviewers take a bathroom break or get a cup of coffee. On Friday and Saturday, we start at 8:00 and run to 11:30; then reassemble at 1:30 and run till 5:00. That allows for five interviews during each session."

"We will interview twenty-five different candidates?" Sarah was wide-eyed as she tried to imagine getting to know that many people.

"Well, in our case, twenty-four candidates, since one of those we invited has declined."

"Which one?" Julia asked.

"Let me see. Oh, here it is—Louise Nakamura Breckenridge, University of Chicago, candidate for a position in modern world history."

"How unfortunate!" Julia said. "she was one of our picks in Louisville. I found her talk fascinating and thought she would be an interesting addition to our department. Did they give you any reason for her refusal?"

"No. It only says that she is unavailable. Could mean anything." Kevin shrugged it off. "That's it for now. Enjoy your evening and get a good night's sleep. Our work starts tomorrow afternoon."

Kevin's dour mood had threatened to spoil the weekend, but the others refused to let him ruin their free afternoon. The lobby shops tempted them, the spa offered tours of their amenities, booksellers were already taking over the main ballroom, old friends poured into the lobby, and, just outside, the crystal blue waters of the harbor invited walks on the beach. In a burst of camaraderie, Julia dragged Kevin with them in their explorations.

That evening, the four of them returned to Sally's Fish House for dinner. Shocked by the high menu prices, they settled for appetizers. Trevor suggested that they share a large Caesar salad, tossed and dressed at table-side, along with a towering display of fresh seafood—oysters, shrimp, Alaskan king crab legs, and lobster tails. Sarah admired the showmanship of the shellfish tower and then ordered an appetizer of salmon *en croute* for her own entrée.

"This will keep my parents and the rabbi happy," she said with a disarming smile.

"Oh, we should have realized that a fish house serving shellfish is not an ideal place to take a Conservative Jew," Julia apologized. "What about the anchovy in the Caesar salad? Is that...?"

"Not a problem. Anchovies don't have shells. And please don't worry about it. I'm used to making accommodations in restaurants."

Dessert featured a platter of cinnamon beignets, accompanied by a chocolate ganache and a jalapeño caramel sauce. For the moment, all was well.

That night, lying sleepless in her bed, Sarah kept remembering her own introduction to Smoky Mountain University at an AHA Convention just like this one. She had stood outside an interview room door while another young college student announced her arrival:

"Doctor Sarah Chomsky, from Columbia University, interviewing for the position in nineteenth-century American history."

All the usual admonitions ran through her head as she waited for her turn.

"Back straight."

"Chin up."

"Remember to smile with your eyes."

"Be interested as they introduce each interviewer. Smile, acknowledge, and repeat each name."

"Try not to stumble over your own feet, and don't miss the seat of the chair."

"Knock nothing over."

"And remember to thank them for the opportunity."

But now, she realized, she had almost no memory of the interview itself. Were Kevin Chalmers and Julia Winthrop part of her interview committee? They must have been, but she couldn't picture them. Nor could she remember any of the questions they asked. Was it all so unimportant, then? Were these interview sessions mere posturings—an elaborate pretense designed to hide the fact that all hiring was random?

Across the room, Julia lay in her own bed listening to the slight squeaks of bed springs that told her Sarah was still awake. She spoke in a whisper.

"Do you plan on tossing and turning all night long?"

"Oh, Julia, I'm sorry. I didn't mean to wake you."

"You didn't wake me. I, too, have trouble sleeping in a strange bed the first night. But you've been so restless. Is something else bothering you?"

"I'm a little worried about the interview process. It's my first time. I'm afraid I'll not think of anything to say, or ask something foolish. I also realize how crucial this all is. In the next three days, we will talk to twenty-four different people, spending a half an hour or less with each one. And then we will make decisions that will change their lives forever, whether for good or ill. That's a daunting responsibility."

"Perhaps you exaggerate your importance. Do you remember the lecture Kevin gave us on the way home from Louisville, the one about not becoming too invested in any one candidate because we were only beginning a long process?"

"Yes, but this is different."

"No, it's not. We will interview twenty-four candidates,

and only six or seven of them will receive an invitation to visit our campus. But those we reject will not go home empty-handed. They are likely to have interviews with other schools for whom they are better suited. And even if we are the only school that interviews a particular candidate, your vote is one of six. No matter how important you may feel your decision to be, it will not change anyone's life all by itself."

"I suppose not."

"And this is not the end of the process. The candidates we accept may have better offers. An individual may change her mind about what she wants to do. Or maybe she'll come to campus and make a fool of herself. A dozen other things could go wrong without it being your fault.

"Your real responsibility in this process is to help us make the best impression we can on candidates we would like to hire. Beyond that, you cannot control what happens. So turn off those horrible images in your imagination. Roll over one last time and snuggle down. Get a good night's sleep and dream of sunlit beaches. We can sleep late in the morning and have a leisurely brunch before we go to work."

Chapter Nineteen

TELL US A LITTLE ABOUT . . .

Thursday, January 7, 2010

W hen Sarah awoke, the sun was streaming into their room, and the digital clock warned that it was already 9:30.

"Good morning, sleepyhead. Are you ready to investigate the hotel's breakfast buffet?"

"I think I'm hungry enough to eat toothpaste."

"I don't recommend that, but the Seaview Breakfast Buffet sounds tempting. They charge more than we would pay for a dinner back home, but they also promise you won't need to eat again until evening."

The corner restaurant featured two walls of floor-to-ceiling windows lined with small two-cover tables. The other two walls and the center of the room offered serving stations and bright displays of local fruits and flowers. An alcove to one side held larger tables for family groupings.

"Should we pick a larger table and wait for our colleagues?"

"Ah, we'll be seeing more than enough of them the rest of

the day. I opt for sunshine and direct access to second helpings."

A distinguished-looking older gentleman with a towel across his arm hovered nearby, waiting to lead them to a window table and hold their chairs. "Will you ladies be ordering the full buffet or only the continental breakfast?"

"Oh, the full buffet, I believe."

"Excellent choice. You won't regret a single mouthful. Do you prefer coffee or tea?"

"Coffee," they answered in unison.

"And juice? In addition to our fresh-squeezed orange juice, we offer apple, pineapple, papaya, guava nectar, or a vegetable blend."

Again, they nodded in agreement at orange juice.

"Perfect. I'll have those ready for you, along with a basket of hot scones, when you return from ordering your entrées. Chef Andre at his corner station will be happy to build an omelette to your specifications or cook your eggs as you prefer. Chef Pierre, on the other side of the doorway, can prepare your blueberry pancakes or a Belgian waffle with strawberries. You are free to help yourself to our sides, pastries, and fruits as you like."

Julia headed straight for the blueberry pancakes, while Sarah made her way to Chef Andre and his omelette station. She watched with delight as he swirled a frothy egg mixture into a hot skillet, added diced tomatoes, sliced mushrooms, and shredded white cheddar cheese, and then sprinkled the whole skillet with a handful of finely chopped fresh herbs.

"it will be my pleasure to deliver your breakfast to your table when it is ready. While you wait, you may wish to help yourself to our meaty sides and prepared fruits."

Sarah and Julia met again at the steam table, where Julia raved over rashers of grilled bacon. "Did you ever see such picture-perfect slices?"

Sarah chuckled. "I'm not much of a bacon expert, but those tiny chicken and apple sausages are calling me."

"Oh dear, I've done this again. You don't eat pork products, either, do you?"

"Don't apologize. Pork and shellfish aren't unmentionables. We just don't eat them if we can avoid it. There are no such restrictions on fruit, however. Have you ever seen such huge berries? And look at those pineapple spears and papaya slices. Such temptations!"

"I'm already planning a second trip around the buffet for fruit and French pastries."

After lingering over their elegant breakfast, Sarah and Julia walked through the lobby, where they met their colleagues, who were headed to lunch.

"We're just going to grab a sandwich before we start interviews," Kevin said. "Will you join us?"

"Goodness, no. We just finished breakfast."

Kevin rolled his eyes. "Well, you girls run along and brush your teeth—or whatever it is you need to do—and we'll meet you in the interview room at 12:30. I would like to go over a plan before we get started."

"Now let's settle in. Everyone looks very professorial. Here is how I thought we might proceed. I will introduce myself and offer a brief description of what makes Smoky Mountain a special place to work. I will then yield to Julia, who, I thought, might describe the diversity of our student body."

"That's disingenuous, isn't it? We have so few..."

"No, I don't think it's misleading. We're all different."

Julia clamped her lips together and refused to force her disagreement further.

"Next, Trevor can make a comment or two about the friendliness of our faculty, and then Sarah can speak as the newest addition to our department, describing her first impressions of the Appalachians. Let's run through it, shall we, and see how it sounds."

Kevin seemed disinclined to allow any discussion as he launched into his introduction. "Good morning. I'm Professor Kevin Chalmers, chair of the history department at Smoky Mountain University and a medievalist by trade."

"Uh, Kevin? It's afternoon."

"Whatever. It'll be morning in the morning. We would like you to know what's special about our school. For me, it's the fact that while our university is young, our buildings and the land they stand on have a long history of service to our country. Our buildings had their origins in a cloistered nunnery that expanded to become an orphanage and a retirement home for the widows and children of Civil War veterans. When the Great Depression forced the nunnery to close, the state purchased the land to create an agricultural center and the home of its veterinarian school. At the end of World War II, we expanded to a full curriculum to meet the needs of returning soldiers. And now we are a full-fledged university, offering graduate work in many fields and serving the varying needs of a booming economy."

He yielded to Julia, who nodded to an imaginary interviewee. "I am Julia Winthrop, associate professor of European history with an emphasis on the Renaissance and Reformation. One thing I love about Smoky Mountain is the diversity of our student body. Not only do we have students of several races, religions, and backgrounds. We also have an amazing spread of ages. Among the students I met last semester were a seventeen-year-old Haitian immigrant with a perfect SAT score and a ninety-two-year-old gentleman who had never attended high school. They were both a delight to teach and leaders in their classes."

"I'm Trevor Monroe, assistant professor of American history, specializing in the twentieth century and finding more and more that my studies require a worldwide point of view. For that reason, I appreciate the camaraderie I have found in the Smoky Mountain faculty. We often cross departmental lines to create courses with contributions from a mixture of subject areas. This spring, several of us are involved in a course exploring the impact of electronic communication. Our lecturers include a novelist from the English department, and professors from journalism, history, psychology, economics, and the hard sciences."

"And I am Sarah Chomsky, the newest addition to the history department. I'm entering my second year as an assistant professor, specializing in the American Civil War and Reconstruction. I was born and raised in New York City, as my accent suggests. I even did my doctorate there, so you can imagine that I thought of the Appalachian Mountains as the edge of the known world. To my surprise, I fell in love with the region. Tennessee is the greenest place I've ever seen. We enjoy a gentle climate, blue skies, fresh air, and open vistas. We live in a small town, but one with a cosmopolitan flavor. It provides an ideal learning environment."

"All right. Good enough. At that point I will ask the candidates to tell us a little about themselves, and it's a free-for-all from then on. The student at the door will let us know when our time is up."

～

O n cue at 1:30, the student announced the first candidate—Doctor Ramona Bishop from the University of Texas. Sarah tried to repress a smile when she recognized the name of her favorite speaker at the Southern conference. She had worried that she might have nothing to say, but now she knew what she wanted to ask.

After several brief discussions about course topics and the exact limitations of the candidate's field of expertise, Kevin turned to Sarah and raised an eyebrow to let her know it was time to speak up.

"Dr. Bishop, I noticed on your application that you are doing a post-doc at the University of Texas. May I ask why you are interested in another one-year position?"

"I'm a realist. I've seen the large number of candidates vying for a limited number of jobs, and I'd rather do another one-year then have no job at all. Each position provides a chance to learn something new—something that will make me a better candidate down the line. Here, after a year at the huge UT campus, Smoky Mountain will give me a chance to work in a much smaller environment, where I can experience a more personal relationship between professors and students. I'm also looking forward to the chance to concentrate on teaching rather than research."

Her response elicited small smiles from everyone at the table as the interview ended on a friendly note.

The next three candidates turned out to be acceptable but less than inspiring. One was coming off a failed tenure decision, while the other two were working as adjuncts and were desperate to find a permanent position, if only for a year.

The fifth and final interviewee of the afternoon was Max Norton, a former Rhodes Scholar now awaiting his doctoral degree from the University of Chicago. Before he came in, Kevin had questioned Julia on his inclusion. "Didn't we agree that we would not bother to interview anyone whose dissertation was still hanging fire?"

"Yes, sir, we did. However, in this case, his application suggested that his dissertation was complete but that he preferred not to use the title 'Doctor' until he received his formal hood during the graduation ceremony in May. Besides, I couldn't bear to reject a Rhodes Scholar."

"Good point. Let's see what he has to say for himself."

Mr. Norton turned out to be as impressive as they had hoped he would be. Tall, handsome, self-possessed, and eloquent, with just a touch of a leftover English accent from his years abroad, he charmed the ladies while managing not to threaten the gentlemen. When Trevor asked him about his interest in a smaller school, his answer was smooth.

"I've been living in the heart of Chicago," he replied, "after spending two years in an English garden. I've traded the countryside for a smog-choked city, and the Appalachians would offer a familiar and welcome retreat."

Once again, the last question fell to Sarah. "I assume your dissertation committee approved your thesis?"

He smiled, as if it was a silly question, but she pursued. "What are your plans for publication?"

And at last he faltered. "Ah, I have not thought about that yet."

The student page ushered Mr. Norton out and then closed the door to allow a wrap-up discussion.

"He didn't answer me, did he?"

"No, he didn't, and that could be worrisome. However, as I've mentioned before, nothing that happens here can be construed as a final decision. I suggest we invite him to campus along with Dr. Bishop so we can observe both of them as they interact with our students. And before he arrives, we can do some further checking on the status of his dissertation."

No one disagreed.

~

Howard Kennedy from Political Science and Marilyn Fitzpatrick from Art History arrived late Thursday evening to join the last two days of interview sessions. On Friday and Saturday, the six professors filled the interview room and formed a daunting panel. The interviews continued all day, and the questions became more monotonous, as did their answers.

During one of their breaks, Sarah grimaced and grumbled to Julia over a much-needed cup of coffee. "Does someone offer courses on how to survive an interview without revealing anything about yourself? Our candidates are beginning to look and sound like little parrots, reciting the words without assigning them any meaning whatsoever."

"Patience, my dear. They all wear a pinstripe suit because that's the way we expect them to dress. In the same way, there are only so many ways they can answer the same tired old questions. Why did you choose history? What's your favorite course? Where do you see yourself five years from now? We are parrots, too, only our feathers are a little more worn."

On Friday, they interviewed candidates for the Early American position. One of the first to arrive was Dr. Elizabeth Bradford from Harvard. Trevor Monroe had observed her talk in Louisville, so the others deferred to him when it came time to question her about the breadth of her knowledge.

"You may remember, Dr. Bradford, that our description of this position included knowledge of early explorers, the development of Latin America, and the history of native American peoples. What can you tell us about your mastery of those related subject areas?"

"Well, it would be hard to talk about the colonists without

a thorough understanding of the people who came before them. I am comfortable teaching such a course should the need ever arise."

"As it will," Kevin interjected. "I gather, however, that you are most comfortable talking about the colonists and, in particular, the Plymouth Rock settlers."

"I admit to a certain amount of bias," she said with a smile. "As a member of the Daughters of the American Revolution and Colonial Dames, I can trace my ancestry from Governor William Bradford, who led the colony for so many years. It's been one of the delightful coincidences of my academic career to discover that I am related—fifth cousins, four times removed, I believe—to Drew Gilpin Faust, the current president of Harvard University, through our mutual descent from the governor."

Kevin brought the interview to a quick close while the rest of the committee tried to look impressed. They repressed their giggles until Dr. Bradford had closed the door behind her.

"Whoo-ey!" Howard Kennedy shook his head in wonder. "Does the history department often get candidates who insist on being so . . . historical?"

"No. Dr. Bradford is an anomaly. That Boston accent is thick, but I'm betting our Board of Trustees will eat it up. She is a Harvard grad whose people came over on the Mayflower. What more could you ask?"

"I'm hoping you have a handsome young Native American waiting in the wings to balance her out," Marilyn Fitz Patrick suggested.

"I'm afraid we don't, but we will talk to a well-spoken Hispanic gentleman who knows more about her history than she does."

And later that afternoon, Gabriel Ramirez proved to be everything Julia had said he was. He spoke of his grandparents, their love of freedom, and their experiences as Mariel Boat People escaping from Cuba and the reign of Castro in 1980. His parents had filled his childhood with stories of how colonists settled America and the doomed struggles of the native Americans to hold on to their tribal lands. He had spent his undergraduate years at Florida International University, where he gained a more global perspective. Then at the University of Florida, he fell under the influence of constitutional historians who deepened his understanding of his adopted country. His mastery of the subject was obvious.

Compared to these two, the other interviewees for the American position had little to offer. They were all competent, well mannered, and trained to repeat a familiar story. Not a single one of them inspired an enthusiastic reaction.

"Bradford and Ramirez could not be more different," Julia said. "I suggest we invite both of them to campus and see which one resonates with our school and student body. If neither of them works out, we can just draw straws from the remaining candidates to find a bland but acceptable replacement."

～

B y Saturday an observer could read exhaustion in the wandering eyes of the interviewers and hear it in the shuffling footsteps of the candidates. Once again, when all nine interviews concluded, only two personalities stood out.

Emily Pottersfield was a petite English woman with a spirit full of curiosity and bright eyes that never seemed to miss a detail. She had completed her education at Lucy Cavendish College in Cambridge and was now doing a post-doc at Cornell while exploring the job possibilities in the United States. Her interview was a delight. She talked about the monarchy, Britain's period of empire building, its war years, and its relationship with the European Union. She impressed everyone with her understanding of world affairs from a unique British perspective.

A second candidate also appealed to the committee. Thomas Etheridge had entered the U.S. Army from his ROTC unit at Penn State and had sped through the junior officer ranks. With his appointment to the rank of major, however, came an assignment to the Army War College at Carlisle, Pennsylvania, and there he experienced a reawakening of his academic interests. After he graduated from the War College with a master's degree, he resigned his commission and applied to Penn State University to earn a doctorate in history. His military background strengthened his understanding of the wars that marked the twentieth century and made him a strong spokesman for those who would find a better way to settle international disagreements.

As they closed the door to their interview room for the last time, everyone sighed with relief. You've done a superb job," Kevin declared." We have six excellent candidates. Starting in February, we'll bring each one of them to campus and from there make our final decisions."

Chapter Twenty

CHANGES OF SEASONS; CHANGES OF HEART

January 10, 2010

Although she did not need a ride from the Nashville Airport, Sarah found David waiting for her when their plane arrived from San Diego. After spending five days with her colleagues, she appreciated David's attentions. Rescuing her suitcase from the pile of luggage loaded onto a baggage cart, she touched Kevin's arm.

"You'll forgive me if I ride back to Birch Falls with my friend. We have a lot of catching up to do. I'm eager to hear what he learned about his shoulder injury during his Johns Hopkins check-up."

"I understand, Sarah. And thank you for all your help this past weekend. I enjoyed watching you ask some penetrating questions. You go ahead. We will see you Wednesday morning."

David took her suitcase in one hand and held her arm with the other. "So, how did it go? Did you and your conspirators find some likely candidates for your open positions?"

"It went OK, but . . ."

"That doesn't sound good."

Sarah laughed at a sudden memory. "My family has a legend concerning my elderly Aunt Lola. At a Sabbath dinner, the family had unexpected guests, and they had to stretch the meal to feed two additional mouths. By the time the chicken platter went around the table and reached Lola, there was nothing left on it except the tail. She claimed the last piece without comment and carved it into several tiny bites. When she finished eating, one of her sisters asked if she had enjoyed the chicken. Her answer was, 'Well, it was good, what there was of it.' Then, realizing how that must sound to a guest, she continued, 'And there was enough of it, such as it was.' That has been a family motto ever since. Here, there were enough suitable candidates, what there were of them. And there were enough of them, such as they were."

"Did you hire anyone?"

"No, not yet. We won't make actual job offers until the six possibilities we've chosen have all visited the campus. And even then, there's no guarantee any of them will accept an offer. It's a never-ending process."

"It sounds like you need a break from academia. But that's good, because I have lots of tidbits to distract you this evening."

"I've been waiting to hear the news. How did your checkup go?"

"I'm fine, Sarah. They cleared and discharged me. Now I just have to avoid the metal detectors in airports."

"And your trip home?"

"Uneventful. Just lonely. What do you say we stop up ahead for some dinner? It's been snowing in Birch Falls, so when we get home we'll want to go straight to your apartment."

Their conversations over dinner were impersonal. David had a few stories about nurses and hospital food, and Sarah amused him with her stories of awkward interview moments. Neither was in a hurry to discuss their responsibilities in the coming months. As in any vacation, with the time drawing to a close, they ignored the clock and the calendar to squeeze the simple pleasures out of each moment they could spend together.

~

Later that evening, David and Sarah relaxed on the couch in front of the fire with Elijah the Cat curled up between them.

"On the evenings when I most missed being at home," Sarah mused, "this is what I imagined—snow on the ground outside but a glowing fire warming my apartment, a purring cat on my lap, and my head resting on your good shoulder."

"I'm not sure I appreciate the order in which you list those," he said. "Why does my good shoulder come in third after the fire and the cat?"

"Because, silly, if we started with a cuddle, we might never get around to the fire or the cat."

"Fair enough, but I'm afraid I have to break this mood. Several things happened while you were in San Diego, and I need to bring you up to date."

She cringed, wondering what little bombshells were going to explode her comfortable world. "Do I need to sit up and take notes?"

"No, it's not all that serious, or at least I hope it's not. The first item has to do with my job. You've met Sam Westerman, our district attorney. He's not my boss, but I spend much of my time working under his direction. Except . . . for the last few weeks, he's been out a lot with stomach problems of some sort. He has seen several doctors, and they've had him on various regimens—some vitamins, medications, stress relievers. So far, nothing has helped, and the longer it goes, the more frightened he becomes. They have scheduled him for exploratory surgery on January 25th, and he's sure they're going to find he has cancer."

"That's terrible, but I'm not sure I see . . ."

He drew a deep breath. "According to my job description, if the DA cannot perform his duties for longer than a week, I become the acting district attorney until he returns to work. And that means I'll be busier than a one-armed paperhanger."

Sarah chuckled despite the seriousness of the subject. "That's a trite comparison. I'll bet you've never hung a roll of wallpaper in your life."

"Well, maybe not, but I've had plenty of experience being one-armed—enough to know how difficult it is to do two things at once. And that's what it will be like. I'll end up doing my job and his job both, which means my free time will evaporate."

"And I will wither away on the vine—is that what you think? On the contrary, it may give me the freedom to get caught up with some of my work. I'll understand. But let's hope it never comes to that."

"From your lips to HaShem's ears. But to move on, I have some good news—something you may hear from Julia—but I want to be the one to tell you first."

"What?"

"Last Wednesday, after you girls went flitting off to sunny San Diego, Bert Wheeler and I dropped into your friend Matt's bar for hamburgers, beer, and the NCAA championship football game between Texas and Alabama. The crowd helped to cheer us up, although since the game was being played in the Rose Bowl, it was another reminder of how cold we were while you were basking in summer temperatures."

"So, the good news is that Alabama won?"

"Well, yes, but that's not what I meant. Bert had just hired an equipment manager for his new athletic complex. He was telling me about this incredible new employee—polite, energetic, reliable, and knowledgeable about many things having to do with sports. When he explained that the young man was still recovering from a serious brain injury, one that had forced him to give up his future career plans as an athlete, I realized who he was describing."

Sarah gasped. "Chad?"

"Yes. Bert had been talking to some of the football staff at the college, and they had told him about Chad. He agreed to talk to him, the two of them hit it off, and Bert hired him on the spot."

"But . . . what about college? What about the rest of his life?"

"Oh, Sarah, don't you see? It's perfect for him. Bert Wheeler Sports will be a protected work environment. It is a charitable organization, reaching out to those in the community who need help. Chad will be a part of that, and perhaps he may never realize how much help he too is receiving. The job makes him a part of sporting life without further risk of physical injury. His tasks will be simple ones, but important in keeping the operation running. He will be self-supporting and independent, but still surrounded by caring supervision. He'll be doing a job he can handle well, and he'll be participating in activities he loves."

"I understand all that, but I've been hoping that somehow . . ."

". . . somehow he could go back to being the old Chad? That will not happen, Sarah. You can't turn back the clock or reverse what has changed. You can only help him move forward."

"Does this mean he is leaving college already?"

"No, Chad's going to finish out the second semester so that he can claim to have had two years of college. Bert is giving him some guidance about what classes to take. There are one or two courses in sports management that will help him become familiar with training equipment, and he's signing up for a basic bookkeeping course. For now, he will work for Bert on Saturdays. By the time school's out in May, the gym will be near completion, and he'll go to work full time."

"If he's happy, I'm happy for him. And I agree it's important for him to remain involved in sports. That's his first love, and he needs to keep his hand in."

"Yes. He'll be inflating footballs and basketballs, true, but also teaching youngsters how to use protective equipment, helping the skinny kids build up their muscles, and teaching the chubby guys to work out with weights. I even had a dream the other night in which Chad was an old man sitting in a corner of the gym, still offering expert advice to eager young athletes."

"I just hope his parents will be supportive about this idea. When Chad talked to me about his injury, he was most concerned about disappointing his father's ambitions for him."

"I think we can count on Burt to make sure they're happy. If need be, I'll drop a quiet word."

Sarah stretched and yawned. "You have been busy, haven't you? David, I hope you realize how grateful I am to have you taking an interest in one of my problem children."

"Hmmm. I hope you feel the same way after you hear about my third bit of news."

"Uh oh! What's that?"

"Let me preface it by telling you that I don't know many details yet. What I do know is that the district attorney's office has received an anonymous whistle-blower letter accusing one Jamison Chandler Cartwright, local factory owner, of violating local, state, and federal regulations concerning environmental protection laws. I assume that he is talking here about the father of your student Olivia Cartwright, the young woman we rescued from a predatory male suitor."

"Oh dear, that's his name, all right. He is a blustering, pompous, and egotistical gentleman—and I use the term 'gentleman' with tongue in cheek. However, I know nothing about him except for his behavior in my office when he and his wife tried to intimidate me with his demands. I don't even know what his company manufactures."

"I understand they make toys for small children. The writer claims to have proof of his accusations, including reports from an independent testing laboratory documenting soil and water contamination and statements from prominent pediatricians about the dangers of such contamination on small children. He also claims to be an employee of the factory and thus vulnerable to retaliatory action if we should ever discover his identity. Therefore, he refuses to turn over any of this evidence without assurances that there will be a full investigation of Cartwright's guilt and responsibility."

"But none of this has anything to do with Olivia's involvement, does it?"

"No. But make no mistake. Investigations like this and the resulting trials turn out to be nasty affairs. Smear tactics, private investigators, incriminating financial statements, family gossip and rivalries—everything will be fair game. Your fair-haired Olivia will not be immune from the fallout, nor will her mother."

"Given the fact that the family business is a major bone of contention between Olivia and her father, you may find that she is cheering for the whistle-blower."

"Or that she IS the whistle-blower."

"You don't believe that!"

"No, I don't. But there will be those who do. I'm violating a confidence by even telling you about this, but knowing how involved you have been in her affairs, I feel obligated to warn you."

"So what happens next?"

"The DA will ask for a preliminary hearing to determine whether the city wants to pursue the matter. At such a hearing, the judge will ask the whistle-blower to turn over any evidence of wrongdoing so that both sides can examine its relevance. Mr. Cartwright will attend the hearing and may have his lawyer present with him if he so desires. He will not, however, have any input beyond answering a question of whether he intends to challenge the accusations. It's like entering a plea of guilty or not guilty."

"So, Mr. Cartwright could admit guilt, promise to clean up his act, pay a fine, and the whole thing would be over."

"Yes, but it's never that easy. If he admitted liability, he would leave the door open for all kinds of other suits. He might as well put up a 'closed' sign and look for a job as a shoe salesman."

"I suppose there's no chance of a judge refusing to hear the case?"

"Not if he's interested in getting re-elected. The public loves juicy stories like this. What worries me is what will happen when the accusation becomes public knowledge. Once the newspapers get hold of such a story, there's no telling . . ."

"His lawyer will understand that danger, too, I suppose."

David grimaced. "That's the other issue. The Cartwright Company has been a client of my father's law firm for as long as I can remember."

"Your father could end up representing Mr. Cartwright in a trial?"

"And, depending on how things go with Sam's surgery, I

could end up as the acting DA in the trial. My father and I would both have to recuse ourselves on grounds of conflict of interest, which would leave the case in the hands of two inexperienced lawyers. That would be a reason for appeal no matter which side won."

He threw up his hands in despair. "I can't even think about it."

"Oh, David, I'm so sorry. I never meant for you to get involved in my student's problems."

"It's not your fault that you teach the daughter of the accused, although I hope the story of that bar room rescue will never come out."

"No one will hear it from me, and I will warn Matt and Olivia, too, if you like. Now, stop pacing back and forth."

"Sorry. This brings back everything I hated about being a lawyer. I have to keep reminding myself that a courtroom trial is better than letting an angry man settle a dispute with a gun."

Chapter Twenty-One

FRIENDS AND FAMILY

Wednesday, January 20, 2010

On the first day of the new semester, Olivia Cartwright dropped by Sarah's office to chat. "Hi, Dr. Chomsky! How was your vacation? All ready for the start of classes?"

"My vacation was productive, thank you. I did a little traveling and a lot of writing, which was a welcome change from the classroom. But this morning, I find I am happy to be back on campus. How about you? How was your Christmas?"

"Not bad, as Christmases go. The family got along without fighting, and my father and I reached some new understandings. Or at least we did until all the wheels came off this last week."

Sarah did not reply. She gave the young woman a questioning look.

"You haven't heard? I thought that fellow you've been dating would have told you all about it by now."

"About what?" Sarah felt guilty about the partial lie, but

she didn't want to get trapped into telling the girl something she might not know.

"Someone among Daddy's employees lodged a complaint against him for using toxic pigments in his plastic extruders."

"Hold on. You just lost me at pigments and extruders. What I don't know about a manufacturing plant would fill a book. As a matter of fact, I don't even know what your father manufactures."

"They are junky children's toys. Here. Let me show you. He insists that I carry some in my book bag all the time, just in case I get a chance to talk about them." She pulled out a small box and emptied a handful of plastic figures onto Sarah's desk.

"These are Pencil Pets. This hole goes onto the end of a normal pencil. Did you know that the metal band that holds a pencil eraser is a ferrule? I didn't either until Daddy gave me a lecture about it when I was six. Anyhow, the end that goes on the pencil has ridges that screw onto that ferrule, and the figures on the pencil pets act like flexible plastic erasers."

"That's clever, actually."

"Kids love them, but my father doesn't deserve much credit for inventing the idea. Do you remember the old PEZ candy dispensers that had cartoon characters on top? Dear old dad just stole that idea and used animals rather than cartoon figures. The first ones were Pencil Pups. They came in a set of five, and there were five different breeds of dogs in the box. They were so popular that he issued additional sets with different dogs. It worked, and kids started collecting them and trading—say, two cocker spaniels for one German shepherd or three beagles for one French poodle.

"When he ran out of dog ideas, he expanded to other animals and changed the name to Pencil Pets. Now we have cats, birds, hamsters and gerbils, forest animals, farm animals, dinosaurs, mythical beasts, and wild animals. The latest additions are zoo animals and this set of circus figures. These also represent an innovation because the circus sets have a human character—a clown, a lion tamer, a trapeze artist, a bareback rider, or the ringmaster—among the tigers and elephants. This group caused the trouble because the designer needed red dye for things like the clown's hair, the lion tamer's jacket, and the bareback rider's horse blanket."

"None of the others ever used red dye?"

"No. Animals don't come in red, except for a bird or two, and father just ignored those."

"Well, I think it's a clever idea and a successful one. I'm quite impressed with how intricate the designs are. You may tell your father I said so, and I am sorry to learn they are causing him so many difficulties. He will need some loving care and careful handling until the trouble dies down."

"He's going to need more than that. You might have noticed that my father does not like to be told what to do. I worry about how he'll behave in the courtroom. He's likely to fly into a rage and threaten to close the plant, or bar all inspectors from his property, or . . ."

"I assume he'll have an excellent lawyer. Part of a lawyer's job is to keep the client from mouthing off."

"Oh, he has a stable full of lawyers. He's used the same firm ever since he opened the plant. They know him well. But can they control his angry tirades? That's a different question."

"But that's not your problem, my dear. Your only job is to be a loving daughter and a hard-working college student. Now, off you go. Let the grownups handle their own affairs."

~

And, for the moment, the grown-ups in Sarah's life had more than enough problems of their own. With the start of a new semester, Julia and Kevin struggled to schedule campus visits with the six candidates they had selected at AHA. Timing was important. If a visit came too soon, the candidate might hesitate, wanting to see what other offers he would receive. If they waited too long, the candidate might have already accepted another position. But other factors played into the matter. Each visit had to fit into the college's calendar of events, the dean's schedule, and the availability of all members of the history department. Sarah soon learned to check with Julia before she scheduled any appointment of her own.

As the date for Sam Westerman's surgery approached, David became more and more distracted. Sarah wasn't sure what worried him the most—the outcome of Sam's surgery or his own ability to handle the DA's responsibilities. The date of the preliminary hearing concerning the whistle-blower complaint depended upon the court's schedule. When the February calendar arrived, it assigned the Cartwright matter to Monday, February 1, eliminating the possibility that Sam would be healthy enough to lead the case. After much discussion and gnashing of teeth, David and his father decided that Michael Feingold, a junior partner of the Cohen law firm, would handle the preliminary hearing for the defendant and Assistant District Attorney Beverley Jacobs, an experienced litigator, would manage the prosecution. David would remain available as a witness representing the city's interests.

Sam checked into the hospital on Friday to start the tests and checks that would prepare him for his procedure, but he wasn't ready to relinquish control of his official responsibilities. He called David on both Saturday and Sunday to discuss upcoming cases. At the end of David's Sunday visit to the hospital, Sam made one additional request.

"This isn't part of your job description, David, but I'd be grateful if you would keep an eye on Mary Alice for me tomorrow. The kids are staying with my mother for the duration. That keeps the children away from the hospital and keeps my mother out of my hair, but it means that Mary Alice will be all alone here waiting for word that I am out of harm's way. She says she'll be fine, but I think she'll need a shoulder to lean on."

"I'll be happy to lend my support. What time is your surgery?"

"It's scheduled for 11:00 AM. The doctor says it should take about two hours, so it will run over the lunch break."

"Great. I'll call her when I get home and pick her up about 10:00 so she can see you before they trundle you off. And then we can grab some lunch in the hospital cafeteria while we wait. I remember the routines from my stay here last spring. The families of all surgery patients use the ICU waiting room, and doctors call the telephone lines there to issue progress reports. She will be in sympathetic company, I promise."

Monday, January 25, 2010

It was a simple plan, but things did not go as everyone hoped. The ICU waiting room welcomed them. David and Mary Alice chatted about local gossip and the quirks that made Birch Falls such a delightful place to live. Mary Alice was interested in hearing about David's relationship with Sarah and was eager to offer him advice on the next steps in his courtship.

Time passed easily until they realized they had been waiting for almost four hours, not the two hours the doctor had promised. Other people had received calls on the bank of phones that lined the back of the room. They had listened, then smiled and hurried off to visit their loved ones. The woman at the reception desk glanced at Mary Alice every time the phone rang, but she never called for the Westerman family. By three o'clock, Mary Alice was pacing the room, and David was pestering the receptionist to check on Sam's progress. It was 4:30 when Mary Alice received her summons to the phone.

The nurse on the line was formal but reassuring. "Mr. Westerman's procedure has taken longer than expected, but he is doing well and there is no cause for alarm. The doctor says the operating team will finish up within the next hour. Then they will move your husband to a recovery room where they will make him comfortable and withdraw him from the anesthesia. The doctor will come for you, give you a full report, and you should be able to see him by early evening. If you have not already done so, you may make arrangements to stay here at the hospital tonight so that you can be with him as he regains awareness."

Mary Alice was pale and shaky as she returned to the couch where they had spent the afternoon. "The nurse says he is doing well, but I cannot see him until this evening. I can't ask you to wait with me here any longer. I know you said you had plans to pick up Sarah and take her to dinner. You must not stand her up. You run along. I'll be fine."

"No. I promised Sam I would stay with you. How's this for a plan? I'll duck out, collect Sarah, and bring her back here. We can all have dinner downstairs, and we'll see you settled into Sam's private room before we leave. I know Sarah will be eager to give you a hug."

"All right. I'll appreciate having company, but I don't think I can eat anything."

"At least have something to drink. You need to stay hydrated."

〜

M ary Alice picked at a salad, while David and Sarah shared the hospital's excuse for a pizza. "Momma Capelli would have a heart attack if she saw this concoction. I should have followed your example and settled for a salad," Sarah said.

"Who is Momma Capelli?"

"Have you and Sam never eaten at Capelli's pizza place up in the hills? We must take you there sometime after Sam has recuperated."

"Will there be a 'Time After?' I can't see anything but darkness ahead." Mary Alice's voice came from far away, and Sarah felt a chill along her spine.

Then came the doctor's call. He met them at the door to the waiting room and led Mary Alice off to a private cubicle. For the first time, David dropped his upbeat attitude, and Sarah realized how worried he was.

"I'm afraid this is terrible news. There have been delays, cryptic messages, and now private consultations. I don't know what's going on, but whatever it is, it's not good."

"Don't second-guess them, David. We'll know soon enough."

They waited for another hour until Mary Alice returned to the waiting room. Her back was straight, her chin held high, and her lips pressed into a firm line. Her face showed no signs that she had been crying—no swollen eyes, no runny nose, no red blotches. But a sheen of moisture below her eyes revealed a steady seepage of tears. She seemed oblivious to the tears as she motioned for David and Sarah to join her in a private corner of the waiting room.

"We have our answer. It's pancreatic cancer—late fourth-stage and already metastasized throughout his body. There is no treatment and no cure. At most, he has a few weeks to live. His long stay in the operating room came about because the surgeons were trying to locate a clinical trial somewhere that might offer hope. There were none that would accept a case so advanced." Her voice seemed almost emotionless, but the tension in her jaw showed how she was controlling herself.

"He's awake now and aware of his diagnosis. They have him on pain killers, so he's resting and seems reconciled to the inevitable. He knows he will never return home, and he's asked me to prepare his letter of resignation from the DA's office. He will remain here in the hospital for several days to make sure his incisions are healing without infection. After that, we will move him to a hospice facility, where the children and I may visit as we like and where the staff is free to administer as much pain relief as necessary to ease his passing. He wants no visitors beyond family for a while, but he asked me to thank you both for everything you've done to help me through this day." With head still held high and tears still leaking, she turned and left the waiting room.

Sarah and David had no words to describe the pure grief they had just witnessed. Clutching each other's hands for support, they left the hospital and drove in silence to Sarah's apartment. At her door, David refused to release Sarah's hand. She turned to stare into his eyes, realizing that they were both crying.

"I don't want to spend the night alone," he whispered.

"Nor do I. I need you tonight."

∿

They awoke the next morning to the insistent meowing of a small black cat who paced across the bed, peering into their faces. "Cut it out, Elijah," Sarah growled at him. "What's the matter? It's too early for your breakfast. The sun is not even up. Curl up and go back to sleep."

"I think I may have stolen his pillow," said a rough voice, and Sarah sat up in alarm. As she did so, the memories came flooding back. It had been a night full of tears—grief bordering on despair, anger at the unfairness of fortune, and fear of the fragility of life itself. But it had also been a night of tenderness, gentle caresses, and rapturous discovery.

"What have we done?" She clutched the blanket around her neck. "What were we thinking? How could we have celebrated a death sentence by indulging our own pleasure?"

"Please don't tell me you regret a moment of last night. Faced with unimaginable future loss, what else is there to do but to seek relief in the immediacy of love?" David tucked a stray curl behind her ear and turned her chin to look into her eyes. "Yesterday offered us a lesson in handling grief. We watched Mary Alice deny the power of her future pain by celebrating the joy of the present. That's the imperative of love, as her marriage to Sam is the embodiment of that love."

"We were witnesses to a marriage about to fall victim to the cruelty of a hideous disease," she lamented.

"And it taught us to honor such a union by picking up the torch. Will you . . ."

"Will I . . . what?"

"Sarah Rebecca Chomsky, will you marry me?"

Without warning, a smile spread across Sarah's face. Her eyes sparkled. "I suppose I should have to, now that you have stolen my honor and led me astray. You understand, I hope, that I come as a package deal. You must earn Elijah's consent as well as mine."

"Not a problem. A catnip mouse can buy Elijah's consent. Too bad his mistress doesn't like mice. Give me back that friendship ring. Maybe I can pawn it while I look for something more appropriate for an engagement."

She grinned at their mutual ease with one another. Teasing, as her parents had taught her, showed trust. "It's about time you did that. Now, if you'll go put the coffee on, I'll think about what I can fix for breakfast. I'm starving!"

Over bacon and frozen waffles, Sarah forced the discussion back to Sam's diagnosis. "I don't mean to spoil your good mood," she warned. "But now that we know what's happened to the Westermans, we must consider how it will affect your work schedule."

"Sam is resigning. I know the mayor wants an orderly transition. I'll be talking to him as soon as I get to the office, and I expect he will name me Acting District Attorney today."

"Which means you'll be involved in the Cartwright trial."

"I'll have oversight on it, but as I explained, I cannot represent the prosecution during the hearings. I'll be there. But ADA Beverley Jacobs, our only trained litigator, will prosecute, with Michael Feingold, a junior partner of the Cohen law firm, for the defense. The preliminary hearing on the whistle-blower case will open on Thursday afternoon."

"May I attend?" Sarah asked, and David hesitated only briefly.

"Sure. It will be open to the public, so if it doesn't interfere with your schedule, I don't see why you shouldn't attend. I understand that it might make your dealings with Olivia easier if you know what's going on in her home life."

"That was my thought. And no, my schedule does not conflict. In fact, it's perfect timing. I finish teaching by eleven on Thursdays."

"Just one other warning. You are welcome to observe the

hearing, but I will not have the time or the freedom to talk to you. It's now part of my job, remember. Whatever happens, we can discuss it that evening—maybe over dinner?"

"Perfect."

Chapter Twenty-Two
SEEING RED

Thursday, January 28, 2010

Sarah gasped when she saw the headlines on the morning paper. "POISON!" in 3-inch letters, followed by slightly smaller type asking, "In the water? In your child's toys?" The lead article was unsigned and carefully worded to remain non-committal. "This paper has learned from a reliable source that the District Attorney's office has received a whistle-blower report concerning the use of a certain hazardous pigment in a local factory." No names, no specifics. Only a threat—a warning of something dangerous lurking in the shadows.

"Irresponsible," she shouted at the news print and then laughed at herself for talking back to an inanimate object. The offending article, however, helped her make up her mind. She had been hesitant to attend today's hearing. Now she knew she needed to hear the details for herself.

Sarah found a seat in the back row in the spectator section of Courtroom III B. She was late by choice, hoping to avoid any conversation with other observers or being noticed by Olivia or other members of her family. Sarah's first experience in a courtroom had been in connection with her teenage divorce, so the judicial atmosphere made her uncomfortable. Still, she couldn't resist smiling at the sight of David on the other side of the room, also trying to make himself invisible.

"All rise. The Pullman County Court is now in session, The Honorable Judge Pearl McCutchen presiding."

A surprisingly small woman, dwarfed by her flowing black gown, entered a door concealed in the panels behind the podium. She pounded her gavel once on the desk. "You may all be seated. We are here assembled to hear depositions concerning Case number 26794, 'The City of Birch Falls and County of Pullman versus The Cartwright Manufacturing Company.'"

She hesitated, looking out at the crowded courtroom. "I was not expecting there to be so much interest at this stage of the matter. You folks must've been reading the headlines in this morning's paper. Please understand that there will be no sworn testimony given today. We are simply dealing with the business details and engaging in an exchange of information that will make our future proceedings go more smoothly."

She frowned again. "We had best start with the counselors assembled here at the front of the courtroom."

As the two lawyers stood up again, a small disturbance broke out among the spectators. A rather scruffy looking fellow—unshaven and dressed in jeans and a sweatshirt—pushed his way to the end of his row and made his way to stand in front of the judge.

She stared at him in surprise. "I beg your pardon, but who are you and what do you want?"

"My name is Jerry Wilson, and I'm here to have my day in court."

"Well, sir, this is not quite how one goes about that. If you are looking for representation, you need to hire a lawyer. If you wish to bring charges against someone, you should start with the police department or, perhaps, the district attorney's office. Whatever the case, you cannot just walk into a court room and ask to be heard. Bailiff, please help Mr. Wilson regain his seat or find a door if he chooses to leave.

"Now then, as I was saying, counselors, you are not the lawyers I expected to see. Will you approach the bench, please?"

She lowered her voice to address the two litigators. "I recognize you both, but neither of you has had much actual courtroom experience, if I'm not mistaken. What's going on?"

"I beg your pardon, Judge McCutchen. I am Beverly Jacobs, Assistant DA and lead counsel for this case. I assumed the mayor would have informed you of our recent developments. DA Westerman has been hospitalized with a serious medical condition that will preclude his fulfilling his duties for the foreseeable future. The mayor has therefore appointed Lt. David Cohen, the city's Police Liaison Officer to serve as the Acting DA until Mr. Westerman can return or until the next election."

"I'm sorry to hear of Mr. Westerman's illness. Please convey my wishes for his early recovery. In the meantime, we will welcome Mr. Cohen's willingness to share his expertise. However, you have not explained why he is sitting in the row seats instead of at the prosecutor's table."

"I understand that he has recused himself from this case because of an ongoing conflict of interest."

"And you, sir?"

"I am Michael Feingold, junior partner at the Cohen Law Firm, representing Mr. Jamison Chandler Cartwright, the factory owner in this case."

"I will address a similar question to you. Why is a junior partner leading this case rather than the head of the Cohen Law Firm?"

"It is my understanding that Mr. Leonard Cohen has recused himself from this case because of an ongoing conflict of interest."

"You two sound like parrots. Would one of you be good enough to explain these conflicts of interest?"

Beverly Jacobs spoke first. "Your Honor, Leonard Cohen and David Cohen are father and son. They agree that they do not want to see a case of this magnitude take on the appearance of 'Family Feud.' They will both attend all sessions and hearings as advisors but will not participate in the actual litigation of the case."

"Fair enough. You may both step back."

Beverly had just reached the prosecutor's table and was moving to sit down when Judge McCutchen called her name. She appeared to bounce off the chair as she stood up again.

"Will you please start the prosecutor's deposition by explaining to the court why everyone, including today's newspaper, is referring to this as the whistle-blower case?"

"Yes, Your Honor. On Monday, January 4th, the district attorney's office received an anonymous letter from someone who claimed to be an employee at the Cartwright Manufacturing Company. He explained that he had accidentally stumbled across an invoice indicating that Mr. Cartwright had ordered five pounds of a toxic and banned red lead pigment from a Chinese company. He was concerned for his safety as well as the safety of others—both those working in the plant and those who might be using the resultant product. After thinking about it for a night, he returned to the same file to find the invoice and make a copy of it. Someone had removed it from the record. That set off more alarms in his mind, and he resolved to pursue the matter on his own."

"Counselor, you keep referring to the letter writer as a male. Does that mean you know his identity?"

"No, Your Honor, although I am not making a sexist

assumption. It is well known that Mr. Cartwright employs almost no women in his factory except for those in a traditional secretarial role. We have no idea who the whistleblower might be, but the odds are high that it is a man."

"And why don't we know who he is?"

"He states in his letter that he fears retribution if he reveals his identity."

"I see. Continue, please."

"Because the factory was closed over the Christmas holidays, the whistle-blower was able to gain access without being detected. He used the opportunity to collect samples and submit them to an independent laboratory for testing. He has promised to deliver the original laboratory results to us to be presented as evidence in the trial. For now, I can tell you only what was tested, not the results themselves. Sample number one came from one of the figures in the most current set of pencil pets."

"Wait! Counselor, I have no idea what a pencil pet is. Could you explain the nature of this item before going on?"

"Certainly, Your Honor. A pencil pet is a small plastic figure that fits over the end of a pencil and serves as an eraser. The figures are usually animals, and they are particularly appealing to grade-school children. In the case of the first sample, the figure in question was a clown wearing a bright red wig. In our office we considered asking for a number of these pencil pets to be distributed among those involved in the trial. However, because of the possibility the red figures are dangerously toxic, we did not do so.

"Sample number two was taken from residue in the dye tank of the extruder that shaped the figures. The third and fourth samples were taken at the wastewater holding pond behind the factory—one from the water in the pond, the other from an area where wastewater appears to be leeching into the surrounding soil."

"And the tests showed . . .?"

"The whistle-blower says all four tests revealed toxic levels of red lead. However, I cannot confirm that because I have not seen the actual reports."

"So far, all I have heard is circumstantial evidence. When will you have access to the reports themselves?"

"The whistle-blower has promised to have them in our hands in time to submit them as evidence in the trial. I do not know, however, when that will be. Our communications go through a double-blind arrangement of private mailboxes and an anonymous courier."

"Do you expect to present any witnesses during the trial?"

"Yes, ma'am, we hope to be able to call for testimony from those who actually run the machinery in the plant as well as outside experts on toxic materials and their effects on human physical and mental development. But again, I cannot yet provide you with any names because we have not had time to identify them."

"You have a hard road ahead of you, young lady. You may step down, at least for the moment. Perhaps the defense will have more to offer."

"Wait! Wait a minute!" Another small scuffle broke out in the audience as Mr. Wilson stood up again and begin waving his hands in the air. "I have firsthand evidence of Cartwright's guilt, and I am willing to testify for the prosecution."

"Mr. Wilson, we are not asking for testimony at this time. As I tried to explain to you, if you have something to say, you need to take it to the proper authorities. Please do not interrupt these proceedings again."

"Cartwright's a murderer, and I can . . ."

"Sit down, Mr. Wilson!"

She took a deep breath and then turned to the witness stand. "Now, Mr. Feingold, let us hear from the defense."

"Your Honor, I have no concrete evidence to present at

this time because it is difficult to prove a negative, particularly when the opposition has failed to offer any positive accusations. I can start, however, by establishing the character of Jamison Chandler Cartwright.

"This man is Birch Falls' finest citizen. We're talking about this city's most important employer. His business pays the salaries of 174 families whose livelihoods depend upon him. He has served on the boards of the March of Dimes, the Pullman County Food Bank, the United Way campaign, and the YMCA. He is a Mason and a Rotarian. For the past several years he has been the president of the Birch Falls Chamber of Commerce. When anything good happens in Birch Falls, you can be sure Mr. Cartwright had a hand in it.

"Jim was born and raised here. He has been a lifelong member of the First Episcopal Church, starting with his years as an altar boy, and he continues to this day to serve his church as a deacon. He was a boy scout and became an eagle scout before he was fourteen years old. In high school he was captain of the football team and president of the senior class. He graduated from Vanderbilt University and went on to earn his MBA at the University of Tennessee. He married a local girl, Emily Peterson, and they recently celebrated their silver anniversary. Jim and Emily have raised a lovely daughter, Miss Olivia Cartwright, who is now a sophomore at Smoky Mountain University. It is ludicrous to think . . ."

"He's no boy scout, and he killed my son, as surely as if he put a gun to his head." Jerry Wilson was on his feet again, waving his arms in the air to gain attention.

"Mr. Wilson! Bailiff! Order in the court!" Judge McCutchen pounded her gavel until the head threatened to fly off. But this time, Jerry Wilson was determined to tell his story. He pulled a switchblade from his pocket and pointed the tip at the elderly bailiff who was reaching for his arm. Those in nearby seats froze in place.

"You will listen to me. Our Timmy was a bright, funny, energetic, and articulate little boy. He had just turned three when he discovered his older sister's pencil pets. At first, I think the bright colors appealed to him, but then he discovered that chewing on them relieved the pain of cutting his last few molars. Within days he forgot how to speak and use the toilet. He suffered convulsions. Now he sits in the corner, rocking, banging his head against the wall, snarling and lashing out at anyone who comes within range. The doctors have diagnosed him with severe and irreversible autism. He will soon have to be institutionalized as a danger to himself and others. That bright, funny, clever little boy is dead, and Cartwright murdered him with a Pencil Pet."

As tears rolled down his cheeks, the distraught man folded his knife, put it back in his pocket, and held out his wrists in submission to the bailiff. A second deputy came into the courtroom from the hall to help remove him.

"Take him straight downstairs to the jail and book him on a charge of contempt of court." Anger had now replaced fear on the judge's face. When she noticed that a reporter stood up in the back of the room and tried to follow the deputies, she shouted at him.

"Forget it, Billy Joel. Your newspaper has already done enough damage with its sensational headlines. Mr. Wilson will have no visitors and give no interviews. Let us continue.

"Mr. Feingold, you mentioned that it is difficult to prove a negative. So it is. How, then, do you intend to go about establishing your client's innocence?"

"I can't predict that, Judge, until I have heard specific charges. So far, there have been none."

"And round and round we go. Approach the bench, both of you. In addition to Mr. Feingold's statement of the obvious, I would remind you both that in a scientific study of any kind, a single set of data points is not enough to prove a conclusion.

Findings are not relevant unless—and until—they have been replicated. Has there been any effort to examine these test results scientifically or to order additional testing to determine the accuracy of the original tests?"

The two lawyers looked at each other and shrugged. As before, Beverly Jacobs spoke first. "May I ask, Judge, whose responsibility it would be to order such additional testing?"

Judge McCutchen appeared to be rather taken aback at the question. "Well, perhaps we need a third-party, someone without a vested interest in the outcome. In this case, I believe that might be the city of Birch Falls." She glanced around the courtroom. "Lt. David Cohen, would you approach, please?"

She lowered her voice and leaned forward to discuss the question with David, who was looking distinctly apprehensive. "Would you clarify your position? Now that you are the acting DA, has someone replaced you as Police Liaison Officer, or are you wearing both hats?"

"This issue has not come up, Your Honor."

"Then I am going to ask you as a representative of the city of Birch Falls to perform your liaison duties by contacting the Environmental Protection Agency's local office. I believe it is their responsibility to conduct any tests to determine the level of danger presented by the pigments being used in the Cartwright's manufacturing facility."

"Yes, ma'am."

"Thank you. That being settled, I believe we may stand adjourned until . . ." She glanced around to confirm the date with the clerk of the court.

"Your Honor, the opening date for this trial is currently set for this coming Monday, February 1st, but that clearly does not allow enough time for . . ."

"Of course, it doesn't. All right. This court stands adjourned until further notice. I will see to rescheduling our opening date and notify all participants by tomorrow. In the meantime, I suggest that all of you keep your wild guesses and opinions to yourselves."

She glanced toward the back of the courtroom, where the reporters were whispering among themselves. She raised her voice to gain their attention. "That goes for you and your newspaper's staff writers as well, Billy Joel. If I see any more inflammatory articles such as the one you published this morning, I shall be seeing red, and I'm not referring to any toxic pigment."

Chapter Twenty-Three

PROPOSALS AND COUNTER-PROPOSALS

January 28–29, 2010

S arah followed the crowd as spectators made their way out of the courtroom. In the hall, she found an empty bench in a spot where she could see David as he came out. She leaned back and indulged in a favorite pastime—people-watching.

She soon realized that everyone she saw was unhappy. She observed angry parents escorting sullen or embarrassed teenagers on their way to juvenile court. Sad middle-aged men and women looking uncomfortable in their new hairstyles, manicures, and high heels avoided each other at the entry to divorce court. Scruffy people of all ages, several of them looking as if they had spent the night in a city jail cell, waited outside traffic court. And lawyers were recognizable with their buttoned-down styles and bulging briefcases. Sarah sighed and closed her eyes.

"Did our proceedings so exhaust you that you have fallen asleep?" a familiar voice asked.

She jerked upright. "Not at all. I have seen enough misery

for one day. I now understand part of what you did not like about being a lawyer, David. Just look at this crowd. This courthouse makes my skin crawl. Did you ever see so many unhappy people in one spot?"

"You must not judge us by our second floor alone. Downstairs, you would find bustling offices with efficient people taking care of business. And on the third floor, well, that's our happy place. There's a room furnished to resemble a comfortable and homey living room. It's our adoption center where excited new parents embrace their forever children. We use the good-sized auditorium for our formal occasions—inducting new police officers, celebrating well-deserved retirements, and swearing-in new citizens. And there's the wedding chapel."

David wiggled his eyebrows. "Hey! That's an idea! Why don't we head up there and see how it's done? The licensing office is still open, and there should be an elderly judge waiting around with nothing else to do."

Sarah laughed and swatted at him. "Don't push your luck."

"A fellow has to keep trying. But you're right. This is a depressing place. Tell you what. The sun has to be over the yardarm somewhere by now, and I could use a drink. Let's head straight to Isolde's."

"I know we agreed to dinner tonight, but I'm not really hungry. It seems a shame to waste a dull appetite on a place as fancy as Isolde's."

"Overruled. A fancy and relaxing dinner is what we need. If you're not hungry, we can just order an appetizer or two."

~

They settled into a banquette while an obsequious waiter hovered nearby. David did not bother to look at the menu. "We'll have one of your appetizer platters to share, Jerome."

"Do you know every waiter in this place?"

"Pretty much. The chef is a good friend, and we help one another now and then." He hesitated and looked at Sarah with a question. "Which do you prefer tonight—French or Italian?"

"M-m-m. I need spicy. Italian, I think."

He nodded at the waiter. "But hold the shellfish, and bring us a bottle of Prosecco, please."

"Sparkling? You are in a frisky mood tonight, aren't you?"

They relaxed into a comfortable silence while Jerome performed his rituals of cork removal, sniffing, sampling, and pouring the wine. When he departed, David raised his glass to Sarah's.

"We have reason to celebrate tonight. My friend the pawn broker returned your ring to me today." He held up a tiny blue velvet box. "Allow me to ask again, this time in public instead of when I have you naked and flat on your back in bed. Sarah Rebecca Chomsky, will you marry me?"

He opened the box and Sarah gasped. "Oh, David, it's exquisite. How . . . ?"

"It's the same ring and the same star sapphire. The jeweler designed it so that he could remove the pearls and replace them with a circle of diamonds when the time was right."

She held out a shaking left hand, and he slid the ring into place. "There is a second piece as well—a solid band that will complete the design on our wedding day." On cue, the pianist launched into several bars of the wedding march and the other patrons in a restaurant applauded.

When Jerome returned with plates and silverware, David and Sarah paid no attention, but when their appetizer platter arrived, they discovered they were both famished.

The center of the platter held a crystal bowl filled with a bruschetta spread. Surrounding it were thin slices of focaccia. The next circle featured cured meats—prosciutto wrapped around slivers of melon, pepperoni, glistening sardines, sopressata and hard salami. Then came an assortment of vegetable products—pepperocini, olives cured in oil, marcona almonds, cherry tomatoes, artichoke hearts, and marinated button mushrooms. The outer ring featured cheeses—wedges of Asiago and fresh Parmesan, provolone, and mozzarella balls—interspersed with homemade rosemary crackers. They demolished it all, except for two sardines, which Sarah carried home wrapped in a plastic bag for Elijah, whose dinner was going to be late.

~

After a weekend spent notifying parents and friends of the new engagement, Sarah was relaxed when she returned to work on Monday morning. The feeling did not last. Summoned to the department chair's office, she was unprepared to find Kevin glaring at her.

"I hear you're engaged now. I hope your love life will not interfere with your responsibilities here."

"No, no. Why would you think . . .?"

"I'm not getting much from you. I asked you to set up the new chapter of Phi Alpha Theta, and I haven't heard a word about your progress."

"Oh. That! Well, to be frank, I don't think it's going to happen."

"As I remember, that wasn't one of your options."

"Maybe it wasn't, but the more I learn, the more I am convinced it's a bad idea."

"Give me one good reason."

"I can give you several. It will not bring in more history majors, which I understood to be your priority. There's no enthusiasm for the idea among our faculty or our graduate students. We don't have enough potential members to qualify, and even those who might qualify will not pay the ridiculous initiation fees required by this so-called honor. Will that do?"

"No, it will not. What's your evidence?"

"All right, I'll give it to you one point at a time, but it's going to take a while. May I sit down?"

"Help yourself."

"You said you wanted a Phi Alpha Theta chapter to increase student interest in becoming history majors. But that's putting the cart before the horse. The home office of PAT needs new inductee names by January each year. The qualifications for undergraduate induction include twelve completed hours of approved history classes, with a minimum of a 3.1 GPA in history and an overall 3.0 GPA. Now, given that we do not require students to declare a major until their fourth semester, there is little chance that they will have completed twelve hours of history course work within their first three semesters because we require so many core courses during the first two years. In addition, the inductions themselves take place only in April or May. Therefore, we can't induct even a student who manages to qualify at the end of his second year until April or May of his third year."

Kevin was shaking his head. "But that would mean the PAT chapter would end up having only seniors as members."

"Yes. And it also means that if we were to apply for new chapter status today, our current seniors could not even qualify for membership because this year's deadline has passed. We could not induct our current juniors until a few days before their own graduation next year. Today's freshman and sophomores could not become members until the end of their junior year. It's hard to sell an idea when the rewards are so far out of reach.

"Now add the $50 initiation fee and ask yourself how many of our students can afford to pay $50 to join this so-called honorary society. I have trouble admiring an honor with a price tag."

"I understand your argument, but how do you explain the fact that so many schools all over the country have successful chapters?"

"Tradition, perhaps. Or maybe the rules have changed. I don't know, but I know that it doesn't sound like a good idea for our campus, at least in the short term. I have another suggestion, however."

"What's that?" Kevin sounded skeptical.

"If we want to get new students excited about studying history, we could start by establishing our own Smoky Mountain Historical Society—open to everyone, with no membership fees and an interesting calendar of programs. We could hold events, like screening important historical films, guest speakers, visits to local historical sites, instruction on genealogical study, and maybe even our own restoration project. We're sitting on an important historical site right here. I think such an organization might encourage the early declarations you are looking for. And in the future, Phi Alpha Theta inductions might become part of the historical society's program."

"You have an answer for everything, don't you?"

"I try. What I'd like to do is take the question to our students. They are the ones who will make or break the organization, whichever one we implement. We could ask Gwen to create a brief questionnaire for the faculty to distribute in each of their history classes."

"Do it, but do it soon."

"Yes, sir, right away."

"Oh, and one more thing. How are your publication efforts coming along?"

Sarah had risen; now she sank back onto her chair. "That's a different story. We've been so busy with the AHA interviews that I forgot to tell you. I have a publishing contract."

"You do? Tell me about it."

"It's a book for Jewish children, explaining the history and traditions of Passover."

"Not your primary field of expertise."

"I suppose not, but it was a wonderful opportunity. At last year's Passover with David's family, I told them the story of how I discovered a tiny kitten on my family's doorstep. I was performing the traditional act of opening the door to allow the spirit of Elijah to enter our hearts. The kitten went straight to our Passover table and helped himself to a bite of brisket. My father, the rabbi, named the cat Elijah, and he has been my constant companion ever since.

"So it was a matter of several coincidences. I have a friend who had just published a children's book on Jewish prayers. It was so popular that she was looking for another idea along the same lines. David's sister, Hannah Steinmark, is a talented artist and asked if she could paint my cat's portrait. David's mother suggested that children would love the story. We worked on it during the semester break. And almost without effort, this story has become a children's book, with illustrations by Hannah Steinmark and text by Sarah Chomsky. With luck, it will be out next month, in time for Passover at the end of March."

"You can not expect me go before a tenure and promotion board and praise your academic talent based on a book about your cat."

"It has historical value."

"But not in your field of study. Come on, Chomsky. Give me a break here. I don't want to lose you. You're doing good work for us, and your students love you, but you have to play by the rules. You have an unfortunate habit of arguing about every expectation. And when we're talking about rules that apply to the whole college, no one cares about your counter-proposals. Just do the work, OK?"

"Yes, sir."

This time she escaped. Her heels clicked on the tiles as she made her way down the hall. She stopped by Gwen's desk to give her some advance notice.

"Clear your desk. I have a project coming up, and I'm going to need a short survey with a copy for every student in every one of our history classes. You might count up the registrations to see how many we will need. I'll bring you the questions as soon as I get them written this afternoon."

Back in her office, Sarah indulged a moment of frustration by kicking off her shoes and sending them flying across the room.

Chapter Twenty-Four

PLAN B

Monday, February 1, 2010

"Whoops! Did I pick the wrong moment to drop by?" Maria Hernandez hesitated in the doorway.

Sarah's face flushed with embarrassment as she turned to face one of her favorite students. "Sorry. When I throw a tantrum, it's short-lived. Come on in while I retrieve my shoes."

"You don't have to do that for me. I'm used to bare feet. And I don't intend to stay long. I just came by to let you know I passed calculus—with a B. That spoils my perfect grade average, but it's so much better than what I deserved in the beginning. I'm still filled with gratitude for everything you did to help me when I thought my world had ended."

"We all need help now and then. You've learned a lot from your experiences in those first few weeks. I hope from now on you'll remember that it's a good idea to have a Plan B."

"Well, I need one now. I have faced the fact that I'm not prepared to go to medical school, but I can not figure out what to do with myself from here. I've always believed I needed to become a doctor to help my people. I don't know what else I could do."

"Oh, there are so many other avenues. You might become a lawyer, an immigrations expert, a social worker, a teacher, a psychologist, a community activist..."

"Like the Obamas?"

"Sure. If you're looking for role models, they are an excellent choice. Remember, they started out to be courtroom lawyers and then discovered they could be of more use on the street corners. Come to think of it, we have a graduate student in the department who works as a community organizer. I'm sure she'd be willing to talk to you about her activities. Would you like me to introduce you?"

"Later, maybe, if I ever have time to decide..."

"The key, my dear, is to take time—time to figure out what you love best and then how you can use that skill to make things better for those around you. And I tell you that in the full awareness that I was just reprimanded for having a counter-proposal—a Plan B."

"Do faculty members get reprimands, too?"

"All the time. That's another one of those rules of life. There's always someone with the right to tell you what to do."

"I don't know whether to feel relieved or discouraged."

"A little of both, I suspect."

"All right. Let's say, just for the sake of argument, that I became a history major. What would you tell me I could do with that kind of degree?"

Sarah tried not to smile at the girl's roundabout way of asking for help. "I would tell you that people hire graduates with history degrees for many jobs. Employers are looking for curious people, people who know how to ask the right questions and then go about finding the answers. They want employees who can test details, recognize the differences between causes and effects, and think. Most of all, I suspect, they want people who can spell and write. History courses teach you all of those things, often without your being aware of it."

"But what about job qualifications? What about career paths?"

"Don't confuse vocational school training and a university education. We are not trying to train plumbers; we're producing thinkers and creators. A plumber ends up with a job; a thinker ends up with a lifetime of wisdom."

Maria's eyes were sparkling with enjoyment at the repartee. "Being a plumber pays better."

"Ah, but being a thinker gives you more to dream about."

"You win. I'd love to be a history major, if only I were sure that when I graduate, I could do something useful with it."

"Maria, I don't want to sound like I'm twisting your arm, but please understand the implications of the questions you are asking. If you decide today that you still want to be a doctor, you will close off all other possibilities. As a history major, or an English major, or a psychology major, you give yourself three more years to look for opportunities to use your education to better help your people. One choice narrows your vision; the other opens vistas."

"I have never thought of it quite that way."

"There's one other aspect we haven't even mentioned. Today's world is evolving at a rate people have never experienced. Technology, computers, instant communications, and artificial intelligence are creating new jobs faster than we can fill them, while traditional career paths are becoming obsolete. The jobs you and your classmates will do when you are middle-aged don't even exist yet. A plumber trained to repair a flush toilet will be useless when thinkers figure out how to vaporize and recycle human waste."

"Oh my! I may never get that image out of my head."

"Sorry. Try this one. It's a little less scatological. I have spent my entire educational experience training to become a teacher. When I was six years old, I'd come home from school, line up my dolls and teddy bears—sometimes the cat —and play school, teaching them everything I had learned that day. Now I am 31 years old, less than two years into my actual career as a college teacher, and I am already almost past my shelf life date. Ten years from now, all college educa-tion may come through virtual classrooms and distance-learning, and I'll be obsolete unless I learn some new skills."

"Once again, you've given me much to think about. Never change that, OK?"

Sarah watched Maria as she left the office, wondering whether her words had helped or hurt. The fine line between advising and interfering was still a murky one. Then she retrieved her shoes from a corner and resettled in a busi-ness-like pose as she reached for her calendar. Before Kevin and then Maria had interrupted her mental scheduling, she had intended to organize her new journal. It was a three-ring binder, with the year's calendar and then a two-page view of the month, followed by a to-do page for each week, and then a day-by-day, hour-by-hour schedule.

She had failed to record anything for the month of January, but it was not too late to jot down the important events on the monthly page as a reminder to herself of when things had occurred. Having noted David's medical appoint-ment, the trip to San Diego, the interview schedule, the cranking up of a new semester, Sam's surgery, the preliminary trial over the Cartwright matter, and the engagement dinner, she turned to the February pages.

She marked the day's date, February 1, with a ribbon and

then turned back once more to the yearly view to make sure of her pre-set obligations. In February, they had scheduled campus visits with the Ren-Ref one-year replacement candidates for Thursday and Friday, the 11th through the 12th and the 18th to the 19th. Valentine's Day fell between the two visits. The Cartwright trial opened on Wednesday, the 24th, followed by the first candidate for the Early American position on February 25th and 26th. Purim finished out the month on the 27th and 28th.

The second Americanist candidate would arrive on March 4th and 5th. Spring break extended from March 12th till the 22nd, which almost corresponded with the opening dates of the Nineteenth Century Studies Conference being held in Tampa starting on the 11th. Sarah noted that meeting on the calendar but realized that if she wanted to attend, she would have to miss the last two days of class before spring break. There was no justifiable way she could warn students against leaving early while doing so herself. Then, too, the conference organizers had not approved her paper submission, so she had no pressing need to attend.

The first Modernist candidate would visit on March 25th and 26th; the second, on the 29th and 30th. Then, after being back for just eight days, Easter break fell from April 2nd through the 5th. And by a quirk of the calendar, it also covered part of Jewish Passover which extended from March 29th through April 6th. Sarah suppressed a cringe as she thought of the family entanglements involved in two Jewish holidays, this year complicated by the news of her engagement to David Cohen. Mrs. Cohen would have plans for Sarah from Purim through Passover.

Sarah shook her head. "Look at that. Those are just other peoples' schedules. I have not entered my own responsibilities—my classes, my writing schedule, my research. And what about other people and their expectations for me?

Hannah is excited about our book coming out, and she expects me to put in appearances in book stores and launch parties. Kevin wants scholarly articles and a new history club. David is sure to ask where he fits into the larger picture. And there will always be students knocking at the door to bring in unexpected problems that only I can solve. It's hopeless."

Irritated by her own failure to prioritize the demands placed upon her by others, Sarah slammed the planner closed. "Who am I kidding? I talk big about always having a Plan B, but I can't even come up with a way to handle Plan A." She buried her face in her hands, feeling hopelessness wash over her. Then a tap on her door pulled her upright again. She put on her best professional expression and called out, "Come in!"

She hadn't expected the visitor to be Trevor Monroe. "Hi! What's up?"

"Got a few minutes? I have a couple of things I'd like to discuss with you."

"Sure. I was just sitting here fussing at myself because I can't get motivated enough to get any new work done. So what can I do for you? Got the upcoming tenure and promotion jitters?"

"Nope. That decision has already occurred."

"You've lost me."

"Only because you're trying to outguess me rather than listening." He laughed. "I'm leaving Smoky Mountain."

"What? Why? When . . .?"

"Sarah . . ."

"OK. I'm sorry. You were saying. . .?"

"I am not cut out to be a university professor. While I love my subject area and enjoy the writing and the research, I hate being in a classroom. Some people enjoy it. I know you do. I've watched you when you walk into a room full of students. No matter what is going on in your own life, you come alive in the classroom. But me? I hate every minute. I don't want to spend the rest of my life doing something I don't enjoy.

"So, over Christmas break, I went to New York, and Genevieve and I hashed out our differences. It turns out that she was not unhappy with me; she worried that I was unhappy with my work. Rather than watch me struggle, she showed me the way by leaving and finding a fresh approach to life. Her solution was to turn her independent company, for which she had total responsibility, over to a larger firm that could provide the guidance and oversight she needed.

"Her small investment company is now a part of a large conglomerate, Adelman and Baxter. They are a real power-house on Wall Street, and they have their fingers in several kinds of investments. One of their branches does nothing but research and analyze the marketplace. And that's where I fit in. They were looking for someone who could take a dedicated historical approach. They were hiring. I interviewed. They offered. I accepted. As of June 1, I will become the head of their new historical analysis department."

"Wow! I am not sure what to say. Congratulations, but . . . I didn't know you were even considering . . . You were in such a good mood in San Diego . . . I assumed it was because your book project was coming along well, and your tenure prospects were looking better."

"No, it was because I already knew what I was going to do. This semester is a pleasure because it will be my last. There are people here I will miss, and I'll miss Birch Falls, too—the clear mountain air, the small-town atmosphere, the green-ness of everything. But in New York, I'll be back together with my wife, and I'll be doing the work I love."

"What did Kevin say when you told him?"

"I haven't told him yet. I had thought about telling everyone at once in a department meeting, but I decided I'd rather make my announcements more personal. I started with you because I knew you would be sympathetic. Julia is next, and then I'll face the lion in his den. Who knows? Maybe he'll be as happy to see me leave as I am."

"Then the dean and the tenure and promotion committee? I don't envy you the next few days."

"A small price to pay. But there's another aspect as well—something I realized in San Diego as I watched all of those eager young candidates pleading their cases. It occurred to me that if I announced now, rather than at the end of the semester, the department might have time to fill my vacancy without having to start that recruitment process all over again. Anyway, there it is, for what it's worth."

"It's worth more than you know. I've been muddling over my own plans without getting very far. David and his parents are pushing for an early wedding. His sister Hannah expects me to commit all my free time to the release of the children's book we have coming out. Julia wants—needs—my help in entertaining all our visiting candidates. Kevin demands that I publish another article or get a book contract, and at the same time he wants me to establish a new extra-curricular activity for our history majors. Meanwhile, my advising class members have been coming in to ask for help in deciding upon a major before their declaration deadline.

"I've scheduled everyone's goals except my own. I used to believe I had a five-year plan for success. Once in a while, I faced criticism for planning so far ahead—for prioritizing my Plan A. Now Kevin has chastised me for always having a counter-proposal, for suggesting a different way to do things. I've lectured my students on the need to have a fallback option—a Plan B. But I've lost all track of what I'm supposed to be doing. Your decision to change directions has brought me up short. Maybe it's time to reconsider my own goals—to define my Plan B."

Chapter Twenty-Five

THE FINE ART OF JUGGLING

Early February 2010

P lan B would have to wait. The month of February opened with a flurry of crises, every one of which demanded immediate attention. To Sarah's surprise, her brief questionnaire about student preferences regarding extra-curricular activities produced a clear vote to establish the Smoky Mountain Historical Society. It also spawned a group of students who wanted to get started. On the day after the vote, Sarah's office email overflowed with questions about the date of the first meeting and her plans for programs. She shook her head in resignation. "There's only one thing worse than having one's ideas rejected," she grumbled to herself. "That's the unbridled enthusiasm of the American teenager who expects the only available grown-up to have all the answers."

By late afternoon, Sarah had created a standard reply: "Thank you for your interest in our new society. Organizational details will take some time, as all such activities must gain the approval of the college administration and board of directors. I have noted your interest and have added your name to a list of potential members. We will notify you as soon as we have permission to proceed." Then she locked her office door and went to visit Julia, hoping for a little tea and sympathy. Instead, as she peeked around the door, she was just in time to witness Julia slam the phone receiver down and hurl her pen across the room.

"Wow! I picked a terrible time, didn't I? I'll come back."

"No, please come in. I need a target."

"Hey, I've been a target all day today, and I'm tired of dodging. What problem has you so riled up?"

"You'll remember Mr. Max 'I'm-so-humble-I-won't-call-myself-doctor-until-I've-received-my-diploma-and-my-hood' Norton? You know, one of our candidates for my one-year replacement? The one I have scheduled to arrive for a campus visit next Thursday, the 11th?"

"Yes . . .?"

"He's gone missing."

"Missing? What does that mean?"

"Missing, as in gone. Disappeared. Absconded. Abducted by aliens. Who knows?"

"Since when?"

"Again, who knows? He hasn't acknowledged my emails or my formal letter inviting him for a campus visit. I called the history office at the University of Chicago, and their secretary informed me they do not know where he is. He hasn't picked up his mail since before Christmas. He hasn't registered for the current semester and hasn't shown up for his part-time job assignment as a TA for several Western Civ. classes.

"I called his home phone number, and his landlady answered. She said he cleared out of his apartment in the middle of the night back in December and took off without paying his last two months' rent. And just now, I talked to his dissertation advisor, who says he has seen nothing of his dissertation except the first two chapters. Norton has not responded to his requests for updates, nor has he put together his defense committee or applied for a graduation date. Like I said, he's missing."

"But that's terrible. He could be dead, or being held captive somewhere, or sick in a hospital and unable to tell them who he is! What are they doing about it? Have they filed a missing persons' report or tried to contact his parents?"

"I gather they don't much want him back. The chair referred to him as 'the department's gadfly.'"

"But his letter of application . . . and his interview with us . . ."

". . . were fakes, just like everything else about him. From what the Chicago people tell me, it looks like we were the last people to see him. How's that for suspicious? My biggest problem now is what to tell Kevin and the dean, both of whom are going to want to know why we have only one viable candidate for my one-year replacement."

"This is not your fault, Julia."

"Yes, it is. I'm the one in charge, and I focused on his claim to have been a Rhodes Scholar. That was a lie, too, I've learned."

"Let's try to put as good a face on it as we can. We're lucky to have discovered the truth now, rather than after he signed a contract with us. The result would be the same if one of our upcoming candidates turns out to have already accepted another job. And, as I remember, the decision to limit ourselves to two campus visits for each position was Kevin's call, not yours."

"Well, all we can do now is hope our Dr. Ramona Bishop turns out to be as qualified a candidate as we think she is."

～

To save herself from a head-to-head confrontation, Julia met with the entire department to make her announcement about the loss of a candidate. She began with the good news, giving her colleagues the dates on which each of the candidates would arrive on campus. She had created a standard schedule to be sure that all the candidates talked with each member of the department, spent some time alone with the students, and visited the support staff they would need if they accepted the job. Each one had several lunches and dinners with members of the department and other members of the faculty, and each one had a late afternoon job talk.

She waited until somebody discovered there were only five interviews scheduled. Then she dropped the news that Max Norton would not be coming. She downplayed his reasons, saying that he had other plans.

"But Julia," Kevin fussed at her, "that means that we have no basis for comparison when we listen to the other candidate for your one-year replacement."

"Well, that can happen for many reasons. You remember that these candidates are interviewing with other institutions. I consider us lucky to have had five acceptances. As for Ramona Bishop, I have every confidence that we are going to find her satisfactory. She is one of those we have already listened to in Louisville. If she does not work out, we have other applicants. We can go back and look at them, but let's not make more work for ourselves unless we have to."

To her own surprise, Kevin accepted that explanation and complimented her for her organizational skills. They spent a few more minutes talking about places to take the candidates for various meals. Then they turned to making sure students were in attendance for each candidate's job talk. Sarah had an answer for that one.

"I already have a list, Kevin. When we announced that we are moving ahead to establish the Smoky Mountain Historical Society, students bombarded me with requests to be a part of that effort. I've explained to them that we have institutional regulations to take care of before we can establish the organization. In the meantime, I'm offering them a chance to become more active within the department. And one of those ways is to attend the job talks and give us a quick written reaction to each one."

"I assume you are screening these students as you go to be sure we don't end up with trouble makers in the mix."

"Yes, sir." Sarah was learning not to take offense when Kevin made a show of throwing his weight around. If it made him feel better, she needed to acknowledge his authority without causing further ill will.

Because the first campus visits would now not start until the 18th, Sarah had time to relax when she and David went out for the first anniversary of their Valentine's Day dinner. However, things did not go as planned because his tensions from work were riding high. Once they had settled into their favorite banquette, David ordered a strong whiskey and soda. That surprised Sarah because he was not much of a drinker. She refrained from commenting, however, and waited to let him lead the conversation wherever he needed it to go. It did not take long.

"I don't know how much longer I can handle doing both my job and Sam's," he confessed, "nor do I know which one I want to give up if I have to choose. My position as liaison officer between the police department and the DA's office is still experimental. I don't think I've had enough time to identify what needs to be done and how well it's going to work.

What I know is that I have to work out an agreement between the police department and the DA, and that's a bit like being my own grandpa."

"What's your biggest worry?"

"The EPA testing at the Cartwright plant."

"Explain, please. I am a newbie, remember?"

"OK. Scenario number one. The EPA tests all come back negative. They find no sign of lead in the toys, in the factory, or in our ground water. The whistle-blower's report turns out to be a false alarm. If that is the finding, the court will have no choice but to dismiss all charges against Mr. Cartwright and his factory. Case closed."

"That would be a relief."

"For you, maybe, but not for the court, which would then have no one to pay the court costs, and not for the lawyers who would have lost a valuable fee."

"What about the whistle-blower? It was his fault. Shouldn't he pay the court costs?"

"Maybe so, but remember, we don't know who he is, and he is not going to jump up and say, 'Hey, it was me.' If we identified him, Mr. Cartwright could sue him for defamation of character, libel, and loss of profit. And the city could demand that he pay all court costs. No, if the judge dismisses the case, the whistle-blower will lie low and lick his wounds."

"What about scenario number two?"

"Aha! In scenario number two, the EPA tests come back all positive. Their independent investigators confirm the whistle-blower's charges. Now we have a full-blown court case, although the charges would fall into two separate bills. The first would deal with questions about Cartwright's personal knowledge and responsibility: what did he know and when did he know it? The second would be a broader issue of who ordered and paid for the lead-based paint, who helped cover it up, who juggled the books, and so on. Those would be criminal charges. Then would come all the liability suits from people who drank the tainted water and others like Mr. Wilson, who could testify to clear and immediate personal injury. Those cases could go on for years. Some enterprising young law firms would stand to rake in the money."

"And is there a third possibility? What happens if the tests show mixed results? What if they are inconclusive?"

"That's the most likely outcome. Time is always the enemy of evidence. That's why it is so vital that we learn the identity of the whistle-blower. The case against Mr. Cartwright may depend upon a whistle-blower being willing to testify in court."

"Do you think he would do so?"

"At the moment, no. But then, we don't know what lies behind this—what his motive is. I remain convinced there's someone out there who knows his identity." David stared at Sarah for a few moments. "Have you . . . have you seen Olivia?"

"Not since the day she dropped by to tell me about the original accusation. I'm not sure why she hasn't been back. Maybe she saw me at the hearing and thought I was being nosy. It's hard to tell with kids that age."

"Well, you are still her advisor, aren't you? Couldn't you just ask her how she's doing, how her parents are holding up, whether she has any new ideas about who the whistle-blower could be . . . things like that?"

"David! No! Are you suggesting that I pump her for information? I can't believe you would even ask that of me. It would be unethical if I gave you information that allowed you to put her father in jail."

"I'm not asking you to spy on her. But you could suggest that she share any suspicions with the police—or with me."

"I still don't feel comfortable doing that. Everyone tells

me to stay out of my students' private lives. That has been your advice, too. But here you are, pushing me to get more involved than I'm willing to do. It's unfair of you. I'd like to go home now."

David straightened his back and gave her a sharp retort. Then he settled back into the banquette, shaking his head. "Sometimes I don't understand you, Sarah. We can't leave now—we've already ordered dinner. And I will not let you flounce out of here like some barnyard hen with ruffled feathers. A simple 'No' would have served just as well if you are not willing to talk to Olivia. That's your choice, and I'll respect it. I had no intention of starting an argument, but I thought we worked together on things like this. It was you who suggested that we try to build bridges between the courthouse and the campus."

"I did, but . . . oh, never mind. How about this as a compromise? I will not pursue Olivia or pump her for information about her family problems. But if she comes to me, I will listen, and, if I think it's appropriate, I'll suggest that she talk to someone involved with the case—either Miss Jacobs in your office or even Judge McCutchen herself. Will that do?"

"Well juggled, my dear. Now, let's see you tackle that steak in true continental style."

Chapter Twenty-Six

PLEASE TAKE A NUMBER

Thursday, February 17, 2010

R amona Bishop's campus visit was a rousing success. She arrived in Nashville Wednesday evening. Kevin met her plane and took her straight to her hotel. The next morning was Sarah's turn. She took Ramona to breakfast in the hotel dining room and then set out for a tour of the campus. Sarah parked in a visitor space near the front gate to avoid the traffic jams in the faculty parking lot. The choice also provided direct access to the cloister gardens. Although it was still winter in the Smokies, blooming daffodils lined the paths, the redbuds were showing color, and several Bradford pears had already burst into their characteristic white marshmallow blossoms.

Ramona gasped as she looked around. "What a gorgeous area! And these Gothic buildings! If I were still a medievalist, I would swear you have dropped me right into the middle of an English landscape."

"You were a medievalist?"

"That's what I started out to do, until wiser and more

experienced professors convinced me that there were better job openings in Renaissance Studies. I switched, but there is still a part of me that resonates with the earlier period."

"Well, your instincts are still right on target. This piece of land used to be a nunnery until the Great Depression forced its closure and the state bought the property for a school. I'm told they modeled the first building on a European monastery."

"The footprint is clear. This was the cloister garden, wasn't it? On the left must have been the abbess's residence, the chapter house, and the nuns' refectory. On the right, that looks like the church, although the original apse and the crossing are missing. And there is the central structure, completing the square, which would have housed the nuns' residence. Am I close?"

"Accurate on every count. If we walk through this next arch, you'll see the buildings they added after the Civil War—an orphanage on one side and a home for widows and elderly parents of soldiers who did not survive the war on the other. The more modern building in the center here is Bailey Hall, which houses our social studies departments. But before we go up to the offices, you need to see what lies at the back of our property.

"This is the area I love the most. On the far left is our veterinary school, complete with the nuns' old barn and pasture. Behind that wooden fence, you'll often find animals here to serve as teaching exhibits. Then comes the original orchard. Some of the trees are well over a hundred years old. And over there in the far corner, you'll find our most curious relic of the nunnery. It's an amphitheater of sorts that the college uses once in a while for outdoor ceremonies."

Ramona's eyes lit up. "Can we get a little closer? That looks like . . . I'm not sure, but that could be . . . a vertical labyrinth."

"What is that?"

"Vertical labyrinth is a psychological term, but it is also used to describe a maze built in a limited space. You usually see labyrinths on flat surfaces. They serve as a pilgrimage substitute, a circular prayer path. For example, there's one in the nave's floor of Chartres Cathedral. Architects sometimes built them like a Roman amphitheater so the path went up and down, resembling the crossing of the Alps. I've heard of them, but I've never seen one until now. Sarah, I've got to get this job to have time to study this one!"

"I'll see what I can do." Sarah laughed, although she knew that Ramona was all but certain to win the position. "But for now, I have to deposit you at the abbess's residence so you can meet our academic dean. After that meeting, someone will escort you to the History Chair's office to discuss our particular opening. You might also keep in mind that Kevin Chalmers is our current medievalist, so you'll have much in common. But you might not want to give him the impression that you're after his job."

By Friday afternoon, Ramona had charmed everyone she met, and a large group of faculty and students assembled in the Bailey Hall lecture hall to hear her job talk. Unlike most candidates, who used the job talk to discuss their dissertations, Ramona used her time to demonstrate her teaching style. Her topic was "Defining the Renaissance." At her prompting, several students volunteered definitions, but when one of them suggested "re-birth," Ramona led them on to her next challenge.

"What died?" she asked.

Most students appeared startled by the very idea, but after a few false starts, they could state the thesis she was suggesting: that a Renaissance only occurred after a period of great cultural destruction. Once they understood that point, she began the heart of her lecture, which turned out to be a massive romp through the history of human civilization. She started with the legends of Noah's flood and the lost city of Atlantis, a geological marker made of a layer of ash deposited some 1100 years BCE, the first examples of writing, the rise and fall of the Roman Empire, and something historians called the Carolingian Renaissance.

She finished with a mischievous grin. "So the great blossoming of art and literature in the fifteenth century—what we refer to as THE Renaissance—was nothing more than the natural result of a terrible century of famine, plague, and warfare. But was it the last Renaissance? That's for you to decide." She sat down and watched as several students, and some faculty, too, turned to each other to debate the issue. The audience filtered out, but their discussions continued. The pertinent phrases echoed down the hall: nuclear war, space travel, electronic communication, email, artificial intelligence.

"Brava! When you send them away still talking about your ideas, you know your talk has been a great success." Julia gave a quick bow accompanied by a gleeful grin. This first campus visit was ending on a high note. "Sarah and I will take you to dinner and then you'll be on your way home for a well-deserved relaxing weekend."

"You have been so welcoming, and I can't tell you how much I appreciate it. You don't need to take me out for dinner one more time. I'm sold on the town, the school, everything."

"You still need to eat, but if you're tired of fancy restaurants, we know just the place to help you relax. How do you feel about pizza?"

"Love it!"

"Great. We'll give you time to freshen up and change into

something more comfortable. Then we'll head up into the hills to a little diner the students have never discovered.

K evin had called a departmental meeting for Monday afternoon. "I had planned this meeting for a vote on the first candidate's qualifications, but I suspect we don't need to vote on Dr. Bishop's suitability. Does anyone object to unanimous approval? No? Then I'll pass that word to the dean with our highest compliments and recommendations. Well done, Julia. Now remind us of who we have coming next."

"Two candidates for our Early American position. Elizabeth Bradford comes in on this Thursday, the 25th, and Gabriel Ramirez arrives the next week, starting on March 4th. I've also made one change to their schedules. Both will give their job talks on those Thursday afternoons."

"Why the change?"

"Because I realized that neither students nor faculty want to hang around campus for an extra hour or two every Friday afternoon. We were lucky this time, and Ramona was entertaining enough to keep people interested, but having a willing audience is critical to a successful presentation."

"Fair enough. We'll see how this goes."

Tuesday, February 23, 2010

S arah regarded Tuesday as her day to get organized for the rest of the week. Her only class, a first-year survey of nineteenth-century American history, finished at 10 AM, which allowed her to spend the rest of the day on chores like paper grading and lecture writing. This Tuesday, however, started off with a problem and promised to get worse. Her reliable little Honda coupe had blinked its 'check engine' light on the drive to campus, and she realized she had missed her scheduled maintenance appointment. She made a mental note to stop for an oil change on the way home that afternoon.

Her office phone was ringing as she opened her door. The caller gave her no time to say hello. "Drop everything! You are a published author at last!"

"Hannah? Slow down, dear heart. What has you so excited?"

"*The Passover Guest!* Our copies are here! Boxes and boxes of beautiful books! Oh, Sarah, you won't believe how good they look. You must see them right this minute. Can you come over? Now?"

"No, I have a class to teach in about twenty minutes, and I haven't even had time to take off my coat. I'm sure they look wonderful, but I must wait."

"Darn! Well, this afternoon will have to do."

"Uh ... I don't think I can ..."

"Yes, you have to. Mother is as excited as I am. She's already called all her lady friends with grandchildren to come by the house this afternoon to buy their copies. I promised you would be there. She wants both of us to autograph the books."

"An impromptu book-signing? Oh, Hannah. I'm at work all day today, and my schedule is full. I can't just up and leave because your mother has ..."

"It's a family occasion, Sarah. Once the ladies have gone home, she is expecting the entire family for dinner. She already has the tuna noodle casserole ready to go in the oven. That's how the Cohens celebrate every major accomplishment, you may remember. Jacob will pick Benjamin up from school and bring him over, and David has promised to come as soon as he can get away from the courthouse."

"Yes, I remember the tuna and noodles, all too well. I wouldn't dare miss it. But I can't be there until late afternoon. Sorry. I'll hurry as much as I can."

Sarah disconnected, but before she could put the phone down it rang again. "Hannah, I told you . . ."

A chuckle greeted her. "It's not Hannah, dearest, it's her irritating brother. I was hoping to catch you before she did, but I gather I have failed. My sister has learned her bullying tactics from our mother all too well."

"David! You know I love your family, but sometimes . . ."

"I know, but they're trying to do something nice for you. Mother is proud that you wrote the text for Hannah's picture book. She wants to show you off to her friends."

"I don't mean to be a grouch, but it's not even nine o'clock, and this is the second crisis I've had to deal with this morning."

"What was the first one? Something wrong?"

"No, just a check engine light this morning reminding me to get an oil change, which is how I planned to spend my afternoon before the phone rang."

"Ah, I can give you a quick fix on that one. I'll pick up a can of oil on the way to the house and top off your dipstick. That will keep your change engine light satisfied for a little while at least. You just go on over to the house and park in front where I can get to the engine compartment."

"You're sweet. Thank you, but now I have to run. I have a class starting in five minutes."

∼

Right after lunch, Sarah reviewed the reading assignment for her Wednesday evening class while she waited for her next advising appointment.

"Hey, Professor Chomsky! If you're busy, I can come back later."

"No, no, I was expecting you. How are you, Chad? I saw you at last Friday's job talk, but there was so much going on at the end that I missed you."

"That new lady was fantastic, wasn't she? It bummed me to realize that she might teach here next year and I wouldn't be around to take a course from her."

Not sure where this conversation was leading, Sarah just raised an eyebrow and waited. Chad gave her a rueful grin and added, "You have heard about my new so-called 'job,' I take it."

"I have, but my informant told me the offer delighted you. You don't sound thrilled to me."

"I'm miserable," he confessed. "Can you stand to listen to me complain?

"The complaint department is open for business." Sarah leaned back in her chair and smiled in encouragement.

"I got excited when Coach Wheeler asked me to be the equipment manager for his new athletics complex, but I thought he was talking about a summer job, not a lifetime commitment. I'm not ready to leave school yet, Professor Chomsky, and I don't want to settle for being a glorified janitor for the rest of my life, either."

"Is that what this job is?"

"Pretty much. I'll be inflating basketballs, and sweeping the floor, and gathering the dirty towels from the locker room. My dad tells me I am lucky to have found someone willing to hire me, given my disabilities, and my mother is relieved to know I will not end up sleeping under a bridge. I don't think anyone realizes how insulting that is."

"I'm sorry."

"It's just . . . that's how everyone has treated me ever since my injury. When I woke up from that coma, my parents told me I would never walk or talk again. The doctors agreed with them, and they kept offering me assistive devices—until I told them in no uncertain terms that their diagnosis was wrong and walked out of the room. Now the medical prediction is that I can never do college-level work, that I can't finish my education, and that I can never hold a responsible job. I think my father is happy that no one expects him to pay for my college education. And no one hears me when I tell them my GPA last semester was a 3.5 and that at midterm this semester, I am carrying a 4.0."

"I suspect they're worried about you. Parents are like that sometimes."

"I understand that they are afraid for me. When I tell them I want to graduate, they are afraid I'll fail, and they don't want to see me hurt. They're so overprotective that they are smothering me. When I mention I'd like to be a teacher, my mother tells me I don't understand my own limitations. But that's not true. I can tell when I'm able to do something, and I know I'd be good in the classroom."

"Then you need to show them, just as you did when you came out of the coma."

"But I don't have the money for college unless I can play football—which they will not let me do."

"There are other sources of funding. Have you talked to Financial Aid?"

"When I applied for my first year, they said my high school grades weren't good enough."

"That was before you started making A's in your college

courses. There's also money available from the state lottery funds. You haven't drawn yours yet, have you?"

"No, because I had the football scholarship."

"Well, the athletic scholarship's gone now, so you should be able to tap into the lottery fund. There's also your own money-making ability. If you work for Bert Wheeler all summer long and deposit your checks in a bank account instead of spending them, you should have enough to pay your own tuition for fall semester."

"You make it sound easy, but I have four semesters to go."

"It won't be easy, but it will be doable. You're still living at home, so you aren't paying for room and board. If you keep this job and work part time––maybe weekends and vacations––you'll have your own money coming in. If you run short, you can always enroll as a part-time student for a semester or two. Lots of people take five or six years to finish. That's no disgrace compared to the satisfaction you'll get from knowing you paid for your own education."

"Thanks, Dr. Chomsky. I should come talk to you more often."

Sarah shook her head as she watched him head down the hall. Not everyone was going to approve of what she had just done, but someone needed to be on Chad's side. "I'll just have to be careful not to say 'I told you so' to David."

Chapter Twenty-Seven

EVERYONE HAS AN AGENDA

Tuesday–Saturday, February 23–27

S arah arrived at the Cohen residence after four o'clock, but the living room was still full of middle-aged ladies waiting to meet the author of *The Passover Guest*. From some inner source of energy, Sarah summoned her best smile and greeted each one as they handed over their new purchases for an autograph. To her own surprise, she enjoyed the recognition. And to be sure, the books were lovely. Sarah had seen several of Hannah's watercolors during Hanukkah, but she had never seen the smaller illustrations or the page layouts. Now the attention to detail on each page delighted her. Mrs. Cohen invited Sarah to read the book to the assembled ladies, and she did so, holding up each illustration.

On the first few pages, the Abraham family prepared for Passover,[1] and as they did so, the mother explained why each step was important—the cleaning, the removal of every trace of leavening from the kitchen, the special tableware, the ordering of kosher ingredients, and preparing special foods. No cat appeared in those first few pages, but somebody had left traces behind. One page had a paw print; another, the tip of a tail disappearing off the page. In an outdoor scene, one hind leg dangled from a tree branch. On another, two bright green eyes peaked from under the porch. Someone left a freshly-caught mouse on the doormat as a gift. When the children decorated the Seder[2] table, two pointy ears poked above the windowsill as a secret watcher observed each step.

The first night of Passover was stormy, and a little black cat—bedraggled and dejected, head lowered and tail dragging—shivered as a passing car hit a puddle and sent a splash of cold water to soak him once again. Inside the Abraham house, however, it was warm and dry. The Passover guests assembled around the Seder table. The children learned the meanings behind this special night as Mr. Abraham read the traditional lines of the Haggadah.[3] They tasted the bitter herbs and other exotic food stuffs, while outside the window, a little black kitten once again peeked over the windowsill.

At the end of the Haggadah, the children learned why there was an empty chair and place setting at the table. "On this special night," Mr. Abraham said, "the spirit of Elijah the Prophet roams the earth, seeking families who will welcome him into their hearts. We leave our door unlocked and an empty place saved at the table, in case Elijah visits us. And we send our youngest child to open the door for his spirit. Timmy, this year it is your turn to open the door."

The little boy approached the door and then jumped back as he heard a noise on the other side. He opened the door, looked up, and saw nothing. Then he looked down and discovered the little black kitten stepping over the doorsill. Giving himself one good shake to get rid of the rain, the kitten sniffed the air and headed straight for the Seder table. He clambered onto the empty chair, placed his two front paws on the table, and looked around. Cousin Ruth, seated next to the empty chair, chose a small bite of brisket from her plate and offered it. The kitten swallowed it without stopping to chew. Several other guests passed their tidbits, and the kitten was soon purring.

Mrs. Abraham frowned. "Samuel, get that cat off the table! He's wet and dirty."

"Now, Martha, who are we to judge? Perhaps someone has named this little cat Elijah. Never let it be said that the Abrahams turned away the stranger—cold, wet, hungry, and afraid—who came to their table on this sacred night."

The book ended with a full-page portrait of Elijah the Cat, painted from a photo of the real Elijah, whose story this was. Sarah beckoned to Hannah, who had done the illustrations, and they linked arms as the room burst into applause. No one clapped louder than David Cohen, standing in the doorway to watch his fiancé and his sister in their moment of accomplishment.

L ater that evening, as the family was finishing the last of the tuna casserole, Hannah broached the subject of other book signings. "I appreciated you being here today, Sarah. I understand how busy you are, but people want to meet you. We have scheduled a a few other signings and selling opportunities. The first is this coming weekend. It's Purim⁴ and we'll all be at the synagogue working on the free meals for the poor. But Rabbi Leibowicz suggested that we could put a small table back by the kitchen where members of the congregation could pick up their copies when they come in to work. I'll handle it, but you may need to spell me once in a while. OK?"

"Sure, that's no problem. I'll be there all day on Saturday and Sunday morning, too."

"Great. Then the following weekend—that's Saturday,

March 6th—that new bookstore, the Book Lair on the Square, has asked us to do a two-hour reading and signing from two to four with snacks and a special appearance by the real Elijah the Cat. They furnish the snacks; we furnish the cat. Will that work?"

Sarah grinned. "I'm not sure I can speak for Elijah. He'll have demands of his own, maybe some leashed walkabouts to relieve the monotony of sitting in his stroller and a week's supply of catnip mice. But sure, we can do that."

"Just one more—so far. The Barnes and Noble store out in the county mall wants us to do a children's program at ten AM on Saturday, March 13th. We would read the book to the assembled children and then have the chance to sell copies to their parents. Oh, and they want the real Elijah to be there, too."

"OK. But before you talk to anybody else, Hannah, let me explain my schedule. We have our spring break coming up from March 13th through the 21st. That's two weekends and the full week in between. During those nine days I am at your disposal. Elijah and I will be happy to go anywhere within reason and talk to any group that's willing to listen. But after that, during the week leading up to Passover, I am unavailable because of my work schedule. You can take a break and let me carry the load when I'm free. Then you can take over when I'm tied up elsewhere. I'll be off work again from April 2nd through the 5th, so I'll be available for the last push."

"Wait a minute, Sarah," David interrupted. "I thought you had a conference in Tampa and a meeting in Charleston during that spring break."

"Changed my mind—or rather, had it changed for me by my department chair. He made it pretty clear that I had better spend that time off working on a major book proposal based on my dissertation. He is right, but I can do it at home whenever and however I please—like the middle of the night in my pajamas. The Elijah talks will provide a welcome balance. Who knows? I might even have time to have a cup of coffee with you once in a while."

Hannah stepped into the discussion again. "Let me remind everyone that our biggest sales opportunity will come between March 30th and April 6th—the eight days of Passover, with the Christian Easter celebration falling right in the middle on April 4th. It was our own rabbi who reminded me that the Easter story celebrates Passover, and many Christians do not understand what Passover means. *The Passover Guest* may interest Christians as they prepare for Easter. But after April 6th, we will be relying on Amazon sales to move the rest of our books."

Wednesday morning dawned dark and foreboding, the heavy atmosphere reflecting Sarah's mood as she contemplated the days ahead. This was her heaviest teaching day, with a topics course before lunch and a three-hour graduate seminar from six to nine in the evening. She usually filled the afternoons with grading or lesson planning, but today she knew her mind would be in the courthouse. The Environmental Protection Agency inspectors were ready to release their findings in the whistle-blower case. David had invited her to attend the hearing, but with another teaching candidate visit scheduled to begin on Thursday, she could not afford the time.

She struggled to concentrate on this evening's class reading, but her eyes kept straying to the clock and its passing minutes and hours. When the phone rang at 4:30, she grabbed it as if it might run away. David's voice sounded noncommittal as he apologized for not for not calling sooner.

"The judge has been chewing my ear off ever since she

dismissed the court. Do you want the quick answer or all the gory details?" he asked.

"Both. Just tell me what happened."

"The trial is over. Judge McCutchen received the EPA reports on Monday, so she had her response ready. To everyone's relief, they found no evidence of lead contamination in the city's water supply or aquifer. Nor did any of the 150 Pencil Pets they tested contain any trace of lead. No one is in any danger. However, the evidence was less clear in two of the new tests they ran. The red streaks they took from the extruder..."

"The what?"

"The extruder. That's the machine that forms and colors the liquid plastic, creating the little guys you see as the finished product. Anyhow, in the extruder they found several traces of red lead along the top lip of the dye tank, although there was no lead in the tank itself."

"I don't understand what that means."

"It means someone dripped the lead onto the edge of the tank but did not put it into the tank. The evidence had been planted where testers could find it."

"Wow!"

"Yeah. They found more red lead in a patch of ground near the retaining pond behind the factory. The whistle-blower had pointed to that spot as evidence that the lead was escaping from the pond when it overflowed. However, there was no trace of lead in the area between the pond and the deposit."

"Which means it didn't flow there. Somebody poured it on the spot."

"Correct. At that point, Judge McCutchen called a halt to the proceedings and went to her ruling. She cleared Jamison Cartwright, his company, and his executive officers of the charges brought against them. The county clerk will expunge the records, and the company is free to resume business bright and early tomorrow morning."

"That's such a relief. Now everyone can quit panicking. The newspaper can get back to reporting actual news, thousands of children will purchase new Pencil Pets, and maybe Olivia can concentrate on her school work again instead of worrying about her father."

"All true, but the judge wasn't through with her ruling. The case itself remains open, and she has instructed the police department to continue its investigation into the identity of the whistle-blower. That leaves open the possibility that Cartwright could come back to court as the accuser, charging the whistle-blower with libel and defamation. We haven't heard the last of this yet."

On Thursday, Sarah's first duty was to meet Dr. Elizabeth Bradford at her hotel, take her to breakfast, and then drive to the campus via the most scenic route. The first views of the old monastic buildings sitting high on a hill overlooking the town always gave Sarah a thrill, but Dr. Bradford did not seem overly impressed. Her only comment was, "What a quaint little town," and her emphasis on the word 'quaint' left little doubt as to her opinion. "Is there anything to . . . to do around here?"

"The town is active, and its citizens support the campus. They turn out in droves for our sporting events and our cultural activities. There's no town-versus-gown rivalry going on."

"How nice."

That lukewarm exchange set the tone for Dr. Bradford's entire visit. She was unimpressed by the school and its location. The students who attended her job talk had picked up on her attitude, and they played upon her weakness. She had talked about the symbolism of the passengers on the Mayflower and their profound influence upon what would become known as the American Dream. The question-and-answer period at the end of her talk gave the students their opening.

"But the pilgrims were troublemakers, weren't they? Local rulers drove them out of two Europe countries before they sought refuge someplace where there was no powerful authority."

"Troublemakers? No. They were righteous, God-fearing people, determined to live as the Bible taught them. They wanted to build a shining city on a hill, to serve as an example to all who saw it. Their leader was the Reverend William Bradford, and no finer man ever lived. He also was my great-great-great-great-great-grandfather."

The sound of snickering from the audience raised a flush on her cheeks.

"What about the way he treated the Indians? Do you believe he was trying to teach them a good Christian lesson when he stole their land and drove them off to starve?"

"Yes," another voice chimed in. "Do you give the Wampanoag peoples equal time in your lectures? They had been living on that land for thousands of years before that little band of self-righteous dissidents showed up."

Stuttering as she struggled to regain control of the audience, Dr. Bradford turned to generalities. "I-I-I give both sides as much attention as they deserve."

"Yeah? According to whom?" A third angry voice joined the attack, and she lost the argument.

The second day of interviews added little to change the eventual outcome. Faculty members and administrators asked the standard questions about teaching methods and research expectations and paid minimal attention when Dr.

Bradford lectured them on how Harvard handled such things. Sighs of relief echoed all over campus when the visit was over.

No one was happier to see her go than Sarah. She headed home in a snarling mood, kicked off her shoes, fed the cat, and poured a glass of wine. At sundown, she lit the Shabbat candles and forgave herself for skipping prayers at the synagogue. She was not in the proper mood for prayers. Besides, Purim began on Saturday, and she had already promised her future mother-in-law that she would help at the synagogue as the ladies of the congregation prepared soup for the hungry. That, too, was a form of worship.

On Saturday, Sarah spent hours in the synagogue kitchen making kreplach, three- cornered pastries filled with potatoes or onions or cheese. Boiled in a rich chicken broth, they would make a healthy meal for those who were in need. It was a mindless task that Sarah accepted with relief. She listened to piped-in music as she worked and let her mind wonder in whatever direction it chose. Thus, she did not notice the two policeman who entered the kitchen until a coworker tapped her on the arm.

"We're looking for Lieutenant Cohen. Someone said he was working back here."

"He's in the all-purpose room, helping to set up the tables for dinner tonight. Follow me. I'll show you."

"David?" she called, waving flour-covered fingers in his direction. "Someone is asking for you." She smiled at the two uniformed patrolmen and headed back to her work station.

A few minutes later, David appeared at her side, grasping her elbow. "I need you, Sarah. Wash your hands and go find your coat. I'll bring the car around and meet you at the back door."

"Why? What's wrong? Where are we going?"

"Jamison Cartwright has been shot."

Chapter Twenty-Eight

MURDER MOST FOUL

Saturday, February 27, 2010

Lights flashing and siren wailing, David wheeled his patrol car in and out of the late Saturday afternoon traffic. In brief spurts between traffic lights, he tried to fill Sarah in on what he knew—which wasn't much.

"Gunshot wound to the head. Janitor found him on the floor and called 911. Shootings always get a full response— fire, EMTs, ambulance, police, newspaper reporters, and Nosy Nellies. From what the patrolman told me, people were swarming all over the place, likely trampling any evidence into the dust. EMTs thought they detected a faint pulse and loaded Cartwright into an ambulance. They hooked him up to an IV and oxygen and headed for the Trauma Center at Riverside General Hospital. You'll remember it, I suppose."

Sarah was remembering all too well—that horrible evening when David was the one bleeding to death and she was the one behind the wheel of the patrol car, dashing to that same hospital to save his life. She shook her head to dislodge the pictures carved into her memory and forced herself to think about the case at hand.

"Was the factory open?"

"No. Deserted except for the one guy emptying the trash."

"So . . . was it . . .?

"Intentional? Self-inflicted? I wondered the same thing, but they didn't find a gun."

"But he was just found innocent of all charges. Why would someone want to kill him now?"

"That's a question for the police to pursue, not you. That's not why I asked you to come along. The chief has sent two patrolmen to the college and the Cartwright residence to round up the family and bring them to the hospital. They only do that when they don't expect the patient to live. I thought you might be a comfort to Olivia."

The scene in the ER was also familiar. Rows of plastic chairs provided no relief for people already in pain or fear. Some cried; others stared into space. Anxious parents held hands as they waited for a doctor's report. A nauseous woman huddled over a waste basket, while her male companion held her hair away from her face.

Across the room, a minor scuffle was taking place. Three uniformed policemen were trying to control one hysterical woman, who kicked out at them with her pointy-toed high heels, screamed in their faces, and refused to let them put handcuffs on her wrists. "He's my husband. I have a right to see him. I want to take him home."

"Ma'am. The doctor will be here to talk to you soon. Please, oh . . . ouch! She bit me!"

Sarah's eyes widened in alarm as she recognized the woman—Emily Cartwright. And nearby, shrinking against the wall as if she wished it would open and swallow her up, stood Olivia. Without hesitation, Sarah went to her and pulled her into the shelter of her arms.

"It's going to be all right, Olivia. Don't be scared. We're here to help."

"I'm afraid they're going to arrest her. She's drunk—as usual. She's drunk by this time every Saturday, but on most days, she doesn't have to face a crisis. She will start throwing things any minute now. And by the time the doctor gets here to talk to us about daddy's condition, she'll be unconscious on the floor."

"You can't help her, but you can be strong for yourself. Has anyone told you what happened?"

"No. They just said that someone shot him, and we needed to come to the hospital."

At that moment David spotted Sarah and approached, not noticing the young woman beside her. He was shaking his head in despair. "DOA."

Olivia looked up in alarm. "DOA? Doesn't that mean 'dead . . . on . . . arrival?'"

"David!" Sarah shouted at him, but he had already realized what he had done. He clamped his hand across his mouth as Olivia crumpled to the floor.

In due time, the chaos sorted itself out. Olivia roused, pale and shaken, but otherwise in control. Sarah found her a bottle of water and explained as best she could what was happening. Mrs. Cartwright, too, calmed down, at least enough to allow the officers to abandon their attempts to handcuff her. Hospital personnel checked her vital signs but refused to give her a sedative because of the amount of alcohol in her system. They settled for bringing her a cup of black coffee and finding her a padded chair in a corner hidden from the rest of the waiting room.

David returned to Sarah and Olivia. "Is there someone we

can call, Olivia? A family member, perhaps, or a close friend of the family—someone who can take charge of the details for a while?"

"Uncle Johnny! Someone needs to notify him! That's Jonathan Cartwright, daddy's younger brother. He and Aunt Judy aren't always on the best of terms with our family, but we all have Sunday brunch together every week. They'll be planning to show up in the morning with their thirteen-year-old twins. I must call them tonight."

"It's best if you leave that to the police, dear. Do you have a phone number?"

She showed David the number on her phone, and he copied it. "Let me see if I can reach him."

Within a few minutes, a younger version of Jamison Cartwright burst into the ER, and Olivia rushed to meet him, throwing herself into his arms as she cried for the first time. "Oh, Uncle Johnny, he's dead. Somebody shot him!"

David interrupted them to introduce himself as the district attorney and to explain what was going on. "The police brought the family here because the first ambulance report said they were stabilizing Mr. Cartwright, but by the time they reached the hospital, his heart had stopped. Attempts at resuscitation failed. Mrs. Cartwright is still demanding to see her husband, but . . ."

"She's dead-drunk herself, isn't she? She always is after a Saturday afternoon drink fest with 'the girls.' So what happens now? Do you need the family here anymore?"

"No. In fact, it would be better if you could take them home, or—better yet—take them somewhere private so that the gossip-hungry public and the newspaper hounds won't have access to them."

"I can take them to our house. Judy and I can put them up for a few days and shield them. Can you tell me how long it will be before you can release the . . . the body?"

"It will be several days. There will have to be an autopsy, and the ongoing investigation will put both the Cartwright residence and the company offices off limits as crime scenes. You might want to consider arranging a private funeral and burial. It's been a long time since this little community had a murder committed here, and every ghoul in town will try to discover what's going on."

Once the Cartwrights had departed, David took Sarah home and then went back to the synagogue. His mother met him with hands on hips, demanding to know where he had gone when there was work to be done. Without revealing details, he explained what had happened.

"Sarah is exhausted after dealing with her student, so I've dropped her off at her apartment. She said to tell you she will be here to help with lunch tomorrow, however. This is a big case, mother, maybe the most important case the DA's office has ever had to handle. You must be patient with me if I'm tied up and can't make a family occasion now and then."

Mr. Cohen had been listening to the details and looked shaken himself. "Jim Cartwright has been my client for over thirty years. I can't wrap my mind around what has happened. But I promise you, son. I'll do whatever I can for you—and the Cartwright family. Just let me know what you need."

"Thanks, dad. I'll need lots of guidance, and I appreciate having you at my back."

David experienced a moment of sheer rage the next morning when he opened the *Birch Falls Gazette* to see the front-page headline declaring MURDER MOST FOUL. "Someone needs to explain to the editor that he is not producing a tabloid for the supermarket counter," he grumbled to himself. Still, he understood that nothing he might say or do would matter to someone more interested in selling newspapers than in printing a factual account. And the murder of a man like Jamison Cartwright was going to sell a lot of newspapers.

~

The month of March began on a high note, with beautiful weather and the promise of even better days to come. No one wanted to remember the adage: "If March comes in like a lamb, it will go out like a lion." After the first flurry of facts about the shooting, the police offered no additional information, and popular interests turned to more relevant matters such as the approach of a long week's break in the routine.

David's office was busy combing the crime scene and reviewing everything they could learn about the factory owner. But most of those details were boring and did not lend themselves to local gossip. Hannah was filling her calendar with book signings and public appearances by Elijah the Cat, and Mrs. Cohen had already started preparations for Passover. The Cartwright family disappeared from public view.

In Bailey Hall, students were planning getaway trips or local parties, while the faculty was busy preparing for their next job candidate. After the debacle of Elizabeth Bradford, their hopes for filling the open American history position rested on a successful visit by Gabriel Ramirez. They had delegated Sarah once more to take him to breakfast on Thursday morning and give him a quick tour of the town on the way to campus. Sarah expected his Latin good looks, but his overwhelming enthusiasm caught her by surprise.

"What a wonderful little town this is," he said. "It reminds me of the stories my grandparents told of Cuban villagers and their sense of community. I miss that in the crowded anonymity of cities like Miami and Tampa."

A little later, as Sarah parked in a visitor slot near the front gate, Ramirez stared at the buildings facing him and said, almost under his breath, "It looks like an old Spanish mission."

"I'm not sure about the Spanish part," Sarah answered, "but these buildings date back to the eighteenth century and used to be part of a Catholic nunnery."

"They make me feel as if I have come home."

His words set the tone for the rest of his visit. He charmed his way from one office to the next, taking delight in everything he learned. And at his job talk, he seduced the students with his first breath. In a deep rich baritone, he began by singing:

"Give me your tired, your poor,
Your huddled masses yearning to breathe free,
The wretched refuse of your teeming shore.
Send these, the homeless, tempest-tossed to me,
I lift my lamp beside the golden door!"

After a brief pause, he spoke. "Do you recognize the words?"

"That's the inscription on the Statue of Liberty," someone volunteered.

"Yes. I shall never forget the first time I heard it. My grandparents were Mariel Boat People, refugees from Castro and the communist takeover of their beloved homeland of Cuba. One summer, when I was about six or seven, my grandparents took me to New York City. We stood at the base of the Statue of Liberty, and my grandfather read those words aloud.

"'That's America speaking,' he said. 'We were the tired, the poor, the homeless, and she took us in. Everything you have is her gift to you. You must never forget her or her words.'

"I have kept that lesson in my heart, and it is the lesson I must pass on. It's why I have studied American history and why I feel I must teach. The story of America begins with the first primitive people to set foot on this land, and it continues today with every refugee who seeks shelter at this golden door and then joins in the effort to light the way for others. I will give you only an example or two today. We will look at others in the months to come."

At the end of the talk, Kevin Chalmers stationed himself at the door to pull the members of his search committee aside. "Are we agreed?" he asked.

"We are."

"Can we make sure we don't lose him? I hate to make him wait until we get back from spring break. There's no telling what other offers he might get between now and then."

"That worries me, too, Julia. With your agreement, I'll take this to the dean this afternoon and push to get an offer on the table before Gabriel leaves tomorrow evening."

The ploy worked, and the History Department left for spring break on Friday afternoon knowing that they had just hired their second new professor. Sarah was as enthusiastic as her colleagues, but overshadowing her relief was the continuing threat of an unsolved murder. Olivia had not returned to classes. That was understandable, but Sarah worried about her.

David kept Sarah informed when he could do so without breaking confidentiality. Thus, she knew that Mr. Wilson, who had shouted out his accusations at Mr. Cartwright in the courtroom, had an airtight alibi for the day of the murder. He and his family had been in Memphis to get a second opinion on their son's condition at Le Bonheur Children's Hospital. Jack Dunlap, Olivia's sometimes escort, had been out of town.

In fact, Cartwright himself had sent Jack to Knoxville to nego-
tiate a deal to make a Pencil Pet of Smokey, the University of
Tennessee's mascot, a Blue Tick Coonhound.

Who else might be a suspect? The whistle-blower was a
person of interest, but David argued that an anonymous
letter-writer was likely to prefer a pen instead of a gun. Olivia
herself had once suggested that almost any of her father's
employees might wish him dead. Sarah feared that the
murderer was a member of the family, the discovery of which
would bring further suffering upon them all. March might
still go out like a lion.

Chapter Twenty-Nine

IRONS IN THE FIRE

March 12–21, 2010

S arah learned several important lessons during the ten days of spring break. Not all of them were pleasant, but each one would serve her well in the coming years. She had worried that the directors of the Jubilee Project would fire her if she cut back on her efforts. She had called Doctor Yearwood to tell him she could not host a local program, only to have him shrug it off as a minor inconvenience. "Don't worry about it," he had said. "Truth is, we have more volunteers than we can use. Somebody else will pick up the date you had scheduled."

When Sarah told David about their brief discussion, he only smiled at her. "That's what happens when you're a little frog in a big pond. It's sometimes better to stay in your little pond where you can feel like the big frog."

For a moment she felt a flash of anger. Then she laughed at how perceptive he was. "OK, you're right. The Jubilee Project was always their show, not mine. I'm better off concentrating on my own projects."

And she was already juggling two efforts of her own. Hannah had scheduled her appearances to introduce *The Passover Guest*. At their first public signing, the entire Cohen family attended, and David had presented each of the authors with an ink stamp bearing Elijah's right front paw print.

"I figured he deserved to 'sign' his own books."

"Is this his paw print? How in the world did you pull that off without letting me see it?"

"Easy. I just carried an ink pad in my pocket until you left me alone with the cat. The hard part was getting the ink off his paw before he left his prints all over your apartment."

Besides the two bookstore book signings, Sarah appeared for 'Story Time' at the local library and gave brief talks at the Rotary Club and Lions Club luncheons, the Methodist Women's Prayer Breakfast, a local writers' critique group, and three private book clubs. Except for the two service club meetings in local restaurants, Elijah accompanied her in his own little traveling stroller. After one such engagement, Sarah complained, "I am still the little frog. Elijah is the one who gets all the attention around here."

The flurry of publicity surrounding *The Passover Guest* had an unexpected but beneficial effect on Sarah's second project, which she referred to as *The Story of Cotton*. It wasn't a catchy title, but it would serve as a placeholder as she worked. It meant she was writing—and making progress—on her first scholarly monograph. And for that, she had to thank *The Passover Guest*. Her audiences at the talks and book signings treated her as a published author. Their acceptance gave her a heady confidence in her own ability, one that carried over when she sat down to work on a more serious project.

The basic structure of *The Story of Cotton* was already in place, thanks to the stubborn insistence of her dissertation advisor, Dr. Les Kaplan. "Keep it interesting," he insisted.

"Your statistics are fine, but they are for your information, not for your readers. I don't want to read statistics. I want you to tell me what you've learned from them. Write for an educated public, not for a narrow-minded and opinionated board of academics."

Sarah had fought him every step of the way. Her fellow students were counting footnotes, while her own advisor was telling her to cut them to a minimum. Every article she found about writing a dissertation insisted upon multiple sources, extensive quotations, and a discussion of theory. Dr. Kaplan wanted a plot line, a hero, a goal, a villain, a crisis, and a satisfying conclusion.

"I'm not writing a novel," she would protest, and he would answer, "Perhaps you should be. Tell a delightful story, and your readers will thank you."

Now, at last, she understood, and with her editing pen in hand she was making her way through the original manuscript, cutting out every dry piece of expository writing and substituting a wonderful story. She plundered her lecture notes for descriptions of interesting characters. She emphasized dramatic moments. And she was learning one more important lesson. Writing was fun again.

March 22, 2010

On the day classes resumed, Sarah felt relaxed and energized even though the history faculty faced an immediate complication. During the following eight days, the last two teaching applicants were scheduled back-to-back. Emily Pottersfield would arrive on Thursday, March 25th; Thomas Etheridge would follow on Monday, March 29th. No one except Sarah had noticed that March 29th was also the first night of Passover. A candidate visit complicated her schedule because she had already agreed to spend the first Seder of Passover with the Jewish Student Association and the second with the Cohen family.

Julia agreed to rearrange the schedule. Sarah would have lunch with Thomas on Monday and take him to breakfast on his second day, thus leaving her free on both evenings. Sarah was not looking forward to the dual roles she would juggle, but she was more than ready to have the whole job search process finished.

The AHA interviews, she had decided, were nothing more than a giant boondoggle, a chance for young professors and aspiring doctoral candidates to travel somewhere interesting at university expense. Why else would six professors from Smokey Mountain University have been willing to travel across the country to San Diego in the dead of winter, during the heaviest period of air travel, and just a week after the most expensive holiday of the entire year? And had it been necessary for the department to read almost 200 multi-page applications, attend several presentations in Louisville, conduct three days of formal interviews in San Diego, and then spend twelve days entertaining the candidates on their own campus? It seemed like a waste of time, since most decisions boiled down to popularity contests. Sarah fumed but pasted a smile on her face and went along with this charade because she knew she, too, was on trial.

The last two candidates were both delightful human beings, full of enthusiasm for their fields of study and eager to embark on a teaching career. Emily Pottersfield had lost some of her British accent after her year at Cornell, so she sounded almost like an American, albeit a sophisticated one. And because of her upbringing as the daughter of a British diplomat, she understood European politics well. She possessed a broad knowledge of the rise and fall of the

British Empire in India. She had a firm understanding of the political positions of the various European states and of the process that was pulling them together into the European Union. And perhaps best from an American point of view, she had no illusions about the crumbling English aristocracy nor about the waning influence of the British monarchy. She struck faculty and students alike as an ideal choice.

But Thomas Etheridge also had a strong appeal. As a former military officer, he carried himself with natural authority. After spending a year studying at the Army War College, his understanding of twentieth-century warfare was unmatched among most other modern historians. His doctoral degree was in American history, but his firsthand knowledge of the greater world extended not only to Europe but to China, Japan, Korea, Southeast Asia, and the Middle East.

"I hate to see us lose somebody like him," Kevin commented at the department meeting on Tuesday afternoon. "He can supply the broad understanding our students need."

"But Kevin," Julia protested, "We advertised for someone with a degree in World History, and he doesn't have it. If we hire him and reject everyone with a world history degree, we might open ourselves to lawsuits."

"Excuse me," Trevor Monroe spoke up for the first time. "I think you are missing an important factor here—my departure. Why not ask the dean for permission to fill my open slot with this ideal American historian? He's been vetted, and he's what you will need. What virtue is there in letting my position sit empty for a year and then repeating the hiring process?"

"Good idea, except for the details. The dean cannot offer anything except a one-year contract without a national advertisement. He can, however, grant a three-year extension within the university to someone with a current one-year contract. We don't know that Doctor Etheridge will accept that kind of offer, because it carries a certain amount of risk and an extra probationary year. But if we agree, I will pose the question to him before he leaves tonight."

Julia and Sarah left the department meeting together and strolled down the hall to their offices. "You should be proud of yourself," Sarah said. "They asked you to recruit three new faculty members, and it looks as if you may have recruited four. If you're not careful, Kevin will make your search responsibility permanent."

"Ah, but the next time I'll know better than to accept it. I am pleased, however, and I have one additional scheme up my sleeve."

"What's that?"

"There's a terrible imbalance in our teaching responsibilities. You three Americanists cover 400 years of history, while three European professors cover almost 4000 years. I know we'll never balance it out, but it's only fair to suggest that we could use a fourth European position. And with a little bit of rearranging, we could put several of us into positions where we are more comfortable in our background knowledge. Kevin is not a huge fan of the Middle Ages. He would love to teach advanced courses in ancient history. He finds anything that happened after Charlemagne—or perhaps the Vikings —to be annoying. I flounder a bit when the Middle Ages give way to the start of the Renaissance. I'm much surer of myself when I get to the Reformation, the Wars of Religion, and the Industrial Revolution. What we need is a dedicated late medievalist with interests that lead into the Renaissance. And next year we will have . . ."

"Ramona Bishop!"

"We should be able to offer her the same scheme as Kevin is proposing for Thomas Etheridge. Even better, I think I can convince the dean that we can add a seventh person to the department at no extra expense."

"That may be a stretch."

"No. Every year, someone quits or goes on sabbatical. With only five or six professors, the school must hire a one-year replacement each time to handle the class load. But with seven of us on board, when one goes on sabbatical, the other six can handle the numbers without the need to launch a job search and hire a one-year replacement."

"And I'm guessing you already have all those figures in hand to prove your point."

"I do."

"I agree, but I wouldn't count on the Dean's ability to follow a logical argument. Give him some time between this proposal and Kevin's request."

March 31, 2010

With the end of the recruitment season, Sarah was feeling more in control of her life—or she had been until Kevin poked his head into her door on Wednesday morning.

"Bright and chipper this morning, I see. What good news can you offer me about our new Smoky Mountain Historical Society?"

She floundered. "Well, I, uh . . . as I've been telling the students, we can't get started until we have permission from the administration."

"Which we received over three weeks ago. Did you not get the message?"

"No, I . . ."

"Get on with it, Chomsky."

Embarrassed and panicked, Sarah dialed the dean's office, only to hear Maria's cheerful voice on the line. "Hi, Dr. Chomsky. How may I help you?"

"Is Martha Wright available?"

"Not right now. She's been in the dean's office for almost an hour. Can I have her call you when she escapes?"

"Please." Putting down the phone, Sarah drew a deep breath and gave herself a quick lecture. "Calm down. You can't go back, but you can fix things from now on. Maybe this is a job for our graduate students. We can talk about it in class tonight.

~

Sarah announced office hours for Wednesday afternoon, although she hoped that no one would show up. She assumed that students would be getting ready for the four-day weekend that would begin tomorrow and run through Easter Monday. To discourage casual drop-ins, she left the office door open only a crack. And to appear busy, she began making notes about the organization of the historical society. Still, her inner conscience would not let her ignore a student who had a legitimate problem.

When Chad Overstreet arrived to announce that his parents were willing to help him finish his college degree, Sarah smiled, but she did not have time to help him integrate his study of history with his love of football. A simple solution occurred to her that might let her slip out of the discussion.

"You know, Chad, there's a graduate student in the department whom you ought to meet. His name is Rick McBride, and he is an assistant football coach at the local high school. He is worried about the lack of safety equipment on the playing field, and I know he has struggled with the same questions you have about career choices. Come see me after the Easter break. I'll arrange for the two of you to get together."

After Chad's visit came Maria Hernandez. "What can I help you with?" Sarah asked.

"Oh, I don't have a problem. I just thought we could talk a bit more about that idea you mentioned—that I could become a community activist."

"I know little more than I have already told you, but . . ." Little reminder bells were going off in Sarah's mind—two students with unique problems but a similar solution. "Did you remember that we have a community organizer in our department?"

"I had forgotten about that. Who is she?"

"Erica Scott is a beginning graduate student this year. She comes to us after getting her degree at Spelman and finding a job here in Birch Falls as a community activist. In class, she mentioned that Michelle Obama is her role model. I'm sure she would love to talk to you. We have class tonight, and she usually arrives early. If you come back this evening around a quarter to six, I'd be happy to introduce you."

With an empty office at last, Sarah leaned back to contemplate how easy it had been to redirect the students to someone better able to handle their problems. "I'm learning," she told herself. "Kevin may not be impressed with sending them to our graduate students instead of the proper university office. But this might be a good way to bring the department together."

Her self-satisfaction buoyed her spirits until another knock at the door brought her back to earth. "They always come in threes," she grumbled. She knew before she opened the door that the visitor would be Olivia.

The young woman was pale and more somber than usual,

but she assumed a determined smile when Sarah opened the door.

"You're busy, Dr. Chomsky, and I won't keep you. I just have two things I need to tell you."

"I'm not all that busy, Olivia. Come in, sit down, and tell me how you're doing."

"Things are falling into place, I think. It was helpful to have spring break come when it did. That gave me some time to get regain my balance and get my thoughts organized." She closed her eyes for a moment, and the smile faded. "I never knew a death in the family involved so much work. I expected my world to stop. Instead, I've had dozens of things to do—sign papers, find documents, change signatures, open safe deposit boxes, empty closets, close offices, notify friends and organizations, cancel memberships, drop subscriptions—the lists just go on. And with a murder investigation ongoing, there's no end in sight."

"I understand. I'm surprised to see you back at school so soon."

The girl's laugh had no humor in it. "School is a good place to hide. But that's not a problem. I wanted to come by and thank you for coming to the emergency room the night daddy died. I was feeling invisible, and it helped me to know that somebody was there for me. Although . . . I don't know how you knew about what had happened."

"You met my fiancé one night at Matt's bar, although he introduced himself then as a member of the police force. He is now the acting district attorney, so the police notify him immediately of all major crimes. Saturday was a Jewish holiday, and we were both at the synagogue helping to prepare a dinner for the poor that would be offered that night. When the office called David in, he recognized the victim's name and asked me to come along in case you needed me."

"I did."

Sarah smiled and changed the subject. "You mentioned two things you needed to tell me."

"Mother and I spent a day in the lawyer's office learning what arrangements daddy had left. His plans were elaborate and detailed. He had arranged for three annuities—one to support my mother in a comfortable lifestyle for the rest of her life; one to pay for my education through a master's degree; and one to pay Uncle Johnny for assuming general responsibility for probate and for managing any trusts that might come into play.

"Then he had put the rest of his holdings—the house, the company, the factory, his stock options—into a trust that will come to me when I turn thirty. Until then, Uncle Johnny will manage the trust fund for me. But there is a caveat. If I have not earned my master's degree in business administration by age thirty, I will have to wait another five years to receive the trust. I believe you could call that 'reaching out from the grave to control my life.'" She grimaced and then continued.

"At any rate, I have given up the idea of earning a double major for my BA because I'm now working under a deadline. I have declared business administration as my major, with history relegated to a minor. And that means you will no longer be my advisor. I regret that because you've been so helpful, but I have to think like a businesswoman because I have a company to run."

"I wish you much success."

The girl's face crumpled. "Can I come back and visit once in a while?"

"I hope you will."

"And can I get a hug?"

"Anytime you need one."

Chapter Thirty

APRIL SHOWERS

Thursday, April 1, 2010

On April Fool's Day, Kevin designated Gwen, the department secretary, as monitor of the women's restroom to prevent a replay of last year's itching powder prank. But unlike the preceding year when a few students were determined to cause trouble, anticipation of an upcoming four-day weekend kept the undergraduates content to finish the day's classes so they could be on the road toward home or some other attraction.

In the Grub Hub, history graduate students congregated to plan the first meeting of the Smoky Mountain Historical Society—a reception for declared history majors during the last week of classes. In the faculty lounge, Kevin posted a tentative schedule of the following year's class offerings. Trevor left early for a flight to New York, and Julia had packed her car for a road trip to introduce Bert to her Georgia family. Sarah had no plans beyond getting through the day. She dreaded the disruption of a new prank, but the day passed without incident.

If truth be told, Sarah needed that long weekend as much as the students did. She slept late on Friday morning and then puttered around the apartment, taking care of a few chores, playing with the cat, and letting her thoughts leap ahead to summer vacation. The sparkling diamond ring on her left hand was a constant reminder she needed to make some decisions. David had been pushing her for several weeks to set a date for their wedding, and he was not in the mood to be told she didn't have time to think about it. The moment for decision-making had arrived.

Sarah and David walked back to the apartment hand-in-hand after prayers at the synagogue. They relished the evening's peacefulness after a social hour that had offered nothing but gossip along with the matzoh crackers and chopped liver.

"I love this time of night when the sky has turned to navy blue and the stars are just beginning to pop out. It's lovely to know I have three entire days of leisure ahead of me."

"And just how do you plan to spend them?" David teased.

"I've been meaning to talk to you about that."

"Well, before you get too far into your plans, let me insert one scheduling note. I promised my mother I would remind you that she is expecting you and Elijah to join us for the last supper of Passover on Tuesday night."

"It's already on my calendar."

"You understand that means more matzoh ball soup and gefilte fish[1], don't you? I don't know about you, but I am almost willing to sell my soul for a bite of leavened bread."

"Oh, please don't. I have designs on your soul."

"Whoa! That sounds interesting."

"David! I was hoping we could spend some time this weekend talking about wedding plans."

"Plans? As in one of your famous five-year plans? I thought we could just pick a date and elope."

"Not a chance! I tried the eloping thing once, remember, and it didn't turn out so well. This time I want all the rituals in place to make sure our bonds are permanent."

They talked late into the night, going over suitable dates on the Hebrew calendar, reviewing the guidelines for marriage as explained in the Torah[2] and regaling one another with stories about horrible wedding excesses they had seen. Their general choices coincided, although the details required negotiations over the next three days. But by April 6, the last day of Passover, they were ready to disclose their plans to the Cohen family.

~

David and Sarah let their excitement carry them through the traditional Passover meal. Then, after the last glass of wine, David cleared his throat and tapped his glass for attention. "We have a series of announcements. We have set our wedding date for June 15th."

"Of what year?" his mother asked. "You can't mean this coming June. That would give me only two months to make plans."

"Mother, dear. We are not children, and we can make our own plans. In fact, we've already settled most of the details. This is only an information session. We are getting married on this coming June 15th. We would like to hold the ceremony in your back yard, if you will permit it, although we have two alternatives if they become necessary."

"But David, while our rose gardens are lovely, they don't leave enough room for the kinds of crowds you can expect."

"We're not having a crowd, father. Sarah can explain."

"We spent hours going over potential lists of attendees, and our conclusion was that we know too many people. And trying to choose among family members, work colleagues, old friends, neighbors—it was just impossible. We agreed that what we want is a small and intimate group. The Torah requires a minyan[3], and that's what we shall have: our two sets of parents, plus Hannah and Jacob. Then there's Rabbi Leibowicz and his wife Sheila, who brought our families together, and Dr. and Mrs. Jankowski. He's a cantor and a vocal music professor. I've gotten to know his family well because we work together at the college as sponsors of the Jewish Students' Alliance. They are the family I join for Passover each year. I'm hoping he will take part in our ceremony by singing some of the prayers. That makes ten for a minyan—all practicing Jews who have taken us into their hearts."

"I agree that it's a suitable minyan. But my dears, what about your attendants? Don't you need a maid of honor, bridesmaids, a best man, groomsmen . . ."

"No, ma'am. Our parents will escort each of us to the altar, as is our long-standing tradition. The attendants you describe are modern—and pretty much shikse[4]—additions. They serve no purpose except to show off how many friends you have. We need just two Jewish witnesses unrelated to us by blood, and Jacob and Mrs. Leibowicz can provide those signatures."

"And what about your wedding gifts and the bridal registry and . . .?"

"We don't need wedding gifts, mother. Sarah and I are both adults with sizable incomes and two separate households. We already have duplicate pieces of furniture and two kitchens with toasters and coffee makers and dishes. It's going to be hard enough sorting out what we want to use in the new house without worrying about where to put the pink alabaster candy dish that arrives as a wedding gift."

Mrs. Cohen appeared to be near tears. "So, no reception, either?"

"After the ceremony, we plan to celebrate with a dinner at Isolde's for the whole minyan."

"But, they often have overflow crowds. What if we can't all get in?"

"It's a Tuesday night, Mrs. Cohen. It won't be a problem." Sarah was trying to be reassuring.

"We've already reserved their piano bar for the evening," David added. "They will set up a formal table for twelve, with room left for dancing. There may also be a few side tables for special friends who drop in later in the evening."

"That sounds lovely, I'm sure, but did you consider our country club?" Mr. Cohen asked. "They might have a larger space, and the rates could be cheaper too, since I am a founding member."

"Dad, it's our wedding, and we have a special reason for wanting to include Isolde's." David and Sarah exchanged private smiles before he launched into a fuller explanation. "The piano bar at the restaurant was the site of our first serious 'let's-get-all-dressed-up' date. It is also the place where we first realized we were falling in love—during a Valentine's Day dinner date. We pledged ourselves to a committed relationship over a dinner there. It's where we got engaged. And it's where we will celebrate our wedding."

"All right. I admit defeat." But Mr. Cohen was not through. "It's your special day—just so long as you include all the traditional rituals. There must be a separate ketubah[5] signing to spell out the duties and responsibilities of your marriage."

"That will work," Mrs. Cohen interrupted. "We'll have a small party for the friends who are not invited to the wedding. We'll serve lots of wine. I can make knishes and a cinnamon babka,[6] and maybe . . ."

"Miriam, please, don't . . . "

"Sorry. I just need to be a part of this."

"You're the mother of the groom, my dear. That's enough. Now, as I was saying, the ceremony may take place in our rose gardens, so long as you erect a fitting chuppah[7] to shelter your altar. You must observe the customs of presenting the bridal ring, the circlings, the glass broken under foot[8], and the seven blessings. I trust Rabbi Leibowicz will guide you through the process."

"I'm sure he will. He's very excited about our wedding."

"He knew before we did?" Mrs. Cohen was about to break into tears again.

"Only because we had to consult him to make sure our date did not fall on one of the forbidden days of the Hebrew calendar[9]. We weren't slighting you, mother."

"I don't mean to put a damper on your plans, my dears. I'm just feeling a little emotional and overwhelmed. It's all happening so fast."

"Speaking of fast . . ." Mr. Cohen stepped in again. "I noticed you slipped right on past that mention of a new house. Have you been house hunting, too?"

"Uh . . . well . . . Something came up two weeks ago. A friend received a surprise promotion that involves a cross-country move. That meant he needed to sell their brand new house. He knew we were engaged, so he had his realtor call us. We went to see it and fell in love with it on the spot. We made an offer, and they accepted. The bank approved a fifteen-year mortgage. Now we're waiting for the paperwork to go through. That's why we went ahead with a June wedding. Once we have a house, it would be a shame not to use it." He grinned at his parents, who now were both looking stunned.

Mrs. Cohen was the first to recover. "So, Sarah, tell us about the house."

"Well, it's in the Black Forest subdivision, close to the college. The address is 1729 Middleton Circle. The house itself is a split level with a two-car garage, build on a sloping lot as a fill-in within a well-developed neighborhood, so the landscaping around us is mature. You enter a foyer with a powder room and coat closet. Then on the main level there's an open floor plan with a living room, dining area, and an eat-in kitchen. Off the kitchen at one end is the laundry and a mudroom leading to the garage.

"Stairs off the living room lead down to an all-purpose room with lots of library shelves and an enormous stone fireplace. There's also a smaller room with a private bath that can serve either as an office or a guest bedroom.

"On the upper level, one side of the hall gives access to the master bedroom with walk-in closets and *en suite* bath. The other side of the hall has two bedrooms with an adjoining bath between them. Again, the arrangement is flexible enough to allow them to be children's rooms, as they are now, or for one to be an office and the other a guest room.

"From the all-purpose room you can walk out onto a covered patio and the yard beyond. It borders on the edge of a golf course but is pretty much out of range of stray golf balls. And above the patio is a small balcony extending out from the master suite."

"It sounds like a forever home, not like the little starter I was expecting," Mr. Cohen commented.

"We're getting a late start. It's time to play catch-up."

∽

Friday, April 16, 2010

Sarah went back to work, pleased that the Cohens had accepted their plans. She was sure nothing could dampen her spirits. But it was April. She should have expected a shower or two.

Only three more weeks of classes remained after Easter break, and semester projects were already coming due. Sarah's graduate class focused on the use of original documents. The topic had been a challenge because the class contained ten students whose areas of specialization spanned times and people as varied as ancient Mesopotamia and modern Russia.

Since she could not master the complete history of the world, Sarah suggested the students teach each other about their areas of specialization. Each one had been in charge of a class session and had described for the class what kinds of documents were available.

Matt Garrison, for example, concentrated on ancient civilizations. For his class, he introduced the use of cuneiform and hieroglyphics, which raised the question of which symbols had been most useful in developing modern writing —pictographs or wedge-shaped representations of sounds. He left them with the challenge of being the first to decipher the markings of Linear A. At the opposite end of the time line, Michael McGarrity, who had spent his military career in Afghanistan, explained the futility of translating Arabic documents written by al-Qaeda leaders spewing propaganda.

The major writing assignment in the class was to pick a single document from their areas of specialization and to identify from it a piece of advice its author might offer to a modern American. It was a quirky assignment, but the students had found it fascinating. On this Friday afternoon, Sarah was reading a paper written by Jean Pendergast, a medievalist and a former nun, who had chosen the writings of Julian of Norwich, a fourteenth-century anchorite. Her title was "'What Julian of Norwich Might Tell a Young Woman about Love."

Jean was a talented writer, and Sarah was enjoying the paper until a series of crashes and shouting interrupted the quiet afternoon. When Sarah went to her door to protest the noise, a young policeman blocked her way.

"Stay inside your office, ma'am. Everything's under control. As soon as we make our arrest, we'll be on our way."

"An arrest? Of whom and for what? This is private property. You can't just waltz in here and grab someone. Do you have a warrant?"

"Yes, ma'am. Right here." He waved it at her but did not show its content. A second policeman appeared in the doorway of a classroom. With him was Trevor Monroe, his arms pulled behind his back.

"Here, Jackson, cuff this guy and hold him for trying to interfere with a policeman performing his duties."

By now the noise had drawn Kevin from his office, and he came charging down the hall, shouting, "What the hell is going on?"

At the door of the classroom, several students clustered, jostling for a better view. Their excited voices added to the chaos.

"Let's everybody calm down. The older of the policemen held up his hands. We have a warrant for the arrest of Miss Olivia Cartwright for the murder of her father, Jamison Cartwright. Turn Miss Cartwright over to us, and we'll let everyone get back to work."

"We will do nothing of the kind, at least not until I see evidence of your authority to make an arrest. And in the meantime, take those handcuffs off my professor. He was just protecting his students."

Sara smiled to herself as she realized Kevin had found his voice of authority. As all eyes turned toward him, a young woman elbowed her way through the crowd of onlookers. She stood, cool and dignified, alone in the hallway.

"It's all right, Dr. Chalmers. I've rather been expecting

this. I'm Olivia Cartwright, sergeant. You were asking for me?" She held out her wrists, ready for her own set of handcuffs.

Sarah gasped and tried to step forward, only to find that Julia had a firm grip on her arm. "Let it be. You will only make matters worse. Best to let David know what has happened and allow him and his authority to take over."

It was an excellent suggestion, and Sarah retreated to her office phone, dialing David's private number. When it went to voicemail, she left a frantic message. "Call me. Your hotshot cops have just arrested Olivia and caused a major uproar on the third floor of Bailey Hall."

As she frowned in frustration, a familiar figure tapped on her door. "I'm sorry, Chad, but this is a bad time. Whatever your problem, I'm afraid it will have to wait until Monday."

"It can't wait, Dr. Chomsky. It's about Olivia. I saw her get arrested, and . . ."

"That's a very private matter. The last I heard, you didn't even know her name."

"A lot has happened since then. We've had several classes together, and I've gotten to know her pretty well. We are not dating yet, but we study together sometimes, and take walks, and talk about school. She told me about her father's death, and I know how upset she has been. Being arrested and taken to jail is going to be very hard on her. And since I have had a little experience along those lines, I thought I might help her handle it."

"Maybe so, but I know no more about what's going on than you do. I can't help."

"Well, it's just . . . If you see her, would you tell her that I am concerned and that I'm available anytime day or night if she needs me?"

"That much I can do, but Chad, please don't go poking around and making more trouble for her."

"I won't. I promise."

Chapter Thirty-One
REVELATIONS

Friday, April 16, 2010

That evening, David tried to explain that he had little control over how policemen handled arrests. Although he agreed that they should not have interrupted a class in session, it was not the district attorney's place to tell them so. "That's the advantage I lost when I gave up the title of 'Police Liaison Officer.'"

"But they shouldn't have tried to arrest Olivia in the first place," Sarah protested.

"That's not for you to judge. Look, Sarah. The police have to operate within certain parameters. They know, for example, that family members or intimate friends commit most murders. Victims almost always know their assailants. In a case of what appears to be an act of passion, they look first to the immediate family. And the Cartwright family is a small grouping. It includes Cartwright's wife, his daughter, and his brother, along with a sister-in-law and 13-year-old twins—a niece and a nephew. Among that group, we know that the brother and his family were out of town when the murder occurred. They were attending an all-day end-of-season basketball clinic in Chattanooga. The parents were chaperones on the school bus; the son was a player; and the daughter was a cheerleader. The bus did not return to Birch Falls Junior High until 4:45 in the afternoon, long after the shooting. So that entire family is in the clear."

"Which leaves the wife and the daughter."

"Yes, with these added bits of information. We have the gun that Jamison Cartwright had registered. Ballistics proved beyond a doubt that it fired the fatal shot, although someone had wiped it clean of prints. Of all the people interviewed so far, only the wife and daughter knew that Jamison Cartwright owned a gun, and only those two knew that he had moved that gun from the house to his office in the days following his trial over lead poisoning."

"OK, but why focus on the daughter rather than the wife?"

"Pure logic. Edith Cartwright has few friends, and those who know her consider her to be a mouse. She has little personality and fewer opinions about anything. She goes out on her own only once a week, on Saturday afternoons, when she joins a group of ladies-who-lunch at the country club. They drink all afternoon and spend more time gossiping than playing bridge. Other than that, she appears infrequently at social events, and even then, she clings to her husband's arm and says nothing. Those women who have known her the longest still don't know her well because she doesn't talk about herself. And none of them could imagine that she might get angry enough to kill someone.

"Olivia, on the other hand, made no secret of her ongoing feud with her father. She complained about how he tried to run her life. You know that to be so, Sarah, because she's talked to you about him. So, if you were a cop, which one would you accuse?"

"There's an old saying that you have to keep a suspicious eye on the quiet ones."

"Maybe so, but it won't stand up in a court of law."

"Neither will pure speculation. The police still have no actual evidence against Olivia, do they?"

"I can't tell you that, even if I knew what else they might have discovered."

"Sometimes I hate the logical lawyer side of you!"

"Hey, I'm just the messenger here. I'm giving you as much information as I can."

"All right. But I need to see her, David. She must be frightened half out of her mind at being locked up in a jail cell."

"You must not try to see her, Sarah. That's the worst thing you could do."

"How so?"

"Because it might look like she was taking you into her confidence. And someone building a case against her could use you to extract the very evidence you think they don't have."

"I don't understand."

"If—no, when—this goes to trial, the prosecution will try to emphasize a history of ill-feeling between father and daughter, and you are aware that they have been fighting for as long as you have known Olivia. The investigators are sure to learn of that black eye Olivia received over fall break, and they will ask you what you knew about it. The lawyer for the prosecution could have you declared a 'hostile witness' so that he could attack you and threaten you until you admitted whatever he wanted you to say. And in this case, you would have to admit that you suspected Cartwright of hitting his daughter."

"That's your job, isn't it? To prosecute the case against her."

"I won't be running the trial, Sarah. I will have to recuse

myself, just as I did in the whistle-blower case. But yes, my office will run the prosecution, and we will follow the rules of law. Those laws permit us to browbeat a hostile witness."

"Well, it sounds to me as if the police already know about the black eye, so there's no need for me to hide it. I'm not ignoring your advice, but in this case my professional responsibilities have to override your concern about how I might handle myself in a trial."

"And what might those professional responsibilities be, pray tell?"

"She's going need an extension for finishing her coursework, and we are less than a week away from the deadline. There's a protocol for postponing exams, too, but both require a great deal of paperwork. If Olivia is not free within the next few days, she risks losing an entire semester's credits. The permissions require her signatures and those of two witnesses, one of them mine as her advisor, along with a full explanation. I need to see her by Monday."

David's displeasure was obvious, but he weakened at the firm set of Sarah's chin. "All right, I yield. But only if you let me accompany you when you visit. I will let the warden know that we will be coming. But Sarah, please promise me you'll be cautious in what you do and say."

"What is it you're so afraid I'll do?"

"Sarah, I trust you, and I know you mean well, but you may not be familiar with all the ramifications of your words. For instance, when you state her reason for needing an extension, what will you say?"

"That she's in jail?"

"No, that's not specific enough."

"OK, she's in jail because the police think she killed her father."

"No. Besides being inaccurate, it makes her sound like a female Oedipus."

"What's inaccurate about it?"

"No one has yet charged her with murder. The correct explanation is that she is being held in protective custody as a material witness to a murder."

"Wow. Lawyers! Why does it matter?"

"Because the law is clear as to how long the police can hold a suspect without a bond hearing. The element of protective custody is the only flexible charge."

"I see why I'll need you, and I'll be happy to have you with me. So, we need to set a time. I teach until 11:20 on Monday, but I'll have time to get the paperwork ready first thing in the morning."

"And I have a lunch meeting that will run until 1:00. Can you meet me at my office around 1:30? We can walk to the jail from there."

~

On Monday afternoon, Sarah and David submitted to the jail's metal detector, emptied their pockets, put their loose belongings in a locker, and entered a small interview room provided with a table and three chairs. In a few minutes, a guard brought Olivia to the room and handcuffed her to one chair.

Olivia spoke first to David. "Who are you? You look like a lawyer. Or a cop. Oh, wait. I recognize you now. You were with Dr. Chomsky that night at the bar when you both rode to the rescue to save my virginal soul from a dastardly gigolo. You are the cop, aren't you?"

Olivia turned next to Sarah, not speaking, but looking belligerent. Then she gave a small, cynical laugh. "Look at your expression. You're already judging me. Orange isn't my color, is it? Why are you here? The guard said something about paperwork?"

"The official reason is that you need to request an extension for each of the courses you are taking. That will give you the entire summer to take your final exams. Once your present difficulties have sorted themselves out, you can contact each of your professors and make suitable arrangements."

"Why bother? By the end of the summer, I could sit on Death Row."

"Don't exaggerate, Olivia. Your situation is not that dire. I don't believe for a moment that you killed your father."

"That makes you a party of one."

"Knock off the tough girl act, Olivia!" David was using his best cop's voice to get her attention. "We're both here to help you. But if you'd rather face a murder rap without any help, just say the word."

"David . . ."

"No, Sarah, don't hush me. I have better things to do with my time than deal with a sulky teenager."

"I'm . . .I'm sorry, Dr. Chomsky. I'm just scared and alone. I don't know who I can trust. Only tough cookies survive in here."

"I've never betrayed your trust, Olivia. I brought David with me because he understands the legal system better than either of us. And he's right. We don't have time to play games. These are the petitions—one for each of your courses. You need to sign each one, and then we will each sign as a witness."

"Just sign? In case you haven't noticed, I'm handcuffed to the chair."

David was already on his feet. "Guard? Will you come in and uncuff this young woman so she can sign some paperwork? I promise she's not an escape risk."

Once they finished the formalities, everyone seemed to relax.

"Is there anything else we can do for you, Olivia? Anything you need?"

"Well, I need an outfit for court. The warden tells me I will have a bond hearing before the end of the week, and I can appear in civilian clothes rather than a jumpsuit that makes me look like a highway warning barrel. But the only other clothes I have are some ratty old jeans and a hooded sweatshirt—what I was wearing when they arrested me—not something to impress a judge with my reliability."

"Can't your mother find something suitable at home?"

"My mother? Hah! She couldn't find her . . . Never mind. I don't know if she even realizes I'm in jail. I used my one phone call Friday night to contact her, but she didn't answer, so I had to leave a message. So far, she hasn't shown up to visit or left a message in return."

"You're not on good terms with her?"

"It's just . . . She drinks, you know. You both witnessed her behavior the night that daddy died. It's how she copes—it's either drinking or throwing things." Again, she gave a cynical little laugh. "And I know from experience what happens when she throws things. You saw my black eye."

"Your black eye? Your mother did that?"

"She didn't mean to, actually. She was mad at my father because he had smoked in the house and used one of her precious cut glass decorations as an ashtray. She threw it at him. She has a powerful arm, but her aim is terrible. She missed him by several feet and hit me square in the face as I walked into the room. Broke my nose, too.

"Anyhow, I was hoping you could go by the house to pick up an outfit for me—slacks, blouse, and a blazer. And maybe you could check on her and make sure she's all right."

"We can do that this afternoon."

～

"I'm doing this only because you asked me to. You have no idea what this woman may be up to." David had been grumbling all the way to the Cartwright mansion at the edge of town.

"No, I don't, but it worries me that she hasn't responded to Olivia's call. She may be ill—or worse. It's just not natural for a mother to ignore the fact that her only child is in jail for murder."

"No one has ever claimed this is a normal family, Sarah." At the house, a car in the driveway suggested that someone was home. They rang the doorbell and waited. When there was no response, David used the heavy brass knocker to show his determination. At last, a small woman in a typical maid's uniform opened the door only wide enough to look out. "I'm sorry," she said. "There has been a death in the family, and madame is in mourning. She is not receiving visitors."

"We are not visitors," David responded. "I am Lieutenant David Cohen of the district attorney's office, and we are here on official police business. Please inform 'Madame' Cartwright that we need to see her—now."

From somewhere across the room came a hazy voice. "It's fine, Matilda. Let the gentleman in. I have been expecting him."

"It's Margaret, ma'am."

"Margaret, Matilda, whatever. Get him a drink."

David frowned, held up a hand, and shook his head at the maid, who then disappeared. "Mrs. Cartwright? Can you turn on the light? It's dark in here with the draperies closed."

"Sorry. The afternoon sun hurts my eyes, but we can have a lamp."

The soft glow revealed a small woman dressed in a ruffled pink peignoir with matching high-heeled mules decorated with tinted pink ostrich feathers. She teetered as she made her way across the room carrying a pitcher filled with a frothy pink liquid. "I was just refilling my supply of strawberry daiquiris. It's so important that one matches one's beverage to one's outfit, don't you think? I prefer a mimosa or tequila sunrise, but the colors are hard to match. Let me pour you a glass even if you are not wearing pink."

"No, no, thank you. We are here on official business. I believe you have met Dr. Sarah Chomsky, who serves as your daughter Olivia's academic advisor." David pulled Sarah forward, giving her a look that warned her not to make him handle this woman by himself.

"We met in my office at the university last year, Mrs. Cartwright. Do you remember?"

"Yes. Olivia talks of you often. But why have you come? To hear my confession?"

"Your confession? What do you mean? Now I'm confused. You know, do you not, that Olivia is in jail for the murder of her father?"

"In jail? That's ridiculous! Everyone knows I did it. Olivia would never . . . Oh, I saw her throw a biscuit at him one time, but it was all in fun. She loved her daddy. Why? I'm sure I don't know, but she did. Can't you tell them to send her home? I haven't seen her in days."

"That's why we're here. We went to visit Olivia today at the jail, and she asked us to check on you to make sure you were all right. She's been worried because she didn't hear from you after her arrest."

"Well, what did she expect me to do—bail her out? Show up to hold her hand?"

"She perhaps needs a little motherly love, some reassurance that someone still loves her."

"The best way I can get her released is to confess. I killed my husband with full intent and justification. For three weeks, I have expected the police to show up so I could admit my guilt. That's why your handsome friend is here, isn't it?"

"No. David, tell her that you're not here to arrest her."

"Mrs. Cartwright, you may remember me from your husband's hearing concerning the use of red lead in his factory. I am the acting district attorney, but I have no power to arrest you or even hear your confession. If you intend to admit your guilt, I will need to call the police and have them bring their recording equipment to document your story. Is that what you want?"

"Yes. I'm tired of hiding the truth."

"This will take some time, and I need to use the police radio in my car to make the call. Sarah, will you come outside with me, please?"

"It's all right, David. We'll be fine here."

"And I need to mix up another pitcher of daiquiris. Someone seems to have finished this one."

"That's unnecessary, Mrs. Cartwright."

"Oh, but it is. Your police will be thirsty."

"No, no, they . . . never mind." He gave up in frustration and headed for the door while Sarah looked around for another topic of conversation to distract the already inebriated woman from having another drink.

She picked up a picture frame from the mantle and smiled. "Is this Olivia as a child? What a beautiful little girl. Tell me about her. What was she like then?"

Chapter Thirty-Two

THE CONFESSION

Monday, April 19, 2010

W ithin a few minutes, a squad car arrived bringing two uniformed policemen armed with recording equipment and microphones. A block behind them, another police car idled, along with an ambulance and two medical technicians. They remained out of sight of the Cartwright house, waiting in case someone needed them.

When the doorbell rang, Mrs. Cartwright jumped up to answer it. She wobbled on her high heels, then tripped over the coffee table, and landed on one knee. David and Sarah both rushed to help.

"Careful! I think you may have twisted that ankle. We must get it looked at before . . ."

"Mrs. C? These men want to do some recording. Where should I put them?" The maid, confused by all the visitors, was wringing her hands.

"They're fine, Mabel. Just invite them in."

"It's Margaret, ma'am."

"Margaret, Mable, Matilda, whoever-you-are. Make yourself useful and refill this pitcher of daiquiris."

Behind her back, David motioned for the two patrolmen to come and help. With quiet efficiency, one policeman positioned Mrs. Cartwright in an easy chair and propped her injured ankle on a footstool. He focused the video camera on her, while the other arranged microphones and a tape recorder. They handed David a microphone and nodded towards him to let him know the tapes were rolling.

"This is District Attorney David Cohen speaking from the Cartwright home at 11097 Hilltop Lane in Birch Falls, Tennessee. With me and speaking to me is Mrs. Edith Cartwright. Also present in the room are Doctor Sarah Chomsky, a history professor from Smoky Mountain University, along with Sergeant Bill Evans and Patrolman Charlie Hastings, both of the Birch Falls Police Department. The date is Monday, April 19, 2010, and the time is 4:18 PM.

"Mrs. Cartwright, I am about to read your rights. You need to listen and confirm that you understand."

'You have the right to remain silent. Anything you say can and will be used against you in a court of law. You have the right to an attorney. If you cannot afford an attorney, one will be provided for you.'

"Do you understand these rights? And do you wish to proceed without an attorney present?"

"I am. I mean, I will. Or I do. Goodness, it sounds like a wedding." She giggled and then choked.

Drawing a long, patient breath, David continued. "All right, then. Will you describe to us your actions on Saturday, March 27th, 2010?

"Every Saturday around here is the same. My husband gets up early to get in a round of golf with his buddies. Then he heads to the factory where he does heaven-knows-what in his office—goes over the books, checks production figures, signs supply orders, and snoops around to be sure everything is in order. He doesn't leave the factory until dinner time, when he heads to a private gentlemen's club to share a steak, a glass of whiskey, and a good cigar with more of his cronies.

"I sleep late and then fuss around, getting ready to join my girlfriends at the country club, where we have several rounds of mimosas and then a long lunch. We spend the afternoon playing bridge and gossiping until it's time for two-for-one happy hour. After two rounds of martinis, the club stewards have to drive me home, where I go straight back to bed." She giggled again.

"So, was this Saturday different?"

"Well, just before I left for the country club, the phone rang and it was Jimmy—that's my husband. You need to know that he had moved his revolver from its usual place in the dresser drawer. He said he needed a gun at the office in case the whistle-blower came after him. So, anyway, he had just discovered that the gun was empty and that he had left the bullets at home. He wanted me to get the box of bullets from his drawer and bring them to him at the office on my way to my bridge game. I objected because it would make me late, but he yelled at me and insisted that I do as he asked. As usual, I did.

"He grabbed the box from me, pulled his gun from the drawer, and fumbled about trying to load it while he went on talking about how much danger he was in. He was never very good at mechanical stuff, so I said, 'Here, let me do it.' I tried to take the gun from him, but he wouldn't let go. So, we struggled over it, and somehow the gun went off. I don't know which of us pulled the trigger, but the bullet creased his upper arm. He grabbed his arm, falling back into the chair and yelling, 'Look what you've done now. I'm bleeding.'

"I just stood there with a gun in my hand, looking at him and thinking how foolish he looked with blood running down his arm. And then I felt a rush of power sweep over me. He was whining, crying, and looking pathetic while I watched. And I realized I could kill him with just one little finger twitch." She grinned, sticking her tongue out between her teeth. "So I did!"

A collective gasp issued from her listeners, not so much because of what she said but because of the obvious joy she took in telling the story.

"What did you do then, Mrs. Cartwright? Did you check to see if he was alive?"

"Oh, there was no need to do that. The bullet went right into his mouth and out through the back of his skull. Splashed his brains all over the wall behind him. He was dead, all right, and I was free for the first time in twenty-four years, seven months, and thirteen days. I was giddy, but I knew enough to wipe my fingerprints off the gun. I used the fancy handkerchief he always wore in his breast pocket. Then I wrapped the gun in the handkerchief and dropped it into my purse, thinking I would have to take it home. But on my way out of the building, I passed a half-full trash can and dropped the gun and handkerchief into it. Then I hurried on to the country club. I was right about being late. I could tell the ladies had been talking about me, so I ordered two mimosas to get caught up. We had a lovely afternoon."

She looked around, proud to have told her story at last, and waited for someone to applaud. The room remained silent as her listeners tried to make sense of what they had just heard.

David was the first to speak. "What do you remember after that—when you went to the hospital?"

"I remember the cops coming to the country club and asking for me. I didn't want to leave because it was just about time for two-for-one martinis, but they insisted. They said my husband was hurt and was on his way to the hospital. They needed me to meet the ambulance there in case the doctors needed my permission to perform surgery. I was angry because I didn't want them trying to save his life. I wanted him dead. But then the doctor came into the emergency room and said they could not restart his heart. They declared him DOA, and I was so relieved I passed out."

The uniformed policeman turned the recorder off and spoke for the first time. "Edith Cartwright, I am placing you under arrest for the murder of your husband, Jamison Cartwright. You have heard your rights, but I will remind you once again that anything you say to us can and will be used against you in a court of law."

"That's fine. I'm just happy I got to tell someone about it. Should I get dressed now so we can go to jail?"

"Ah, no . . . I think you're fine as you are. That's the outfit that will show on the film, so . . . uh . . . Besides, I think we'll run you over to the hospital rather than the jail. We need to be sure you haven't injured your leg. We'll get you a nice private room in the Detox Center. You'll be under guard, but you'll be more comfortable than in a jail cell. The nurses will find you something more suitable to wear when they help you into the bed. You can have some dinner, get a good night's sleep, and be more alert in the morning for some tests they'll need to run."

"Can I have just one more little drink? All that story-telling made me dry."

He nodded to Sarah, who passed her a half-empty glass. "Sergeant Evans, give the EMTs a call and have them bring in a transport chair."

Mrs. Cartwright waved the medical technician away so she could finish draining the last daiquiri. Then she ensconced herself in the transport chair, waved goodbye to

David and Sarah, and leaned forward to get a better look at the ambulance.

"Oh, I've never ridden in one of those. Will you blow the siren and everything?"

"We can do that if you wish, ma'am. Most folks don't want to draw attention to themselves and their problems."

"I do. It could be the last bit of fun I have for a rather long time."

As David and Sarah settled into the patrol car, Sarah shook her head. "I'm mind-boggled. Are most confessions that honest and outspoken?"

"Sometimes they are. If the perpetrator has been dealing with guilt, the chance to tell the truth can be a great relief. Here, though, we may have just seen the effects of alcohol loosening the tongue. It wouldn't surprise me if, in the future, she denies the whole story."

"Oh, my, and this is what you deal with, day after day?"

"No, I admit, this day has been more bizarre than most."

"What happens next? What will they do with her at the hospital?"

"The fuss over her ankle has been a ruse. I don't think she hurt it, but it is a face-saving measure to ensure her cooperation until we can get her locked up."

"Locked up?"

"Oh, yes. She's a confessed murderer, after all. She's headed straight for the detoxification unit—the drunk tank. I had a private word with the ambulance driver while she was being loaded into the back. He needed to know that she is already displaying symptoms of delirium tremens."

"What's that? I've heard the term, but I don't know what it means."

"It's a stage in severe cases of alcoholism. The patient has been drunk over a long period—enough so that her body is used to operating under a high level of alcohol content. She appears to be sober and in control after drinking an amount that would put most folks under the table. Trouble arises after several hours without a drink, because her body cannot adjust. Blood pressure rises, respiration increases, heart rate goes up, nervous shaking and twitches begin, and most times the patient hallucinates."

"I wondered about how normal Mrs. Cartwright appeared to be after drinking two pitchers of those horrible pink daiquiris."

"That was my first clue. Another appeared within her confession—her sudden outbursts of violent behavior. On the day of the murder, she headed to the country club for her first mimosa of the day. She told us how frustrated she was that she was going to be late with that first drink. And then, unable to control herself or her impulses, she shot her husband. And later that day, she was waiting for a martini when the police arrived to take her to the hospital. We witnessed how violent and out of control she was there."

"And she insisted on that last drink before she left the house today."

"It's the last one she will have for a very long time."

"Meaning that she will become violent before the night is over."

"That's why they must be in a hurry to get her locked into the detox ward. But the problem is more serious than just random violent behavior. The deprivation can be fatal. They will have to watch her and treat her with various medications to mimic the effects of drinking, thus slowly weaning her metabolism off alcohol. The drying out process can take weeks if it succeeds at all."

Sarah shuddered. "It sounds horrible. I think I'll go home and have an enormous glass of milk."

"I don't think you have to worry, my dear. I've seen how you react to alcohol. You fall asleep after your second drink—long before the alcohol can take over your metabolic functions. At any rate, that milk will have to wait until we go back to the jail and spring Olivia."

"Can we get her out tonight?"

"Sure. That's one advantage of being the district attorney. I can't make an arrest, but I can order a release."

Sarah pondered for a few minutes. Then she raised the question that had been haunting her.

"What will happen to Mrs. Cartwright, assuming she kicks her drinking problem? Will they charge her with first degree murder? Ask for the death penalty? I know Olivia is going to wonder the same thing."

"I don't think she will ever go to trial. I wouldn't want to try the case. First, I doubt that she will ever return to a sober life style. The drunk tank treatment may help, but it seldom provides a cure for a dedicated alcoholic. My best guess is that the courts will find her incompetent to stand trial, and she will spend the rest of her life in the hazy comfort of a residential mental health treatment center. But even if she manages a complete cure, she will have recourse to claiming a classic case of battered wife syndrome. She could get off scot-free."

"I'm glad. She's already paid a heavy price for choosing the wrong husband."

∼

At the jail, David took control of releasing Olivia. "I know you'll want to talk to her, Sarah, but it will be easier—less emotional—to let the guards tell her that she is free to go. They will get her civilian clothes, her other belongings, and the paperwork she will have to sign. Then they can tell her that we are waiting for her in the outside hallway. I'm assuming it will be best to take her to her dorm room rather than home."

"Yes, I agree, but I have another thought. Olivia and Chad Overstreet have become good friends this past school year. The day they arrested her, he came to see me and asked me to tell her to call if she needed him—that he would be available day and night. Because of his own stay in jail, he thought he could understand her feelings in a way that others could not.

"I'm thinking of calling him and asking him to come down to the jail to take her wherever she wants to go. I doubt she needs us tonight, and I'm certain she need not hear all the technical details of what will happen next. She can get those questions answered as they occur to her. What she needs tonight is a shoulder to cry on and a protective arm to support her."

"It's perfect. Do you have his number?"

"I do. He insisted I enter it in my phone."

"Then call him, while I get the guards moving."

When Chad answered the phone, Sarah told him what had happened. "Can you come down to the jail and take her back to campus?"

"I'm on my way!"

If Sarah had any doubts about the wisdom of calling Chad, the smile that lit Olivia's face as she emerged through the double swinging doors was enough to confirm the choice. Without a glance at David and Sarah, Olivia rushed into Chad's warm embrace. "Thank you," she whispered.

Chad held her for a moment and then grasped her shoulders to pull her away. "No time for tears," he warned. "You are free, and it's time to celebrate. Tell me. What food did you miss most while you were in jail?"

The question surprised Olivia. She hesitated before answering, "Ice cream! Dessert was always lime Jell-O."

"How well I remember. But I know just how to fix it. There's a Steak'n'Shake on our way back to campus. How does one of their big chocolate milkshakes sound?"

"Heavenly!" Then she seemed to notice that Sarah and David were watching. "You arranged this, didn't you? I'm grateful, but I . . ."

"I understand. Run on and enjoy your ice cream and your freedom. We can talk on Monday."

That conversation on Monday was one of the most difficult that Sarah had ever experienced. Olivia's face crumbled with the realization that her mother had sacrificed her own freedom for the sake of her daughter. "Why would she do that? And why did you let her confess to something she . . .?"

"She confessed because it was true. She did it, Olivia. She fired the fatal shot."

"You can't know that. Maybe she's just covering for my . . . maybe . . ."

"We can know that she's guilty. The police kept several minor details about the shooting as secrets from the press—details only the killer could have known. And in her confession, which I heard, your mother included every one of those secret details. She left no doubt as to her guilt."

"What's going to happen to her? Where is she? When can I see her?"

"The police have hospitalized her in the detoxification center, where they are letting her regain her sobriety. No one has access to her except her doctors. They will notify you when it's safe to let her see you. You must be patient, but if it's any comfort, Lieutenant Cohen tells me that she may not ever stand trial. They intend to offer her a plea deal. She will admit to firing the weapon but claim justification based on the battered wife syndrome. It's going to take a while, Olivia, but it's going to be all right."

"And in the meantime, . . . What do I do? How do I survive this?"

"Your aunt and uncle are ready to provide a sense of family. Chad is offering his strength to lean on. When you have your mother back, she will need your love and understanding. And you have a legacy—an inheritance that represents your father's confidence in you. You're going to be fine, Olivia."

Chapter Thirty-Three

MAY FLOWERS

Saturday, May 1, 2010

S arah awoke in a panic. She had been dreaming of a May Day filled with poisonous black flowers and a never-ending drive to a hospital as David lay in the passenger seat, his life blood pouring away. She had not suffered that nightmare for some time, but on this first anniversary, every terror-stricken moment flooded back. She lay staring at the ceiling, willing her heart to quit pounding. In another few moments, she realized that the pounding was actually a knock at her front door.

She struggled into a robe and slippers, tiptoed over a sleeping cat, and opened the door to find a package resting on the doorstep. A red satin bow decorated the box and secured an envelope. The message inside was brief:

Flowers didn't seem right for this day, but they tell me chocolates are always welcome. Will pick you up at eleven for brunch in the mountains and a walk in the woods. I love you more than yesterday, but less than tomorrow. D.

The Hideaway Inn was a log house hidden in one of the hollows that dotted this side of the Appalachian Mountains. It featured a huge log-burning fireplace, several tables for two, and an open kitchen managed by two middle-aged women dressed in pioneer garb. The menu for the day appeared as a chalked message on a child's blackboard. Today's offering included fresh squeezed orange juice or a bloody Mary; an egg white omelette flavored with spinach, scallions, and fresh herbs; homemade sausage patties; toasted slices of banana bread; and strawberry jam made from the first crop of the year.

David and Sarah had become regular customers after their first trip the previous year. They had been celebrating David's release from the hospital and the last day of Sarah's probationary year as a college professor. Their relationship, however, had been much in doubt. They returned several times, each one marking an additional step in their journey together. On this morning, the women in the kitchen welcomed them as family, fed them well, and asked what today's occasion might be.

Sarah grimaced, but David spoke without hesitation. "A year ago, we stood on your threshold, not sure whether we should turn away forever or give our friendship one more chance to bloom into something rich and wonderful. As you've seen, your little hideaway convinced us to keep trying. And in about six weeks, we will be back again, this time for a honeymoon brunch." The two women nodded to each other as if they had known all along it might come to this. And perhaps they did.

～

No trip to the mountains would have been complete without the accompanying walk in the woods. The small kitchen garden beyond the inn featured a path that led off into the trees. Someone kept the path cleared so that walkers could concentrate on their surroundings rather than watching every step they took.

The way led them to a footbridge crossing a small stream. In the stream, tiny tadpoles swarmed and waited to grow their frog legs. In the branches above them, birds twittered and squirrels scurried up tree trunks with nest-building materials. Patches of sunlight allowed mountain laurels to burst into flower, while pockets of deep shade sheltered shy little violets and snowdrops. Where the terrain was level, groves of blooming dogwoods and redbud trees flourished. On steeper slopes, pines and stately oaks secured the ground.

Sarah breathed deeply, trying to draw in all the lovely scents of nature. She gasped, covered her nose with her hand, and grabbed David's arm to stop him from taking his next step.

"Sh-h-h! Don't move. They'll see you."

"Who?"

"Mrs. Pugh and her family. Look. Aren't they adorable?" She was grinning with delight as the skunk, tail held high, led her three small kits across the path. "They remind me of Elijah at that age."

"I'm sure he smelled better."

"Those little ones wouldn't . . ."

"Don't kid yourself. They can spray. They just don't direct the spray very well yet. You don't want to be anywhere close when they are practicing."

At the top of the next rise, someone had installed a bench, and Sarah sank down gratefully. "Time for a break. Maybe if we don't move, some other family—somebody softer and sweeter-smelling—will pay us a visit."

"With my luck, it'll be a family of raccoons. You know, the ones with sharp teeth that carry rabies."

"OK, how about a possum? No rabies there."

"No, but they aren't very cuddly, and they smell terrible."

"Rabbits?"

"I was thinking more like a coyote pup or a mountain lion cub."

"Right—with Mama coming right behind! Where did you learn to be so romantic?"

"I don't need animal families to cuddle. I have you right here."

"That's better." Sarah leaned into his encircling arm. "I was just thinking. This may be the most peaceful moment we will have in the next six weeks. You have all that mopping up to do regarding the Cartwright affair, and I am facing three more weeks of final exams and graduation hoopla. And after that? Parents and wedding stuff."

"Fun times."

"Right. And why are you looking at me that way?"

"I was just thinking how much you have changed in the past year."

"Is that good or bad?"

"I meant it in a good way. Remember? When we first met, you were all about your five-year plan for your life. You knew what you would do at every four months' segment of every year. If you didn't have a name written into your book, you had no time for its owner. You intimidated the hell out of me."

"Oh, silly! I wasn't that bad, was I? Hmmm. Maybe I was, and yes, I have changed. I've learned that we cannot plan in advance for the best things that happen."

"Well, whatever you've learned, I like you better this way. I

—in contrast—have had to learn to think—and plan—before I leap. We've been good for each other in that way. Look at what we've accomplished in the past month. On the first weekend, we planned an entire wedding. On the second, we bought a house. During the third weekend, we convinced both sets of parents that we know what we are doing. And on the fourth, we solved a murder. We make a great team."

"So, what's going on, David? I sense a message that something else is on your mind."

"OK, I have a big decision to make, one that will affect both our lives, and I have no five-year plan to guide me."

Sarah was studying his face. "Whatever it is, we can figure it out. Talk to me."

"You may remember that when Sam first got sick and asked me to fill in as acting district attorney while he was in the hospital, I didn't hesitate to take on the job because it was for only a short time. Then we got the news that his illness was terminal. The mayor asked me to stay on until he could call a special November election, and again I agreed with no problem. But now the Democratic party bosses want me to stay on and then run for election in November 2012, and that's a whole unique situation. Everyone tells me I'll be a shoo-in, which is nice to hear but . . . It also means giving up on the police liaison office. I don't think I'm willing to do that. But I also don't know how well I would do in that position if some newcomer moved in as district attorney."

"I see your dilemma."

"It's more than a dilemma; it's no longer a choice between being a cop or a lawyer. Now there are four balls bouncing in my court."

"Four?"

"My father turns sixty-five this year. That's retirement year. He says he isn't ready to give up the reins of the business yet, and I believe him. He's strong and healthy. But his age must be a factor in my decision, because, like it or not, I will inherit that law firm someday. So, should I become the cop, the defense attorney, the prosecutor, or the liaison officer who tries to mediate among the other three?"

"Well, first, I think you are complicating the issue. There's little chance that you'll ever go back to being a cop. Amazing though your artificial shoulder is, you haven't tested it on a firing range. Nor have you kept up with your physical training. And, if I remember, you promised both your mother and me that you would never rejoin the police force.

"Your father is not likely to drop dead just because he now fits some insurance company's actuarial tables. He could live to be a hundred years old with his fingers still on the pulse of his law firm. So, you have only the two current possibilities—running for district attorney or returning to the job of police liaison officer. Quit confusing that actual issue."

"Yeah, you're right. But how do I decide between them? Which of the two would you choose to marry?"

"I won't answer that, because I've already chosen to marry you, no matter what your job title may be. My choice must not be a factor in your decision. Which position will make you happiest?"

"I don't know."

"Let's concentrate on the district attorney's job for the moment. What worries you about running for that office?"

"I can do the day-to-day work of a DA. What bothers me most is becoming a politician. Instead of fighting crime, how much of my time would I spend on politics—wheeling and dealing, making campaign promises, raising money from people who have more cash than conscience, giving speeches, kissing babies, shaking hands, eating cold chicken. Ugh! Not only does it sound miserable; I know I would be miserable at doing it. I've often said I've never known an honest politician. Could I be the exception, or would politics drag me down to the common level?"

"I'm not sure you can know the answer to that until you've tried it." Sarah squeezed his hand. "I trust you to do what's best. Besides, it's not a once-in-a-lifetime decision. The office comes up for re-election every four years. You'll have plenty of chances to change your mind."

"You're a wise woman, Sarah Chomsky. Thank you."

She meant the smile on her face to be reassuring, but David could tell that something else had intruded upon her thoughts. He waited as she leaned back to watch the clouds sailing above them.

"We've clarified the direction of my path today. How's yours coming along?"

"What?" Sarah's thoughts had been far away, and she struggled to refocus on David's questions.

"You turned pensive on me. What are you thinking?"

"To be honest, my five-year plan hasn't been all that much help. I've had to add a few side trips along the way. All that five-year talk isn't my idea, you know. I didn't invent it. The college imposed it upon me with its deadlines for achieving tenure. They've also established their markers along the way, and I can't change those. All I can do is try my best to conform to their pre-conceived notions."

"I still don't understand the full implications of the tenure process. Can you explain it to me so I know what you're going through?"

"It boils down to just three areas. The first is teaching. A new professor has to be proficient in running a classroom and holding the students' interest. At the end of each course, students fill out an evaluation form in which they rate the professor's performance in many areas—like being on time for class, making assignments clear, listening to opposing views, being available for office hours, and grading speed.

Their answers can be brutal. So far, I've been lucky. My student evals put me in the top ten percent of the faculty.

"The second category is research. The administration expects us to make important contributions to knowledge within our specific areas of expertise. In layman's terms, that means delivering conference papers, writing articles for specialized and juried journals, and publishing at least one book with a well-respected university press. And each of those examples of our research must receive favorable reactions from our peers. A critical review is a kiss of death if it appears just as the tenure decision comes up for debate."

"How are you doing on that score?"

"I am pretty much on target there, I think. I presented a paper at the Southern last fall. *The Nineteenth-Century Studies Journal* has accepted my article on slaves and their use of water symbolism and returned the manuscript for minor revisions. Best of all, I have finished the early draft of my book on the role of cotton in the Civil War. I have sent query letters and sample chapters to several southern university presses. And now I'm waiting for responses, although that can take months, maybe even a year or more."

"The third category?"

"Service refers to what I am contributing to the expertise of the university and its faculty—expanding my department's course offerings, serving on university-wide standing committees, and getting along with my colleagues and cooperating as we work on common goals.

"I think Kevin was worried about me on that score last year, but he is now impressed with me because I established the Smoky Mountain Historical Society. The 'Welcome to History' party the graduate students organized last week was a rousing success. And he's giving me credit for it. Lots of our new undergraduates signed up for membership, and several volunteered to work on plans over the summer.

"I'm also now a member of the faculty Honors Committee, which oversees honors project done by our top students. Their finished products get sent out for binding and then go into our permanent library collection as examples of what our students can do. Committee members read the projects and give them a final stamp of approval."

Sarah made a small face before continuing. "I could be in trouble there. I angered a senior member of the economics department by vetoing his honors student's project. The topic was interesting and well handled, but the grammar was atrocious, and the typing even worse. I refused to accept the paper until the young man produced a clean copy, and his advisor called me 'an obsessive-compulsive old maid grammar Nazi.' He also suggested that when I came up for review, he would have a few things to say about my lack of collegiality."

"Uh-Oh!"

"Yeah! I think I recovered somewhat when the boy's father asked to see the paper. He told the committee chair that it looked like something produced when the legendary 1000 chimpanzees found themselves in a room with 1000 typewriters. But you never know how long someone will hold a grudge. I've learned to be more circumspect in expressing my opinions.

"Anyway, that's where I stand at the moment. I know what I have to do in the next three years to ensure that they will offer me tenure. That path is clear and well-marked. My crisis will come three years from now, when I have to decide which fork in the road to follow."

"I don't understand why you see getting tenure as a fork in the road. I thought that was the ultimate goal."

"So did I, but it's not. At least, it shouldn't be. I've now seen what happens to those who accept tenure. Tenure means safety and—all too often—stagnation. The winners get to take a sabbatical, and then they have ten more years when it doesn't make much difference what they do. They don't have to write a book or research a new topic or even please the students. They just go to class, teach from old notes, and show up at faculty meetings. After their ten-year hiatus, they can try to perform miracles again and apply for a full professorship that brings a little more money and a little more prestige. But if they don't want to bother, they don't have to do a thing. They can just ride their tenure out until they're old enough to retire. Too many take that choice, and the profession is poorer for it.

"I guess I've discovered that university professors are ordinary people, not shining stars of intellectualism. Julia tells me that is a common reaction among many young academics, and she assures me that I'll get over my disillusionment. But I don't know, David. I enjoy being in the classroom, too, but sometimes it isn't enough. I don't feel the same degree of joy that I experienced while reading my book to a group of rapt five-year-olds."

"What is it you see as your other choice?"

"The choices differ for everyone. We just witnessed Trevor Monroe giving up any chance for tenure for a job on Wall Street. For me, the other fork leads to a career in creative writing. I love writing, and I'm learning that I'm good at it. When I read a detail of historical data, my creative imagination weaves a story around it.

"The conventions of academic history frustrate and bore me. I don't want to write another history of the 1864 Battle of Franklin with its statistics and diagrams and logistics. The real story belongs in a novel like *The Widow of the South*, about the old woman who allowed her plantation house to become a field hospital during the battle. Later, she turned her land into a cemetery for unidentified southern soldiers buried in a mass grave nearby. I want to write a great story for the reading public. I don't care about giving a few dozen of my colleagues another footnoted treatise.

David watched her face light up as she talked and realized he was seeing a side of her that she usually kept well hidden. "You're a natural-born story teller, aren't you? Why not do both? Can't you hold down a tenure-track position and teach your classes with enthusiasm, but write your historical novel on your own time?"

"I've asked myself the same question. They are both full-time jobs, so time is the limiting issue. But worse, academics are not tolerant of those who seek fulfillment beyond the boundaries of the university. I've already received a formal letter from the Tenure and Promotion committee, informing me that my *curriculum vitae* may not include *The Passover Guest* in my list of publications."

"Why not?"

"They said it showed neither rabbinical authority nor scholarly preparation."

"It's a children's book!"

"Therefore, it's not important."

"But readers love it!"

"I know, I know. I also have to admit that I enjoyed the couple of weeks I spent promoting the book. The book signings, the rapt expressions on the faces of small children, the enthusiasm of their parents—all those things made me feel like an actual author, and I loved it." She paused and chuckled to herself. "Even if I didn't have rabbinical authority!"

"It sounds to me as if you've already made your decision to follow the road less traveled," he suggested. "You asked me which of my choices would make me happiest. Have you asked yourself the same question?"

"My situation differs from yours, I think, because the alternatives are not equal. The road to tenure offers safety—a guaranteed job for as long as I care to teach, a good income with generous health and retirement benefits, a comfortable lifestyle with few risks."

"Wait a minute. I make a hefty salary, Sarah, and I can support a family without the need of a wife's monthly paycheck. Don't let money stand in the way of what you want to do with your talents."

"It's not just a matter of money, David, and I'm not questioning your ability to support me. The lesser road is full of dangers that threaten my sense of self-worth. It offers no guarantees, no protection against misadventures and malicious reviews, no promises of success or the respect of friends and colleagues. It's almost a sure formula for failure. Most writers would starve to death, were it not for their day jobs. The chances of writing a best seller are minuscule. And worst of all, should I choose that path, there's no opportunity to have a do-over. Once I turn my back on academia, it's out of reach for good.

"If I stay at the university, though, I can keep dreaming of writing the great American novel. That path will always branch off, available any time I find my enthusiasm for teaching has disappeared. But so long as I have students who inspire me, I suspect I'll choose the safer path. And I will squirrel away all the great plot lines I conjure up in my fertile imagination, hoping that their time may come in due course.

"So the answer to the question about doing both is obvious. I can teach and write—but not at the same time. I only hope I will recognize when it's time to make the switch. It may arrive when a tenure offer comes through or not until I'm a doddering old lady. Your job will be to keep reminding me of how lucky I am to have that choice."

MIRIAM COHEN'S FAVORITE RECIPES

Like mothers everywhere, Mrs. Cohen harbored conflicting wishes. First, she hoped that her new daughter-in-law would not be a better cook than she was. That would be embarrassing. But she also wanted to pass on all her family recipes to Sarah so that she could be sure David would continue to enjoy his favorite meals with his new family. Here are a few of the recipes Miriam taught Sarah. Not all of them were Jewish in origin, but all were familiar dishes at the Cohen dinner table.

TUNA NOODLE CASSEROLE

Noodle dishes have always been a favorite on Jewish tables, and this one may have originated as a childhood staple in homes where a hot meal was more important than its individual ingredients. How does one persuade a small child to eat strongly-flavored tuna? By hiding it under the noodles. Here, Miriam seems to have upped the argument by declaring the dish reserved for special occasions. And so it persisted, long after the children had developed more sophisticated tastes. It was also suitable for breaking the fast of Yom Kippur because of its mild flavors and easy preparation.

INGREDIENTS

- 6 oz. uncooked no-yolk egg noodles
- 1 tbsp. olive oil
- 1 tbsp. unsalted butter
- 1 cup finely chopped onion
- 1 cup thinly sliced celery
- 3 tbsp. all-purpose flour
- 2 ¼ cups low-fat 1% milk
- ½ cup frozen green peas, thawed
- 1 ½ tbsp. chopped fresh dill
- 1 tsp. finely grated lemon rind
- 1 tbsp. fresh lemon juice
- 1 tsp. dry mustard (such as Colman's)
- ½ tsp. kosher salt
- ¼ tsp. black pepper
- 1 (5-oz.) can solid white albacore tuna packed in water, drained and broken into chunks
- ¼ cup whole-wheat panko (Japanese breadcrumbs)

DIRECTIONS

Fill a large saucepan with water; bring to a boil. Add noodles; cook 3 minutes or until al dente. Drain.

Heat a 10-inch ovenproof skillet over medium heat. Add oil and butter; swirl until butter melts. Add onion and celery; sauté 6 minutes or until tender. Sprinkle flour over pan; cook 45 seconds.

Add milk, stirring constantly. Stir in peas and next 7

ingredients (through tuna). Remove pan from heat; gently stir in noodles.

Spread into 9x13 baking pan; cover and refrigerate until ½ hour before serving time.

Heat oven to 350°F and bake for thirty minutes or until heated through. Sprinkle breadcrumbs and cheese over top. Broil 2 minutes or until topping is lightly browned.

A chopped Mediterranean salad of romaine lettuce, cherry tomatoes, and cucumbers, enhanced with kalamata olives, feta cheese, and cannellini beans, makes a tasty accompaniment. Serve with grilled pita wedges.

POPPY SEED CAKE

Jewish tradition associates this poppy seed cake with the holiday celebrations of Purim, but the Cohen family spent most Purim holidays helping at the synagogue to provide free meals for the needy. Mrs. Cohen knew, however, that her children loved this cake, so she added it to their other special occasions.

INGREDIENTS
- 1 cup poppy seeds
- 1 cup low-fat milk
- 2 tbsp. honey
- 1 cup (2 sticks) unsalted butter, room temperature
- 1 ½ cups sugar
- 4 eggs, separated at room temperature
- 3 tbsp. lemon zest
- 2 tbsp. fresh lemon juice
- 1 ½ tsp. vanilla
- 1 cup low-fat sour cream
- 2 ½ cups all-purpose flour

- 1 tsp. baking soda
- 1 tsp. salt
- Powdered sugar, for dusting

Lemon frosting glaze:
- 1 cup powdered sugar
- 2 tbsp. fresh lemon juice

Warm lemon glaze:
- 1 cup powdered sugar
- 3 tbsp. fresh lemon juice
- 1 tbsp. water

DIRECTIONS

Preheat oven to 350°F. Grease a 9- or 10-inch Bundt cake pan (12-cup capacity) and set aside.

In a small saucepan, combine poppy seeds (whole or ground*), milk, and honey. Stir till combined and bring to a boil over medium heat, stirring constantly. Let mixture boil for 1 minute, then remove from heat and let stand for 20 minutes.

Place poppy seed mixture into a mixing bowl along with butter and sugar. Beat on high until all ingredients are mixed. Add egg yolks to the mixture and beat again on high. Add lemon zest, lemon juice, vanilla, and sour cream and beat until blended.

Sift together flour, baking soda, and salt. Gradually add wet ingredients to dry, using an electric mixer to beat everything together until well combined. Scrape the sides of the bowl to make sure all dry ingredients are moistened.

In a separate clean mixing bowl, beat egg whites to stiff peaks. Gently fold the egg whites into the poppy seed batter. Pour the batter into the Bundt pan. Do not fill beyond three-quarters full. or your cake might overflow during baking. Smooth the batter on the top so it is flat and even all the way around the pan.

Bake cake in preheated oven for 55-65 minutes. When the edges darken and pull fully away from the sides of the pan and the cake browns all the way across the surface, it's done.

Let the cake cool for exactly 10 minutes, and then invert it onto a flat plate. Tap the Bundt pan gently to release the cake. If your cake sticks, use a plastic knife to loosen the cake around the center tube and sides. Allow cake to cool completely.

Top with your choice of powdered sugar or lemon glaze (cooled or hot).

*Grinding the seeds into a paste before mixing will cause a darker and softer cake. Leaving the seeds whole will give a light-colored crumb but a crunchier texture.

Rosh Hashana is the first day of the Jewish New Year, and because it represents the sixth day of Creation, it becomes a festive occasion. As the celebrants prepare for a call to repentance, they also pray for the blessings of a sweet year to come. For that reason, most of the foods served on Rosh Hashana are sweet—flavored with honey, apples, and vegetables with a high sugar content. The following three recipes are typical.

BEEF BRISKET WITH TOMATO GRAVY

. . .

INGREDIENTS

- ¼ cup minced garlic (about 12 cloves)
- 2 tbsp. finely chopped fresh rosemary
- 2 tbsp. freshly ground black pepper, more to taste
- 1 tbsp. kosher salt, more to taste
- 2 tsp. light or dark brown sugar
- 1 tbsp. crushed red pepper
- 1 tbsp. smoked or hot paprika
- 1 8-to-9-lb. whole brisket, trimmed (see note)
- ¼ cup extra virgin olive oil
- 3 cups chopped yellow onions (about 2 large onions)
- 1 35-oz. can plus 1 28-oz. can (about 7 cups) peeled tomatoes and liquid
- 1 ¼ cups fruity white wine

DIRECTIONS

Preheat oven to 450°F.

In a bowl, combine garlic, rosemary, pepper, salt, brown sugar, red pepper and paprika. Place brisket fat-side up in a large, deep roasting pan (about 13 by 16 inches) and rub all over with mixture. Roast brisket, uncovered, for 20 minutes.

While brisket cooks, pour olive oil into a large saucepan over medium heat and add onions. Sauté, stirring occasionally, until onion softens, about 5 minutes. Add tomatoes and their liquid, bring to a boil, then reduce to a simmer. Stir occasionally, breaking tomatoes with a spoon or whisk. Simmer uncovered for 10 minutes and season to taste with salt and black pepper. Remove brisket from oven. Reduce oven temperature to 325.

Pour 1 cup wine and the tomato sauce over brisket. Cover pan as tightly as possible with foil and roast for 3 ½ hours, turning once at 2 hours and again at 3 hours, each time carefully replacing foil.

Transfer brisket to a platter. Allow sauce to settle for a moment in pan; using a slotted spoon, transfer to a blender, allowing fat to strain out. Purée until smooth, adding remaining ¼ cup wine. Season to taste with salt and black pepper.

Slice brisket diagonally from thinnest end in ¼-inch slices. Serve with sauce.

HONEY-ROASTED CHICKEN

This is another way to ensure that even the main course of a Rosh Hashanah dinner conveys the idea of sweetness.

INGREDIENTS

- 3 ½ to 4 lbs. whole chicken without giblets
- 1 small handful of fresh rosemary sprigs
- 1 small handful of fresh thyme sprigs
- Peel from one small lemon, sliced
- 2 garlic cloves
- 2 large onions, peeled and sliced
- Salt and pepper
- ¼ cup olive oil
- 3 tbsp. honey, divided
- ½ cup white wine
- ¼ cup chicken broth
- Fresh rosemary and thyme sprigs for garnish (optional)

. . .

D IRECTIONS

Preheat oven to 400°F.

Whisk together ¼ cup of olive oil, 1 tbsp. of honey, and 1 tbsp. fresh lemon juice. This is the basting mixture.

Season the cavity of the chicken with salt and pepper; pack loosely with half of the fresh rosemary and thyme sprigs, sliced lemon peel, garlic cloves, and a few pieces of the sliced onion. Truss the chicken. Season the chicken with salt and pepper.

Line the bottom of roasting pan with foil. Toss remaining onion slices with 2 tbsp. of olive oil and leaves of the rosemary and thyme sprigs. Spread evenly on bottom. Place the chicken breast side down onto the bed of onions. Pour half of the basting mixture over the chicken, using a brush to coat it evenly.

Cover the roasting pan with foil and vent. Roast for 45 minutes.

Take roasting pan out of the oven, remove the foil (reserve), and flip the chicken to breast side up. Brush the rest of the basting mixture evenly onto the top of the chicken. Cover again with the vented foil and roast for 45 minutes longer.

Reduce oven heat to 375°F. Let the chicken continue to roast another 20-30 minutes until the skin is brown and crisp.

Chicken is done when the skin is nicely browned, and the internal temperature reaches at least 170 ° F as measured on a food thermometer at the thickest part of the thigh.

Place chicken on a carving board. Cover it with foil to keep the heat in and let it rest.

Strain the pan drippings from the roasting pan into a small saucepan and let settle. Skim about half of the fat/oil from the top of the liquid. Add ½ cup of white wine, ¼ cup of chicken broth, and 2 tbsp. of honey to the pan. Whisk to blend.

Heat the sauce over medium heat. Bring to a light boil and let it simmer for about 2 minutes, whisking constantly.

Remove the honey sauce from heat and season with salt and pepper to taste.

Carve the chicken. Drizzled each serving of meat with some of the honey sauce. Garnish with fresh thyme or rosemary, if desired, for a pretty and aromatic presentation.

HONEY CAKE

INGREDIENTS
- 3 ½ cups all-purpose flour
- 1 tbsp. baking powder
- 1 tsp. baking soda
- ½ tsp. salt
- 4 tsps. ground cinnamon
- ½ tsp. ground cloves
- ½ tsp. ground allspice
- 1 cup vegetable oil
- 1 cup honey
- 1 ½ cups granulated sugar
- ½ cup brown sugar
- 3 eggs
- 1 tsp. vanilla extract
- 1 cup warm coffee or strong tea
- ½ cup fresh orange juice
- ¼ cup rye or whisky (see Note)
- ½ cup slivered or sliced almonds (optional)

· · ·

DIRECTIONS

Preheat the oven to 350°F.

Lightly grease the pan(s). An angel food cake pan (9-inch) works best, but you can also use a 10-inch tube or Bundt cake pan, a 9-by-13-inch sheet pan, or three 8-by-4 ½-inch loaf pans. For tube and angel food pans, line the bottom with lightly greased parchment paper.

In a large bowl, whisk together the flour, baking powder, baking soda, salt, and spices. Make a well in the center and add the oil, honey, sugars, eggs, vanilla, coffee, orange juice, and rye or whisky. (Note: If you prefer not to use the whiskey, replace it with an equal amount of orange juice or coffee.)

Using a strong wire whisk or an electric mixer on low speed, combine the ingredients well to make a thick batter, making sure that no ingredients stick to the bottom of the bowl.

Spoon the batter into the prepared pan(s) and sprinkle the top of the cake(s) evenly with the almonds. Place the cake pan(s) on 2 baking sheets stacked together and bake until the cake springs back when you touch it gently in the center.

For angel and tube cake pans, bake for 60 to 70 minutes; loaf cakes, 45 to 55 minutes. For sheet-style cakes, the baking time is 40 to 45 minutes. This is a wet batter and, depending on your oven, it may need extra time. Cake should spring back when gently pressed.

The menu for a Passover Seder is traditional and allows the cook relatively few choices. For example. each diner receives a special plate that contains three matzah (unleavened bread), a shank bone (the sacrificial lamb), a hard-boiled egg (a temple offering), bitter herbs (horseradish, endive, or romaine lettuce stems), charoset (a paste of apples, nuts, and wine), and a vegetable such as an onion or boiled potato to be dipped in salt water.

Cooks may also find that canned versions of other traditional foods such as gefilte fish and matzo ball soup are readily available in kosher groceries, but they taste much better when homemade.

G EFILTE FISH

I NGREDIENTS
- 2 celery stalks
- 2 medium yellow onions, peeled
- 3 large carrots, peeled or scraped
- 1 ½ lbs. boneless, skinless salmon, whitefish or striped bass fillets, cut into 2-inch pieces
- ½ lb. boneless, skinless trout, pike or carp (or a mixture of two), cut into 2-inch pieces
- 10 chives
- 3 tbsp. chopped parsley, tarragon, dill and/or a combination
- 3 large eggs, lightly beaten
- 1 tbsp. vegetable oil
- 4 to 6 tbsp. matzo meal
- ½ tsp. ground black pepper
- 1 head radicchio or endive, or both, for serving
- Prepared horseradish, for serving

. . .

D IRECTIONS

Fill a large, wide pot with 10 cups of water and place over high heat. While bringing to a boil, coarsely chop and add to the pot 1 onion, 1 celery stalk, 1 carrot and the fennel bulb. Add the peppercorns and 1 tsp. salt. Once water is boiling, reduce the heat and simmer, uncovered, while preparing the fish.

Coarsely chop the remaining onion, celery stalk and 1 carrot, then pulse in a food processor until finely chopped. Add fish, chives and 2 tbsp. parsley, tarragon and/or dill, and keep pulsing until fish is chopped but not mushy.

Move the fish mixture to a medium bowl and add eggs, oil, matzo meal, 1 ½ tsps. salt (or more to taste) and the ground black pepper, and mix well with your hands.

Put your hands in a bowl of cold water. Using your hands, mold the fish mixture into a 3- by 2-inch oval patty (about 2 ozs) and gently place on a platter. Repeat with the remaining fish mixture, dipping your hands in water as needed.

Pop the third carrot into the simmering broth and gently add the patties to the pot. Cover and cook for about 20 minutes until patties are firm.

Use a slotted spoon to remove the fish and carrot from the poaching liquid to cool on a plate. Slice the carrot diagonally into thin rounds.

Place each patty on a leaf of radicchio or endive or both. Set the sliced carrot rounds on top of each patty. Garnish with the remaining tbsp. of fresh herbs and serve warm or at room temperature with horseradish, preferably homemade.

If making a day ahead, refrigerate, covered, then return the patties to room temperature before serving.

. . .

Matzo Ball Soup

Ingredients

Chicken stock:
- 1 5-lb. chicken, cut into 8 pieces
- 1 lb. chicken wings, necks, and/or backs
- 2 large yellow onions, unpeeled, quartered
- 6 celery stalks, cut into 1" pieces
- 4 large carrots, peeled, cut into 1" pieces
- 1 large parsnip, peeled, cut into 1" pieces
- 1 large shallot, quartered
- 1 head of garlic, halved crosswise
- 6 sprigs flat-leaf parsley
- 1 tbsp. black peppercorns

Matzo ball mixture:
- 3 large eggs, beaten to blend
- ¾ cup matzo meal
- ¼ cup schmaltz (chicken fat), melted
- 3 tbsp. club soda
- 1¼ tsp. kosher salt

Assembly:
- 2 small carrots, peeled, sliced ¼" thick on a diagonal
- kosher salt
- 2 tbsp. coarsely chopped fresh dill

- coarsely ground fresh black pepper
- reserved breast meat

DIRECTIONS

Bring all ingredients and 12 cups cold water to a boil in a very large (at least 12-qt.) stockpot. Reduce heat to medium-low and simmer until chicken breasts are cooked through, about 20 minutes.

Transfer breasts to a plate (remaining chicken parts are strictly for stock). Let breasts cool slightly, then remove meat and return bones to stock.

Shred meat. Let cool, tightly wrap, and chill.

Continue to simmer stock, skimming surface occasionally, until reduced by one-third, about 2 hours. Strain chicken stock through a fine-mesh sieve into a large saucepan (or airtight container, if not using right away); discard solids. You should have about 8 cups. Stock can be made 2 days ahead. Let cool; cover and chill.

Keep reserved chicken meat chilled.

Mix eggs, matzo meal, schmaltz, club soda, and salt in a medium bowl (mixture will resemble wet sand; it will firm up as it rests). Cover and chill at least 2 hours. Mixture can be made 1 day ahead. Keep chilled.

Bring chicken stock to a boil in a large saucepan. Add carrots; season with salt. Reduce heat and simmer until carrots are tender, 5–7 minutes. Remove from heat, add reserved breast meat, and cover. Set soup aside.

Meanwhile, bring a large pot of well-salted water to a boil. Scoop out 2-tbsp portions of the matzo ball mixture and, using wet hands, gently roll into balls.

Add matzo balls to water and reduce heat so water is at a gentle simmer (too much bouncing around will break them up). Cover pot and cook matzo balls until cooked through and starting to sink, 20–25 minutes.

Using a slotted spoon, transfer matzo balls to bowls. Ladle soup over, top with dill, and season with pepper.

J ewish families love having an excuse to throw a party, and the more festive the occasion, the more elaborate become the food preparations. These last two recipes illustrate that principle.

P UFF PASTRY KNISHES

I NGREDIENTS
- 2 sheets puff pastry (1 box), thawed at room temperature
- 2 large Yukon gold potatoes or 1 large russet (Idaho) potato
- ½ tsp. salt
- ¼ tsp. pepper
- 2 tsp. olive oil
- ½ lb. ground beef
- 2-3 tbsp. olive oil
- 1 small onion, or ½ large onion, finely diced
- 2 garlic cloves, minced
- ½ tsp. cumin
- ½ tsp. paprika
- 1 tsp. salt
- ½ tsp. black pepper
- 1 egg

. . .

D IRECTIONS

Pre-heat oven to 375°F.

Remove puff pastry from freezer and let sit on counter for 20-30 minutes until it has softened a bit and can easily be unfolded.

Peel potatoes. Boil potatoes in salted water for 20 minutes, or until fork tender. Drain water and mash potatoes using a masher, ricer or heavy fork. Add ½ tsp. salt, ¼ tsp. pepper and 2 tsp. olive oil to potatoes and mix.

´In a large sauté pan, heat olive oil. Sauté onions and garlic until translucent. Add cumin, paprika, salt and pepper. Add meat and brown until cooked through.

Drain excess oil and liquid from meat.

Lightly roll out puff pastry with rolling pin. Cut each puff pastry sheet into 6 squares.

On each square add approximately 1-2 tsp. of potato and 1-2 tsp. of meat mixture. Fold each corner of the puff pastry square up until they touch. Pinch and twist tips down to form the knish.

Brush with lightly beaten egg. Bake until golden brown, around 25-30 minutes.

Serve with spicy brown mustard.

Note: Other fillings include cheese, sauerkraut, sautéed onions, any or all of which can be added to potato mixture.

C INNAMON BABKA

D OUGH INGREDIENTS

• 3 cups King Arthur or Red Mill Unbleached All-Purpose Flour

- 2 tbsp. Baker's Special Dry Milk
- 2 tsp. instant yeast,
- ¼ cup sugar
- 1 ¼ tsp. salt
- ½ to 2/3 cup lukewarm water
- 1 large egg
- 5 tbsp. unsalted butter, room temperature
- 1 ½ tsp. vanilla extract

FILLING INGREDIENTS
- ½ cup brown sugar, packed
- 4 tsp. cinnamon
- 1 tbsp. King Arthur Unbleached All-Purpose Flour
- 4 tbsp. unsalted butter, melted
- 2 tsp. water
- ½ cup diced pecans or walnuts, toasted if desired
- ½ cup golden raisins

GLAZE AND TOPPING
- 1 large egg, beaten with a pinch of salt
- 2 tbsp. King Arthur Unbleached All-Purpose Flour
- 1 tbsp. brown sugar, firmly packed
- ½ tsp. cinnamon
- pinch of salt
- 1 tbsp. unsalted butter, cold

DIRECTIONS
Measure flour by gently spooning it into a cup, then sweeping off any excess.

Combine all the dough ingredients (starting with the lesser amount of water), mixing until everything is moistened. Add more water if necessary to enable the dough to come together. Cover the bowl and let the dough rest for 20 minutes. Then mix and knead it until it's soft and smooth.

Place the dough in a lightly greased bowl, cover, and allow the dough to rise for about 1 ½ to 2 hours, until it's quite puffy.

Make the filling: Just before you're ready to shape the dough, combine the sugar, cinnamon, and flour. Stir in the melted butter and water until evenly incorporated. Set aside.

Make the topping: Combine the flour, sugar, cinnamon, and salt until evenly incorporated. Work in the butter until coarse crumbs form. Set aside.

Shape the dough into a 9" x 18", ¼"-thick rectangle. If the dough "fights back," cover the dough and let it rest for 10 minutes to relax the gluten, then stretch it some more.

Smear the dough with the filling, coming to within an inch of the edges.

Scatter the nuts and raisins atop the filling.

Starting with a short end, roll the dough gently into a log, sealing the seam and ends.

Using a pair of scissors or a sharp knife, cut the log in half lengthwise (not crosswise) to make two pieces of dough each about 10" long; cut carefully, to prevent too much filling from spilling out.

With the exposed filling side up, twist the two pieces into a braid, tucking the ends underneath. Place the twisted loaf into a lightly greased 9" x 5" loaf pan.

Brush the loaf with the egg glaze. Mix the topping ingredients until crumbly and sprinkle it over the loaf.

Cover the loaf, and let it rise until it's very puffy and crowned a good inch over the rim of the pan, 1 ½ to 2 ½ hours. Towards the end of the rising time, preheat your oven to 350°F.

Bake the bread for 40 to 50 minutes, tenting with

aluminum foil during the final 15 to 20 minutes of baking; the loaf should be a deep-golden brown and a digital thermometer into the center of it should register about 195°F.

Remove the babka from the oven, and immediately loosen the edges with a heatproof spatula or table knife.

Let the babka cool for 10 minutes, then turn it out of the pan onto a rack to cool completely.

NOTES

4. REVELATIONS

1. kosher: fit to eat or consume; following all the Jewish dietary laws.
2. rabbi: learned one; a Jewish scholar or teacher; one who teaches Jewish law or serves as the leader of a Jewish community.

5. RETURNING STUDENTS

1. High Holy Days, ten days of personal reflection and repentance.
2. Rosh Hashana: the first two days of the new year, falling sometime in early autumn. It introduces the High Holy Days, ten days of personal reflection and repentance. Jews mark the first day by prayers and the blowing of the shofur or ceremonial horn, after which families share a festive meal and joyful wishes for the coming year.
3. Observant Jews avoid speaking or writing the name of G_d. Instead, they use a euphemism such as this word, which means 'the name.'
4. Yom Kippur: The Day of Atonement; the holiest day in the Jewish calendar. Jews mark it by a 25-hour fast, prayers, and repentance.
5. Oy veh: A Yiddish expression used to express dismay, or frustration, or exasperation.

6. FALL IS A BEGINNING, NOT AN END

1. synagogue: the building in which Jews meet as a community for prayers and other community activities.

7. TRICKS OF THE TRADE

1. Conservative Jewish family: Conservative Jews belief that the Jewish faith constantly evolves to meet the needs of its believers. They adhere to most of the traditional beliefs and practices but allow modifications made necessary by modern conditions.

8. A FLURRY OF SOCIAL OBLIGATIONS

1. The sabbath begins at sundown on Friday and ends at sundown on Saturday. Prayer services to mark the sabbath take place in the evening and the following morning.
2. Bat mitzvah: religious initiation ceremony for a girl on the first day after her twelfth birthday. A girl speaks about a Jewish tradition of her choosing as an indication that from this day forward, she is an adult, responsible for her own actions and required to observe all the traditions of her faith.
3. Shabbat candles: Jewish women light two candles shortly before sunset on Friday evenings to usher in the Sabbath.
4. The recipe for their apple kugel appeared in *What Grows in Your Garden?*
5. shofar: a ceremonial instrument originally used as a battle symbol. It is usually made from a ram's horn and lacks keys to change its pitch. Its sound depends on the blower's skill in shaping his lips.
6. Recipes for these holiday dishes appear on pages 339-344.

9. DAYS OF ATONEMENT AND RECONCILIATION

1. Yom Kippur: The Day of Atonement; the holiest day in the Jewish calendar. Jews mark it by a 25-hour fast, prayers, and repentance.
2. tuna noodle casserole: recipe appears on pages 335-337.
3. Poppy Seed Cake: recipe appears on pages 337-339.
4. challah: a Jewish bread, either braided, or, on Rosh Hashanah, a round loaf.

17. WHICH PATH WILL YOU FOLLOW?

1. Hanukkah: An eight-day celebration commemorating the rededication of the Temple in 165 BC by the Maccabees after its desecration by the Syrians. It is marked by the successive lighting of eight candles.
2. menorah: a nine-branched candelabrum.
3. miracle of the oil: The Maccabees had only enough oil to burn a candle for one night, but it lasted for eight—enough time to discourage the Syrian attackers.

27. EVERYONE HAS AN AGENDA

1. Passover: an eight-day holiday in early spring, commemorating the escape of the Israelites from Egyptian slavery, as told in the Torah, or the first five books of the Old Testament. Among the traditions is the banishing of all leavening agents not only from the menu itself but from the kitchen where the cook prepares it.
2. Seder: the ritual family meal celebrated at the start of Passover. The contents of the meal and the prayers and readings that accompany them are traditional.
3. Haggadah: A liturgy describing the events of the Exodus.
4. Purim: a joyous and sometimes rowdy festival commemorating the defeat of Haman, a Persian leader who planned to kill all the Jews living under Persian rule.

30. APRIL SHOWERS

1. matzoh ball soup and gefilte fish: recipes appear on pages 345-348.
2. Torah: the first five books of the Hebrew Bible, or the entire collection of Jewish law. The Torah says little about marriage except to define its purposes as: to unite with someone they love for the rest of their lives. to please God. and to allow their two souls to merge into one and form a complementary and mutually supportive partnership.
3. minyan: a group of ten or more Jewish men (or women) over the age of 13; a requirement for the holding of a public worship service.
4. shikse: non-Jewish women; often used to describe those who are showy or overblown.
5. ketubah: the marriage contract, outlining the husband's responsibilities toward his future wife after marriage. Traditionally they include a roof over her head, clothes on her back, food on her plate and sex. In a more modern ceremony, it may also cover the possibility of divorce and a wife's responsibility toward her husband.
6. knishes and babka: these recipes appear on pages 349-352.
7. chuppah: a canopy under which the bride and groom stand for their marriage ceremony. It symbolizes the home they will build together.
8. The breaking of a glass: The most unusual part of the Jewish marriage ceremony, it is a reminder of the destruction of the Jewish temple, and more generally, an admonition to remember Jewish history even in one's happiest moments.
9. forbidden days of the Jetwish calendar: days on which work is not allowed—including holidays, festivals, fast days, and, of course, the Sabbath.